P9-DTI-850

BLOOD AND SAND

BLOOD
AND
SAND

Vicente Blasco Ibáñez

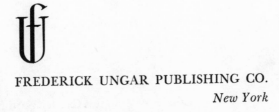

FREDERICK UNGAR PUBLISHING CO.
New York

Translated from the Spanish
Sangre y arena by Frances Partridge

Second printing, 1966

Printed in the United States of America

Library of Congress Catalog Card No. 62-12957

INTRODUCTION*

One of the secrets of the immense power exercised by the novels of Vicente Blasco Ibáñez is that they are literary projections of his dynamic personality. Not only the style, but the book, is here the man. This is especially true of those of his works in which the thesis element predominates, and in which the famous author of *The Four Horsemen of the Apocalypse* appears as novelist of ideas-in-action. It is, of course, possible to divide his works into the "manners" or "periods" so dear to the literary cataloguers, and it may thus be indicated that there are such fairly distinct genres as the regional novel, the sociological tale and the psychological study; a convenient classification of this sort would place among the regional novels such masterpieces as *La Barraca* and *Cañas y Barro*—among the novels of purpose such powerful writings as *La Catedral, La Bodega* and *Sangre y Arena*—among the psychological studies the introspective *La Maja Desnuda*. The war novels, including *The Four Horsemen* and the epic *Mare Nostrum,* would seem to form another group. Such nonliterary diversions as grouping and regrouping, however, had perhaps best be left to those who relish the task. It is for the present more important to note that the passionate flame of a deeply human purpose welds the man's literary labors into .a larger unity. His pen, as his person, has been given over to humanity. He is as fearless in his denunciation of evil as he is powerful in his description of it; he has lived his ideas as well as fashioned them into enduring documents; he reveals not only a new Spain, but a new world.

While Blasco Ibáñez does not desire to be known as regional novelist—nor does a complete view of his numerous works justify such a narrow description—he has nevertheless in his earlier books made such effective and artistic use of

*This introduction by the noted critic and Harvard lecturer, Isaac Goldberg, was written in 1922, when Blasco Ibáñez was still alive. The Spanish author died in 1928, Goldberg in 1938.

i

regional backgrounds that some critics have found this part of his production best. Speaking from the standpoint of durable literary art, I am inclined to such a view. Yet is there less humanitarian impulse in *The Four Horsemen* than in these earlier masterpieces? Whether Blasco Ibáñez's background is a corner in Valencia, a spot on the island of Majorca, a battlefield in France, or Our Sea the Mediterranean—the cradle of civilization—his real stage is the human heart and his real actor, man.

Upon his election to the Cortes—Spain's national parliamentary assembly—Blasco Ibáñez naturally turned, in his novels, to a consideration of political and social themes. Beginning with *La Catedral* (The Shadow of the Cathedral), one of the most powerful modern documents of its kind, he took up in successive novels the treatment of such vital subjects as the relation of Church to State, the degrading and backward influence of drunkenness, the problem of the Jesuits, the brutality and psychology of the bull-fight. In all of these works the writer is characterized by fearlessness, passion and even vehemence; yet his ardor is not so strong as to lead him into conscious unfairness. A fiery advocate of the lowly, he yet can cast their shortcomings into their teeth; they, in their ignorance, are accomplices in their own degradation, partners in the crimes that oppress them. They slay the leaders whom they misunderstand; they are slow to organize for the purpose of bursting their shackles. This appears in *La Barraca* (one of the so-called regional novels) no less than in *La Catedral, La Bodega* and other books of the more purely sociological series. In varying degree, applied to a nation rather than to a class, this fearless attitude is evident in *Los Cuatros Jinetes del Apocalipsis* and *Mare Nostrum,* in which is assailed the neutrality of Spain during the late and unlamented conflict. This unflinching determination to see the truth and state it is also discernible in a most personal manner; the sad inability of such noble spirits as Gabriel Luna *(La Catedral)* or Fernando Salvatierra *(La Bodega)* to solace themselves with a belief in future life is perhaps an exteriorization of the author's own views, even as these revolutionary spirits are, in part, embodiments of himself.

In the bulk of the noted Spaniard's books there is waged, on both a large scale and a small, the ceaseless, implacable struggle of the new against the old. This eternal battle early formed an appreciable part of even the writer's short fiction. His old seamen look with scorn upon the steam vessels that replace their beloved barks; his vintners regret the passing of the good old days when sherry sold high and had not yet been ousted from the market by cheap, new-fangled concoctions; his toilers begin to rebel against ecclesiastical authority; some of his heroes are even capable of falling in love with Jewesses or with women below their station (*Luna Benamor, Los Muertos Mandan*); everywhere is the fermentation of transition. His protagonists—red-blooded, vigorous, determined—usually fail at the end, but if there are victories that spell failure, so are there failures that spell victory. It is the clash of these ancient and modern forces that strikes the spark which ignites the author's passion. He is with the new and of it, yet rises above blind partisanship. His dominant figures, chiefly men, are representative of the Spain of tomorrow; not that *mañana* which has so long (and often unjustly) been a standing reproach to Iberian procrastination, but a tomorrow of rebirth, of rededication to lofty ideals and glowing realities.

In *Sangre y Arena (Blood and Sand,* written in 1908) Blasco Ibáñez attacks the Spanish national sport. With characteristic thoroughness, approaching his subject from the psychological, the historical, the national, the humane, the dramatic and narrative standpoint, he evolves another of his notable documents, worthy of a place among the great tracts of literary history.

His process, like his plot, is simple; whether attacking the Church or the evils of drink, or the bloodlust of the bull ring, his methods are usually the same. He provides a protagonist who shall serve as the vehicle or symbol of his ideas, surrounding him with minor personages intended to serve as a foil or as a prop. He fills in the background with all the wealth of descriptive and coloring powers at his command—and these powers are as highly developed in Ibáñez, I believe, as in any living writer. The beauty of Blasco Ibáñez's descriptions—a beauty by no means confined to the pictures he summons to the mind—is that, at their best, they rise to interpretation. He not only brings before the eye a vivid image, but communicates to the spirit an intellectual reaction. Here he is the master who penetrates beyond the exterior into the inner significance; the reader is carried into the swirl of the action itself, for the magic of the author's pen imparts a sense of palpitant actuality; you are yourself a soldier at the Marne, you fairly drown with Ulises in his beloved Mediterranean, you defend the besieged city of Saguntum, you pant with the swordsman in the bloody arena. This gift of imparting actuality to his scenes is but another evidence of the Spaniard's dynamic personality; he lives his actions so thoroughly that we live them with him; his gift of second sight gives us to see beyond amphitheatres of blood and sand into national character, beyond a village struggle into the vexed problem of land, labor and property. Against this type of background develops the characteristic Ibáñez plot, by no means lacking intimate interest, yet beginning somewhat slowly and gathering the irresistible momentum of a powerful body.

Juan Gallardo, the hero of *Blood and Sand,* has from earliest childhood exhibited a natural aptitude for the bull ring. He is aided in his career by interested parties, and soon jumps to the forefront of his idolized profession without having to thread his way arduously up the steep ascent of the bull fighters' hierarchy. Fame and fortune come to him, and he is able to gratify the desires of his early days, as if the mirage of hunger and desire had suddenly been converted into dazzling reality. He lavishes largess upon his mother and his childless wife, and there comes, too, a love out of wedlock.

But neither his powers nor his fame can last forever. The life of even Juan Gallardo is taken into his hands every time he steps into the ring to face the wild bulls; at first comes a minor accident, then a loss of prestige, and at last the fatal day upon which he is carried out of the arena, dead. He dies a victim of his own glory, a sacrifice upon the altar of national bloodlust. That Doña Sol who lures him from his wife and home is, in her capricious, fascinating, baffling way, almost a symbol of the fickle bullfight audience, now hymning the praises of a favorite, now sneering him off the scene of his former triumphs.

The tale is more than a colorful, absorbing story of love and struggle. It is a stinging indictment brought against the author's countrymen, thrown in their faces with dauntless acrimony. He shows us the glory of the arena—the movement, the color, the mastery of the skilled performers—and he reveals, too, the sickening other side. In successive pictures he mirrors the thousands that flock to the bullfights, reaching a tremendous climax in the closing words of the tale. The popular hero has just been gored to death, but the crowd, knowing that the spectacle is less than half over, sets up yells for the continuance of the performance. In the bellowing of the mob Blasco Ibáñez divines the howl of the real and only animals. Not the sacrificial bulls, but the howling, bloodthirsty assembly is the genuine beast!

The volume is rich in significant detail, both as regards the master's peculiar power and his views as expressed in other words. Once again we meet the author's determination to be just to all concerned. Through Dr. Ruiz, for example, a medical enthusiast over tauromachy, we receive what amounts to a lecture upon the evolution of the brutal sport. He looks upon bullfighting as the historical substitute for the Inquisition, which was in itself a great national festival. He is ready to admit, too, that the bullfight is a barbarous institution, but calls to your attention that it is by no means the only one in the world. In the turning of the people to violent, savage forms of amusement he beholds a universal ailment. And when Dr. Ruiz expresses his disgust at seeing foreigners turn eyes of contempt upon Spain because of the bullfight, he no doubt speaks for Blasco Ibáñez. The enthusastic physician points out that horseracing is more cruel than bullfighting, and kills many more men; that the spectacle of fox hunting with trained dogs is hardly a sight for civilized onlookers; that there is more than one modern game out of which the participants emerge with broken legs, fractured skulls, flattened noses and what not; and how about the duel, often fought with only an unhealthy desire for publicity as the genuine cause?

Thus, through the Doctor, the Spaniard states the other side of the case, saying, in effect, to the foreign reader, "Yes, I am upbraiding my countrymen for the national vice that they are pleased to call a sport. That is my right as a Spaniard who loves his country and as a human being who loves his race. But do not forget that you have institutions little less barbarous, and before you grow too excited in your desire to remove the mote from our eye, see to it that you remove your own, for it is there."

Juan Gallardo is not one of the impossible heroes that crowd the pages of fiction; to me he is a more successful portrait than, for example, Gabriel Luna of *The Shadow of the Cathedral*. There is a certain rigidity in Luna's make-up, due perhaps to his unbending certainty in matters of belief—or to be exact, matters of unbelief. This is felt even in his moments of love, although that may be accounted for by the vicissitudes of his wandering existence and the illness with which it has left him. Gallardo is somehow more human; he is not a matinée hero; he knows what it is to quake with fear before he enters the ring; he comes to a realization of what his position has cost him; he impresses us not only as a powerful type, but as a flesh and blood creature. And his end, like that of so many of the author's protagonists, comes about much in the nature of a retribution. He dies at the hands of the thing he loves, on the stage of his triumphs. And while I am on the subject of the hero's death, let me suggest that Blasco Ibáñez's numerous death scenes often attain a rare height of artistry and poetry—for, strange as it may seem to some, there is a poet hidden in the noted Spaniard, a poet of vast conception, of deep communion with the interplay of Nature and her creatures, of vision that becomes symbolic. Recall the death of the Centaur Madariaga in *The Four Horsemen of the Apocalypse,* dashing upon his beloved steed, like a Mazeppa of the South American plains, straight into eternity; read the remarkable passages portraying the deaths of Triton and Ulises in *Mare Nostrum;* consider the deeply underlying connotation of Gabriel Luna's fate. These are not mere dyings; they are apotheoses.

Doña Sol belongs to the author's siren types; she is an early sister of Freya, the German spy who leads to the undoing of Ulises in *Mare Nostrum.* She is one of the many proofs that Blasco Ibáñez, in his portrayals of the worldly woman, seizes upon typical rather than individual traits; she puzzles the reader quite as much as she confuses her passionate lover. And she is no more loyal to him than is the worshipping crowd that at last, in her presence, dethrones its former idol.

Among the secondary characters, as interesting as any, is the friend of Juan who is nicknamed Nacional, because of his radical political notions. Nacional does not drink wine; to him wine was responsible for the failure of the laboring class, a point of view which the author had already enunciated three years earlier in *La Bodega;* similar to the rôle played by drink is that of illiteracy, and here, too, Nacional feels the terrible burdens imposed upon the common people by lack of education. Indicative of the author's sympathies is also his strange bandit Plumitas, a sort of Robin Hood who robs from the rich and succors the poor. The humorous figure of the bullfighter's brother-in-law suggests the horde of sycophants that always manage to attach themeslves to a noted—and generous—public personage.

The dominant impression that the book leaves upon me is

one of power—crushing, implacable power. The author's paragraphs and chapters often seem hewn out of rock and solidly massed one upon the other in the rearing of an impregnable structure. And just as these chapters are massed into a temple of passionate protest, so the entire works of Blasco Ibáñez attain an architectural unity in which not the least of the elements are a flaming nobility of purpose and a powerful directness of aim.

Once upon a time, and it was not so very long ago, it was the fashion in certain quarters to regard Blasco Ibáñez as impossible and utopian. The trend of world events has greatly modified the meanings of some of our words and has given us a deeper insight into hitherto neglected aspects of foreign and domestic life. Things have been happening lately in Spain (as well as elsewhere, indeed!) that reveal our author in somewhat the light of a prophet. Or is it merely that he is closer to the heart of his nation and describes what he sees rather than draws a veil of words before unpleasant situations? Ultimately these situations must be met. The Spain of tomorrow will be found to have moved more in the direction of Blasco Ibáñez than in that of his detractors.

The renowned novelist is but fifty-two, energetic, prolific, voluminous; besides more than a score of novels thus far to his credit he has written several books of travel, a history of the world war, has traveled in both hemispheres and made countless volumes of translations. He has now a larger audience than has been vouchsafed any of his fellow novelists, and his future works will be watched for by readers the world over. That is a rare privilege and imposes a rare obligation. Blasco Ibáñez has it in him to meet both.

ISAAC GOLDBERG

CHAPTER ONE

Juan Gallardo lunched early that day, as he always did before a bullfight.

He ate nothing but one slice of roast meat; his bottle of wine stood untasted on the table in front of him. He must stay completely sober. He drank two cups of strong black coffee, lit a long cigar, and sat with his elbows on the table and his chin in his hands, dreamily watching the other guests as they gradually filled up the dining-room.

Ever since he had received the full rank of matador in the Madrid bull-ring several years ago, he had always stopped at this hotel in the Calle de Alcalá, where the landlord and his wife treated him as one of the family, and he was the idol of waiters, porters, kitchen-boys and chambermaids. Once, as the result of being badly gored in the arena, he had had to stay on for quite a long time, sitting wrapped in bandages in a suffocating atmosphere of iodoform and cigar smoke; but this unfortunate experience had left no deep impression on his mind. With typical Andalusian superstitiousness he felt that the hotel was in some way lucky to him, and that no real disaster could happen to him while he was staying in it. There would be the usual accidents of his profession of course—torn clothes or torn flesh; but he wouldn't meet the fate of his comrades, the thought of whom haunted him even in his moments of triumph.

On bullfight days he liked to linger on in the dining-room after his early lunch, watching the other guests (mostly foreigners and visitors from the provinces) who passed him unconcernedly by, but who turned to look at him when one of the servants told them that the handsome, well-dressed young man with the clean-shaven face and black eyes was Juan Gallardo—El Gallardo himself, the famous matador. Their curiosity helped him pass the agonizing time of waiting until he was due at the bull-ring. How slowly they passed, those

5

hours of suspense, of vague subconscious fears and self-doubts! This was far the worst part of his profession. He couldn't go out into the streets, for he must save all his energy and agility for the ordeal of the arena; nor could he spin out his meal, for he must eat little and finish early, so as to arrive with no weight on his stomach.

He sat on at the head of the table with his face between his hands and a cloud of fragrant smoke floating in front of him, casting rather conceited glances from time to time at any women who might be looking at him with interest.

Conscious as he was of being a public hero, he thought he could read admiration in their eyes. They would be thinking how handsome and smartly dressed he was. And forgetting his anxiety for the moment, he instinctively dropped into the mannerisms of a man used to striking an attitude in front of the crowd, sat up straighter in his chair, flicked the cigar-ash from his cuffs, and gave a twist to the ring which covered a whole joint of one of his fingers with an enormous diamond, flashing its colours like the magic rainbow in a drop of water.

He let his eyes pass complacently over his well-cut suit, his hat lying on the next chair, the slender gold chain which ran between his waistcoat pockets, the pearl tie-pin which seemed to throw a milky light on to his dark face, his shoes of Russian leather, and his silk socks decorated with embroidery and drawn threads like the stockings of a cocotte.

A strong waft of subtle English scent came from his clothes and his shining black hair, which he now smoothed back from his forehead with an arrogant gesture for the benefit of his feminine audience. Not bad at all. He was pleased with his appearance—what other bullfighter was more distinguished-looking and more irresistible to women?

But suddenly his anxieties returned. His eyes lost their brilliance, his chin sank between his hands again, and he puffed away desperately at his cigar with his gaze lost in a cloud of tobacco smoke. He thought impatiently of the coming evening, and wished he were already returning from the bull-ring, exhausted and dripping with sweat, but full of the joy of

6

having triumphed over danger, and of eagerness for pleasure and the satisfaction of his appetites in the few days of relaxation ahead of him. God willing he would again emerge safe and sound; then he would eat like a wolf, get rather drunk and go and find that music-hall singer he had seen on his last visit but had had no further chance to pursue. In his life of continual movement from one side of Spain to another there was never time for anything.

Some admirers were now coming into the dining-room, eager to greet their hero before they went off to lunch. They were *aficionados*[1] of long standing, who wanted to adopt young Gallardo as their new favourite, giving him good advice and reminding him every few moments of some past idol of theirs, like Lagartijo or Frascuelo. They spoke to him in a friendly patronizing way, while he gave them the formal title of Don, according to the tradition by which the bullfighter, risen from the social subsoil, is considered to belong to a different class from his admirers. Their admiration was tempered with a great many reminiscences of the past, designed to make the young man feel the superiority of age and experience. They talked about the old bull-ring of Madrid, where only the best bulls and bullfighters used to be seen, and coming closer to the present they trembled with emotion as they spoke of El Negro. El Negro was Frascuelo.

"I wish you could have seen him. . . . But you were all babies then, or not even born."

Other poorly dressed and hungry-looking characters now began to pour into the dining-room: unknown journalists representing papers only read by the *toreros*[2] who were praised or criticized in them; men of dubious occupation, who as soon as they heard of Gallardo's arrival came to pester him with adulation and requests for tickets. In the general excitement they mingled indiscriminately with the big business men and public officials in heated discussion of the politics of the bull-ring.

Everyone came up in turn to pat Gallardo on the back or

[1] Knowledgeable bullfighting enthusiasts.
[2] Professional bullfighters of all sorts—matadors, picadors and banderilleros.

7

shake him by the hand, to a running accompaniment of questions and exclamations:

"Hullo, Juanillo. . . . How's Carmen?"

"Fine, thanks."

"And your old lady? Señora Angustias?"

"Splendid, thanks. She's at La Rinconada."

"And how about your sister and the kids?"

"Same as usual."

"And that ridiculous brother-in-law of yours?"

"He's fine too. Talks too much, as usual."

"No more brats on the way?"

"No—thank God!"

He bit his finger-nail by way of emphasizing the negative, and then in his turn began to question the newcomer, about whom he knew nothing except that he was a bullfighting enthusiast.

"And how's your own family? All right? Well, that's fine. Sit down and have a drink."

Then he tried to find out something about the bulls he would be fighting in an hour or so, for all these people had come straight from seeing the animals taken to their pens at the bull-ring. Also, with professional curiosity, he asked for news from the Café Inglés, a great centre for aficionados.

This would be the first bullfight of the spring season in Madrid, and Gallardo's supporters had high hopes of him, based on the accounts of other *corridas*[1] they had read in the papers. He was the matador most in demand at the moment. Ever since the Easter bullfight at Seville—the first important one of the year—Gallardo had gone from town to town killing bulls. By August and September he would be spending his nights in the train and his afternoons in the arena, with no time to rest. His agent at Seville was being driven crazy by letters and telegrams, and didn't know how to fit so many offers of contracts into the short time available.

Yesterday afternoon he had appeared at Ciudad Real, and had had to get into the night train for Madrid still wearing his

[1] Bullfights. Six bulls are killed during most *corridas*, on special occasions sometimes eight.

full costume. He had hardly slept at all, though the other passengers had squeezed up close together to give him a little more space, and a chance of a few short naps before he risked his life for them next day.

His admirers praised his physical toughness and the reckless courage with which he hurled himself on the bull at the moment of execution.

"We shall see what you can do this afternoon," they said enthusiastically. "We all expect great things of you. If you're as good as you were at Seville you'll put plenty of noses out of joint."

Then they went off home to lunch, so as to be in good time at the bull-ring. Gallardo, finding himself alone, and unable to bear his nervous restlessness, was just getting up to go to his room when a man holding two children by the hand pushed his way in through the glass doors of the dining-room, regardless of the servant's intervention. When he saw the matador he advanced towards him with a seraphic smile on his face, dragging the children behind him and not seeming to notice where his feet were carrying him. Gallardo recognized him.

"How are you, old chap?"

And the usual questions about the health of the family began all over again. Then turning to his children the man said solemnly:

"Well, you've been asking and asking to see him, and here he is, just like his picture!"

The two children gazed with awe at their hero, whose portrait they had looked at so often on the posters which decorated the walls of their poor little house: a supernatural being, whose exploits and success had been the first objects of their admiration.

"Juanillo, kiss your godfather's hand."

The younger of the two little boys pressed the bullfighter's right hand with a small red mouth, recently polished by his mother for the occasion. Gallardo patted his head absent-mindedly. This was one of his many god-children. His

9

admirers were always getting him to stand godfather to their children, hoping in this way to provide for their future; one of the penalties of fame was that he must always be appearing at christenings. This particular godson reminded him of his early difficulties, and he felt a certain gratitude to the child's father for having believed in him when no one else did.

"And how's business, old chap?" Gallardo asked. "Going all right?"

His friend pulled a wry face. He made a living by his dealings in the market of the Plaza de la Cebada—a living, but nothing more. Gallardo cast a sympathetic glance at his shabby Sunday-best suit.

"You'd like to see the fight, wouldn't you? Go up to my room and Garabato will give you a ticket. Good-bye, old fellow. Buy yourselves a little something." And while his godson seized his right hand and kissed it again he gave each child a couple of duros. Their father dragged away his offspring with apologies and thanks, hardly aware in his confusion whether he was expressing gratitude for the children's presents or the ticket for the bullfight.

Gallardo waited a little, so as to give them time to leave his room. Then he looked at his watch. One o'clock! What a long time still to go before the corrida!

He had left the dining-room and was making for the stairs when a woman wearing an old shawl came out of the porter's office and firmly barred his way, paying not the smallest attention to the servants' protests.

"Juaniyo! Juan! Don't you know me? I'm La Caracola, Señora Dolores—poor Lechuguero's mother."

Gallardo smiled at the chattering little old woman with her dark wrinkled face and burning eyes—the eyes of a witch; and guessing what the end of it all would be, his hand began moving to his pocket.

"Nothing but trouble, son! Trouble and misery! When I heard you were to be fighting today I says to myself: 'I'll go and see Juaniyo; he won't forget his poor friend's mother, I'll be bound.' But how handsome you are, boy! All the women crazy for you, of course. Things are very bad with me, son. Not a vest to my back, not a bite to eat all day. Only a little drop of liquor. Pepona lets me live in her house out of pity; it's a decent five duro house. You come along there, they'll be glad to see you. I brush the girls' hair and take messages to the gentlemen. Oh! if only my poor boy was still alive! You've not forgotten Pepiyo? Remember the day he died . . . ?"

Gallardo put a duro into her withered hand and tried to escape from the flood of gabbled words, now tremulous with tears. Devil take the old hag! Why must she come and remind him, just before a fight, of poor Lechuguero the comrade of his early days, whom he had seen killed almost instantly, gored to the heart, in the bull-ring at Lebrija when they were both *novilleros*.[1] Ill-omened old wretch! He pushed her aside, but passing as lightly as a bird from self-pity to gaiety she burst into voluble praise of the bravery of young bullfighters who robbed the public of their money and women of their hearts.

"You deserve the Queen of Spain herself, my beauty! Señora Carmen had better take care some other girl doesn't grab you. Can't you give me a ticket for this afternoon, Juaniyo, so as I can see you kill?"

The old woman's shrill cries and gesticulations made the hotel servants laugh, distracting their attention from the inquisitive and importunate crowd which had collected in the doorway, attracted by the matador's presence. Quietly slipping past the hotel servants, a mob of idlers, beggars and newspaper-sellers now invaded the hall.

Boys with bundles of papers under their arms pulled off their caps and shouted excitedly:

"El Gallardo! Hurrah for El Gallardo! *Olé!*"

The bolder spirits seized him by the hand and shook it long and violently, determined to make the most of this moment of access to the great national hero whose picture had been in all the papers. Then they encouraged the others to share in their triumph, shouting:

[1] A matador in the apprentice stage, who fights young bulls (under four years old) or in some cases old bulls, or those defective in size, vision or horns.

"Shake him by the hand! He won't mind! He's a good chap!" They were almost prepared to go on their knees to the torero in their enthusiasm.

Others, with unshaven chins and dressed in worn-out clothes which had once been smart, shuffled round their idol in down-at-heel shoes and took off their greasy hats to him, calling him 'Don Juan' to mark their superiority to the rest of the noisy disrespectful crowd. They complained of their poverty, and asked for money, or—braver still—for a ticket for the bullfight, although they had every intention of selling it immediately.

Gallardo laughingly defended himself from this jostling avalanche, but the hotel staff were too much impressed by his popularity to come to his rescue. He emptied all his pockets, blindly distributing silver coins among eager outstretched hands.

"There! That's the lot! The bank's broke! Get along with you!"

Pretending to be annoyed by this flattering popularity, he thrust his way through the crowd with muscular agility and ran quickly upstairs, while the servants, freed from the restraint of his presence, pushed the mob of intruders back into the street.

Gallardo passed the open door of the room occupied by Garabato, and saw his servant busy among trunks and boxes getting ready his clothes for the bullfight.

As soon as he was alone in his own room, the excitement and gaiety caused by the admiring crowd faded. Now the worst moments of the day were upon him: those last anxious hours before he started for the bull-ring. Bulls from the Miura herd and the critical audience of Madrid! When he was face to face with danger it seemed to intoxicate him and stimulate his courage; but now that he was alone the thought of it filled him with a superstitious dread, increased by the very fact that it lacked definite shape.

He felt crushed, as if exhaustion from his bad night had suddenly overtaken him. He longed to stretch himself on one of the beds at the far end of the room; but returning anxiety about the terrifying, uncertain future drove away his desire to sleep.

He walked restlessly up and down the room, and lit another cigar from the stub of the one he had just finished.

What was in store for him during the Madrid bullfighting season? What would his enemies say of him? How would his rivals fare? He had killed many Miura bulls; after all they were only bulls like the rest, but he couldn't help thinking of his comrades who had been killed in the arena, nearly all victims of animals from this herd. No wonder that every matador insisted on an extra thousand pesetas in his contract when he had to fight bulls of this breed.

He prowled nervously round the room, stopped to stare stupidly at various familiar belongings, and then threw himself into an armchair as if seized with sudden weakness. He looked at his watch repeatedly. Not two o'clock yet! How slowly the time passed.

He longed for the time to come for him to dress and go to the bull-ring and so put an end to his nervous tension. The crowds, the noise, the general curiosity, his desire to appear calm and at ease before an admiring public, and, above all, the proximity of real physical danger would instantly efface this lonely agony, this isolation from every external stimulus, in which he found himself face to face with something very like fear.

In an effort to distract his thoughts he felt in the breast-pocket of his jacket and brought out his pocket-book and a heavily scented letter. Standing by the window which let the dim light from the patio into the room he studied the envelope, which had been handed to him on his arrival at the hotel, admiring the delicacy and elegance of the handwriting.

Then he drew out the letter, inhaling the elusive perfume which came from it with delight. Ah! It was such small details as these that revealed the aristocrat and the woman of the world.

Gallardo liked to drench himself in scent, as if his body was tainted with the bitter smell of his early poverty. His enemies jeered at this habit, even going so far as to cast aspersions on his virility. His admirers smiled indulgently at his weakness, but sometimes had to turn their heads aside, almost sickened by the strong aroma that hung about him. He took a whole scent-shop about with him on his travels, and his body was anointed with feminine perfumes when he entered the arena, among dead horses, blood-stained entrails and dung.

When he was fighting in the bull-rings of the south of France some cocottes among his admirers taught him how to mix exotic scents together.

But the perfume that came from this letter! It was the perfume of the writer; it had a delicate and intangible quality which seemed to be the emanation of her aristocratic body. He called it 'my lady's perfume'.

He read and re-read the letter with a proud, delighted smile. It wasn't long, only half a dozen lines; a greeting from Seville wishing him luck in Madrid and congratulating him in advance on his expected success. It was a letter which would in no way compromise the writer if it should go astray. From the beginning, 'My friend Gallardo', written in a hand whose elegance delighted the eye, to the end, 'Your friend Sol', the style was amicable but cold and formal, and struck a note of superiority, of condescension rather than equality.

As he studied the letter with the respect for literacy of an uneducated son of the people, the matador could not suppress a feeling of annoyance, as if he had received a slight.

"What a girl she is!" he murmured, "always on her high horse. Why, she writes to me as *Usted!*[1] *Usted!* To me!"

But he smiled with pleasure at his memories. This chilly style was for letter-writing only, part of the equipment of the lady of fashion, the precaution of the woman of the world. His annoyance soon turned to admiration.

"She knows her way about all right!"

And a certain professional satisfaction was apparent in his smile—the pride of the lion-tamer who by praising the strength of the animal he has conquered only enhances his own glory.

[1] The formal mode of address.

14

While Gallardo was still looking at the letter his servant Garabato came in and out of the room, carrying clothes and boxes which he put down on one of the beds.

He was quiet and deft in his movements and seemed to take no notice of the matador's presence. For the last few years he had accompanied him everywhere as personal servant and sword-handler[1] in the ring. He had begun his bullfighting career in the provincial *capeas*[2] at the same time as Gallardo; but bad luck had come his way just as fame and advancement had been the lot of his comrade. He was small, swarthy and of poor muscular development, and a twisted badly-healed scar made a white scrawl across his thin, wrinkled, prematurely aged face. It was the result of a goring which had nearly been the death of him in some provincial bull-ring, and beside this fearful wound there were others disfiguring the hidden parts of his body.

He had escaped with his life by a miracle, but the cruellest part of it was that people laughed at his misfortunes and had seemed to enjoy seeing him trampled and ripped by the bulls. At last his pig-headed obstinacy yielded to adversity and he resigned himself to being the attendant and confidential servant of his old friend. He was Gallardo's most fervent admirer, although he sometimes abused his confidence and intimacy by criticism or advice. There were times when he thought he could have done better than his master, had he been in his shoes. Gallardo's friends were amused by the frustrated longings of the sword-handler; but he took no notice of their mockery. Give up bullfighting? Never. So that his past career should not be utterly forgotten, he combed his coarse hair into two shining curls over the ears and still wore it long at the nape of his neck in the pigtail of his youth, that caste-mark which distinguishes bullfighters from ordinary mortals.

When Gallardo was angry with him this adornment was always the object of his noisy outbursts.

[1] Responsible for the sword and muleta. He must be ready to hand a new sword when needed, and performs various other functions.

[2] Informal bullfights or bull-baitings in village squares. Amateurs as well as aspirant toreros take part.

"So you want to wear a pigtail too, you good-for-nothing! I'll soon cut that rat's-tail off for you, you insolent wretch!"

Garabato received these threats with resignation; but he took his revenge by retiring behind a silent air of superiority and only responding by shrugging his shoulders when his master returned in high spirits from a successful afternoon in the ring and asked with childish vanity:

"Well, what did you think? I was good, wasn't I?"

He had kept from the old days his habit of addressing his master as *tu*. He couldn't have spoken to him in any other way, but this privileged *tu* was accompanied by a respectful and serious expression. It was the familiarity of squire to knight-errant.

Down to the neck he was a bullfighter, but the rest of his body seemed half tailor, half valet. The lapels of his suit of English cloth, a present from his master, were full of pins, and there were needles and thread stuck in one of the sleeves. His thin dark hands were neat and deft as a woman's.

When he had put every item of the matador's costume ready on the bed, he counted over the various objects so as to make sure that nothing was missing. Then he advanced to the middle of the room, and without looking at Gallardo said brusquely but as if to himself:

"Two o'clock!"

Gallardo looked up with a start, as if only just aware that his servant was in the room. He put the letter in his pocket and slowly moved towards the bed, apparently wishing to postpone the moment when he must dress himself.

"Is everything there?"

Suddenly his pale face flushed scarlet and was distorted with anger, and his eyes opened widely as if in horrified surprise.

"What are these clothes you've put out for me?"

Garabato pointed to the bed, but before he could speak his master's wrath had exploded violently upon him.

"Don't you know the first thing about your job, damn you? What are you thinking of? A corrida in Madrid, bulls from the Miura herd, and you put out my red suit, just like the one

16

poor Manuel el Espartero used to wear! Anyone would think you hated me, you wretch, and wanted me to die!"

The more he thought about the enormity of his servant's defiance of ill luck, the more furious he became. The idea of wearing a red suit in the bull-ring at Madrid after what had happened! His eyes flashed and became bloodshot with anger as if some treacherous attack had been made on him, and he seemed to be about to lay violent hands on poor Garabato.

A discreet knock at the door cut short this scene.

"Come in."

A young man entered the room, dressed in a light-coloured suit with a red tie, carrying his Córdovan hat in a hand covered with large diamond rings. Gallardo immediately recognized him, with the aptitude for remembering faces peculiar to those who depend on the applause or disapproval of the crowd, and his anger was at once transformed into smiling amiability, as if the visit were an agreeable surprise to him. All he could remember about the newcomer was that he came from Bilbao and was an enthusiastic admirer and *aficionado*. What in the world was his name? He knew so many people. What could it be? The one thing he was sure of was that he was an old friend and must be addressed as *tu*.

"Come in and sit down. This is a surprise! When did you arrive?"

His friend sat down, with the pleasure of a devotee entering the sanctum of his idol, and was obviously determined to stay where he was till the last possible moment, enjoying the distinction of being called *tu* by the maestro, and of calling him Juan at every other word, so that walls, furniture and anyone going along the passage should be aware how intimate he was with the great man. He had arrived from Bilbao that morning with the sole object of seeing Gallardo and would be returning next day. He had read about his triumphs; the season had begun well. He was sure to do splendidly this afternoon. He had seen the bulls put in their pens this morning and had noticed a black animal which would certainly be a worthy adversary for Gallardo. . . .

17

But the matador cut short these prophecies somewhat brusquely.

"Excuse me a moment; I'll be back soon."

And he left the room and went towards a door with no number on it at the end of the passage.

"What clothes shall I put out?" Garabato called after him, in a voice made all the harsher by his desire to show subservience.

"The green one; the brown; the blue—whichever you like." And Gallardo disappeared through the door, leaving his servant smiling maliciously. This hurried flight at the moment when it was time to dress was nothing new—'pissing with fright' was what they called it in the profession. And his smile expressed the pleasure he felt at seeing once again that the greatest masters of the bullfighting art, and the bravest, suffered the same symptoms of anxiety as he had done before going into the ring in the old days.

When Gallardo came back to his room some time later, safe from the danger of having to relieve himself in his bull-fighter's suit, he found he had a new visitor. This was Doctor Ruiz, a much-loved physician who had spent the last thirty years signing medical certificates and attending bullfighters wounded in the Madrid ring.

Gallardo had a great respect for him as a leading practitioner of science, but at the same time teased him affectionately about his good nature and personal untidiness. In this he followed the custom of the uneducated masses, who are more ready to recognize a man's wisdom and skill if his slovenliness and eccentricity mark him out from the rest.

He was short and had a prominent stomach; his broad face, rather flattened nose and fringe of dirty yellowish-white beard contributed to give him a faint resemblance to a bust of Socrates. When he was standing, his bulky and pendulous paunch seemed to wobble behind his full-cut jacket in time to his words; when he sat down this same part of his anatomy rose up under his meagre chest. His clothes, which looked dirty and shabby even after very little wear, seemed to float around his unharmonious body as though they belonged to someone

18

else—so obese were those parts dedicated to digestion and so scrawny those required in locomotion.

"He's a saint," Gallardo used to say. "A wise man but a bit cracked as well; he's as good as gold and he'll never be rich. Whatever he has he gives away, and he takes what anyone chooses to pay him."

Two great passions filled his life, bulls and the Revolution—some vague and tremendous revolution which was bound to come and sweep away the existing state of things in Europe. His was an anarchistic republicanism which he couldn't be bothered to explain and which only expressed itself in the form of destructive and negative statements. Bullfighters all treated the good doctor like a father; he called them all *tu*, and he had only to receive a telegram from any far corner of Spain for him to leap instantly into a train and go to the assistance of one of the 'boys' who had been gored in the ring, with no hope of reward beyond whatever they felt like giving him.

It was a long time since he had seen Gallardo, and he embraced him warmly, pressing his flabby stomach against that steel-hard body.

"And what about that Republic, doctor? When's it coming, eh?" asked Gallardo, with Andalusian irony. "El Nacional, says it'll be any time now."

"What do you care about it, you rascal? Leave poor Nacional in peace, he'd much better learn to be a better *banderillero*.[1] And as for you, what you ought to be thinking about is how to go on killing bulls better than God himself. What a splendid afternoon we shall have, eh? They say that the bulls . . ."

But at this point the young man who had seen the bulls penned interrupted the doctor with the news that he had noticed a black bull which had taken his fancy, and of which great things could be expected. Gallardo's two visitors, who had passed some time alone and silent in the room together

[1] A torero whose job is to place up to four pairs of banderillas (wooden sticks with harpoon points) in the bull's withers, to tire it and make it lower its head. He is on foot and is sometimes called a peon. Each matador employs four.

during his absence, were now confronting each other and he felt it was time for an introduction. But what was he to call the friend who spoke to him as *tu*? He scratched his head, and frowned thoughtfully, then hesitated no longer.

"Look here, what *is* your name? I'm sorry—but you know I see so many people."

The young man concealed his disappointment at being forgotten by the maestro behind a pleasant smile, and gave his name. As soon as he heard it Gallardo was aware of a rush of memories from the past, and amended his forgetfulness by adding after the name, "a rich mine-owner from Bilbao". Then he introduced "the famous Doctor Ruiz", and the two men, united by their common enthusiasm, began talking about the day's bulls as if they had known each other all their lives.

"Sit down, both of you," said Gallardo, pointing to a sofa at the end of the room. "You won't disturb me. Talk away and don't bother about me; I'm going to get dressed. We're all men here!"

And he took off his suit. Sitting in his underclothes under the arch which separated the drawing-room from the bedroom, he gave himself over into the hands of Garabato, who opened a bag made of Russian leather and took out of it a feminine looking toilet-case.

Although his master's face was already smoothly shaved, Garabato lathered it once more and passed the razor over his cheeks with a speed born of daily practice. After washing himself, Gallardo returned to his chair and the servant covered his hair in brilliantine and scent, combing it into curls on the forehead and temples; then he dealt with the sacred badge of his profession, his pigtail.

Carefully he combed out and plaited the long lock which adorned his master's nape; and then, interrupting his operations, he fixed it with two hairpins to the top of his head, leaving its final arrangement till later. Next he must attend to the matador's feet, and he took off his socks, leaving him dressed in nothing but his vest and silk drawers.

Gallardo's powerful muscles swelled beneath these thin garments. A hollow in one thigh revealed a deep scar where the flesh had shrunk after a goring. There were white weals on the dark skin of his arms—traces of old wounds—and his brown hairless chest was criss-crossed by two irregular purplish lines left by two other bloody incidents in the ring. The flesh of one of his heels was violet-coloured and had in it a round hollow like the mould for a coin. A smell of clean manly flesh emanated from this athletic body, and combined with the strong odour of feminine perfume.

Garabato knelt at his master's feet, his arms full of cotton-wool and white bandages.

"Just like the gladiators of ancient times," said Doctor Ruiz, breaking off his conversation with the man from Bilbao. "You've become a Roman, Juan."

"Old age, doctor," answered the matador with a tinge of melancholy. "We're all getting older. When I had to fight hunger as well as bulls in the capeas I didn't need all this stuff. My feet were made of iron then."

Garabato pushed small wads of cotton-wool between his master's toes, and put a layer of it over the insteps and soles; then taking out the bandages he began to wrap them round in tight spirals like the bindings of an Egyptian mummy. He finished this operation by securing the ends with tiny stitches, with a needle and thread from his sleeve.

Gallardo stamped on the ground with his bandaged feet which seemed to have become more solid, stronger and more agile in their wrappings. His servant next pulled on his long stockings, which reached to the middle of his calf and were as thick and supple as gaiters; these would be the only protection his legs would have beneath his fighting suit.

"Take care they aren't wrinkled—you know, Garabato, I can't bear baggy stockings;" and standing in front of the looking-glass he surveyed himself from all sides and bent down to smooth out the wrinkles for himself. Garabato now pulled on pink silk stockings to hide the white ones, and Gallardo slipped his feet into a pair of pumps selected from several which his servant had laid out for him on a chest, all quite new with white soles.

Then began the real business of dressing. The servant held out his knee-breeches of tobacco-coloured silk heavily embroidered with gold at the seams, and Gallardo pulled them on, leaving the thick cords with their gold tassels hanging loose. These cords, pulled tight below the knee, would constrict the legs and give them extra strength; they were called *machos*.

Gallardo told his servant to pull them as relentlessly tight as he could, and at the same time he swelled out his leg muscles. This was an operation of vital importance, for a matador must always wear his machos extremely tight, and Garabato quickly and skilfully rolled up and fastened the cords out of sight under the breeches, with tassels hanging.

Next the servant held out a fine lawn shirt with goffered frills on the breast, as smooth and fine as a woman's blouse. After he had fastened it he tied the long tie which divided the torero's chest with a thin red line and was lost behind his waistband. The most complicated item of clothing still remained—a strip of silk more than four yards long, which seemed to fill the whole room as Garabato manipulated it with practised mastery.

The matador stood beside his friends at the other end of the room, tucking one end of his sash into his belt.

"Take care now," he said to Garabato, "do your feeble best." And revolving slowly on his heels he gradually approached his servant while the sash wound itself around his waist in even circles, giving him a look of added slenderness. Garabato regulated the position of the silk band by means of quick movements of his hands; in one turn the sash would be folded double, in the next it would open out flat again, and all the time it was moulding the matador's waist smoothly, without wrinkles or unevenness. Gallardo was pernickety and hard to please where his personal appearance was concerned, and he stopped several times in the course of his spinning journey, to go back and improve what had been done.

22

"That's not right," he said crossly. "Do be more careful, Garabato, damn you!"

After many such halts Gallardo reached the end of the sash, and his servant deftly stitched and pinned until his master's clothes were literally all in one piece. It would be impossible now for him to get out of them without the help of scissors and other hands, unless a bull tore them off him in the ring, and they finished undressing him in the infirmary.

He sat down again and Garabato unfastened the pigtail from the top of his head where it was pinned, and fastened it to the *moña*—a black rosette, which was all that was left of the hair-net of early bullfighting days.

The maestro stretched himself, as if he wanted to put off getting finally into the rest of his costume; he asked Garabato for the cigar he had left on his bedside table, and inquired what time it was, as all the clocks seemed to be fast.

"Early still. The boys aren't here yet—I don't like getting to the ring early. Everything gets on one's nerves so when one's waiting!"

At this moment one of the hotel servants came in to say that the carriage with the *cuadrilla*[1] was waiting outside.

The time had come! There was no excuse whatever to delay his departure. He slipped his gold-embroidered waist-coat over his sash, and on top of that his brilliant jacket with its massive embroidery, as heavy as a piece of armour and flashing like fire. The tobacco-brown silk could only be seen on the inside of the sleeves and in two triangles on the shoulders. Almost all the fabric was covered by the heavy frogging and gold embroidery in the shape of flowers with coloured stones for centres. The epaulettes were of solid gold embroidery with tassels of the same material, and the jacket was edged with a thick gold fringe which quivered at every step. In the gold edged pockets the corners of two silk handkerchiefs could be seen, red like the tie and sash.

"My *montera*."

[1] The troupe of toreros working under a matador, including picadors and banderilleros.

Garabato opened an oval box and very carefully took out the round black matador's hat, trimmed with two pompons which stood out on each side like ears. Gallardo put it on, taking care that his moña should be uncovered and hang in the middle of his back.

"Now my cloak."

From the back of a chair Garabato took the cloak known as the *capa de paseo*, a princely affair made of silk of the same colour as the suit and as heavily embroidered with gold. Gallardo slung it over one shoulder and looked at himself in the glass, well satisfied with the effect. Pretty good—now for the bull-ring!

His two friends hurriedly said good-bye, meaning to find a cab and follow him. Garabato was carrying a large bundle of red cloth under his arm with the hilts and points of several swords projecting at each end.

When Gallardo reached the entrance-hall of the hotel he saw that an excited crowd was gathered outside, as if something momentous had just happened, and he could also hear a buzzing from a larger throng out of sight.

The landlord of the hotel and his family came forward with hands outstretched, as though they were speeding him on a long journey.

"Good luck! May all go well with you!"

The servants shook him by the hand, forgetting all social distinctions in the emotion of the moment.

"The best of luck, Don Juan!"

He smiled round at them all, ignoring the apprehensive expressions of the women of the hotel.

"Thanks, many thanks. See you later."

He was a different man now. The moment he put his glittering cloak over his shoulders his face had lit up with a carefree smile. He was pale with the damp pallor of a sick man; but he smiled with the joy of living and of going to meet his public, adopting this new attitude with the instinctive ease of a man used to posing before the crowd.

He swaggered along with a handsome man's arrogance,

24

swinging his hips under the gorgeous cloak, and puffing at the cigar he carried in his left hand.

"Let me pass, gentlemen, please! Many thanks! Many thanks!"

He made his way through the crowd of shabby enthusiasts who crowded round the door of the hotel, trying to keep his fine clothes from being dirtied. They couldn't afford a ticket for the corrida, but they weren't going to miss the chance of shaking the great Gallardo by the hand or even touching his clothes.

A carriage was waiting by the pavement, drawn by four mules handsomely caparisoned with tassels and bells. Garabato had already hoisted himself on to the box seat with his bundles of cloth and swords. Inside were sitting three bull-fighters with their fighting capes laid across their knees; they wore suits of as bright a colour as the maestro, and as richly embroidered, but in silver only.

Jostled by the crowd, defending himself as best he could from eager hands, Gallardo managed at last to reach the step of the carriage and was unceremoniously helped up by his admirers.

"Good afternoon, gentlemen," he said curtly to his cuadrilla. He took the back seat beside the step so that everyone could see him, and smiled and nodded acknowledgement of the shouts and greetings of a group of working-women and newspaper boys.

The spirited mules started forward, filling the street with the cheerful jingling of bells. The onlookers parted to let them pass, but many hung on to the carriage in imminent danger of falling under its wheels. They waved hats and sticks; a shiver of excitement ran through the mob—one of those contagious impulses which sometimes sweep like wildfire through a crowd, making them shout without knowing why:

"Hurrah for the brave toreros! *Viva España!*"

Gallardo, pale and smiling, waved his hand, repeating "Thank you, thank you!" He was moved by the enthusiasm which surrounded him and proud of the fame which made them couple his name with his country's.

25

A string of ragged boys and dishevelled girls were running after the carriage as fast as their legs would carry them, as if they expected some extraordinary event at the end of the drive.

For the last hour the Calle de Alcalá had looked like a river of carriages running between two banks of pedestrians all making for the outskirts of the town. Every conceivable sort of vehicle, ancient and modern, took part in this confused and noisy migration, from prehistoric wagonettes to motor-cars. The trams were full to overflowing, with passengers crowded on their steps. Buses collected fares at the corner of the Calle de Sevilla, while the conductors shouted: "Bull-ring! Bull-ring!" Mules with tasselled harness trotted by with a gay tinkling of bells, drawing open carriages full of women in white mantillas, with bright flowers in their hair; every few moments a cry of alarm went up as some child, threading its way across the road through the stream of traffic, emerged with the agility of a monkey from between the carriage wheels. Motor horns hooted; drivers shouted; newspaper-boys hawked leaflets with pictures and descriptions of the bulls which were to fight this afternoon or portraits and biographies of famous bull-fighters. Now and then the dull hum of the crowd rose to a crescendo of excitement. Among the Municipal Guard in their dark uniforms were gaudily dressed riders mounted on thin miserable hacks, their legs swathed in yellow padding, wearing gold-embroidered jackets and wide beaver hats with a pompon at the side like a cockade. These rough-looking horsemen were the *picadors*,[1] and perched behind each of them on the high Moorish saddle was the *monosabio*[2] who had brought his horse from the stable, dressed like the devil in red.

The cuadrillas went by in open carriages; the golden embroidery on the toreros' clothes flashed in the afternoon sun, dazzling the eyes of the crowd and seeming to inflame the general excitement. "There goes Fuentes!" "That's

[1] Mounted toreros who enter the ring after the preliminary cape work, and insert the points of their pikes into the bull's tossing muscle when he charges the horses.
[2] Servants to the picadors, who help them mount, kill wounded horses, etc.

26

El Bomba!" And delighted at having recognized these heroes they followed the vanishing carriages with eager eyes, anxious to miss nothing of the show.

From the top of the Calle de Alcalá, the whole of this broad straight street could be seen lying white under the sun, with its rows of trees beginning to turn green under the breath of spring, its balconies black with onlookers, and the swarming crowds making their way on foot or in carriages towards the fountain of La Cibeles.

At this point the street took a turn uphill between lines of trees and tall buildings, and the view was blocked at the far end by the Puerta de Alcalá, standing white against the blue sky, in which floated a few wisps of clouds like lonely swans.

Gallardo sat in silence, responding to the ovation of the crowd with a fixed smile. He had not uttered a word since his greeting to his banderilleros, who were pale and silent too, oppressed by fear of the unknown. The toreros had no need to keep up with each other the swagger they assumed before the public.

The crowd seemed to know by instinct that this was the last cuadrilla on its way to the bull-ring. The street urchins who had been running after the carriage shouting for Gallardo had dropped behind and scattered among the traffic; all the same, people looked round as if they knew that the famous matador was coming, and slackening their pace, lined the pavements to get a better view of him.

The women in the carriages in front turned when they heard the jingling bells on the mules' harness. A wordless roar of enthusiasm came from some of the groups on the pavement; hats were waved, and sticks flourished.

Gallardo acknowledged their salutations with an automatic smile, but he seemed preoccupied and hardly aware of his surroundings. Beside him sat El Nacional, the banderillero in whom he put most trust, a big, tough-looking man ten years older than he was, with a serious expression and eyebrows that met in the middle. He was well-known in the profession for his kindness of heart, his honesty and his interest in politics.

27

"Well, you can't complain of Madrid, Juan," said El Nacional, "you're going down all right with the crowd."

But Gallardo seemed not to hear, and answered as if voicing his innermost thoughts: "I feel in my bones that something's going to happen this afternoon."

When they got to La Cibeles the carriage stopped. A funeral procession was coming from the direction of the Prado on its way to La Castellana, cutting right across the stream of traffic in the Calle de Alcalá.

Gallardo turned even paler than before as he gazed with horrified eyes at the cross, and the party of priests who broke into a melancholy chant as they looked—some with indignation, others with envy—at all these godless people bent on enjoying themselves.

The matador quickly took off his hat and his banderilleros followed his example—all except El Nacional.

"Take your hat off, damn you!" cried Gallardo furiously, glaring at him as if he were going to strike him, in the confused belief that this act of defiance would bring about some appalling misfortune.

"All right, I'll take it off," said El Nacional with the sulkiness of a thwarted child, as he saw the cross moving away. "I'll take it off—but to the dead man."

They had to wait for a considerable time to let the long procession go by.

"What bad luck!" Gallardo muttered in a voice trembling with rage. "Who on earth was responsible for bringing a funeral across the road to the bull-ring? Devil take them! I told you something was going to happen today."

El Nacional smiled and shrugged his shoulders.

"Superstition and fanatical rubbish! You can't expect God or Nature to be bothered with things like that."

This remark, which increased Gallardo's irritation, seemed to relax the tension among the other toreros, and they began to laugh at their companion, as they always did when he aired his favourite phrase: "God or Nature."

Once the road was clear, the carriage started off again at

28

full speed, forging a way through the other vehicles which were converging on the bull-ring. On arrival at the ring it turned to the left and made at a slower pace towards the door which led to the stables and bull-pens. Gallardo received a further ovation when he and his banderilleros got out of their carriage. Again he pushed his way through the crowd, trying to save his clothes from dirty contacts, smiling his greetings, but keeping his right hand hidden, for everyone was trying to shake it.

"Make way there please, gentlemen! Thank you!"

The great courtyard between the bull-ring and the wall surrounding the outbuildings was full of people anxious to get a glimpse of the toreros before taking their seats. Above the heads of the crowd could be seen the mounted figures of the picadors and the *alguacils*,[1] in seventeenth-century costume. On one side of the yard were brick buildings one storey high with vines trained round their doors and pots of flowers in their windows: these made up what was virtually a small town of offices, workshops, stables, and houses for the stable-boys, carpenters and other servants of the bull-ring.

The matador made his way laboriously through the crowd, hearing his name spoken excitedly everywhere.

"Gallardo! Here's El Gallardo! *Olé! Viva España!*"

And surrendering himself completely to the homage of the public, whose idol he was, he strode along, serene and self-satisfied, as if arriving at a party being given in his honour.

Suddenly two arms were thrown round his neck, and a strong smell of wine assailed his nostrils.

"Here's a fine randy fellow for you! Hurrah for the brave toreros!"

He was a respectable-looking tradesman, who had been lunching with some friends, who were now watching him smilingly from a little way off. He let his head fall on to the matador's shoulder and seemed disinclined to move, as though he meant to drop asleep there out of excess of excitement; but

---

[1] Mounted bailiffs, who communicate the orders of the president to the toreros. There are usually two.

with the help of his friends Gallardo was at last freed from this endless embrace. When he saw that he had been parted from his hero the man burst out into drunken shouting: "Hurrah for these fine fellows! If only foreigners from every country in the world would come and see what a real torero is like, they'd die of envy! They may have ships . . . they may have money. . . . But that's nothing! They've got no bulls or men as brave as these. . . . *Olé!* Long live my country!"

Gallardo crossed a large white-washed hall, quite bare of furniture, where the other bullfighters were collected surrounded by groups of admirers. Then he pushed through the crowd blocking a doorway and came into a narrow dark room, at the far end of which lights were burning. It was the chapel. The altar-piece was an old picture of the Virgin of the Dove. On the table were four candles, and some sprays of dusty moth-eaten artificial flowers stood in cheap pottery jars.

The chapel was full of people. The poorer aficionados were collected together at the back to get a good sight of the great men. Bare-headed in the semi-darkness, they sat on chairs and benches or squatted on the ground, most of them with their backs to the Virgin and gazing eagerly towards the door ready to call out a name at the first glimpse of a glittering gold-embroidered jacket.

There was hardly a murmur for the banderilleros and picadors—poor devils who were going to run as great a risk as the maestros. Only the most fanatical aficionados knew their nicknames.

Presently there began a prolonged muttering, and a name was passed from mouth to mouth.

"Fuentes! . . . It's Fuentes!"

The tall slender torero walked gracefully up to the altar, with his cloak slung on one shoulder, and went down on one knee with as much style as an actor; the candle-light was reflected in the whites of his dark gypsy eyes, and shone on his tense, agile and charming figure. After saying a prayer he crossed himself, got up and walked backwards to the door without taking his eyes from the Virgin, like a tenor who leaves the stage bowing to his audience.

Gallardo's piety took a less elaborate form. He entered hat in hand, with his cloak gathered round him, still with his swaggering walk; but as soon as he came face to face with the Virgin he fell on both knees and became absorbed in prayer without noticing the hundreds of eyes which were fixed on him. He was shaken to the depths of his simple Christian soul by fear and remorse. He prayed for protection with the fervour of an ignorant man who lives in constant danger and believes in every sort of supernatural influence, adverse or favourable. For the first time that day he thought of his wife and his mother. Poor Carmen waiting for a telegram, far away in Seville! And Señora Angustias peacefully feeding her hens in her farmyard at La Rinconada, without knowing for certain where her son was fighting that day! And there was that terrible presentiment of his that something would go wrong this afternoon! "Virgin of the Dove, protect me! I will do right, I will renounce sin. I will live as God commands."

He left the chapel with his superstitious mind fortified by this empty repentance, but still deeply moved, and with troubled eyes which didn't see the people round him.

Outside in the room where the other bullfighters were waiting he was greeted by a clean-shaven man dressed in black, who seemed embarrassed.

"Curse my bad luck!" murmured the matador moving on. "Didn't I say something would happen today?"

It was the chaplain to the bull-ring, who had arrived from the suburb of La Prosperidad, carrying the holy oil hidden under his coat. He was an enthusiastic aficionado, and had been engaged in a dispute for many years with another priest from the centre of Madrid who claimed a better right to conduct the religious services of the bull-ring. He brought with him a neighbour who acted as his sacristan in exchange for a ticket for the corrida. On bullfighting days he used to choose one of his friends or protéges to occupy the sacristan's seat, take a cab at the expense of the management, put the holy vial under his jacket, and set out for the bull-ring, where two front seats were reserved for him close to the entrance to the bull-pens.

The priest entered the chapel with a proprietary air, and was scandalized by the behaviour of the public. All had their heads uncovered but they were talking loudly, and some even smoking.

"This is not a café, gentlemen. Please go outside at once. The corrida is just going to begin."

This news caused a general exodus, during which the priest took out his hidden oil and put it away in a painted wooden box. After which he hurried away so as to get to his seat before the entrance of the cuadrillas.

The crowd had vanished. No one was to be seen in the courtyard except men dressed in gold-embroidered silk, horsemen in yellow with wide-brimmed hats, the alguacils and the servants on duty in their blue and gold liveries.

The toreros were rapidly forming up under the archway which led into the arena: in front were the maestros; some distance behind came the banderilleros; and behind them in the courtyard were the rearguard, the fierce-looking steel-clad squadron of picadors, smelling of hot leather and horse-dung and riding on skeleton horses with one eye bandaged. At the very end, like the baggage-train of an army, were the teams of mules which were to carry away the carcasses—strong, restlessly fidgeting animals with shining coats; their harness was trimmed with tassels and bells, and the national colours were on their collars.

At the far end of the archway, above the wooden barrier which closed its lower half, was a bright semi-circle, in which could be seen a patch of sky, part of the roof of the bull-ring and some of the seats, densely packed with a teeming crowd, among which fans and papers fluttered like coloured butterflies. A strong draught swept out through this archway, like the breath from an enormous lung, bringing with it a harmonious buzzing, as of distant music guessed at rather than heard.

32

All round the archway were peering heads, heads by the score; the spectators nearest to the entrance were craning forward, trying to be the first to get a sight of the heroes of the day.

Gallardo took his place among the other matadors, greeting them with a grave nod of the head. No one spoke; no one smiled. Each man was plunged in his own thoughts, or following his imagination far afield, or thinking of nothing whatever—with that vacuity of brain peculiar to strong emotion. They expressed their anxious tension by altering and re-altering the set of their bright-coloured cloaks, leaving them to hang loose from one shoulder, or folding the ends round their waist so that their legs could move more freely in their casings of silk and gold. Every face was pale, not with a dull pallor but with the ghastly gleam of agitation. They thought of the invisible arena with the peculiar terror that is reserved for things which happen on the other side of a wall, and for indefinite dangers guessed at but not seen. How would the day end?

Two horses could now be heard trotting along under the arcades outside the bull-ring. These were the alguacils in their short black capes and broad brimmed hats trimmed with red and yellow feathers. They had just finished clearing the ring of intruders and now came and stationed themselves in front of the cuadrillas like outriders.

The doors of the archway and the wooden barrier were thrown wide open. The great ring was revealed, the arena itself, that circular space in which the afternoon's tragedy was to be enacted for the delight and excitement of fourteen thousand spectators. The confusion of harmonious sound grew louder until it emerged in the form of gay spirited music from a brass band, a triumphal march which made the audience swing to its rhythm. Now let the heroes of the day come forward!

Blinking at the sudden change, the toreros stepped out of the darkness into the light, out of the silence of the quiet archway into the roar of the arena, and a wave of excitement ran through the crowded tiers of benches, as the audience stood up to see better.

As soon as they stepped into the arena the bullfighters seemed at once to dwindle in size in the immensity of their surroundings. They looked like puppets, glittering in the sun which struck rainbow lights from their gold embroidery, and the crowd was thrilled by their stylish movements just as a child is excited by some marvellous toy. The whole ring was swept by a wild gust of enthusiasm; the audience was electrified. They clapped, they shouted, the music blared; and in the middle of this universal tumult the cuadrillas advanced slowly and solemnly from the entrance to the president's box, making up for the shortness of their steps by the grace with which they moved and swung their arms. In the circle of blue sky above the ring white doves were fluttering, terrified by the roar arising from this crater made of bricks.

The toreros felt like new men as they advanced into the arena. It was not for money only that they risked their lives. They had left their terrors and doubts behind outside. Now they were in the ring; now they were face to face with their public; this was reality. And their desire for glory, their longing to excel their comrades, their pride in their own skill and strength blinded these simple primitive men, made them forget their fear and infused them with animal courage.

Gallardo was transfigured. He drew himself to his full height as he walked along with conquering arrogance, looking triumphantly around as if his two companions did not exist. The ring and the audience were all his. He felt himself at that moment capable of killing every bull that existed in the pastures of Andalusia and Castile. He knew that the applause was for him; that the thousands of pairs of feminine eyes gazing out from beneath white mantillas in the galleries and boxes were fixed on him alone; there was no question of that. The public adored him, and as he stepped forward, accepting their ovation to himself with an insolent smile, he cast his eyes over the rows of seats, knowing exactly where the biggest groups of his supporters were collected, and trying to ignore those tiers where the friends of the other toreros were sitting.

They all bowed to the president, montera in hand, and then the brilliant procession broke up, while one of the alguacils caught the key thrown him by the president in his plumed hat. Gallardo walked to the side of the ring where his most enthusiastic devotees were sitting and handed over to them his beautiful processional cloak, which was seized by eager hands and spread over the barrier as the sacred symbol of their partisanship.

The more ardent of his supporters stood up, waving hands and sticks, and shouting:

"Show us what the boy from Seville can do!"

And he leant against the barrier smiling proudly, repeating to all of them:

"Thank you. He'll do his best."

His adherents were not the only ones to gaze at him in eager expectation of intense excitement to come. He was a matador who gave the whole crowd hopes of what aficionados call *hule*,[1] and such *hule* was liable to lead to a bed in the infirmary. They all believed it was his ultimate fate to die in the ring, and this gave their applause a sort of homicidal frenzy, a savage intensity like that of the misanthrope who followed an animal-tamer everywhere in the hope of at last seeing him devoured by his wild beasts.

Gallardo scoffed at some of the older aficionados—grave professors of tauromachy who believed that no accident could happen to the bullfighter who followed the rules of his art. Rules indeed! He had no idea what they were, nor any desire to learn them. Courage and confidence were the qualities needed for victory. His meteoric success had been achieved by blind reliance on his bravery and physical prowess, and the crowd had been roused to transports of admiration by his wild recklessness.

He hadn't advanced in his career by slow steps, like most of the other matadors, nor by serving the maestros for long years as banderillero. He had no fear of the bulls' horns. 'Hunger gores more savagely.' The important thing was to

[1] Frenzied excitement.

35

rise quickly in his profession, and the public had watched him start straight away as a matador and become immensely popular in a few years.

They admired him for the same reason that made them certain of his eventual fate: his defiance of death inspired a morbid excitement in them. They paid him such attentions as are received by a prisoner in the condemned cell. This torero held nothing back from them; he would give them everything he had, even his life. He was worth the money he cost. And they applauded and cheered their hero with the brutality of those who like to watch danger from a safe place. The more cautious among them shrugged their shoulders; they knew that his methods were suicidal, and they muttered:

"All very well while it lasts . . . !"

Trumpets and drums sounded as the first bull rushed into the ring. Gallardo stood close to the barrier where his supporters were sitting, in an attitude of motionless disdain, with his unadorned working cape on his arm, confident that the eyes of the whole crowd were fixed on him. This bull was for someone else. He would come to life when his own bulls appeared. But the applause at his comrade's cloak-play roused him from his immobility, and in spite of his intentions he advanced towards the bull and carried out several feats which showed more audacity than skill. The audience burst into applause of his daring.

When Fuentes killed the first bull and went up to the president's box, bowing to the crowd, Gallardo's face turned paler, as if any sign of approval which was not for him amounted to a deliberate insult. Now it was his turn; now they would see great things—he was not sure what form they would take, but he was bent on astonishing the audience.

The second bull had hardly appeared before Gallardo seemed to dominate the ring with his agility and his eagerness to shine. His cloak was never far from the animal's muzzle. One of the picadors of his cuadrilla, called Potaje, was thrown from his horse and lay helpless in front of the bull's horns, but the maestro seized the creature by the tail and pulled with such herculean strength that it turned round until the picador was safe. The audience applauded wildly.

During the placing of the banderillas Gallardo stood in the passage between the barriers, waiting for the signal for the last phase. El Nacional was challenging the bull in the middle of the arena, with the darts in his hand. No graceful movements or superb daring here: it was a question of earning his daily bread. He had a family of four children far away in Seville, and if he died they would never find another father. He would do his duty but no more; he would place his banderillas as if it were part of the day's work of bullfighting, seeking neither applause nor hisses.

When both banderillas were in position some of the huge audience applauded while others gave vent to muttered complaints of the banderillero:

"Get up to the bull, why don't you? And keep out of politics!"

And El Nacional, unable to make out what they were saying, smiled like his master, and said, "Thank you! Thank you!"

When the trumpets and drums gave the signal for the bull to be killed, Gallardo again leapt into the ring, and the crowd moved in their seats, buzzing with excitement. This matador was the man for them! Now they were going to see something!

He took the folded *muleta*[1] and the sword, handed him over the barrier by Garabato, walked with short steps to the president's box, where he stopped, holding up his hat in one hand. Everyone craned forward, devouring their idol with their eyes. His formal dedication of the bull was inaudible, but the sight of the tall slender figure, with his chest arched backwards to give more strength to his words, aroused more enthusiasm in the crowd than the most eloquent ovation. As he ended his speech he made a half turn, and threw his montera on the ground. The applause was thunderous. *Olé* the boy from Seville! Now they would see the real thing! And the spectators exchanged glances, silently promising each other a

[1] A piece of crimson serge draped over a stick, used by the matador in the final stage.

terrific thrill. A shiver ran through the rows of seats, as if in the presence of something awe-inspiring and sublime.

The silence of strong emotion suddenly fell on the great throng; it was as if the bull-ring were empty. The entire life of these thousands of people was concentrated in their eyes. None of them seemed to breathe.

Gallardo advanced slowly towards the bull with the muleta in front of his stomach like a flag; in his right hand he held the sword, swinging like a pendulum in time with his steps. Turning his head for a second he saw that El Nacional and the rest of his cuadrilla were behind him with the cape, ready to help him.

"Out of the ring, all of you!"

His voice rang through the silent arena as far as the highest rows of seats, and was answered by a roar of delight. " 'Out of the ring all of you!' He said 'Out of the ring'! What a man!"

Now he was quite alone and close to the bull, and immediately silence fell once more. Very calmly he unfolded the muleta, spread it out and took a few steps forward till it was almost touching the muzzle of the animal, which stood amazed and bewildered by his audacity.

The audience hardly dared breathe, much less speak, but their eyes were bright with admiration. What a nerve! He stamped impatiently with one foot on the sand, trying to incite the animal to charge, and with a bellow of rage the creature hurled its huge bulk and sharp horns against him. The muleta passed over the horns, which grazed the tassels and fringes of the matador's suit; but he held his ground, only arching his torso backwards. The crowd roared its appreciation of this pass with the muleta. "*Olé*! . . ."

The great beast turned and charged again, and again the pass was repeated and greeted by a roar from the audience. Frustrated and infuriated, the bull returned to the attack, but each time the man repeated his pass with the muleta, moving within a strictly limited space, and emboldened and as it were intoxicated by the proximity of danger and the admiration of the crowd.

Gallardo felt the animal's hot breath; his face and hands were splashed with its slaver. This close and physical contact gave him a sense of familiarity with the bull as if it were a friend who was to allow him the glory of killing it.

For a few seconds the creature stood quite still, as though tired of the game, gazing with sombre eyes at the man and his red cloth, as if in its dim intelligence it were aware of some trap, and knew that it was going to be led from attack to attack, to death itself.

Gallardo felt his heart beat high with the excitement of approaching triumph. Now! . . . Describing a circle with his left hand he let the muleta roll itself round the stick, while he raised his right hand to the level of his eyes, holding the sword pointed at the nape of the bull's neck. A tumult of cries of surprised protest broke from the crowd.

"Not yet!" cried thousands of voices. "No! No!"

It was too soon. The bull was badly placed; it would charge again and he would be caught. He was disobeying all the rules of his art. But what did such a desperate character care for rules, or even for his life?

Suddenly he threw himself forward on the sword at the same moment that the bull hurled itself at him. It was a ferocious, brutal encounter. For a second the man and the animal seemed to be part of a single mass, and to move together without it being possible to make out which was master. Part of the man's body and one arm was between the two horns, while the bull struggled with lowered head to toss the small figure in its gold and many-coloured clothes, which always eluded it.

At last the two broke apart; the muleta lay on the ground like a torn rag and the matador emerged empty-handed, staggering for several yards from the violence of the shock. His clothes were in disorder; his tie floated loose outside his waistcoat, ripped out and torn by the bull's horns.

The bull was still carried along by the impetus of its charge, with the red handle of the sword standing out from its broad neck, where it was buried up to the hilt. Suddenly it stopped short in its career, rocked forward with a painful curtsying motion; its forelegs doubled under it, its head sank lower till the bellowing muzzle touched the sand, and it subsided full length in the convulsions of its final agony. . . .

It was as if the whole bull-ring were collapsing with a clatter of falling bricks, as if the crowd were about to fly in panic. They all stood up, pale, trembling, waving their arms and gesticulating. Dead! What a magnificent *estocada!*[1] For the space of a second they had seemed to see the matador impaled on the bull's horns; but instead of falling bleeding to the ground, there he stood, still a little giddy from the shock, but smiling. Their amazement only increased their enthusiasm.

"What a monster!" they shouted, finding no better word to express their admiration. "What a savage!"

Hats were hurled into the arena, and a thunderous ovation greeted the matador as he made the rounds of the barrier and stood before the president's box with outstretched arms. There were shouts from all sides that he should be given the bull's ear. Never had this honour been better deserved. An estocada such as this was a rare thing to see. And the excitement swelled even higher when one of the bull-ring servants came forward and presented him with a dark triangular piece of bleeding flesh—the tip of one of the animal's ears.

The third bull had already entered the ring, but still the applause for Gallardo went on, as if the public couldn't recover from its astonishment and nothing else that could happen in the corrida could be of the slightest interest.

The other toreros did their best to attract the attention of the audience, their faces pale with professional jealousy; but the applause they received sounded faint and spiritless. Shaken by the delirious excitement of a moment ago the crowd gave only half their minds to what was now happening in the ring. Heated arguments had begun between the spectators. The supporters of the other matadors were recovering from the wild frenzy that had possessed the whole amphitheatre, and they began to criticize Gallardo. Very brave. Very brave;

[1] Sword-thrust.

reckless—suicidal even; but you couldn't call it art. His supporters, who admired their idol's daring above everything else, became even more insolent and aggressive towards those who tried to cast doubts on the miracles of their own particular saint.

The audience's attention soon began to be distracted from the ring by confused movements among the benches. Suddenly a violent commotion broke out in one sector; people were standing up; arms and sticks were waving. The other spectators turned their backs on the arena and began staring towards the centre of agitation and the large painted numbers on the inside barrier which indicated the different blocks of seats.

"There's a fight in No. 3!" they shouted delightedly. "Now they're at it in No. 5!"

Soon the contagion had spread like wildfire through the whole crowd, and everyone stood up trying to see over the heads of his neighbours; but all that was visible was the slow ascent of the police from tier to tier till they reached the group where the disturbance was going on.

"Sit down!" shouted the more peaceable, annoyed at being prevented from seeing the arena where the toreros were still in action.

Gradually the wave of mass excitement subsided and the rows of heads dropped back into line with the rings of seats. The corrida went on. But the audience still seemed to be in a state of nervous agitation, which they manifested by unfair animosity or scornful silence directed at certain bullfighters. Exhausted by their recent emotional outbursts, they now found the spectacle dull, and relieved their boredom by eating and drinking. Refreshment-sellers circulated between the barriers throwing up what was asked for with marvellous dexterity. Oranges flew like yellow balls to the highest benches in a straight line from seller to buyer as if a thread was pulling them. Bottles of mineral water were opened, and the golden wine of Andalusia bubbled into glasses.

Soon a murmur of interest ran round the amphitheatre. Fuentes was just advancing into the ring with the banderillas in his hand and everyone expected a display of unusual grace and skill. He walked slowly out alone, as calm and self-possessed as if it were the beginning of a game. The bull followed his movements with curious eyes, astonished to be confronted by only one man after the previous hurly-burly of outspread cloaks, cruel pike-thrusts in the neck, and horses coming close to its horns as if offering themselves to be attacked.

The man seemed to hypnotize the animal. He approached so close that he was able to touch the creature's head with the point of his banderillas; then he ran lightly to the far side of the ring, with the bull following him as if fascinated. It seemed entirely in the matador's power and obeyed his every movement, until Fuentes, deciding that the game had lasted long enough, extended both his arms with a banderilla in each hand, drew his slim graceful figure up on tiptoe and advancing towards the bull with magnificent coolness, fixed the coloured darts firmly in the astonished beast's neck.

Three times he performed this feat amid roars of applause. Those who prided themselves on their connoisseurship now got their own back for the general outburst of enthusiasm Gallardo had provoked. Here was a real maestro! This was pure art!

Gallardo stood by the barrier wiping the sweat from his face with the towel Garabato handed him. Afterwards he drank some water, turning his back on the arena so as not to see his comrade's success. In the world outside the bull-ring he had that fellow-feeling for his rivals which common danger provokes, but here in the arena all were enemies, and their successes caused him as much pain as if they were insults. It seemed to him now that the general enthusiasm for Fuentes was robbing him of his great triumph.

On the appearance of the fifth bull, which was for him, he leapt into the ring determined to astonish everyone.

If a picador fell he spread his cape and with a series of passes drew the bull to the far side of the ring, till at last it stood still in utter bewilderment. Then he would touch its muzzle with one foot, or take off his montera and lay it between the horns. Or he would take advantage of the animal's dazed state to expose his stomach to it in a daring challenge or kneel before it as though he meant to lie down under its nose.

The older aficionados began to mutter their disapproval. Monkey-tricks! Such horse-play wouldn't have been put up with in the old days! But their complaints were drowned in shouts of applause.

When the signal for the banderillas was given the crowd was amazed to see Gallardo take the darts from El Nacional and advance with them towards the bull. There was a cry of protest. They all knew his weakness in banderilla play; that was only for those who had risen in their careers step by step and had passed many years as banderilleros to the maestros before they became matadors. Gallardo had begun at the other end, killing bulls from the time he first appeared in the ring.

"No! No!" yelled the crowd.

Doctor Ruiz banged on the barrier and shouted:

"Leave that alone, my boy! You're the only one who really knows how to kill!"

But when Gallardo was moved to recklessness he cared nothing for his audience and was deaf to its advice. In the midst of the din he went straight up to the bull, and before it could move he had placed both banderillas. It was clumsily done, and one fell out as the bull started back in surprise. But that didn't matter. The public, ever indulgent to its idol, smilingly applauded his daring. Growing more reckless Gallardo placed another pair of banderillas, ignoring the protests of the crowd. A third time he repeated the feat, again unskillfully, but with such fearlessness that what would have provoked hisses in another was received with admiring enthusiasm. What courage! And what astonishing luck he had!

The bull was now carrying four banderillas instead of six, and those so badly fixed that it hardly seemed to be aware of any discomfort.

"He's still fresh!" shouted the aficionados; but Gallardo walked boldly up to him, sword and muleta in hand and his montera on his head, trusting to his lucky star.

"Out of the ring, all of you!" he cried again. Aware that

43

there was someone who had disobeyed his order still close
behind him, he turned his head. Fuentes was standing a little
way off, with his cape over his arm, pretending not to have
heard and ready to come to his help, as if he expected an
accident.

"Leave me alone, Antonio," said Gallardo angrily and yet
respectfully, as if he were speaking to an elder brother. His
manner was such that Fuentes shrugged his shoulders as if to
disclaim all responsibility, and moved slowly away, confident
that his help would be needed at any moment now.

Gallardo spread his muleta right over the head of the bull,
which instantly charged. A pass. "*Olé*!" roared the enthusiasts.
But the animal turned suddenly and again hurled itself at the
matador with a violent toss of its head which tore the muleta
out of his hands. Finding himself disarmed and pursued he had
to run for the barrier, but at this moment Fuentes distracted
the bull with a flourish of his cape. As he ran Gallardo guessed
by whose intervention the creature had been brought to a
standstill, and instead of jumping over the barrier he sat down
on the step and remained there for several moments only a
few paces from his enemy. This display of coolness at the end
of his flight brought him a round of applause.

He recovered his muleta, carefully arranged the red cloth,
and once more approached the bull, but less calmly this time;
a murderous rage possessed him now, a longing to kill this
brute which had made him run before the eyes of so many of
his admirers.

He hardly played the bull at all. He judged that the decisive
moment had come and he braced himself, with the muleta low
and the hilt of the sword close to his eyes.

Again the audience shouted their fears:

"Not yet! No! Aaah!"

A cry of horror came from all sides; in one movement the
crowd rose to its feet with starting eyes, while women hid
their faces or convulsively clutched at the arm nearest them.

As the matador made his thrust his sword struck a bone,
and delayed by this mishap he was caught by one of the horns

44

and hooked upwards by the waist. The splendid strong muscular body hung suspended like a pathetic dummy, until the powerful beast with a toss of its head sent him flying several yards away, and the torero fell heavily in the dust with arms and legs sprawling, just like a frog dressed in silk and gold.

"He's killed! He's gored in the stomach!" came from the benches.

But Gallardo got to his feet among the men who rushed to his rescue with capes. He smiled; he passed his hands over his body and then shrugged his shoulders to show that he was all right—a shaking, that was all, and a torn sash. The bull's horn had not penetrated further than the strong silk of his belt.

He turned to pick up his sword and muleta, but none of the audience sat down, guessing that the next encounter would be short and terrible. Gallardo advanced blindly towards the bull, as if he disbelieved in the deadliness of the horns now that he had escaped unharmed from them, prepared to kill or die, but it must be at once, without delays or precautions. Either the bull or himself! Everything turned red before him as if his eyes were injected with blood. He heard the crowd imploring him to keep calm as if their voices came from another world.

He made only two passes with the cape and then suddenly, quick as thought, like a spring released from its catch, he threw himself on the bull driving home the sword with a lightning thrust. His arm reached so far over the horns that as he drew back one of them grazed him, sending him staggering for a few steps; but he kept on his feet, and the animal rushed madly to the opposite side of the ring and fell with its legs doubled under it and its head touching the sand, where it lay till the *puntillero*[1] came to finish it off with his dagger.

The crowd went mad with delight. A splendid corrida! They were glutted with excitement. Gallardo gave them their money's worth all right—the entrance money and interest too! The aficionados would have something to talk about for at least three days when they met in the café. What courage!

[1] Who gives the *coup de grâce* to a mortally wounded bull.

45

What ferocity! . . . And Gallardo's supporters looked round them aggressively in case anyone disagreed with them.

"He's the finest matador in the world. If anyone denies it he's got me to reckon with!"

The rest of the corrida hardly attracted any attention. Everything seemed insipid and colourless after the feats of their idol.

When the last bull fell on the sand, a swarm of boys, aficionados of low class and bull-ring apprentices, invaded the arena. They surrounded Gallardo and escorted him from the president's box to the exit. They pressed round him, trying to shake his hand or touch his clothes, and finally the wilder spirits, struggling out of the grasp of El Nacional and the banderilleros, seized the maestro by the legs, hoisted him on their shoulders, and carried him in triumph all round the ring and the galleries, out into the street.

Gallardo took off his hat and waved it at the cheering crowds. Wrapped in his gorgeous processional cloak he was carried along like a god, erect and motionless above the sea of caps and Córdovan hats.

As he drove down the Calle de Alcalá in his carriage, hailed by the crowds who had not seen the bullfight but had already heard of his triumphs, a smile of pride and pleasure in his own prowess lit up his pale sweating face.

El Nacional was still feeling anxious about the maestro's tossing and terrible fall; he asked if he was in pain and whether Doctor Ruiz shouldn't be called.

"No: a mere touch. . . . No bull alive can kill me."

But as though he had remembered his earlier fears even in his moment of triumph, as though he detected an ironical expression in El Nacional's eyes, he added:

"I often get those feelings before I go into the ring. Womanish fears. But you're not far wrong, Sebastián. What is it you always say? . . . God or Nature? That's it. Neither God nor Nature has anything to do with bullfighting. Every man must get along as best he can, with his own skill and courage; he'll get no help from heaven or earth. You're a clever chap Sebastián; you ought to have studied for a profession."

46

And with the optimism born of success he treated the banderillero like a man of learning, forgetting how he normally jeered at his involved theories.

When he got to his hotel the hall was full of admirers waiting to embrace him. To judge from their exaggerated accounts, his exploits had become distorted out of all recognition on the way from the bull-ring to the hotel.

Upstairs, his room was full of friends, men who called him *tu* and imitated the countrified accent of shepherds and cattle drovers, as they slapped him on the back and cried: "You were fine! Absolutely splendid!"

Gallardo escaped from his enthusiastic welcomers and went into the passage with Garabato.

"Go and send off a telegram to them at home. You know: 'Same as usual'."

Garabato made excuses. The hotel people would see to it. He must help his master undress.

"No: I want you to do it. I'll wait. . . . And there's another telegram you must send. To that lady. You know—Doña Sol. Put 'Same as usual' in that one too."

CHAPTER TWO

After the death of Señor Juan Gallardo, a respectable cobbler with a shop under an archway in the suburb of La Feria, his wife Señora Angustias mourned his loss with suitable grief; but at the same time in her heart of hearts she felt the relief of someone who rests after a long march, or lays down an overwhelming burden.

"My poor darling! He's with God now! He was so good! So hard-working!"

In the twenty years of their life together he had caused her no more unhappiness than the other women of the district had to put up with. Out of the three pesetas which his work brought him most days of the week, he gave one to Angustias for house-keeping money and kept the other two for his own personal expenses and entertainment. After all, he had to repay his friends' hospitality; and the wine of Andalusia, though it is one of the glories of God, is far from cheap. Then of course he must go to the bull-ring. . . . What is a man supposed to be doing in this world if he neither drinks nor goes to bullfights?

Señora Angustias had to keep all her wits about her in order to bring up her two children, Encarnación and Juanillo. She worked as charwoman in the wealthier houses of the neighbourhood, she took in sewing, hawked around clothes and jewellery for a friend who was a pawnbroker, and made cigarettes with the skill she had acquired as a girl when Juan was courting her and used to wait for her, eager and attentive, at the gate of the tobacco factory.

She never had to complain of infidelity or cruelty. When the cobbler arrived home drunk and supported by his friends in the small hours of Sunday morning, his affection and high spirits were still with him. Angustias had to pull him indoors by force, because he would persist in standing in the street clapping his hands and serenading his portly spouse in a drivelling tone of voice with long-drawn-out love songs. And when at last she got the door shut behind him, depriving the neighbours of a source of much amusement, Juan would insist on satisfying his drunken sentimentality by a sight of the children, who were asleep in bed, kissing them and sobbing over them and all the while continuing to sing the praises of Señora Angustias, the "best woman in the whole world". In the end the good woman always relaxed her severity and burst out laughing; then she undressed him and put him to bed like a sick child.

It was his only failing, poor fellow! No leanings whatever towards women or gambling. It was selfish of him to insist on being well dressed while his family went about in rags, and to divide his earnings so unequally, but he made up for it by sporadic generosity. Señora Angustias remembered proudly how on fiesta days Juan used to make her put on her Manila shawl and her wedding mantilla and would walk by her side in his white Córdovan hat carrying his silver-handled stick, with the children in front, through the gardens of Las Delicias, just as though they were tradespeople from the Calle de las Sierpes. On the days of cheap bullfights he would treat her handsomely to glasses of Manzanilla in La Campana or a café in the Plaza Nueva before going to the ring. Now all that was left to the poor woman of those happy times was a pleasant but faded memory.

Señor Juan fell ill with consumption, and for two years his wife had to nurse him and at the same time work harder than ever at her various jobs so as to make up for the daily peseta he no longer gave her. At last he died in hospital, resigned to his fate because he had come to the conclusion that life without Manzanilla and bullfights was worthless. His last looks of love and gratitude were for his wife, as if his eyes were trying to tell her she was "the best woman in the whole world".

When Señora Angustias was left alone her situation was no worse than before; on the contrary she had more freedom than during those last two years, when her husband had weighed more heavily on her than her children. She was a woman of energetic and decided character, and she at once began to make plans for her son and daughter. Encarnación was now seventeen and was working at the tobacco factory, thanks to a friend of her mother's youth who had now become forewoman there. Juanillo had ever since babyhood spent his days under the archway in the suburb of La Feria watching his father at work, and Señora Angustias was determined he should become a shoemaker. She took him away from school, where he had learnt to read very badly, and apprenticed him at twelve years old to one of the best shoemakers in Seville.

Now the poor woman's troubles began.

Oh, that boy! The son of such respectable parents . . . yet every day, instead of going to the shop, he was off to the slaughter-house with some young hooligans who used to meet by a seat in the Alameda de Hércules and dare each other to make passes with a cape in front of th oxen, amusing the drovers and slaughtermen but getting knocked down and trampled on more often than not. Señora Angustias, who sat up at nights sewing so that her son should be decently dressed and have clean shirts to go to work in, would find him hanging about at the door, afraid to come in but too hungry to keep away, with his trousers torn, his jacket filthy and his face covered in bruises and scratches.

His mother would add slaps and beatings with a broom handle to the knocking-about the treacherous oxen had given him; but the hero of the slaughter-house put up with everything as long as he got his daily bread. "Beat me, but give me something to eat." And with appetite sharpened by violent exercise he swallowed stale bread, mouldy beans and rotten stockfish—all the damaged goods that the thrifty woman could find in the shops to keep her family going as cheaply as possible.

Busy as she was all day scrubbing floors in other people's houses, it was only in the evenings that she could keep an eye on her son, or go to his master's shop to ask how the apprentice was doing. She used to return from the shoemaker's breathless with rage, promising herself that the little devil would get a good thrashing.

Most days he never went near the shop at all; he spent the morning at the slaughter-house and the afternoon with a gang of other boys at the top of the Calle de la Sierpes hanging round the toreros out of a job who used to gather in La Campana, wearing new clothes and smart hats and boasting of their exploits, but none of them with more than a peseta in his pocket.

Juanillo gazed at these superior beings, enjoying the fine figure they cut and the effrontery with which they bantered the girls. It filled him with awe to think that each of these men owned a silk suit embroidered with gold, which he wore when he walked before the crowd with bands playing.

Señora Angustias' son was known as Zapaterín[1] to his disreputable friends, and it pleased him to think he had a

[1] Little shoemaker.

nickname, like nearly all the great figures of the bull-ring. That was a beginning at least. He wore a red handkerchief round his neck which he had filched from his sister, and let his hair fall over his ears in thick locks which he smoothed down with saliva. He liked his drill shirts to be gathered in at the waist with plenty of pleats. His trousers were old ones of his father's, altered to fit him by Señora Angustias; he wanted her to cut them high in the waist, tight over the hips and full in the leg, and was ready to weep with humiliation when she refused to fall in with his ideas.

A cape! If only he had a fighting cape of his own, instead of having to borrow this coveted object from his more fortunate friends for a few moments at a time! In the lumber-room at home there was an old mattress-cover from which Señora Angustias had taken the wool to sell when she was hard up. Zapaterín spent a morning shut up in this room while his mother was out cleaning the Canon's house. With the ingenuity of a shipwrecked mariner left to his own resources on a desert island he managed to cut out a fighting cape from the damp frayed material. Then he threw a handful of red dye, bought from the chemist, into a saucepan of boiling water and dipped the old linen in it. Juanillo was delighted with the result. A brilliant scarlet cape, which would be greatly envied at the village capeas! It only wanted drying, so he hung it up in the sun between the neighbours' white clothes. The wind blew the dripping rag against the nearest garments staining them with red, and a concert of threats, oaths and abuse of the ugliest sort aimed at his mother and himself, accompanied by clenched fists, obliged Zapaterín to take down his glorious cape and make off, with his face and hands covered with red as if he'd just done a murder.

Señora Angustias was a strong, stout, moustachioed woman, who feared no man and was respected by other women for her energy and determination. But she was powerless to control her son. What was to be done? She had laid violent hands on every part of the boy's body, and broken broomsticks on him, but with no result. He must have the hide of a buffalo. He was used to being butted by calves, cruelly trampled by cows and beaten by the drovers and slaughtermen (who had no mercy on the scallywag would-be bullfighters), so that his mother's thrashings seemed to him natural, the normal continuation at home of his life outside, and he accepted them without the slightest intention of reform, but simply as a payment for his food. And he went on hungrily chewing dry crusts, under blows and curses from his mother.

As soon as he had satisfied his appetite he took advantage of the liberty that Señora Angustias' frequent absences gave him, and fled from the house.

It was in the Café de La Campana, for many years the meeting-place of aficionados and clearing-house for bullfight gossip, that Juan used to hear the thrilling news: "There's a corrida tomorrow, Zapaterín."

The villages in the surrounding province celebrated the feast days of their patron saints by capeas with experienced bulls, and aspiring toreros would hurry off, in hopes of being able to say on their return that they had spread their cloaks in such famous rings as Aznalcóllar, Bollulos or Mairena. They walked by night, with their capes over their shoulders in summer, or wrapped round them in winter, with empty stomachs and talking about nothing but bulls.

If the village were several days' journey away they would camp in the open unless they were allowed to sleep in the hayloft of some inn out of charity. They made short work of any ripe grapes, melons or figs that came their way. Their only worry was lest some rival party, some other rough cuadrilla, should have had the same idea and arrive at the village before them.

When they reached their destination, tired and footsore from their long tramp and with mouths and eyes full of dust, they went straight to the mayor, and the leader of the group made a speech in praise of the talents of his party. They thought themselves lucky if municipal generosity provided them with a lodging in the inn stables, and a dish of stew which was cleaned up in a few seconds.

The village square had been converted into a ring with carts and boarded scaffolding, and here old bulls were let loose—mountains of flesh covered with scars and scabs, with huge sharp horns; beasts that had seen fighting in provincial fiestas for many years; veterans whose cunning and knowledge of the game was such that they were said to 'understand Latin'.

The local boys poked sticks at the bulls from places of safety and the crowd got more amusement from the 'toreros' from Seville than they did from the animals themselves. They spread their capes, trembling with fear, but comforted a little by the fullness of their stomachs. When they were knocked down everyone was delighted. If one of them suddenly took fright and ran for safety behind the palisade, the cruel villagers would receive him with insults, strike at his hands clutching the barrier and beat at his legs to make him go back into the ring.

"In you go again, you coward ! Show your face to the bull you shirker!"

Occasionally one of the 'matadors' would be carried out of the ring by four friends, white as a sheet, with glassy eyes and hanging head, his chest heaving like a broken bellows; but when the vet arrived on the scene he reassured everyone. There was no blood to be seen, the boy was only suffering from the shock of being tossed several yards to fall on the ground like a sack of potatoes, or of being trampled under foot by one of these enormous bulls. A pail of water was emptied over his head and when he recovered his senses he was regaled with a draught of aguardiente from Cazalla de la Sierra. After this princely treatment, back he had to go into the ring again.

When it began to grow dark and there were no more bulls loose, two of the cuadrilla took the best cape they had among them and went round the stands holding it out by the corners and asking for money. Coppers rained down on the red cloth, in large or small quantity according to the amusement the strangers had given the villagers; and when all was over they set off on their tramp home, knowing that their credit at the

53

inn was exhausted. Often they quarrelled on the way over the division of the coins tied up in a handkerchief.

All the rest of the week would be given over to describing their exploits to their friends who had stayed at home, who listened to them wide-eyed. They talked of their *veronicas*[1] at El Garrabo, of their *navarras*[2] at Lora, or of a dreadful goring which had happened at El Pedroso, imitating the airs and attitudes of the real professionals, who were sitting a short way away consoling themselves for their failure to get contracts by boasting and lies of every description.

Once Señora Angustias was without news of her son for more than a week. At last she heard a vague rumour that he had been hurt in a capea at Tocina. Heavens above! Where in the world was that? And how could she get there? She believed he was dead, and wept bitterly; all the same she decided to make the journey, but while she was planning it Juanillo arrived in person, pale and weak but talking of his accident with manly pride.

It was nothing: a jab in the buttock a few inches deep, which he was shamelessly eager to exhibit to all the neighbours, assuring them that he could put his finger in without reaching the end of it. He was proud of the smell of iodoform which hung about him, and told everyone how well he had been treated in Tocina. It was the best village in Spain. The richer inhabitants—the aristocracy as one might call them—had taken a great interest in him; the mayor had been to see him and had paid his return fare. He still had three duros left, which he handed his mother with princely generosity. His satisfaction was even greater when some of the toreros in La Campana took notice of him and inquired after his wound. They were real toreros too—this was fame indeed, at fourteen years old!

After this accident he stopped going to the shoemaker's shop altogether. His wound and his greater experience of bulls had increased his self-assurance. He would be a bull-fighter; nothing else would satisfy him! Señora Angustias gave

[1], [2] Different passes with the cape.

up all attempts at controlling him, seeing them to be useless. She tried to ignore her son's existence. When he returned home in the evenings at supper-time, his mother and sister used to give him his plate of food in silence, as if to crush him with their disapproval, but he munched away quite unmoved. When he was late they didn't keep so much as a crust of bread for him and he had to go out again just as empty as he had come home.

At nights he was to be found in the Alameda de Hércules with a lot of other young delinquents, apprentices, criminals and toreros. Sometimes the neighbours would see him talking in the streets to young men whose airs made the girls laugh, or to more dignified gentlemen who had been given feminine nicknames by the scandalmongers. Now and again he sold newspapers or boxes of sweets to the ladies who sat in the Plaza de San Francisco during Holy Week. When the Feria was on he hung about outside the hotels hoping to catch an 'Englishman' who would engage him as a guide. All tourists were Englishmen to him.

"Milord! . . . I'm a bullfighter!" he would say when he caught sight of a foreign-looking stranger, as if his profession was an irresistible qualification.

And to prove the fact he took off his cap and let down his pigtail—which he usually wore coiled on top of his head.

His companion in misfortune was a boy of his own age called Chiripa—a stunted, mischievous-looking orphan who had been wandering round Seville ever since he could remember, and impressed Juanillo with his greater experience. One of his cheeks was scarred by a bull's horn and Zapaterín thought this a much greater mark of distinction than his own invisible wound.

Once a lady tourist, eager for local colour, got into conversation with the two little toreros outside the door of her hotel, admired their pigtails and listened to the story of their exploits and was preparing to give them some money when Chiripa said in a sentimental voice:

"Don't give it to him; he's got a mother, but I'm all alone in the world. A chap doesn't value his mother till he loses her."

And Zapaterín, overcome with sadness and remorse, let the other boy take all the money, and muttered:

"Yes—that's true all right."

But this outburst of filial affection didn't prevent Juanillo from carrying on just as before—only putting in an occasional appearance at home and often taking long journeys away from Seville.

Chiripa was a past master of the vagabond life. On bullfight days he was determined that he and his companion should get into the ring somehow or other, by means of such stratagems as climbing walls, slipping in among the crowd or softening up the bull-ring servants by pitiful entreaties. It was unthinkable that there should be a bullfight and they shouldn't see it—after all they were members of the profession! When there were no capeas in the province they could always go and practice with their capes on the young bulls in the pastures of Tablada; but such attractions of Sevillian life didn't satisfy their ambition.

Chiripa had travelled about quite a bit, and he used to tell his companion about all the things he had seen in distant parts of Spain. He had become an expert in the art of travelling for nothing, by stowing away on trains. Zapaterín would listen enthralled to his descriptions of Madrid, that city of dreams whose ring might almost be called the cathedral of bullfighting.

One day a young man amused himself at their expense outside a café in the Calle de la Sierpes by telling them that they would make a lot of money if they went to Bilbao, there weren't so many bullfighters there as in Seville. So the two boys started off, with empty pockets and no other equipment than their capes—real fighting capes, the cast-offs of toreros whose names appeared on posters, which they had picked up for a few coppers in an old clothes shop.

They crept into trains and hid under the seats, but hunger and other needs forced them to come out and face their fellow passengers, who ended by pitying their plight, laughing at the queer figures they cut with their capes and pigtails, and giving them what was left of their provisions. When they stopped at a station and the railway officials chased them, they ran from coach to coach, or even tried to climb on the roofs, where they crouched till the train started off again. Quite often they were caught, pulled out of the train by the ears with blows and kicks, and left standing alone on the platform while the train vanished into the distance like a lost hope.

Then they used to wait for the next, bivouacking in the open air; or if they found they were being watched they walked across the fields to the next station, hoping for better luck there. And so at last they arrived at Madrid after an adventurous journey of several days, with some long waits and more than one thrashing. They gazed admiringly at the groups of unemployed bullfighters in the Calle de Sevilla and the Puerta del Sol, and even ventured to ask these superior beings for a little money to continue their journey—quite without success. One of the bull-ring servants who came from Seville took pity on them and let them sleep in the stables; he even procured them the treat of seeing a corrida of young bulls in that famous arena, which, however, seemed to them less imposing than the one in their home town.

Then they grew frightened by their own boldness, and by the fact that their journey's end seemed no nearer than before. They decided to go back to Seville in the same manner as they had come, but this time they enjoyed their stolen railway trips more. They travelled to several small villages in the provinces, following vague rumours of fiestas or capeas there. In this way they got as far as La Mancha and Estremadura, and if bad luck forced them to go on foot they took refuge in the huts of the credulous, good-natured peasants, who were amazed at their youthfulness, their daring and their bombastic talk, and took them for real toreros.

This wandering existence taught them a primitive cunning for the satisfaction of their needs. They would crawl round farmhouses on their stomachs, robbing kitchen gardens without anyone seeing them. They waited for hours for a solitary hen to come close enough for them to wring her neck, and then

57

went on their way again, stopping later to light a fire of dry wood and devour the poor bird, charred and half-raw, as voraciously as little savages. They were more frightened of farm dogs than of bulls. They were difficult brutes to fight, and they used to rush out with fangs bared, as if they were enraged by the boys' strange appearance and suspected they were enemies with designs on the property they guarded.

Several times when they were asleep near a station waiting for the next train a pair of Civil Guards came up to them, but when they saw the red bundles the vagabonds were using for pillows the guardians of law and order were pacified. They quietly took off the boys' caps and uncovered their pigtails—then they went away laughing, without further inquiries. Obviously they weren't thieves—only aficionados going to a capęa. There was in their tolerance a combination of love for the national sport and respect for the inscrutable future. Who could tell whether one of these ragged miserable-looking boys might not one day become a star performer—a hero who would dedicate bulls to kings, live in princely style and have his exploits and sayings described in the newspapers?

But an evening came when Zapaterín was left all alone in a village in Estremadura. The two boys were trying to astonish the country folk who had come to see the 'famous bullfighters come all the way from Seville' by placing the banderillas in the neck of a particularly crafty old bull. Juanillo had fixed his pair and was standing by the barrier enjoying the approval of the public, which took the form of tremendous thumps on the back and offers of glasses of wine, when a sudden horrified exclamation startled him out of his daze of glory. Chiripa was no longer to be seen standing in the ring. There was nothing left of him but the banderillas rolling in the dust, one shoe and his cap. The bull was fidgeting as if irritated by some impedi-ment, and on one of its horns was a bundle of clothes like a doll. Tossing its head violently it freed itself of the shapeless package, from which a crimson jet spouted, but before it could reach the ground it was caught and turned over on the other horn. At last the luckless bundle fell on the sand, and lay there limp and still, with blood pouring from it as wine gushes from a punctured wine-skin.

The herdsman lured the bull out into the corral with the help of a team of oxen, for no one dared go near it; meanwhile poor Chiripa was carried on a straw mattress to a room in the town hall which was used as a prison. His friend saw him lying there with his face as white as chalk, his eyes dim and his body red with the blood which could not be staunched by the cloths dipped in vinegar and water with which they were bathing his wounds, for lack of anything better.

"Good-bye, Zapaterín!" he sighed. "Good-bye, Juanillo!" and spoke no more. The dead boy's companion set off back to Seville, overcome by horror and unable to forget those glassy eyes, that groan of farewell. He was afraid. He would have run like a hare if a peaceable cow had crossed his path. He thought of his mother and her good advice. Perhaps it would be better to be a shoemaker and lead a quiet life. However these ideas only lasted as long as he was alone.

When he arrived at Seville he fell at once under the sway of the prevailing atmosphere. All his friends hurried up to ask for every detail of poor Chiripa's end, even the professional bull-fighters in the Campana showed a sympathetic interest in the death of the little chap with the scarred face who had run errands for them so often. Fired by the interest he aroused, Juan gave rein to his lively imagination and described how when he saw his friend tossed he had rushed at the bull and seized it by the tail and performed other stupendous feats, without being able to save poor Chiripa.

The terrifying memory faded at last. He would be a bull-fighter; nothing else would do for him. If others could, why shouldn't he? He thought of the mouldy beans and stale bread he got at home; of the shifts he was put to to get a new pair of trousers; of the hunger that was his constant companion on his expedition to the capeas. Moreover he felt a violent longing for all the pleasures and luxuries life had to offer; he looked with envy at carriages and horses; he stood about outside grand houses staring through the iron gates at

59

their handsome oriental-looking patios, with tiled archways, marble pavements and murmuring fountains scattering showers of pearly drops, night and day, into basins embowered in green leaves. He had made his choice. He would kill bulls or die. He would be rich, acclaimed by the public and written about in the newspapers, even if it cost him his life. He despised the inferior ranks of the profession. He saw the banderilleros risking their lives as the maestros did, for thirty duros a corrida, with no prospect at the end of a hard and dangerous life but to start some wretched little business with their savings or take a job at the slaughter-house. Some died in hospital; most of them begged from their younger comrades. No banderillas for him; no long years of submission to a maestro, as member of his cuadrilla. He would start killing bulls straight away; he would make his first entry into the ring as a matador.

*　　*　　*　　*　　*

Poor Chiripa's accident gave him a certain ascendancy over his friends, and he got together a ragged cuadrilla which followed him to the village capeas. They admired him because he was the bravest and the best dressed among them. Zapaterín was now nearly eighteen and several girls of easy virtue, attracted by his manly beauty and the glamour attached to his profession, quarrelled noisily for the honour of looking after him. He also possessed a so-called godfather, an elderly patron and ex-magistrate, who had a weakness for handsome young bullfighters, and whose intimacy with her son outraged Señora Angustias so much that she used to break out into the most obscene expressions she had learnt when she worked at the tobacco factory.

Zapaterín dressed in well-fitting suits made of English cloth and a smart hat. His female associates saw that his collars and shirt fronts were spotlessly white, and on special occasions he wore over his waistcoat a double gold chain like a woman's. This had been lent him by his elderly friend; it had already been worn by other young men at the outset of their careers.

He mixed with the professional bullfighters, and could afford to stand a glass of wine to old banderilleros who liked to talk about their famous masters. It was said that there were certain patrons who were backing this boy and were only waiting for a good moment to launch him at a novillada in the Seville bull-ring.

Zapaterín was in fact a matador already. One day at Lebrija, when an extremely lively young bull was loosed into the arena, his companions egged him on to try his fortune. "Do you dare have a go?" And he had a go. Afterwards, emboldened by the ease with which he had got through this crucial test, he went to every capea or farmhouse where young bulls were to be killed.

The owner of La Rinconada, a rich farm with a small bull-ring, was an enthusiast for bullfighting, and there were always meals and a hayloft at the disposal of any half-starved aficionados who wanted to amuse themselves by fighting his cattle. Juanillo had been there with his friends in his days of poverty and had eaten and drunk to the health of the land-owner. They would arrive on foot after a two days' walk, and the proprietor would look at the dusty little troupe with their bundles of capes and say solemnly:

"The one of you who does best will get his railway fare back to Seville."

For two days the farm owner sat smoking on the balcony of his ring, while the boys from Seville fought his young bulls and were often knocked down and trampled in the process.

"That's no good, you clumsy idiot!" he used to say when a pass with the cape had been bungled. Or: "Get up, you coward! A glass of wine'll help you get over your fright," to a boy who still lay stretched on the ground after the bull had passed over his body.

Zapaterín killed a young bull in a style so much to the taste of its owner that he was invited to sit at the master's table, while his friends stayed in the kitchen, dipping their horn spoons into the same steaming pot as the shepherds and farm labourers.

"You've earned your railway ticket, my boy. If you don't lose your nerve you'll go far. You've got talent."

As Zapaterín began his return journey to Seville in a second-class railway carriage, while his cuadrilla tramped home on foot, it seemed to him that a new life was beginning for him, and he cast looks of envy at the vast farm with its extensive olive-groves, its cornfields and mills, its pastures stretching away into the distance where thousands of goats grazed and bulls and cows lay chewing the cud. What riches! If only one day he could be the owner of something of the sort!

The news of his success in the village novilladas reached Seville and brought him to the notice of those restless and insatiable aficionados who were always on the look out for the rise of a new star to eclipse the old ones.

"He looks a promising lad," they said to each other, watching him walk down the Calle de las Sierpes with short steps and arrogantly swinging arms. "We must see what he can do when it comes to the real thing."

For them, and for Zapaterín also, the 'real thing' meant the arena of the Seville bull-ring, and the young man was soon to find himself face to face with reality. His protector had bought him a second-hand fighting suit, cast off by some unknown matador. A novillada was being organized on behalf of a charity, and some influential aficionados eager for new blood got him included in the programme.

Señora Angustias's son refused to be billed as Zapaterín, a name he was anxious to forget. No nicknames for him, to remind the grand people he would be friends with in future of his humble origins; no subordinate position in the ring. He wanted to be known by his father's names, he wanted to be Juan Gallardo.

All the inhabitants of the La Feria district hurried to the bull-ring, full of patriotic and noisy enthusiasm. The people from La Macarena and the other working-class suburbs were roused to special interest also. A new Sevillian matador! . . .

There weren't enough seats for everyone, and thousands waited outside the ring, eager for news.

Gallardo fought, killed, and was knocked down by a bull without being wounded. He kept his audience on tenterhooks by his recklessness, which more often than not turned out luckily and provoked deafening roars of applause. Aficionados whose judgement was respected smiled delightedly. He still had much to learn; but he had courage and eagerness, which were more important than anything.

"Best of all he goes right in to kill, and once there he never leaves the bull."

The matador's girl friends were frantic with excitement, waving and gesturing hysterically, their eyes full of tears, their mouths pouring out loving endearments in broad daylight which they generally kept for the hours of darkness. One threw her shawl into the arena; another went one better by sending her blouse and stays to joint it; while a third tore off her skirt. Some of the spectators laughingly seized hold of the girls, to prevent them hurling themselves into the ring or stripping themselves naked.

On the other side of the amphitheatre the old magistrate was smiling tenderly through his white beard to see how bravely the boy was comporting himself and how well his bullfighter's suit became him. When he saw him knocked down by the bull he threw himself back in his seat, almost fainting. That was too much for him to stand.

The husband of Gallardo's sister Encarnación was sitting in the second row, looking proud as a peacock. He was a saddler, a sedate and disapproving man, who had fallen in love with the cigarette-maker and married her, but on the express condition that he would have nothing to do with that bad lot, her brother.

Gallardo was offended by his brother-in-law's unfriendliness and never attempted to set foot in his shop, which was in the suburb of La Macarena, nor had he ever dropped calling him *Usted* when he met him sometimes of an evening in Señora Angustias' house.

63

"I'm going to see them pelt your good-for-nothing brother with oranges," he said to his wife when he set off for the ring.

But here he was greeting the matador from his seat, calling him *tu*, and 'Juanillo', and bursting with obvious pride when the young torero heard his shouts and responded to them with a movement of his sword.

"He's my brother-in-law," said the saddler, hoping to impress the people sitting next him. "I always thought that boy would come to something. My wife and I have helped him of course. . . ."

Gallardo's final exit was triumphal. The crowd rushed forward as if they wanted to eat him in their delight. It was thanks to his brother-in-law that order was restored; he protected him with his own body and led him away to the hired carriage, where he sat down by his side.

When they arrived at the little house in the suburb of La Feria a large crowd was following them, cheering so loudly that everyone came out to their front doors. News of the matador's success had got there before him and all the neighbours hurried forward to look at him and shake him by the hand.

Señora Angustias and her daughter were waiting at the door of their house. The saddler almost lifted his brother-in-law down in his arms, shouting and waving in a proprietary fashion to prevent anyone from touching him, as though he were a sick man.

"Here he is, Encarnación," he said, pushing him towards his wife. "Roger de Flor[1] himself!"

Encarnación had no need to ask any more questions, for she knew that her husband thought of this historical personage as the embodiment of all greatness—a belief based on a confused recollection of books read long ago—and that he would only use his name when it was a question of a prodigious success.

Some excited neighbours who had been at the corrida complimented Señora Angustias:

[1] A soldier of fortune of the Middle Ages.

"Blessed be the mother who bore such a brave son!" they cried, looking admiringly at her prominent abdomen.

The poor woman's eyes were full of wonder and doubt. Was it really her Juanillo that everyone was running after so enthusiastically? Had they all gone crazy?

Then suddenly she threw herself upon him, as if all the past was obliterated, as if all the worry and rage he had caused her had been a dream, as if she were now confessing to a shameful error. Her large plump arms were round the torero's neck, and her tears wetted his cheek.

"My son! Juaniyo! . . . If only your poor father could see you!"

"Don't cry, Mother. . . . You must be happy today. You wait! God willing you shall have a new house and your friends will see you ride in your own carriage, with a Manila shawl that'll make them die of envy!"

The saddler acknowledged these promises of future splendour, by nodding repeatedly at his wife who hadn't recovered from her dazed astonishment at this sudden change of heart.

"Yes, Encarnación . . . there's nothing the boy can't do if he tries. He's Roger de Flor all over again!"

That night nothing was talked about in the bars of the working class quarter except Gallardo's success.

"He's the torero of the future. He's been biding his time and now he's ready . . . that boy will drive all the Córdovan champions out of the ring!"

These assertions were animated by the proud rivalry of Seville with Córdova, which also produced fine bullfighters.

From this day Gallardo's life was completely transformed. His social superiors greeted him as an equal and invited him to join them at their café tables. The girls who had saved him from hunger and looked after his clothes found themselves gradually cold-shouldered and treated with smiling contempt. Even his elderly protector discreetly withdrew into the background after one or two rebuffs, and transferred his tender feelings to other youthful toreros.

The managers of the bull-ring sought him out, and flattered

him as though he were already a celebrity. When his name was on the placards they were sure of success; every seat would be taken. The populace applauded 'Señora Angustias' son' wildly, repeating stories of his courage; Gallardo's fame began to spread all over Andalusia. The saddler was always to the fore, and without ever being invited, took upon himself the function of protecting his brother-in-law's interests. A hard-headed man (in his own opinion) and very experienced in business matters, he saw his future career clearly marked out for him. "What your brother needs," he would say as he got into bed beside his wife, "is a practical man to look after his interests. How would it be if he made me his manager? A splendid thing for him. And for us. . . ."

The saddler pictured to himself the great wealth that Gallardo would one day enjoy, and at the same time thought of his own five children and those that would certainly follow, for he was a man of tireless and prolific conjugal fidelity. Perhaps the matador's fortune might one day come to his nephew. Who could tell?

For a year and a half Juan fought in novilladas in the best bull-rings in Spain. His fame even reached Madrid, whose aficionados were anxious to see the 'Sevillian boy', of whom they had heard so much from the newspapers and from their knowledgeable Andalusian friends.

Arrived in the capital, Gallardo swaggered along the pavement of the Calle de Seville and past the Café Inglés, surrounded by friends from his own country who now lived in Madrid. The pretty girls smiled at his gallantries and fixed their eyes on his thick gold chain and large diamond rings, jewellery bought with his first earnings and on the credit of those to come. A matador must show that he has plenty of money by his personal adornment and his generous hospitality. How far away now the old days seemed when he and poor Chiripa had wandered along this same pavement in terror of the police, and gazed admiringly at the bullfighters, and collected the butts of their cigars!

Things turned out well for him in Madrid. He made

friends and collected a group of admirers on the look out for something new, who declared that he was the 'torero of the future', and that he should already have been formally presented as full matador.

"He's bound to make bags of money, Encarnación," said his brother-in-law. "Millions even, if he doesn't have an accident."

The family circumstances had completely changed. Gallardo now mixed with the gentry of Seville, and he didn't care for his mother to go on living in the same little house of the days of her poverty. For his own part he would have liked to move to the best street in the town, but Señora Angustias was faithful to the La Feria district which she loved with that devotion to the scenes of their youth that simple people develop as they grow older.

They now lived in a much better house. His mother didn't need to work any more; the neighbours paid court to her, seeing her as a generous lender in future times of distress. Besides his flashy heavy personal jewellery, Juan possessed that chief treasure of every bullfighter—a powerful sorrel mare, with a cowboy saddle and a horse blanket trimmed with many-coloured fringes. He used to ride her through the streets with the sole object of receiving the homage of his friends, who greeted his stylish appearance with loud *Olés*. For the present this satisfied his craving for popularity. Sometimes, too, he would join some of his upper class friends in a gay cavalcade and ride out to the pastures of Tablada to look at the cattle on the eve of a corrida.

"When I receive the *alternativa*,"[1] he was always saying, as if all his plans for the future depended on this event. This was the moment when he hoped to realize various projects with which he wanted to surprise his mother, though the poor woman was already quite frightened by all the comfort which had suddenly invaded her house, and couldn't possibly have envisaged any improvements.

[1] The formal initiation of a novillero as a full matador; he is given the sword and muleta by the senior matador of the corrida, and has to kill the first bull with it.

At last the day of the alternativa came—the day of Gallardo's public recognition as matador.

A famous maestro presented him with the sword and muleta in the middle of the Seville bull-ring, and the crowd went mad with delight when they saw him kill the first of his formal[1] bulls with a single sword thrust. A month later this doctorate in tauromachy was confirmed in the Madrid bull-ring, when another no less celebrated maestro gave him the alternativa in a corrida of Miura bulls.

He was no longer a novillero; he was a matador, and his name figured on the placards beside those of heroes he had worshipped from afar in the days when he was going round to village capeas. He remembered waiting for one of them, and asking him for help, when his train passed through a station near Córdova. That night he had something to eat, thanks to that brotherly feeling that exists between wearers of the pigtail, and which may prompt a matador living in princely style to give a duro and a cigar to the needy wretch who is learning the rudiments of cloak play.

Engagements began to pour in upon the new matador. There were people curious to see him in every bull-ring in the Peninsula. The bullfighting newspapers spread abroad his photograph and the story of his life, distorted by the addition of many romantic episodes. No matador had more contracts. He was clearly going to make a lot of money.

His brother-in-law Antonio scowled and grumbled to his wife and mother-in-law about this success. What an ungrateful fellow! It was always the way with people who rose quickly in the world. He had worked so hard for Juan too; never giving in to the impresarios, when they were making arrangements for novilladas! Yet now that he was a maestro Gallardo had made a quite recent acquaintance his manager—Don José, who was no relation whatever, but had the prestige of being an aficionado of long standing.

"He'll regret it," he concluded. "A man only has one

[1] Bulls conforming in age, size, etc. to the requirements for a formal bullfight.

68

family. Where else can he find the affection he gets from those who've known him from a child? Well, he'll be the loser. I would always have treated him like the real Roger. . . ."

But here he stopped short, swallowing the rest of the famous name, for fear of being laughed at by the banderilleros and aficionados who frequented the house and had not failed to take stock of the object of the saddler's historical passion.

With the good nature of a successful man Gallardo gratified his brother-in-law by giving him the supervision of the house he was building, with *carte blanche* as to expenses. Money came into the matador's hands with such amazing ease that he wasn't sorry Antonio should get hold of some of it, as a compensation for not being made manager.

He was now able to fulfil his dream of building a house for his mother. Having passed most of her life scrubbing the floors of the rich, poor thing, she should now have a beautiful patio of her own, with marble floors and tiled dados, and rooms furnished as the gentry's were, and servants—plenty of servants—to wait on her. He shared her feeling of faithful affection for the suburb where he had spent his miserable childhood. It pleased him to dazzle and impress the same people who had employed his mother as charwoman, and give a handful of pesetas to those who used to take their shoes to his father to mend, or perhaps had given him a crust of bread when he was starving. He now bought up several old houses, amongst others the one with the archway under which his father had worked; he had them pulled down and was building a fine house which was to have white walls, grilles painted green, a porch lined with coloured tiles, and a gate of elaborate iron-work through which could be seen the patio with its fountain in the middle and its marble columns with gilded cages full of song-birds hanging between them.

Antonio's pleasure at being given a free hand over the direction of these building operations received a check from a terrible piece of news.

Gallardo had a sweetheart. It was now full summer and he was rushing all over Spain, from one bull-ring to another, killing bulls and being applauded by huge crowds; yet almost every day he wrote a letter to a certain girl who lived in the suburbs, and when he had a short respite between one corrida and the next, he used to leave his companions and take the train back to Seville to spend the night in amorous conversation with his sweetheart.

"You see what he's up to?" exclaimed the scandalized saddler to 'the bosom of his family', as he described them, namely his wife and mother-in-law. "He gets himself a sweetheart, and never a word to the family, which is the only thing that matters in this world. So his lordship wants to get married! He's tired of us, no doubt, the shameless fellow!"

Encarnación's coarsely handsome face expressed her emphatic agreement: she rather enjoyed disapproving of her enviably fortunate brother. Yes, he was shameless, and always had been.

But her mother disagreed.

"No, indeed he's not. I know the girl, and her poor mother used to work at the factory with me. Good as gold, a nice-mannered little thing, and pretty too. . . . I've already told Juan that as far as I'm concerned he can go ahead . . . and the sooner the better."

The girl was an orphan, living with her uncle and aunt who kept a small grocer's shop in the district. Her father had been a dealer in spirits, and had left her two shops in the neighbourhood of La Macarena.

"It's not much," said Señora Angustias. "But the girl doesn't come empty-handed; she's got a little something of her own. And as for clothes . . . Jesus! You should just see what she does with those little hands of hers; all the embroidered stuff in the bottom drawer she's filling for herself!"

Gallardo had a dim recollection of playing round the cobbler's shop with her when he was a boy, while their mothers were gossiping together. She had been as dark and quick as a lizard, with gypsy eyes—the irises densely black like drops of ink, the whites blueish and the tear-ducts pink. She ran as nimbly as a boy on thin stick-like legs, and her hair flew wildly round her head in rebellious curls like black snakes. Then he lost sight of her and didn't see her again till many years later, when he was a novillero and already beginning to make a name for himself.

It was at the Feast of Corpus Christi, one of the few fiestas when women abandoned their oriental seclusion indoors and came out into the streets wearing white lace mantillas and carnations pinned to their breasts. Gallardo saw a tall girl, slim but strong, with her slender waist belted in between firm and ample curves which showed all the vigour of her youthful body. Her face, pale as milk, blushed red when she saw the young torero and she dropped her large bright eyes behind her long lashes. 'That girl recognizes me,' Gallardo thought conceitedly. 'She must have seen me in the ring.'

But when he followed the girl and her aunt, and found that it was Carmen, his childhood playmate, he felt amazed and bewildered at the marvellous transformation of 'the little dark lizard' of former days.

All the neighbours gossiped about their courtship, and felt that it was in some sense a credit to the district.

"That's the way I am," said Gallardo to his friends in his lordly fashion. "I don't want to be like the other toreros and marry a young lady, all hats, feathers and flounces. I stick to my own class. Give me a fine shawl, an attractive figure, a girl who knows how to walk. . . . *Olé!*"

His friends were eager to defend his choice. She was a fine girl all right! What a figure! Enough to drive a man mad. And from a good family too! But the bullfighter frowned. No more joking, eh? And the less they all talked about Carmen the better.

Some evenings as they exchanged loving words through the grille, her dark face framed among the pots of flowers, they would be interrupted by the waiter from a neighbouring wine shop, carrying a tray with glasses of Manzanilla. This was the traditional Sevillian custom of treating courting couples; it was called 'paying the rent'.

The matador drank one glass and offered the other to his girl, saying to the waiter:

"Go and say thank you to these gentlemen for me, and that I'll look in there later on. And tell Montañes that he's not to take any money from them. Juan Gallardo will settle the bill."

And as soon as the conversation with his betrothed was finished he would go over to the wine shop where the originators of the compliment were waiting; sometimes they would be close friends, sometimes strangers who wanted to drink a glass of wine with the matador.

During the winter after his return from his first tour as full matador, he used to spend the cold nights at the grille of Carmen's window, wrapped in a short full-cut cloak made of greenish cloth embroidered with a design of leaves in black silk.

"They say you drink too much," sighed Carmen, pressing her face against the iron bars.

"Rubbish! . . . My friends treat me and I treat them back, that's all. After all a torero is . . . a torero; he can't be expected to live like a monk."

"They say you go with bad women."

"All lies! . . . That was long ago before I knew you. Good heavens! I'd like to know what cad has been putting such ideas into your head. . . ."

"And when shall we be married?" she went on, cutting short her lover's indignation.

"As soon as the house is finished. I wish to God it could be tomorrow. My ridiculous brother-in-law won't get on with it. He knows he's doing all right so he let's everything slide "

"I'll arrange everything once we're married, Juaniyo. You'll see how well I'll manage, and how your mother'll love me."

And so they went on planning for the wedding which all Seville was talking about. Carmen's uncle and Señora Angustias discussed it whenever they met, but in spite of that the torero hardly ever entered his sweetheart's house, as if some formidable prohibition closed the door to him. They both preferred to talk through the grille in the customary way.

The winter passed. Gallardo went hunting on the estates of several country gentlemen who addressed him as *tu* in a patronizing way. He had to keep fit by constant physical exercise until the corridas began again. He was afraid of losing his strength and agility.

His most indefatigable propagandist was that same Don José who now acted as his manager and spoke of him always as 'my matador'. He took a hand in everything that concerned Gallardo, recognizing no prior claims even among his family. He had a private income of his own and his life was entirely absorbed in talking about bulls and bullfighters. According to him corridas were the only interesting things in the world, which was divided among nations of two different sorts: the favoured ones with bull-rings, and all those other sad countries where there was no sun, no gaiety, no Manzanilla, yet where people still thought themselves happy and important although they had never seen even a bad novillada.

He put a warlike energy and a fanatical faith into his interest in bullfighting. Still young, but stout and bald, with a fair beard, this father of a family who was so cheerful and laughter-loving in ordinary life could be fierce and obstinate when his neighbours in the bull-ring maintained a different opinion from his own. He felt himself capable of fighting the whole audience in defence of a torero whom he admired, and his loud protests often interrupted the applause when he felt it was not deserved.

He had been a cavalry officer, out of interest in horses rather than in war. He retired from the service because of his stoutness and his obsession with bulls, and thereafter spent his summers watching corridas and his winters talking about them. If only he could be the guide, mentor and manager of a matador! When he became aware of this longing all the maestros were provided with managers, so that Gallardo's advent was a stroke of luck for him. The slightest doubt cast on the merits of his hero made him turn crimson with anger, and the argument would soon become a personal one. He used to describe, as if it were some glorious episode in a war, how he had come to blows with two evil-minded aficionados who had been criticizing 'his matador' for being too reckless.

73

The newspapers seemed to him quite inadequate to broadcast Gallardo's fame, and on winter mornings he would go and sit at a sunny corner at the top of the Calle de las Sierpes where he would be sure to see most of his friends.

"Ah—there's only one real man among them!" he would say aloud as if talking to himself, pretending not to notice who was coming by. "He's the best in the world! Anyone who thinks otherwise had better say so! He's the only one!"

"Who?" asked his friends, making believe not to understand him for their own amusement.

"Who do you think? . . . Juan of course."

"Juan who?"

"What Juan could it be?" (With an expression of indignant surprise.) "As if there were more than one Juan! Why Juan Gallardo."

"Good heavens man!" some of them said, "anyone would think you went to bed together! Perhaps it's you who are going to marry him?"

"Only because he doesn't want to," Don José answered roundly and with idolatrous fervour. Then seeing some more friends approaching he forgot their banter and began all over again!

"No—there's only one real man among them! The best in the whole world! If you don't believe me, just say so. . . . I'm here to answer you!"

*　　*　　*　　*　　*

Gallardo's wedding was a great event. It was also the beginning of life in the new house, of which the saddler was immensely proud, showing off the patio, the columns and the tiles as if he had made them with his own hands.

They were married in San Gil, before the Virgin of Hope, known as La Macarena. As they left the church the sun was shining on hundreds of Chinese shawls embroidered with exotic flowers and brilliant-coloured birds worn by the bride's friends. A member of the Cortes was best man. Amongst the black or white felt hats worn by most of the guests could be seen the shining top hats of Gallardo's manager and other gentlemen, enthusiastic supporters, who smiled with pleasure and felt they had gained in popularity from standing beside the torero.

All day long alms were distributed at the door of the new house. Many poor people came from distant villages attracted by news of this splendid wedding.

A grand repast was served in the patio, and photographers arrived to take pictures for the Madrid newspapers, for Gallardo's wedding was an event of national importance. The melancholy twanging of guitars went on far into the night, accompanied by hand-clapping and the rattle of castanets. Girls stamped their little feet on the marble pavement, with their arms arched above their heads, while their shawls and petticoats swirled around their graceful figures swaying to the rhythm of sevillanas. Bottles of good Andalusian wine were opened by the dozen; glasses of heady sherry, rough Montilla and pale perfumed Manzanilla from Sanlúcar passed from hand to hand. Everyone was tipsy, but their drunkenness had a gentle nostalgic flavour which needed no outlet but sighs and singing. Often several songs would start up at once, all with some sad refrain about death, prison and 'poor Mother'— that eternal theme of the Andalusian muse.

At midnight the last guests went home, and the newly-married pair were left alone in the house with Señora Angustias. The saddler departed with his wife, an expression of gloom on his face. He was drunk, and angry too, because no one had taken any notice of him all day. As if he were of no account! As if Gallardo's family didn't exist!

"We're being turned out, Encarnación. That girl with her innocent little face means to be the mistress now. There won't be any room for us; the house will be full of children, you'll see...."

And the prolific husband became indignant at the thought of the matador's future family coming into the world with the sole object of ruining his own.

But time passed; a year went by, and Antonio's prophecies

had not come true. Gallardo and his wife appeared at every fiesta, dressed with all the showy elegance suitable to a rich and popular couple—she in shawls which drew cries of admiration from poorer women, he flashing his diamonds. He was always ready to pull out his purse to stand someone a drink or give money to the beggars who flocked round him. Copper-skinned gypsy women, witchlike and garrulous, besieged Carmen with promises of a lucky future. She would soon have a child, God bless her!—a baby boy more beautiful than the sun. They could tell by the whites of her eyes. She was half-way through her time already. . . . But though Carmen dropped her eyes and blushed with pleasure and bashfulness, though the matador drew himself up, proud of his work and hoping it would bear fruit, no child appeared.

Another year passed, and still their hopes weren't realized. Señora Angustias grew sad when people talked to her of this disappointment. She had other grandchildren, Encarnación's children, who passed much of their time in her house on the saddler's instructions, doing everything they could to please their uncle. But their grandmother was trying to make up to her son for her past unkindness, and she longed for a son of his to bring up in her own way and surround with all the love she had stinted his father of during his unhappy childhood.

"I know what it is," said the old woman sadly. "Poor Carmen has too much to worry about—you should see the way she gets when Juan is on his travels."

In winter time, the season of rest, the torero stayed at home or went into the country hunting, or for trials of yearling bulls. Then all was well. Carmen seemed happy in the knowledge that her husband was not in danger. She laughed at anything and everything, ate well, and a healthy colour came into her cheeks. But as soon as it was spring and Juan left home to fight in bull-rings all over Spain the poor girl grew pale and sickly looking and seemed to fall into a distressing stupor, her eyes wide with fear and ready to shed tears at the least provocation.

"He's got seventy-two corridas this year," said the friends of

76

the family counting up his engagements. "He's more sought after than any of them."

And Carmen gave an unhappy ghost of a smile. Seventy-two afternoons of anguish, sitting like a criminal in the condemned cell, longing for the arrival of the telegram in the evening, yet dreading to open it. Seventy-two days haunted by vague superstitions, fearing that a word left out of a prayer might influence the fate of her absent husband. Seventy-two days of living a life of painful unreality in this peaceful house, of seeing the same faces, the same daily happenings slipping by as gently and smoothly as if nothing extraordinary were happening in the world, hearing her sister-in-law's children playing in the patio and the song of the flower-seller in the street—yet knowing that all the while, far away, very far away in unknown cities before millions of eyes, her Juan was fighting with wild beasts, seeing death itself pass close to his breast with every movement of the red cloth in his hands.

Oh! those corrida days, days of fiesta, when the sky seemed bluer and the deserted streets echoed under the feet of passing holiday-makers; when guitars thrummed and there was singing and hand-clapping in the wine shop at the corner. Carmen used to leave the house, poorly dressed, with her mantilla over her eyes as if she dreaded meeting anyone, and take refuge in one of the churches. Her simple faith, peopled with anxious superstitions, sent her from altar to altar, weighing in her mind the virtues and miracles of each sacred image. She went to San Gil, the church which had witnessed the happiest day of her life; she knelt before the Virgin of La Macarena and gazed through the warm light of the dozens of tapers she had ordered to be lit at the dark face of the figure with its black eyes and long lashes, which many said so singularly resembled her own. She put her trust in La Macarena; she was not called 'Our Lady of Hope' for nothing. At this very moment she was certainly protecting Juan with her divine power.

But suddenly doubts and fears tore a breach in her faith. The Virgin was a woman, and women can do so little! They

77

are destined to suffer and weep, just as she was weeping for her husband, just as the Virgin had wept for her Son. She must seek more potent help. And with the egotism of suffering she left La Macarena without a qualm, like someone who forgets a useless friendship, and went to the church of San Lorenzo, in search of Our Lord Jesus of Great Power. The sculptor Montañes had carved this terrifying image of the Man-God with his crown of thorns, sweat and tears on his cheeks and his cross by his side.

The tragic sadness of the Nazarene as he stumbled over stones, bowed down by the weight of the cross, seemed to bring some comfort to the poor wife. Lord of Great Power! The vague but grandiose title calmed her. If only the Deity in his purple and gold velvet would listen to her sighs, and the prayers she muttered over and over so hastily, trying to get as many words as possible into the time—surely Juan would come safely out of the arena where he was fighting at that very moment! At other times she would give money to the sacristan, light tapers and spend hours on end watching the wavering reflection cast by their orange tongues on the image, imagining that she saw smiles of consolation and expressions of kindness in the changing lights and shadows on that varnished face, fancying it promised her happiness.

Our Lord of Great Power had not deceived her. When she got home there was the blue folded paper. She opened it with a shaking hand: 'Same as usual.' She could breathe again, she could sleep like the criminal who is granted a momentary respite from execution; but in another two or three days the torments of uncertainty, the terrible fear of the unknown, were with her again.

In spite of her love for her husband Carmen had moments of rebellion. If only she had known what her life would be like before she married! Now and then she would feel impelled to go and see her sisters in misfortune, the wives of the other toreros of Juan's cuadrilla. Perhaps they would have some news.

El Nacional's wife, who kept a wine shop in the same district, received the maestro's lady calmly and seemed surprised at her fears. She had got used to the life. Of course her husband must be all right since she had had no news of him. Telegrams were expensive things, and a banderillero didn't make much. If the paper-boys weren't shouting about an accident then there hadn't been one. And she went on serving her customers, as if her dull mind were insensitive to the impression of fear.

At other times Carmen crossed the bridge and went to the Triana district to see the wife of Potaje the picador, who led a gypsy existence in a hovel like a fowl-house, surrounded by dirty dark-skinned children whom she ordered about and terrified with stentorian shouts. She was proud to be visited by the maestro's lady, but ready to laugh at her anxieties. There was nothing to be afraid of. If you were on foot you could always get away from the bull, and Señor Juan Gallardo had a rare way of throwing himself on the brutes. Hardly anyone got killed by bulls. The worst thing was when a man fell off his horse. Everyone knew what happened to the picadors, it was just one dreadful fall after another all their lives long. If sudden death in some frightful accident didn't get them they'd die mad as like as not. That was what would happen to poor Potaje; it was a hard life just for a handful of duros—while others. . . .

She didn't finish her sentence, but her eyes were full of protest against the injustice of fate and against the fact that as soon as a young man got a sword in his hand he took all the applause, the popularity and the money for himself, without risking his life any more than his humbler companions.

Little by little Carmen grew accustomed to her new existence. The cruel hours of waiting on bullfight days, the visits to churches, the superstitious vacillations, all had to be accepted as incidents necessary to her life. Besides, her husband's good luck and the continual discussion at home of the events of each fight, gradually familiarized her with danger. She learnt to think of a brave bull as a noble animal which had come into the world for the sole purpose of bringing fame and money to matadors.

She had never been to a formal corrida. Since the day she had seen her future husband in his first novillada she had never returned to the ring. She felt she hadn't the courage to watch a bullfight, even if Gallardo was not appearing in it. She would faint with terror if she saw other men facing danger dressed like her Juan.

After they had been married three years, the matador was wounded in the Valencia ring. Carmen didn't hear of it at once. The telegram arrived at the usual time, with the message 'Same as usual'. This was the well-meaning work of Don José, Gallardo's manager, who came to see her each day and made use of every stratagem to prevent her reading the papers, so that the news was kept from her for over a week.

When Carmen at last heard of the accident through the indiscretion of some neighbours, she wanted to jump into a train at once and go and look after her husband, who she felt sure was being neglected. But there was no need. Before she could start, the matador arrived home, pale from loss of blood and under orders to rest one leg for some time, but gay and cheerful enough to reassure his family. From that moment the house was like a shrine, with hundreds of people passing through the patio to salute Gallardo ('the greatest man in the world') who sat in a basket chair with his leg up on a stool, peacefully smoking, as though his flesh was not torn by a horrible wound.

Doctor Ruiz who had arrived with him at Seville pronounced him well in less than a month, marvelling at the vigour of his constitution. In spite of his long experience of surgery, he was always surprised by the speed with which bullfighters recovered. The bull's horn, filthy with blood and excrement and often splintered by blows, broke through the flesh and ripped it, combining deep penetration with extensive bruising. Yet these appalling wounds healed much more easily than those of ordinary life.

"I don't understand it. It's a mystery," said the old doctor with a puzzled expression. "Either these boys' flesh is tougher than other people's, or the horn—dirty as it is—has some curative power we don't understand."

Not long afterwards Gallardo began fighting again, with his enthusiasm quite unaffected by his goring in spite of his enemies' predictions.

After four years of marriage, the matador sprang a great surprise on his wife and mother. They were going to be land-owners—landowners on a really big scale, with properties stretching to the horizon, with olive groves, mills, vast flocks of sheep: an estate, in fact, as fine as any belonging to the richest men in Seville.

Gallardo had the typical craving of a torero to be a country gentleman and own horses and cattle. Bullfighters are not attracted by town property and stocks and shares, nor do they understand them. The bull makes them think of the green plains; the horses remind them of the country. Their constant need of exercise and movement, hunting and walking during the winter months, turns their minds to the ownership of land.

The only wealth that Gallardo believed in was that of the owner of a farm and great herds of cattle. Ever since the days of his poverty when he had wandered by footpaths, through olive groves and pastures, he had cherished the fervent longing to possess acres and acres of land of his own, guarded from intruders by barbed wire fences.

His manager was aware of his desires. He it was who looked after all the matador's interests, collecting the money due from different impressarios, and keeping accounts which he tried in vain to explain to Gallardo.

"That's all gibberish to me," said the torero, not at all dissatisfied with his ignorance. "I know how to kill bulls—that's all. Do what you like, Don José. I trust you. I know you'll do the best for me."

And Don José, who hardly gave any thought to his own affairs (which he left to the inexpert management of his wife) brooded day and night over the matador's fortune, investing it at good interest, with the cupidity of a money-lender.

"I've found what you want," he said one day in a pleased

81

voice. "A farm as big as the whole world, and—what's more—very cheap. An absolute bargain. We'll sign the deeds next week."

Gallardo asked where the farm was and what was its name.

"It's called La Rinconada."

His dearest wish had been fulfilled.

When Gallardo went with his wife and mother to take possession of the farm, he showed them the hayloft where he had slept with his companions in poverty, the room where he had dined with the master of the house, and the little bull-ring where he had killed a yearling bull and so won for the first time the right to travel in a train without hiding under the seat.

CHAPTER THREE

In the winter, when Gallardo was not at La Rinconada, a party of his friends used to gather in the dining-room of his Seville house and spend the evenings with him.

Among the first arrivals were the saddler and his wife, whose two youngest children now lived with the matador. It was as though Carmen hoped to forget her own sterility and the oppressive silence of the great house by having them with her; and partly from natural affection and partly at the instigation of their parents the children were always kissing and petting their beautiful aunt and their generous and popular uncle.

Encarnación was now as fat as her mother, with a figure grown shapeless through constant child-bearing, and the beginnings of a moustache to emphasize the advancing years. She smiled sycophantically at her sister-in-law, apologizing for the trouble the children gave her. But before Carmen could reply, the saddler interrupted:

"They're all right, my dear. You know how fond they are of their uncle and aunt. The little girl adores her Auntie Carmen. . . ."

So the two children stayed on, as if the house were their own, guessing what their parents expected of them with infantile cunning, and lavishing fondness and caresses on these rich relations, of whom everyone spoke with such respect. When supper was over they kissed the hands of Señora Angustias and their parents, and flung their arms round the necks of Gallardo and his wife, before going up to bed.

Their grandmother sat at the head of the table. When the matador had guests—usually people of some social position—she tried to refuse the place of honour.

"No," Gallardo would say, "I must have my mother presiding at my table. Sit down, Mamma, or we won't have any supper." And he gave her his arm to her chair, lavishing affectionate endearments on her as though to make amends for the pain he had caused her in his vagabond youth.

Whenever El Nacional paid what he seemed to regard as a duty visit to the maestro's house of an evening, the conversation became more lively. Gallardo usually wore a handsome sheepskin waistcoat, like a country gentleman's, and was bareheaded, with his pigtail smoothed forward nearly to his forehead. He welcomed the banderillero with bantering geniality. What were the aficionados saying? What lies were they telling now? And how about the Republic?

"Garabato, give Sebastián a glass of wine."

But El Nacional shook his head. He wouldn't have any wine; he never drank. Wine was the cause of the backwardness of the working classes. When they heard this everyone burst out laughing, as if it was just what they had been waiting for, and the banderillero began on his favourite theme.

The only person who sat in silence with a hostile expression in his eyes was the saddler. He detested El Nacional and looked upon him as an enemy. The banderillero too was a faithful and prolific husband, and a swarm of brats clung round his wife's skirts in the wine shop. The fact that Gallardo and Carmen were godparents to the two smallest made a fresh bond between the matador and El Nacional. What hypocrisy! Every Sunday he brought the two children, dressed in their best, to kiss their godfather's hand, and the saddler turned pale with indignation every time they received a present.

They were robbing his own children. Perhaps the banderillero was even dreaming that part of Gallardo's fortune might some day come to his godchildren. It was sheer theft! And he wasn't even a relation either!

When he didn't take El Nacional's remarks in sulky silence or with an expression of hatred, he attacked him openly, saying that anyone who spread disaffection among the people was a public danger and ought to be shot.

El Nacional was ten years older than his master. When Gallardo was just beginning to fight in capeas he was already a banderillero in a recognized cuadrilla. He had lately returned from South America, where he had been killing bulls in the ring at Lima. At the outset of his career he had enjoyed a certain popularity because of his youth and agility, and had even been spoken of for a short while as 'the torero of the future', the aficionados of Seville hoping that he would outshine matadors from other towns. When he returned from his travels, with the prestige of rumoured successes in distant lands, people crowded into the bull-ring at Seville to see him kill. Thousands were turned away. But at this crucial testing time 'his heart failed him' as the aficionados say. He placed the banderillas with aplomb, like a serious and conscientious workman carrying out a prescribed task; but when the time to kill arrived, the instinct of self-preservation proved stronger than his will, and kept him at a distance from the bull where he couldn't make full use of the advantages of his height and his strong arm.

El Nacional had to renounce the highest honours of tauromachy. It was the banderillas for him—that was all. He resigned himself to being a journeyman of the art, serving others younger than himself, and earning a *peon's*[1] wage so as to provide for his family and put by a few savings to start a small business later on. His good nature and sense of honour were proverbial in the profession. The matador's wife was

[1] A torero who works on foot, under the matador's orders.

fond of him, seeing him as a sort of guardian angel of her husband's fidelity. When in summer Gallardo and his cuadrilla went out on the spree to a *café chantant* in some provincial town, looking for amusement after dispatching bulls in a series of corridas, El Nacional would sit silent and solemn among the singers in their transparent dresses with their painted faces, like some early Father of the desert among the Alexandrian courtesans.

It was not that he was shocked, but he felt sad when he thought of his wife and little ones waiting for him in Seville. According to him all the vice and corruption in the world was the result of lack of education, and these poor women could certainly neither read nor write. As he believed the same defect in himself to be the source of his own insignificance and want of intelligence, he saw in it the cause of all human wretchedness and degradation.

In his early youth he had been an iron-founder, an active member of the Workers International, and an attentive listener to those more fortunate fellow-workmen who could read out loud pamphlets about the welfare of the proletariat. At the time of the National Militia he played at soldiers and belonged to one of the battalions who wore a red cap as a sign of federalist sympathies. He spent whole days in front of the platforms erected in public places where societies, political and otherwise, were in permanent session and where orators followed one another, day and night, holding forth with Andalusian eloquence about the divinity of Jesus or the rise in the cost of living. Then came a time of repressive measures, and a strike left him in the difficult position of a man marked out for his subversive views and rejected by every workshop in turn.

He had always enjoyed going to bullfights, so at twenty-four years old he became a torero just as he might have chosen any other profession. Besides, all his years spent listening to political pamphlets had not been in vain; he had learned a lot, and spoke with indignation of the anomalies of modern society. However little success he achieved as a torero, he would earn more and have a better life than as a skilled workman.

Remembering the days when he shouldered a musket as a National Militiaman, his friends nicknamed him El Nacional.

Even after many years spent in the bullfighting profession he still spoke of it apologetically, excusing himself, as it were, for being a member of it. The committee of his district had expelled from the Party all who supported the 'reactionary' and 'barbarous' sport, but they made a special exception in his favour and kept him on their register.

"Of course bullfighting's reactionary," he used to say in Gallardo's dining-room, "a bit like the days of the Inquisition, if you see what I mean? People need to read and write just like they need bread, and it's bad that they spend their money on us instead of on schooling. That's what they say in the pamphlets I'm sent from Madrid. . . . But the Party don't think too badly of me, and since Don Joselito gave them a piece of his mind the committee have agreed to keep my name on the register."

His calm seriousness, quite unruffled by the jokes and comically exaggerated rage with which the matador and his friends greeted these announcements, manifested his serene satisfaction at the honour paid him by his political comrades.

Don Joselito, an eager and loquacious schoolmaster who was head of the district committee, was a young man of Jewish extraction who brought the zeal of the Maccabees to the political struggle, and fancied that his dark ugly face pitted by smallpox had a certain resemblance to Danton's. El Nacional always listened open-mouthed to what he had to say.

When Gallardo's manager, Don José, and his other friends brought up every sort of extravagant argument, and teasingly attacked El Nacional's beliefs after dinner at the maestro's house, the poor man used to scratch his head, quite at a loss.

"You're gentlemen and you've been educated. I can't read or write. I'm just a tomfool like the rest of the lower classes. But if only Don Joselito was here! By jingo, if you could hear him! He talks like an angel!"

Next day, to bolster up his beliefs which were perhaps a little shaken by all this mockery, he would go and see Don

Joselito, who seemed to take a savage pleasure in showing him what he called his chamber of horrors. He had returned to the country of his persecuted ancestors and made a collection of souvenirs of the Inquisition, which were now set out in one of the class-rooms with the meticulous vindictiveness of a fugitive from justice reconstructing the skeleton of his gaoler, bone by bone. There was a bookcase full of parchment-bound accounts of *autos-de-fé* and lists of questions for the interrogation of prisoners under torture. On one wall hung a white banner with the dreaded green cross, and in the corners were heaped instruments of torture, whips, and any other horrifying device for cleaving and tearing human flesh that Don Joselito had been able to pick up in junk-shops—all carefully docketed as possessions of the Holy Office.

El Nacional's simple good-natured heart swelled with indignation at the sight of these rusty irons and the green cross.

"Good heavens! And there are still some people who'll tell you . . . By jingo! I wish I had some of them here!"

The desire to make converts made him take every opportunity to air his beliefs, without fear of ridicule but also without any trace of aggressiveness, and always amiably. In his opinion anyone who was indifferent to the state of things and was not a member of the Party was 'a poor ignorant wretch' whose salvation depended on learning to read and write. For his part, he modestly declared that he was past reclaiming; he was now too slow-witted to learn, but he held the whole world responsible for his ignorance.

Often when the cuadrilla was travelling from one province to another in the summer-time and Gallardo had moved into a second class carriage with the rest of his 'boys', a country priest or a couple of monks would join them.

The other peons nudged each other and winked, looking at El Nacional, whose manner became more solemn and portentous in face of the enemy. The two picadors, Potaje and Tragabuches, rough aggressive young men fond of practical joking and vaguely hostile to the cloth, egged him on under their breath.

"Now you've got him where you want him! . . . Give it him straight! . . . Let him have it! You know how."

The maestro glared at El Nacional with all the unquestioned authority of chief of the cuadrilla, and the banderillero was at first obediently silent; but his simple desire to make converts got the better of him, and one insignificant remark was enough to start him on an argument with his fellow-travellers. He was trying to convince them of the truth—which consisted in a jumbled collection of odds and ends put together from what he had heard Don Joselito say, and delivered with heat.

His companions exchanged glances, astonished by this display of learning, and pleased that one of themselves should be able to hold his own with professional men and even get them in a corner—for his adversaries were seldom well educated.

Amazed by El Nacional's violent arguments and the laughter of the other toreros, the priests at last had recourse to extremes. How was it possible for men who risked their lives so often not to have God constantly in mind? No doubt their wives and mothers were praying at that very moment!

The faces of the cuadrilla became serious and a little apprehensive as they thought of the amulets and medals which had been sewn to their fighting suits by their women's hands before they left Seville. The matador's dormant superstitiousness was roused and he burst out in exasperation against El Nacional, whose impiety he felt was endangering his own life.

"Be quiet! and stop your blasphemies. I'm sorry gentlemen, he's a good chap but his head's been turned by all the rubbish they tell him. . . . Shut that big mouth of yours, and don't answer me, curse you!"

And Gallardo overwhelmed the banderillero with threats and oaths in order to pacify these men who held his future in trust.

El Nacional took refuge in scornful silence. Nothing but ignorance and superstition, and all through being unable to read or write. And with the unshaken persistence of a man who only possesses two or three ideas and is determined not to let go of them come what may, he started the argument all over again a short while afterwards, paying no attention to the matador's anger.

His irreligion didn't leave him even in the arena, surrounded by peons and picadors who had said their prayers in the chapel and entered the ring hoping that the sacred objects sewn to their clothes would preserve them from danger.

When an enormous heavy thick-necked bull with a coat of inky black fell to his share, El Nacional took his stand at a little distance, with arms outstretched and the banderillas held ready, shouting insultingly:

"Come on, priest!"

The 'priest' charged furiously at El Nacional who fixed the darts firmly in his neck as he rushed by, proclaiming triumphantly:

"One for the clergy!"

Gallardo always ended by laughing at his extravagances.

"You're making me ridiculous; people will think we're just a gang of heretics. It's not everybody likes that sort of thing you know. All a bullfighter is expected to do is fight bulls."

But he was very fond of his banderillero, and never forgot his loyal devotion which more than once had reached the point of self-sacrifice. El Nacional minded not at all when he was hissed for placing the banderillas anyhow in a dangerous bull, so as to be done with it quickly. He had no desire for glory; he fought only to earn his living. But when Gallardo advanced sword in hand on a tricky bull, the banderillero stayed close behind him, ready to help him lower the brute's head with his heavy cape and his strong arm. Twice when Gallardo had been rolled in the sand, on the point of being gored, El Nacional had hurled himself at the bull, forgetting children, wife, wine shop and all, prepared to die to save his master.

When he arrived in Gallardo's dining-room in the evening he was greeted like one of the family. Señora Angustias felt that affection for him that binds together people of humble station who find themselves among their superiors.

"Come and sit by me, Sebastián. Won't you really have a drink? . . . Come and tell me how business is doing? Are Teresa and the children all right?"

Then El Nacional would run over yesterday's sales: so many glasses of wine over the counter; so many demijohns delivered at houses; and the old woman listened with the attentive interest of one who has known poverty and understands the value of money down to the last centimo.

Sebastián would go on to tell her how he hoped to enlarge his business. A licence to sell tobacco in his wine shop would suit him down to the ground. Gallardo might be able to use his influence to get it for him, but he hesitated to ask such a favour of him.

"You see how it is, Señora Angustias. The tobacco trade is a government matter, and I have my principles. I'm a federalist; I belong to the Party, and the committee too. What would they say?"

The old woman was outraged by his scruples. What he had to do was to bring as much bread as he could home to his family. That poor Teresa! With so many babies!

"Don't you be such a silly, Sebastián. Get all those cobwebs out of your brain! Now don't answer me. Don't start on all the dreadful things you always say. Remember I'm going to Mass at La Macarena tomorrow. . . ."

But Gallardo and Don José, who were sitting smoking and drinking brandy at the other side of the table, wanted to get El Nacional talking, so that they could laugh at his notions; so they baited him by insulting Don Joselito—an impostor who went about unsettling ignorant people!

The banderillero took their ridicule meekly. Cast doubts on Don Joselito! It was too absurd even to make him angry. It was just as if people tried to injure his other idol, Gallardo, by saying he didn't know how to kill a bull.

However as soon as the saddler—whom he couldn't abide—joined in the mockery, he lost his calm. Who was that blood-sucking hanger-on of the maestro's to argue with him? And losing all restraint, he ignored the matador's wife and mother, and Encarnación (who was pursing up her hairy lip in imitation of her husband and looking contemptuously at him) and launched himself head foremost into an exposition of his theories, with as much warmth as if he were addressing his committee. For lack of better arguments he heaped abuse on the beliefs of his tormentors.

"The Bible? All rubbish! . . . The creation of the world in six days? Rubbish! . . . Adam and Eve? Rubbish! . . . It's all lies and superstition."

This word 'rubbish' that he used instead of an even more disrespectful one, fell from his lips in an extraordinary tone of contempt.

The story of Adam and Eve had always been a subject of sarcasm to him; he had thought about it a great deal, during hours of quiet semi-drowsiness when travelling with the cuadrilla, and had discovered an irrefutable argument drawn entirely from his own inner consciousness: How could all the human beings in the world possibly be descended from a single couple?

"My name is Sebastián Venegas, and yours, Juaniyo, is Gallardo; and you, Don José, have your own surname. Everyone has his own, and when the names are the same people must be relations. If we were all grandchildren of Adam, and Adam's name was—Perez, for instance, we should all be called Perez. That's right, isn't it? . . . Well then as we've all got different surnames there must have been a great many Adams, and so what the priests tell us is all— *rubbish*! Reactionary superstition! It's education we want, and instead the clergy take advantage of our ignorance. You see what I mean?"

Gallardo flung himself back in his chair exploding with laughter, and greeted the banderillero's speech by imitating the bellowing of a bull. His manager solemnly stretched out his hand and congratulated him:

"Shake hands! Magnificent! Better than Castelar!"

Señora Angustias, poor old woman, was terrified at hearing such things in her house when she felt her life to be near its end.

"Be quiet, Sebastián! Shut your wicked mouth, or out into the street you must go! I won't have such things said in my house! If I didn't know what you're really like, that you're a good man. . . ."

But she forgave the banderillero in the end, remembering how devoted he was to her Juan and what he had done for him in moments of danger. Besides it was a great comfort to her and Carmen to have this honest, steady man in the cuadrilla, for the matador was irresponsible, and left to himself could be easily lead astray by his desire for women's admiration.

The enemy of Adam and Eve knew a secret of his master's which made him sometimes fall silent and serious when he saw him at home with his mother and Carmen. If these women only knew what *he* knew!

In spite of the respect that every banderillero feels for his matador, El Nacional had once ventured to speak frankly to Gallardo, presuming on his seniority and their long friendship.

"Look here, Juaniyo, all Seville knows about it! It's the talk of the town; it's sure to get round to your family in time, and then the fat'll be in the fire! Señora Angustias sobbing her heart out and poor Carmen half frantic. . . . Remember the row about that singer? Yet that was nothing to this one— she's much more dangerous."

Gallardo pretended not to understand. He was both worried and flattered at the thought that the whole town knew the secret of his love affair.

"But who and what are you talking about?"

"Who do you think? . . . Why Doña Sol, of course; that fine lady who gives everyone so much to gossip about. The niece of the Marqués de Moraima, the cattle breeder."

And as the matador only smiled in silence, gratified that El Nacional was so well-informed, the banderillero went on holding forth, in the style of a preacher who is disillusioned by the world.

"The first thing a married man ought to see to is that there's peace in his home. Women! . . . They're all the same . . .

rubbish! They all act the same in the same circumstances, and it's nothing but foolishness to poison your life by flying from one to the other. In the twenty-five years I've lived with my Teresa I've never deceived her once, not even in my thoughts, although I'm a torero and I've had my good times and more than one girl has made eyes at me."

Gallardo burst out laughing. The banderillero was talking like a Father Superior. And this was the man who wanted to make mincemeat of every monk he met!

"Nacional, don't be an idiot. One is as one is, and if women want to come one's way—well, let them come. Life's not so long, after all! One of these days I may leave the ring feet foremost. Besides you don't know what real ladies are like . . . If you knew that woman!"

Then he added candidly, as if he wanted to banish El Nacional's look of sadness and disapproval:

"I love Carmen dearly, you know that. I love her just as much as ever. But I love the other one too. It's different . . . I can't explain. Different, that's all!"

And the banderillero could get no more out of Gallardo.

Some months earlier in the autumn, at the end of the bull-fighting season, the matador had a chance meeting in the church of San Lorenzo.

He was taking a few days off in Seville before going to La Rinconada with his family. When his rest period came round nothing pleased him more than to live quietly in his own house, enjoying his freedom from endless train journeys. Killing more than a hundred bulls a year, with all the dangers and fatigue involved, was not so exhausting as those months of travelling from bull-ring to bull-ring all over Spain.

These journeys were made in full summer, under the crushing heat of the sun, across scorched plains and in ancient carriages whose roofs seemed to be on fire. Though the water-bottle was refilled at every station, it was not enough to quench the cuadrilla's thirst. Moreover the trains were generally packed with passengers, on their way to the ferias to see the corridas. Many a time Gallardo would hurry to the

93

station immediately after killing his last bull and still dressed in his fighting suit, flashing like a coloured meteor through the crowds of travellers and their piles of luggage.

Then he would arrive, exhausted, at a town in full fiesta, with streets decorated with streamers and triumphal arches, and have to submit to the ordeal of being a public hero. His supporters would be waiting at the station to accompany him to his hotel. They were full of high spirits after a good night's rest, and crowded round expecting to find him as expansive and forthcoming as if it gave him the greatest pleasure in the world to see them.

Often there was more than one corrida. He had to fight three or four days in succession, and at nights, worn out with physical fatigue and lack of sleep after the violent emotions of the day, he would throw convention to the winds and sit outside the door of his hotel in his shirt-sleeves, enjoying the coolness of the street. His cuadrilla used to put up at the same hotel, under the wing of their matador, like schoolboys with their master. Sometimes one of them ventured to ask leave to go for a walk through the brightly-lit streets or to the fair-ground.

"Miura bulls tomorrow," the maestro would say. "I know those walks of yours. You'll come back at dawn after several glasses too many, or under the weather from some scrape or other. . . . No; you can't go out. It'll be soon enough after the corrida."

When it was all over, if they had some days free before the next bullfight in another town, the cuadrilla would linger where they were, and take advantage of being away from their families to indulge in wine, women and general dissipation among their admirers, who imagined their whole life was spent in this fashion.

The matador had to make the most fantastic journeys in order to fit in with the dates of the various fiestas. After leaving one town to fight at the opposite end of Spain, he would have to come all the way back again four days later, for a corrida in a place almost next door. So that the summer months were spent zig-zagging across the country in trains.

"If all my journeys during one summer could be put in a straight line," Gallardo used to say, "they would reach to the North Pole at least."

At the beginning of each season he would set out quite eagerly on his travels, thinking of his audiences impatiently waiting for him after talking about him all the year round; of the chance friendships he might strike up; of the adventures with women; of the life he would lead in the different hotels—so eventful, so full of excitement and change compared to his placid existence in Seville or the mountain solitude of La Rinconada.

But after a few weeks of this dizzy career, earning five thousand pesetas every afternoon, Gallardo began to pine for his family like a child away from home.

"Oh, to be in my cool house in Seville, with poor Carmen polishing away at everything till it shines! And Mamma cooking her delicious meals!"

When he came home at the end of the season Gallardo forgot his fame and his honours with relief, and gave himself up to the enjoyment of ordinary life.

He would sleep late, forget about railway timetables, think about bulls without emotion. Nothing to do today, nor the next, nor the next! His family seemed more cheerful and even in better health now that they had him with them for a few months. His longest journeys ended at the Calle de las Sierpes or the Plaza de San Fernando. He would set out with his felt hat on the back of his head, swinging his gold-headed cane and admiring the big diamonds on his fingers.

There were usually several people waiting to see him in the porch, standing by the iron gate looking in at the sunny patio with its freshly whitewashed walls—sunburnt men, reeking with sweat, dressed in dirty blouses and hats with wide, frayed brims. Some were agricultural labourers passing through Seville, who thought it the most natural thing in the world to come and ask help from the famous matador. They called him 'Señor Juan'. Others were fellow townsmen, who addressed him as '*tu*' or 'Juaniyo'.

Gallardo's memory for faces was phenomenal and he often recognized friends of his schooldays or his roving adolescence.

"Business going badly, eh? Times are hard for everyone." And before his amiability could lead them on to greater intimacies, he turned to Garabato who stood with his hand on the gate.

"Ask the Señora to give everyone a couple of pesetas."

And he went on out into the street whistling, satisfied with his own generosity and finding life sweet.

As he passed the wine shop, Montañes' children and some of the neighbours came to the door, smiling and curious, as if they had never set eyes on him before.

"Good day, gentlemen! . . . Thank you, but I won't have a drink."

He waved aside the admirer who came out to meet him with a glass in his hand, and walked on. In the next street two old friends of his mother's stopped him to ask him to be godfather to the grandchild of one of them. Her poor daughter might give birth at any time now, and her son-in-law hadn't dared approach Gallardo, though he was one of his most ardent supporters, and had more than once got into a fight in defence of his hero.

"But good heavens! Do you all take me for a wet-nurse? I've got more godchildren than there are children in the orphanage."

To get away from them he suggested they talk it over with his mother, and hear what she had to say. And he walked on again, not stopping till he reached the Calle de las Sierpes, though he waved a greeting to some and let others have the honour of walking proudly beside him for the whole world to see.

He looked in at the Forty-five Club to see if his manager was there; this was an aristocratic and exclusive club, as its name showed, where bulls and horses were the sole topics of conversation. Its members were rich aficionados and cattle-breeders, whose oracle was the Marqués de Moraima.

One Friday afternoon when Gallardo was on his way to the

Calle de las Sierpes, he took it into his head to turn aside into the church of San Lorenzo.

There was a row of smart carriages drawn up in the little square for this was the day when all the best people in the town went to pray to the miraculous image of Our Lord Jesus of Great Power. Ladies dressed in black, wearing beautiful mantillas, were getting out of their carriages, and men followed them into the church, attracted by so much feminine elegance.

Gallardo went in too. A torero must take every opportunity that offered to rub shoulders with people of high social position. Señora Angustias' son felt a thrill of pride when rich aristocrats greeted him and beautifully dressed ladies whispered his name and exchanged glances.

Besides, he was a devotee of Our Lord of Great Power. He put up with El Nacional's talk about "God or Nature" without feeling shocked, as he would have listened unmoved to abuse of someone known only by hearsay. His ideas of the Divinity were vague and imprecise; but he had known the Virgin of Hope and Jesus of Great Power all his life, and would allow no one to say a word against either of them in his hearing.

In his rough manly way he was moved by the agony of Christ with the cross over His shoulder; and the pale sweating suffering face reminded him of friends he had seen lying in the bull-ring infirmary. He must propitiate this all-powerful Deity, and he fervently repeated paternosters as he stood before the image in whose dark eyes the lights of the wax tapers shone like red stars.

A movement among the kneeling women in front of him caught his attention, ever on the alert for signs and portents which might guide him in his dangerous career.

A tall slender woman was passing among the worshippers; she was strikingly beautiful, and wore a light-coloured dress and a large hat trimmed with feathers, beneath which flamed the shining gold of her hair.

Gallardo knew her. She was Doña Sol, the Marqués de Moraima's niece, known in Seville as the Ambassadress. She

97

made her way between the kneeling women, ignoring their interest in her and seeming to accept and enjoy their glances and whispering, as a natural homage which she expected to follow her wherever she went.

The exotic elegance of her dress and her enormous hat made her conspicuous among the other sombrely clad figures. She knelt down and bent her head in prayer for a few seconds; then her clear greenish-blue eyes flecked with gold began to wander tranquilly round the church, as if looking for someone she knew among the audience of a theatre. When they rested on a friend's face they seemed to smile, and then moving on again they met the eyes of Gallardo, who was looking at her fixedly.

The matador was far from modest. Used to being the focus of interest of thousands of people in the arena, he honestly believed that wherever he went all eyes must be on him. Many women had confessed, at confidential moments, that when they first saw him in the ring they had been overcome with emotion, interest and desire. Doña Sol's eyes did not fall before the torero's; on the contrary she continued to stare at him with the cold haughtiness of a great lady, until the matador, ever respectful towards riches and position, had to look away. 'There's a fine woman!' he thought. 'I wonder if she's for me?'

Outside the church he was reluctant to go away, and waited near the door hoping to see her again. The beating of his heart told him that something extraordinary was happening. He felt a mysterious presentiment like that which in the ring made him disregard the protests of the audience and launch himself into the wildest audacities, always with splendid results.

When she came out of the church she turned her head and looked at him with a strange expression, as if she had guessed that he would be waiting at the door. She got into her carriage with two women friends, and as the coachman whipped up his horses she turned again and looked at the matador with a slight smile curling her lips.

Gallardo was preoccupied all that afternoon. He thought of his previous love-affairs, triumphs achieved through his recklessness as a torero, conquests which filled him with pride and made him believe himself irresistible. Now he felt ashamed of them. This fine lady who had travelled all over the world and was the uncrowned queen of Seville—she would be a conquest indeed! His admiration for her beauty was combined with the respect of the former ragamuffin for riches and noble birth. If only he could succeed in attracting such a woman! What greater triumph could he possibly have?

His manager was a great friend of the Marqués de Moraima and mixed with the best society of Seville; he had sometimes talked about Doña Sol.

She had returned to Seville a few months ago after an absence of several years, and all the young men of the town were wild about her. Her long stay abroad had filled her with enthusiasm for all that was characteristically Spanish, and she was enamoured of popular customs, declaring everything "very interesting . . . very artistic". She went to bullfights wearing the costume and adopting the attitudes of one of the charming ladies painted by Goya. She was an athletic young woman, an expert rider and sportswoman, and she was often to be seen galloping her horse through the country round Seville, wearing a black riding-habit with a short jacket cut like a man's, a red scarf, and a white hat on her helmet of golden hair. Sometimes she would carry a *garrocha*[1] slung across her saddle, and would go out with a party of friends to bait bulls on some country estate—a rough and dangerous sport in which she delighted.

She was not a young girl. Gallardo vaguely remembered having seen her as a child in the gardens of Las Delicias, sitting beside her mother, covered in white frills like the expensive dolls in the shop windows, whilst he, poor little wretch, ran under the carriage wheels looking for cigar ends. She must be the same age as himself—nearly thirty, but so radiant, so different from other women! She was like an exotic bird, a bird of Paradise in a pen full of plump glossy hens.

Don José knew her whole history. Doña Sol was a wild

[1] A stick tipped with a goad, used in bull-baiting.

eccentric creature! Her romantic name suited her original and independent character.

When her mother died she inherited a fortune, and got married, in Madrid, to a man a good deal older than herself but who, as Spanish Ambassador to the principal courts of Europe, could satisfy her desire for splendour and novelty.

"How that girl amused herself, Juan!" said the manager. "The heads she turned all over Europe during those ten years! Her life was like a geography book with foot-notes in cypher on every page. When she looks at a map every capital city must have its crops of memories for her. And the poor Ambassador! I'm sure he died of frustration, because there was nowhere left for him to go to. That girl stuck at nothing. Her husband would be sent to represent us at some foreign court or other, and before the year was out the Queen or Empress of the country in question would be writing to Spain to ask for the recall of our Ambassador and his formidable consort. The newspapers used to call her the 'irresistible Spaniard'. Oh yes! crowned heads were crazy about her! Queens trembled at her arrival, as though she were the cholera. At last there was nowhere left for the poor Ambassador to exercise his talents except the South American Republics; but as he was a man of high principles and had been the friend of kings he preferred to die. . . . And don't imagine for a moment that the young lady found sufficient scope among those who eat and make merry in royal palaces. If only half of what's said about her is true! . . . She's an extremist: it must be all or nothing; if not the highest in the land, well then the lowest will do. I've heard it said that when she was in Russia she went after one of those long-haired anarchists—a young man with a pretty face who didn't care much for her because she interfered with his schemes. Just for that very reason she followed him about everywhere, until he was caught and hanged. Then they say she had an affair with a painter in Paris, who painted her portrait half naked with one arm over her face so as not to be recognized, which was reproduced on all the match-boxes. That may not be true; or exaggeration at least. What does seem to be certain is that she took up with a German composer, who wrote operas. You should hear her play the piano! Or sing! Just like one of those sopranos who came to the theatre of San Fernando last Easter. And don't imagine she only sings in Italian; she knows a bit of everything; French, German, English. I've heard her uncle, the Marqués de Moraima (who between ourselves is a bit of an ass), say at the Forty-Five Club that he believes she even knows Latin! . . . What a woman! Eh, Juanillo? Interesting, isn't she?"

The manager described Doña Sol's sensational and erratic career with genuine admiration; whether it was all true or false did not seem to matter much. Her birth and wealth inspired him with respect, as they did Gallardo. He was smiling with approval as he talked, though the same behaviour in some other woman would have led to a stream of ribald comments.

"She leads a model life here in Seville, I must say," he went on, "which makes me wonder if some of the stories about her are false. A question of sour grapes perhaps!"

He laughingly repeated some of the accounts of Doña Sol's adventures which had been going the rounds of the clubs in the Calle de las Sierpes. She could be as enterprising and brave as any man at times. When the Ambassadress came to live in Seville, a court of admirers had formed itself around her.

"Just think, Juanillo. A really smart woman, such as we're not used to here, with clothes and hats bought in Paris, perfume from London; known to have been the friend of kings . . . It's as if she was marked with the brand of the finest herds in Europe. . . . They were all mad about her, and she allowed them certain liberties, you know, mistaking familiarity for something better; when they weren't free with words they would be free with their hands. . . . Well, it came to slaps at times, Juanillo, or even worse. That girl's a caution. It seems she can fence, box like an English sailor, and has even learnt ju-jitsu. So it comes to this: if a man lays hands on her she hardly seems to be annoyed; she just takes hold of him with her lily-white hands and tears him apart. Now people fight shy of her, but she has made enemies who go about speaking ill of her—some of them making up lies about their successes with her, and others saying she's not a beauty.

"But Doña Sol is in love with Seville it seems. After so many years spent in cold foggy countries she can't have enough of our deep blue sky and golden winter sunlight. She raves about our country customs. You'd think she was an English tourist come to Seville for the first time to see Holy Week; yet she was born here! She means to spend the winters here and the summers abroad, she says. She's tired of court and palace life and the people she used to mix with . . . she's been made a member of one of the most popular of the charitable confraternities, and spends a lot of money on Manzanilla for the brothers. Some evenings she fills her house with guitarists and dancers—any local girls who are learning to sing and dance. They bring their teachers and their parents and even their distant relatives with them, and they all stuff themselves on olives, sausages and wine, while Doña Sol sits in her chair like a queen asking for all the Andalusian dances, one after another. It's like some king one reads about, who used to have whole operas performed for himself alone. The servants she brought here when she came go round, stiff and solemn as judges, wearing evening-dress and carrying glasses of wine to the dancers, who get so drunk they pull their whiskers and throw olive-stones in their faces! Fine goings on! Then in the mornings Doña Sol sends for an old gypsy called Lechuzo who gives her lessons in guitar-playing in the traditional style. When her guests don't find her with a guitar in her hands, it's an orange. The oranges that girl has eaten since she came! And still she's not tired of them! . . ."

So Don José rambled on, describing Doña Sol's eccentricities to the matador.

Four days after Gallardo had seen her in the Church of San Lorenzo, his manager came up to him in a café in the Calle de las Sierpes, and said mysteriously:

"You're in luck, my boy! Who do you think has been talking to me about you?"

And putting his mouth close to the torero's ear he whispered: "Doña Sol!"

She had been asking him about 'his matador', and saying she would like to meet him. He looked such an original character! So typically Spanish!

"She says she's seen you in the ring several times; once in Madrid, I'm not sure where else. She admired you; she realizes you're a very brave man. So you see she's taken quite a fancy to you! What an honour! It looks as if you'll be brother-in-law or something of the sort, to all the kings in the pack!"

Gallardo smiled modestly, dropping his eyes, but well aware of his handsome figure, and not seeming to find what his manager told him either extraordinary or difficult to believe.

"But I don't want you to have any illusions, Juanillo," Don José went on. "Doña Sol wants to have a closer view of a bullfighter for the same reason that she takes guitar lessons from Lechuzo. Local colour, that's all. 'Bring him to Tablada the day after tomorrow,' she said to me. As you know there's to be a bull-baiting at Moraima's cattle ranch; the Marqués has arranged a fiesta for his niece. We'll go together; I've been invited too."

Two days later, in the afternoon, the maestro and his manager rode out of La Feria dressed for the bull-baiting. People came to their doors or lingered on the pavements to see them go.

"They're off to Tablada," they said.

The manager was riding on a bony white mare, and wore country clothes: a thick jacket, cloth breeches and yellow gaiters with cowboy leather leggings over them. The matador had chosen to put on the bizarre costume that toreros used to wear in private life before modern customs had decreed that they should dress like everyone else. On his head was a round velvet hat with a strap under the chin. He wore no tie, but the collar of his shirt was fastened by two diamonds and other larger ones flashed from the goffered frill down the front. His jacket and waistcoat were of wine-coloured velvet trimmed with black frogs and braid, his sash of crimson silk, and his tight-fitting breeches moulded his muscular thighs and were fastened at the knee by black ribbon garters. His gaiters were amber-coloured with leather fringes from top to bottom, and his short boots of the same colour were almost hidden by the wide Moorish stirrups, leaving only his silver spurs visible. On his saddle-bow was a gaudy Jerez blanket with coloured tassels hanging down on both sides, over which he had thrown his grey overcoat with black trimmings and a red lining.

The two riders galloped along, each carrying over his shoulder, like a lance, a garrocha made of strong fine-grained wood with a button protecting the steel point. They were cheered as they passed through the working-class quarter. *Olé!* Women waved at the handsome pair.

"Good luck to you! Have a good time, Señor Juan!"

They put spurs to their horses to get away from the swarms of children running behind them, and the narrow streets with their white walls and blue pavements echoed to the rhythmical impact of hoofs.

When they reached the quiet street of aristocratic houses with projecting iron grilles and glassed-in balconies where Doña Sol lived, they found other arrivals sitting motionless on their horses outside the door, leaning on their goads. They were relations or friends of the lady of the house, and they greeted the matador with genuine friendliness, obviously glad that he was to be of the party.

The Marqués de Moraima came out of the house, and mounted his horse at once.

"My niece will be down directly. You know what women are—they take so long to get ready!"

He said this with his usual sententious solemnity, as if all his words were oracles. He was an elderly man, tall and bony, with large white whiskers framing a mouth and eyes which had kept an almost childish air of innocence. Courteous and moderate in his speech, with polished manners but few smiles, the Marqués de Moraima was a nobleman of the old school; he nearly always wore riding clothes, hated town life and was bothered by the social demands his family made on him when they were in Seville, from which he was always eager to escape among his shepherds and drovers whom he treated with friendly familiarity. He had almost forgotten how to write for lack of practice, but as soon as anyone started talking about brave bulls, cattle or horse-breeding or agriculture, his eyes sparkled with the assurance of a connoisseur.

The sun's brilliance was suddenly dimmed. The sheet of golden light which covered one side of the street grew paler. People looked up at the sky. A dark threatening cloud was crossing the strip of blue stretching between the eaves of the houses.

"Nothing to worry about," said the Marqués solemnly. "As I came out of the house I saw the wind blowing a piece of paper along. We shan't have rain from that quarter."

Everyone looked reassured. It couldn't possibly rain if the Marqués de Moraima said it wouldn't. He understood the weather better than any old shepherd, and there was no danger of his being mistaken.

Then he went up to Gallardo.

"You'll have some magnificent corridas this season—I've some splendid bulls for you! They ought to die like good Christians. I wasn't altogether satisfied, you know, this year. The poor brutes deserved better of you."

At this moment Doña Sol appeared, holding up the skirt of her black habit to show her high grey leather riding-boots. She wore a man's shirt with a red tie, a jacket and waistcoat of purple velvet, and a small round velvet hat jauntily askew on her curly hair.

Though her figure was voluptuously feminine she jumped on her horse with the agility of a boy, and took her garrocha from a servant. She greeted her friends, apologizing for being late, but her eyes sought out Gallardo. Don José pricked forward his mare so as to make the introduction, but Doña Sol was too quick for him and rode up to the torero.

Gallardo felt deeply disturbed by her presence. What could he find to say to this magnificent woman?

He saw that she was holding out a slender scented hand, and in a sudden access of confusion he seized it in the firm grasp which was more accustomed to holding a sword. But her little pink and white paw, instead of cringing under this rough involuntary grip which might easily have produced a cry of pain from another woman, returned the pressure firmly and then freed itself with ease.

"Delighted to meet you. I'm glad you could come."

And Gallardo, dazedly aware that he must make some answer, stammered the phrase he used to aficionados:

"Thanks. And how are the family? Well I hope?"

Doña Sol's ripple of laughter was lost in the sound of horses' hoofs on stones as they set off. She put her horse into a trot, and the other riders followed, in a convoy around her, with Gallardo bringing up the rear, still ashamed and confusedly aware that he had made a fool of himself.

They galloped through the outskirts of Seville beside the river leaving the Torre del Oro behind them, along yellow sandy tracks through shady gardens, and out on to a main road bordered by small inns and eating-houses.

When they reached Tablada they saw a crowd of people and carriages, forming a dark mass against the green grassland, beside the fence which separated the paddock from the animals' enclosure.

The broad stream of the Guadalquivir ran along beside the paddock; on the opposite bank rose the hill of San Juan de Aznalfarache crowned by a ruined castle, and farm-houses shone white among the silver-grey of the olives. Far away on the horizon, against a blue sky with fleecy clouds, Seville could be seen, with the line of its houses dominated by the imposing bulk of the Cathedral, and the exquisite Giralda glowing softly pink in the evening light.

The riders forced their way through the large crowd with difficulty; the fame of Doña Sol's eccentricities had brought nearly all the ladies of Seville to the scene. Her friends greeted her from their carriages as she passed, admiring her beauty in her mannish habit. Her cousins, the daughters of the Marqués —some unmarried, some accompanied by their husbands— begged her to take no risks:

106

"For heaven's sake, Sol! Don't do anything rash!"

The bull-baiters rode into the enclosure and were greeted with cheers from the country-people who had come to the fiesta.

When the horses saw and smelt their enemies they began to rear and buck, whinnying as the firm hands of their riders restrained them.

The bulls were in a group in the centre of the enclosure. Some were quietly grazing, or lay ruminating with heads low on the brownish winter grass. Other less tractable animals were trotting towards the river pursued by the prudent old bell-oxen, jingling their cow-bells; meanwhile the herdsmen helped them round up the stragglers by slinging well-aimed stones at their horns.

For some time the riders were motionless and seemed to be holding a conference, while the crowd looked on impatiently, eager for developments.

The first to ride out were the Marqués and one of his friends. They galloped towards the herd, and when they got close to them, reined in their horses and stood up in their stirrups, waving their garrochas and shouting loudly. A powerful-looking black bull detached itself from the others and galloped off to the far end of the enclosure.

The Marqués had every reason to be proud of his herd, which consisted entirely of fine, carefully bred animals. These were not beef-producing oxen, with thick, rough dirty coats, clumsy hoofs, hanging heads and huge crooked horns. They were alert and lively, so strong and heavy that the ground shook and clouds of dust rose beneath them; with coats as smooth and shining as those of well-groomed horses; eyes full of fire; thick and proudly-carried necks; short legs; thin tails; clean, well-shaped horns with sharp points as if they had been fashioned by hand, and small round hoofs—so hard that they cut the grass like steel.

The two riders galloped after the bull, hustling it from either side and cutting it off when it tried to make for the river; until the Marqués, spurring on his horse, caught up with it and drove his garrocha into its rump with sufficient force to make it lose its balance and roll over on the ground stomach upwards, with its horns stuck in the ground and its feet in the air.

The rapidity and ease with which the cattle-breeder had carried out this feat produced a burst of applause. Well done, old fellow! No one understood bulls better than the Marqués. He handled them as if they were his own children, looking after them from their birth in the cowsheds to the day they went off to the bull-ring to die like heroes who deserved a better fate.

Other riders were now eager to go out and win the applause of the crowd, but Moraima gave the preference to his niece. If she wanted to try her luck it was better for her to go out at once, before the herd had become infuriated by constant attacks.

Doña Sol put spurs to her horse which had been plunging about in terror of the bulls. The Marqués wanted to go with her, but she wouldn't let him. No; she would rather have Gallardo, who after all was a torero. Where was Gallardo? The matador took his place beside her, still silent with shame at his own awkwardness.

They galloped together straight towards the herd. Doña Sol's horse reared up several times into an almost vertical position, refusing to advance; but she mastered it and forced it on again. Gallardo waved his garrocha, roaring aloud as he always did in the arena to incite the bull to attack.

It was easy enough to cut out one animal from the herd. It was a white bull with red-brown patches, a thick pendulous neck and sharp-pointed horns. It galloped to the far end of the enclosure as if it had its *querencia*[1] there, which it wanted to get to, and Doña Sol galloped after it, followed by the matador.

"Take care, Señora," Gallardo shouted. "It's an old bull, and may be tricky! Be careful it doesn't turn on you!"

This was exactly what happened. As Doña Sol was preparing to make the same stroke as her uncle's, turning her horse at an angle so as to plant the garrocha in the bull's rump and overthrow it, the creature suddenly doubled back as if it realized its danger and took up a menacing stand in front of its attacker.

[1] Part of the arena where a bull feels at home, and makes its stand.

Doña Sol's horse rushed on at such a pace that she couldn't control it, with the bull after her—no longer pursued, but pursuing.

She had no thought of flight. Thousands of people were watching her; she was afraid of the laughter of her women friends and the sympathy of the men, and she reined back her horse and confronted the bull. Holding her garrocha under her arm like a picador she drove it into the neck of the animal as it rushed forward bellowing, with lowered head. A stream of blood reddened the massive shoulders, but still it rushed forward, carried on by the impetus of its charge, seemingly unaware of the widening wound, till it got its horns under the horse's belly, shook it and lifted it off the ground.

The rider was thrown from her saddle and a cry of horror was heard from the hundreds of onlookers. The horse forced itself from the horns, and galloped away like a mad thing, with its stomach stained with blood, the girths broken and the saddle flapping loose.

The bull turned to follow it; but at that very moment something nearer at hand attracted its attention. It was Doña Sol, who instead of lying still on the grass had got to her feet, picked up her garrocha and was bravely preparing to challenge the bull once more. It was an action of insane courage, but her thoughts were on her audience; better a challenge to the death, rather than any compromise with fear and ridicule!

No shouts came from the direction of the palisade now. The crowd stood paralysed in terrified silence. The other riders were approaching at full gallop in a cloud of dust, but their help would be too late. The bull was already pawing the ground and lowering its head to attack the small reckless figure who dared to threaten it with her goad. One blow of those horns and all would be over. But at this critical moment a savage roar distracted the bull's attention and something red passed before its eyes, like a flash of fire.

It was Gallardo, who had thrown himself off his horse and dropped his garrocha so as to snatch the coat from his saddlebow.

"Eeeh! . . . Come on!"

The bull came on. It found the crimson coat-lining a worthier adversary than the figure in purple and black, still standing stupefied by danger with her goad under her arm.

"Don't be afraid, Doña Sol. I've got him now," said the torero, pale with emotion, but smiling and sure of himself.

With no other weapon but his coat he played the bull, gradually drawing it away from the lady, and avoiding its furious attack by dexterous twists and turns.

The crowd forgot its recent alarm and began to applaud loudly. What luck! to come to an ordinary bull-baiting and find it turn into what amounted to a formal corrida! To see Gallardo fight, and all for nothing!

The matador warmed to the violence of the bull's attack, and forgot Doña Sol and everything else, concentrating entirely on defending himself. The infuriated beast, finding that the man had again slipped away unharmed from between its horns, turned and charged again, only to come up against the shield of red cloth.

At last, tired out, it stood still on trembling legs, with head hanging and muzzle covered in foam; Gallardo took advantage of its bewilderment to take off his hat and lay it between the horns. A great howl of delight from the palisade greeted this act of bravado.

Then Gallardo heard cries and jingling of bells behind him and a crowd of herdsmen and bell-oxen surrounded the bull and slowly drew it off to join the rest of the herd.

He looked round for his horse. It was accustomed to the proximity of bulls and hadn't moved. He picked up his garrocha, mounted, and cantered off towards the palisade—prolonging the applause of the crowd by the slowness of his approach.

The riders who had escorted Doña Sol back to safety were enthusiastic in their praise. His manager winked, and said mysteriously:

"Well, my boy, you haven't wasted much time! Very good. Very good indeed! She's as good as yours now."

Doña Sol was sitting in a landau with the Marqués'

daughters, outside the palisade. Her cousins crowded round her, anxiously feeling her all over to see if she had suffered from her fall. They made her drink several glasses of Manzanilla to counteract the shock, but she smiled in a superior and detached way at their feminine agitation.

When she saw Gallardo come riding through the crowd between waving hats and outstretched hands, she smiled more warmly:

"Come here, my Cid Campeador. I want to shake hands with you."

And once again they exchanged a long hand-clasp.

The afternoon's adventure was discussed that evening in the matador's house, for the whole of Seville was talking about it. Señora Angustias was as delighted as if she were hearing about a successful corrida. Her son saving the life of one of those grand ladies! Long years of domestic service had made her look up to the aristocracy with admiration and respect. Carmen was silent, not knowing quite what to think.

Several days passed without Gallardo having any news of Doña Sol. His manager was away with a hunting-party of friends from the Forty-Five. But one evening just as it was getting dark Don José sought the matador out in a café in the Calle de las Sierpes frequented by aficionados. He had got back from his hunting-party a few hours earlier and had found a note from Doña Sol waiting for him, asking him to go and see her at once.

"Good heavens, man, what a brute you are!" said the manager, dragging the matador out of the café. "She's been expecting you to go and see her all this time. She's stayed at home evening after evening, hoping to see you turn up every moment. You can't go on like that, you know. After being introduced, and all that happened, you really owe her a visit—just to ask how she is."

The matador stood still and scratched his head under his felt hat.

"The fact is," he muttered uneasily, "the fact is . . . I'm ashamed. Well, I've said it now: that's what it is—I'm ashamed. I'm no saint, as you know; I'm not slow with women usually and can find a few things to say to a girl as well as any other man. But not to this one. She's a lady and as learned as Lepe,[1] and when I'm with her it comes over me what an ignorant brute I am, and I daren't open my mouth for fear of making a fool of myself. No, Don José . . . I'm not going! And what's more, I oughtn't to go!"

But the manager, confident of persuading him, led him on towards Doña Sol's house, telling him as he went about the interview he had just had with the lady. She had seemed quite offended by Gallardo's neglect. Everyone in Seville had been to see her after her accident; he was the only one to stay away.

"You know a torero ought to keep in with important people; it's part of his education. You must show them you're not a ploughboy brought up in the stables. When such a grand lady singles you out and is waiting for you to make the next move! . . . Stuff and nonsense! I'll come with you."

"Ah! If you'll come too!"

And Gallardo seemed to breathe again, as if a load were off his mind.

They arrived at Doña Sol's house. The patio was built in the Moorish style, with horseshoe arches of fine workmanship in many colours, reminiscent of the Alhambra.

The evening silence was broken by the gentle monotonous plash of the fountain into a basin where goldfish flicked their tails. In the four arcades with panelled ceilings, separated from the patio by marble columns, the torero saw antique cabinets, dark paintings of pale-faced saints, old pieces of furniture with rusty iron-work and so riddled with wormholes that they looked as if they had received a charge of grape-shot.

A servant showed them up the wide marble staircase, and the torero looked round in wonder at the retables with faded figures on a gold background; at the crudely sculptured virgins taken from old altars, decorated with faded paint and dim gilding; and the tapestries of the soft colour of dead leaves,

[1] A proverbially learned Bishop.

with borders of flowers and apples surrounding scenes of the Crucifixion, or of hairy cloven-hoofed satyrs who seemed to be engaged in a corrida with some scantily dressed young ladies.

"What it is to be ignorant!" he said to his manager in astonishment. "I thought they only had this sort of thing in convents! . . . But it seems these people like them too!"

As they went upstairs the servants turned on the electric lights, though the dying splendours of the sunset still shone in at the windows.

There were fresh surprises in store for Gallardo. He had been proud of the heavy, richly carved furniture upholstered in showy silk he had bought in Madrid, which seemed to shout aloud the amount of money it had cost him. And now he felt disorientated by the sight of these fragile delicate chairs in white or green, the tables and cupboards of simple design, the walls painted in one colour only with no further adornment than a few small pictures, far apart, hanging from thick cords. All this refined and subtle luxury had been achieved by the carpenter's skill. He felt ashamed of being so deeply impressed, and also that he should ever have thought his own house represented the height of luxury. What it is to be ignorant! He sat down cautiously, afraid the chair would break under his weight.

The entrance of Doña Sol put an end to his reflections. He saw her now as he had never seen her before, without hat or mantilla, her shining hair uncovered and seeming to justify her romantic name. Her perfectly white arms appeared from the silk sleeves of a Japanese kimono crossing over her bosom and exposing the whole column of her enchanting neck, whose pale golden skin was encircled with the two lines called Venus's necklace. When she moved her hands, precious stones of all colours flashed from the curiously fashioned rings covering her fingers. Gold bracelets tinkled on her cool forearms, one made of oriental filigree with some cabbalistic inscription, and other heavier ones with amulets and strange charms hanging from them, which she had brought back from her travels.

As she talked she crossed her legs with masculine freedom, while a red embroidered slipper of diminutive size, with a high gold heel, swung from her foot.

There was a buzzing in Gallardo's ears, a mist before his eyes: all he could see clearly was a pair of pale eyes fixed on him with an expression which was both caressing and ironical. He smiled to cover his emotion, but it was the stiff artificial baring of teeth of a child who wants to be polite.

"No, Señora. Thank you very much. It wasn't anything," was all he could stammer, when Doña Sol thanked him for what he had done at Tablada.

However, little by little he began to recover his presence of mind. The lady and his manager were talking about bulls and this suddenly gave the matador assurance. She had seen him in the ring more than once, and remembered the chief circumstances in detail. Gallardo was proud to think that she had watched him and that her memories of him were still so fresh.

She had opened a lacquer box decorated with exotic flowers, and now she offered the two men some gold-tipped cigarettes which had a strange and pungent aroma.

"They have opium in them; they're very nice."

And she lit one for herself, following the coils of smoke with her greenish eyes, into which the light shone, making them look like pools of liquid gold.

The torero was used to strong Havanas and he inhaled his cigarette with some curiosity. It tasted of straw—feminine rubbish! But the strange perfume gradually seemed to dissipate his timidity.

Doña Sol was gazing at him intently and asking him questions about his life. She wanted to go behind the scenes of his fame and glory, to see from within the wretched wandering life of a torero before he had been acclaimed by the public; and Gallardo, suddenly self-confident, talked and talked, describing his early days, dwelling with proud insistence on his humble origins, but leaving out anything he was really ashamed of in his adventurous adolescence.

"How interesting! How fascinating!" And the beautiful

114

woman turned her eyes away and seemed lost in contemplation of something invisible.

"He's the best of them all!" exlaimed Don José in a burst of enthusiasm. "Believe me, Sol, this young man has no equal. And he can take a tossing too!"

Like a proud father describing his son's prowess, he ran over all the wounds Gallardo had received in the ring, describing them as minutely as if he could see them through his clothes. Doña Sol's eyes followed this anatomical journey with obvious admiration. He was a real hero; bashful, reserved and simple like all men of action.

The manager said he must go. It was past seven o'clock and they would be waiting for him at home. But Doña Sol stood up and tried to detain him with smiling insistence. They must stay. They must dine with her; it was an informal invitation, but she was alone that evening, as the Marqués and his family had gone to the country.

"I shall be quite alone. . . . I won't hear another word; I insist. You must share my frugal meal."

And she left the room at once, as if there could be no denying her commands.

The manager protested. No, he really couldn't stay; he had only got back that afternoon and had hardly seen his family. Besides, he'd asked some friends in. As for the matador it was quite right and proper that he should stay. The invitation was really intended for him.

"But you really mustn't go," said the torero in desperation. "Good heavens! don't leave me alone. I don't know what to do; I don't know what to say."

A quarter of an hour later Doña Sol returned, in a different costume. Instead of the exotic negligée in which she had received them she was now wearing one of the dresses from Paris which were the envy and admiration of her friends and relations—a Paquin model.

Don José again excused himself. He must go, there was no help for it; but 'his matador' should stay. He would take a message to his house to tell them not to expect him.

Again Gallardo cast an anguished look at him, but the manager's expression reassured him. "Don't worry," he murmured as he went to the door. "I'm not a child you know. I'll tell them you're out with some aficionados from Madrid."

What torments the matador endured during the first moments of that dinner! The aristocratic and imposing splendour of the dining-room intimidated him; he and his hostess seemed lost in it, as they sat opposite one another in the middle of the great table, with its enormous silver candlesticks fitted with electric lights and pink shades. He was filled with awe of the dignified servants, who moved about with impassive ceremony, as if they were accustomed to everything, and nothing their mistress did could astonish them. He was ashamed of his clothes and his manners, feeling that they were out of keeping with his surroundings.

But this first feeling of fear and embarrassment gradually faded. Doña Sol laughed at his abstemiousness—his reluctance to taste the different dishes and wines. Gallardo looked at her admiringly. She certainly had a good appetite! After the finical over-niceness of the young ladies he had met, who seemed to think it bad form to eat at all heartily, he was astonished by Doña Sol's voracity and the stylish manner in which she carried out her nutritive functions. Mouthfuls of food disappeared between her rosy lips without leaving any trace of their passage; her jaws worked away without diminishing the beautiful serenity of her face; and she lifted her glass to her mouth without letting the smallest drop fall on the front of her dress, like a coloured pearl. This was surely how a goddess must eat and drink.

Encouraged by her example Gallardo ate and above all drank heartily, trying to find in the different exquisite wines he was offered a cure for the nervousness which left him shamefaced and only able to smile at everything and repeat: "Thanks very much."

The conversation became more animated. The matador's powers of speech were returning to him, and he told Doña Sol amusing anecdotes of his professional career, ending with

116

stories of El Nacional and his remarkable theories, and the doings of his picador Potaje—a barbarian who swallowed hard-boiled eggs whole, was half an ear short because one of his comrades had bitten it off; and who, when he was carried to the bull-ring infirmary wounded, fell on the bed with such a heavy thud of muscular limbs and steel combined that his long spurs went right through the mattress and had to be cut out afterwards.

"How extraordinary! How interesting!"

Doña Sol smilingly listened as he described the lives of these rough men, always face to face with death, whom she had hitherto only admired from a distance.

After the champagne Gallardo's transformation was complete, and when they rose from the table he offered the lady his arm, amazed at his own audacity. This was surely what was done in the fashionable world? . . . He wasn't so ignorant of social behaviour as he might seem at first sight.

Coffee was served in the drawing-room, where the matador caught sight of a guitar, obviously the same one on which Lechuzo gave lessons to Doña Sol. She offered it to him, asking him to play her something.

"But I don't know how! I'm the most ignorant man in the world! I don't know how to do anything except kill bulls!" If only the puntillero from his cuadrilla had been there! He drove women crazy with his clever guitar-playing.

There was a long silence. Gallardo was sitting on the sofa puffing at an excellent cigar, while Doña Sol drowsily smoked one of her scented cigarettes. The torero felt overcome by the torpor of digestion; he hardly spoke and gave no sign of life except a stupidly fixed smile.

Doña Sol seemed bored by his lack of response; she sat down at the grand piano and her strong fingers made the keys resound to the gay rhythm of a malagueña.

"*Olé!* That's good—very good!" said the torero, struggling to fight back his drowsiness.

After the malagueña she played some servillanas, and then

some melancholy oriental-sounding Andalusian airs, which she had learnt by heart in her enthusiasm for everything local.

Gallardo interrupted her singing with exclamations, just as if he had been sitting in front of the stage at a *café chantant*.

"Bravo! Let's have another one!"

"Do you like music?" the lady asked.

"Oh, very much." Gallardo had never asked himself this question before; but of course he liked it.

Doña Sol now abandoned the lively rhythms of folk-song and passed gradually into the slower, more solemn harmonies, which the music-loving matador recognized as 'religious'.

There were no interruptions from Gallardo now. He felt a delicious lethargy stealing over him; his eyes were closing; he realized that if this concert went on much longer he would certainly fall asleep.

To prevent this catastrophe, he gazed at the beautiful woman who sat with her back to him. Mother of God! what a magnificent body she had!

His dark eyes followed the line of her round white neck crowned by its aureole of waving golden curls. An absurd idea was running through his bemused mind, keeping him awake by its teasing promptings: "What would that girl do if I walked softly up behind her, step by step, and kissed her lovely neck?"

But his thoughts did not lead him to action; she inspired him with invincible respect. Also, he remembered what his manager had told him: how arrogantly she disposed of unwelcome advances with that technique she had learnt abroad for reducing a strong man to helplessness. He went on staring at her white neck surrounded with its golden halo, through the mists which were spreading in front of his eyes. He was falling asleep! He was terrified that at any moment a loud snore would interrupt her incomprehensible but presumably splendid music. He began pinching his legs to keep himself awake; he stretched his arms; he covered his mouth with his hand to stifle his yawns.

Some time passed. Gallardo was not sure whether he had been asleep or not. Suddenly Doña Sol's voice broke in on his uneasy somnolence. She had put down her cigarette, which lay sending up spirals of blue smoke, and was singing again, softly but in a voice trembling with passion, and accompanying herself on the piano.

The torero leant forward to hear what the words were. He couldn't understand a thing. It was some foreign song or other. "Damn it, why can't she sing a tango or something? And she expects a man to keep awake!"

Doña Sol's fingers ran lightly over the keys, while her eyes wandered round the room, her head thrown back and her breast swelling to her song.

It was "Elsa's Dream", the lament of the fair-haired virgin for her strong handsome warrior, unconquered by men and tender and timid with women.

She was singing as if in a trance, a quiver of passion running through her words, and tears of emotion in her eyes. This strong, simple warrior could almost be the man who now sat behind her. . . . Why not?

He hadn't Lohengrin's legendary appearance; he was rough and awkward; but she could still see, with all the vividness that a powerful impression makes upon memory, the gallantry with which he had come to save her the other day, and the smiling confidence with which he had fought the savage bull, just as Wagner's heroes fought terrifying dragons. Yes: he was *her* warrior.

And shaken from head to foot by a wave of voluptuous terror, giving herself up as conquered beforehand, she believed that she could feel the sweet danger approaching her from behind. She imagined her hero, her champion, rising slowly from the sofa with his dark eyes fixed on her; she heard his cautious footsteps; she felt his hands on her shoulders, then a fiery kiss on her neck, a seal of passion which would make her his slave for ever. . . . But the rhapsody ended, and nothing had happened; she felt no other impact beyond the thrill of her own trembling desire.

Disillusioned by his restraint she took her hands from the keys and turned round on the piano-stool. Her warrior was sitting on the sofa opposite, half buried in cushions, trying for the twentieth time to relight his cigar, and opening his eyes meanwhile as widely as possible to keep off encroaching drowsiness.

When he saw her looking at him, Gallardo stood up. Ah! the great moment was coming! Her hero was coming to her, to crush her passionately in his manly arms, to conquer her and make her his own.

"Good night, Doña Sol. I must go, it's late. You must be tired."

Surprised and piqued, she stood up too, and scarcely knowing what she did held out her hand to him. He was as awkward and simple as a real hero should be!

Thoughts passed through her mind in rapid succession—of the conventions, of all those restraints which no woman ever forgets even in her moments of greatest abandon. What she longed for was impossible! The very first time he had come to her house, and not the smallest pretence of resistance! To go to him unasked! But as she took the matador's hand she met his eyes—eyes which knew how to look at her with passionate intensity, trusting to the mute tenacity of his timid hopes, his silent desires.

"Don't go. . . . Come! Come."

And she said no more.

CHAPTER FOUR

A NEW reason, deeply satisfying to his vanity, had now been added to those which made Gallardo proud of his personal appearance.

When he talked to the Marqués de Moraima he looked at him with almost filial affection. This man in his countryman's clothes, this rough centaur with garrocha and leather leggings, was a distinguished personage, who had the right to cover his breast with crosses and ribbons, and wear an embroidered coat with a gold key sewn to the tail when he went to the Royal Palace. His remote ancestors had come to Seville with that king who had expelled the Moors, and had been rewarded by the gift of vast domains taken from the enemy—of which only the plains where the present Marqués' bulls were pastured were left. Subsequent generations had been friends and councillors of their reigning sovereigns, and had squandered most of their fortune on the splendours of court life. This good-natured unaffected nobleman, whose illustrious lineage was not entirely forgotten in the simplicities of country life, had become in a sense a close relation of Gallardo's.

The cobbler's son was as proud as if he had really become a member of this noble family. The Marqués de Moraima was his uncle, and though it was not a legitimate relationship and couldn't be publicly avowed he consoled himself by thinking of the power he exercised over one of the clan, thanks to a love affair which seemed to mock at all the laws and prejudices of class. All these gentlemen, who had hitherto behaved to him with the condescension of noble aficionados to a torero, were now his cousins, or relations of one sort or another, and he began to treat them as equals. Since Doña Sol talked to him about them with cousinly familiarity he thought it right to respond in the same style.

His life and habits had entirely changed. He seldom went into the aficionados' café in the Calle de las Sierpes. There were a good sort of people collected there, simple and friendly, but of very little importance: small tradesmen, workmen who had become employers, clerks, people of no profession who supported life in some unknown way, without any apparent occupation except talking about bulls.

Gallardo used to walk past these cafés, greeting his admirers, who eagerly beckoned to him to join them. "I'll be back in a moment," he would say. But instead he would sit down in another establishment in the same street, an aristocratic club decorated in an imposing Gothic style, where the servants wore knee breeches and there was silver plate on the tables.

Señora Angustias' son felt a thrill of complacency every

time that he passed between the club servants erect as soldiers in their black suits, or when the steward came forward to take his hat and stick, looking like an alderman with a silver chain round his neck. He enjoyed being surrounded by so many important people.

The younger men sat in tall chairs talking about horses and women, and the number of duels that still went on in Spain, for they were all touchy about points of honour and the obligations of a brave man. In an inner room people were practising fencing; in another they gambled from early afternoon till dawn. They all tolerated Gallardo, as one of the oddities of the club; he was a 'presentable' torero, who dressed well, spent a lot of money and knew the right people.

"He's very well educated," the members used to say confidently, realizing that he knew just about as much as they did.

Don José's sympathetic personality and excellent connexions served as guarantee for the torero in this new existence; and, besides, the shrewdness he had acquired in his early street-urchin days helped Gallardo make himself popular with these smart young men, all of whom seemed related to each other.

He gambled heavily. It was the easiest way of getting into closer touch with his new friends. He played and he lost, with the proverbial bad luck of a man who is fortunate in other undertakings. He used to spend most of his nights in the Criminal's Den, as they called the gambling-room, and he very seldom came away a winner. The club was proud of his ill-luck.

"Gallardo was cleaned out last night," the members told each other. "He must have lost at least eleven thousand pesetas."

And this reputation of being a heavy plunger, as well as the calm with which he took his losses, made his new friends respect him the more as a prop of their favourite occupation.

This new passion rapidly took hold of the matador. The excitement of play began to obsess him to such a degree that he was once or twice forgetful of the fine lady who stood first in his affections. Gambling with the cream of Seville society! Treated as an equal by these young aristocrats, thanks to the fellow-feeling that common emotions and loans of money engender!

One night a large electric lamp suddenly crashed down on the table. In the total darkness and confusion that followed Gallardo's voice rang out commandingly:

"Keep calm, gentlemen! Everything's all right. We'll go on with the game. Let's have some candles."

And the game went on. His companions admired this masterful speech even more than the way he killed bulls.

Gallardo's manager was questioned by his friends about the matador's losses. He was ruining himself, they said: at this rate he would spend everything he got from bullfighting on play. But Don José smiled scornfully, and redoubled his praise of his hero.

"This season we've got more contracts than anyone. We shall soon be tired of killing bulls and making piles of money. Let the boy have his fun. This is the reward of his labours; it's why he's what he is—the best man among them all!"

Don José felt that the general admiration for the calm way his idol lost money added new lustre to his glory. A matador couldn't be expected to behave like other men and count every centimo. Besides it gave him as much satisfaction as a personal success to see Gallardo accepted by an exclusive club, which was by no means open to everyone.

"He's the man of the moment," he would say aggressively to anyone who criticized the torero's new mode of life. "He doesn't go about with scallywags and sit about in bars, like the other matadors. Why? Because he's the favourite torero of the aristocracy, and he likes it too. The others are envious."

The club was not Gallardo's only haunt in his new life; he also went sometimes to the Forty-Five, which was a sort of senate-house of tauromachy. It was not easy for bullfighters to gain access to it; the more distinguished and respected aficionados could voice their doctrines more freely in their absence.

During the spring and summer the Forty-Five used to occupy the hall of their premises and overflow out into the street, where they sat in basket chairs waiting for telegrams with reports of the corridas. They paid little attention to the accounts in the Press; besides they wanted to hear the news before it appeared in the papers. The telegrams used to arrive at about nightfall, and would come from every town in the Peninsula where there had been a bullfight. After the members had listened gravely while the message was read aloud, they would argue about it and fill in the gaps left by the laconic telegraphic style.

They were extremely proud of this occupation; it gave them an importance above ordinary mortals to sit quietly outside their club enjoying the fresh air and receiving the certain knowledge, without any bias or exaggeration, as to what had happened that afternoon in the bull-rings of La Coruña, Barcelona or Valencia, as to how many ears a certain matador had been awarded, or how another had been hissed—while all the time their fellow-townsmen remained in abysmal ignorance, and would have to go about their business and wait till the evening papers came out later that night. However, when there had been an accident, and a telegram arrived announcing that some local torero had received a terrible tossing, these dignified gentlemen were softened by their patriotic feelings and would impart the momentous secret to a passing friend. The news would circulate through the cafés of the Calle de las Sierpes in a flash, and nobody doubted it for an instant. It was in one of the telegrams received by the Forty-Five.

Gallardo's manager was inclined to disturb the gravity of the club by his noisy and aggressive enthusiasm; but he was an old friend, and they put up with it, laughing at his mono-mania. It was quite impossible for reasonable people to discuss the merits of different toreros with Don José. Often when they were talking about Gallardo among themselves—'a brave chap, but not a great artist'—they would cast anxious glances towards the door.

"Look out, here comes Pepe," and the conversation came to a sudden standstill.

In came Pepe waving a telegram.

"Have you heard the news from Santander? Here you are:

124

'Gallardo, two estocadas, two bulls, and an ear for the second.'
What did I tell you? He's the best of them all!"

Often the telegram received by the Forty-Five was quite
different; but the manager only gave it a quick scornful
glance, and burst out into loud protests:

"Lies! Envious lies! Mine is the one that counts. This is
just jealousy of my boy's success."

The club members all laughed at Don José, tapped their
foreheads, and made jokes about 'the best man of them all'
and his comical manager.

But he had succeeded by gradually insidious means in
getting Gallardo accepted into the Forty-Five Society. First
the torero went there under the pretext of looking for his
manager; in the end he was sitting among the members, many
of whom were no friends of his and supported rival matadors.

The Society's premises were decorated with what Don
José described as 'character'. There were deep dados of
Moorish tiles, and on the immaculately white walls hung
posters of old corridas, stuffed heads of bulls famous for the
number of horses they had killed or for having wounded a
noted matador, and processional capes and swords presented
by certain maestros after cutting off their pigtails and retiring
from the profession.

Servants in evening dress waited on the members, who wore
country clothes—or shirt-sleeves in hot weather. In Holy
Week and at the time of other important fiestas, when
aficionados from all over Spain arrived at the Forty-Five, the
servants wore powdered wigs and red and yellow livery with
knee breeches, like footmen to the royal household, as they
took trays of Manzanilla to these rich gentlemen, many of
whom had taken off their ties.

On the arrival of the senior member, the Marqués de
Moraima, the others made a circle round him, sitting in
their deep arm-chairs while the distinguished cattle-breeder
presided over the conversation from a higher chair, much like
a throne. They always began by talking about the weather.
Most of them were breeders or prosperous farmers whose

incomes were derived from the soil and depended on the vagaries of the climate. The Marqués used to expound the knowledge he had gained in the course of long journeys on horseback over the plains of Andalusia—those interminable deserts like an earthly sea, where the bulls lie like basking sharks among grass-covered waves. On his way to the club he invariably caught sight of a piece of paper being blown by the wind, and on this he based his forecasts. They would talk for days on end about the drought, that cruel scourge of the southern pastures; and when, after long weeks of anxious expectation, the sky clouded over and distilled a few big warm drops, the landowners smiled happily at each other and rubbed their hands, while the Marqués would say sententiously as he watched the large round spots on the pavement:

"Thank God! Every drop is worth five duros."

If it wasn't the weather they talked about, then it would be cattle, and more especially bulls which they referred to with affection as if they were linked to them by some affinity. The other breeders listened to the Marqués' views with respect, recognizing the weight given his words by superior wealth. The aficionados, who never left town, admired his skill in breeding brave bulls. What a lot that man knew! He talked of the difficulties involved in rearing cattle with an obvious conviction that his profession was an important one.

Out of every ten yearlings tested for potential 'bravery' eight or nine would be handed over to the butchers. Only one or two proved themselves sufficiently aggressive under the steel of the garrocha to qualify for the ring, and a life apart with every sort of care lavished on them.

"A ranch which breeds brave bulls is not a business," the Marqués said. "It's a luxury. You get four or five times as much for a fighting bull as you do for a beef bull, of course. But look at the cost!"

They must be constantly watched over, their food and drink carefully regulated; they must be moved from one place to another according to changes of temperature.

Each bull cost more to keep than a whole family; and when it was ready it still needed the utmost care until the very last moment, so that it shouldn't disgrace itself in the arena, but be a credit to the herd whose brand was on its neck.

The Marqués had come to blows with the impresarios of more than one bull-ring, because he refused to let his animals go into a pen with a band playing just above it. The noise of the instruments worried the noble creatures, so that by the time they entered the ring they would have lost all their courage and calm.

"They're just the same as us," he said fondly, "except that they can't talk! The same? There are some that are much better."

And he told them about Lobito, an old bull who was leader of one of his herds. He wouldn't sell him not if he was offered the whole of Seville with the Giralda thrown in. He used to gallop over his huge estates, and as soon as he came in sight of the herd to which this treasure belonged, he only had to call out "Lobito!" and Lobito would leave his companions and trot up to the Marqués, rubbing his wet and friendly muzzle against his boots; yet he was an immensely powerful animal and the rest of the herd went in terror of him.

Then the breeder would dismount, take a piece of chocolate out of his saddle-bag and give it to Lobito, who showed his gratitude by nodding his great head with its colossal horns; and with one arm over the bull's neck the Marqués would advance calmly into the middle of the herd, though they fidgeted and looked fierce, resenting the presence of a man among them. There was nothing to fear.

Lobito walked like a watch-dog, covering his master with his body and looking round him with blazing eyes as if to impose good behaviour on his companions. If one of them was bold enough to come forward and sniff at the Marqués he would be met by the leader's threatening horns. Or if several grouped together to bar the way, Lobito would open a passage through them with his powerful head.

As the Marqués related the doings of some of the animals that had come from his ranch his shaven lips and white whiskers trembled with affectionate emotion.

"Bulls are the noblest animals in the world! If men were more like them, things would be a lot better. Poor old Coronel over there now. Do any of you remember that splendid beast?"

He pointed to a large sumptuously framed photograph, of himself as a much younger man dressed in hunting clothes, among some little girls in white frocks in the middle of a meadow. They all seemed to be sitting on a black mound with two horns at one end. This shapeless dark seat was Coronel. The enormous bull was fierce with the rest of the herd but all gentleness and devotion with his master and his family. He was like one of those mastiffs who savagely attack strangers but allow the children of the house to pull their ears and tails, putting up with all their devilries with good-natured grunts. The Marqués used to take his daughters to see him when they were still very young, and he used to sniff at their little white skirts as they clung timidly to their father's legs, or, suddenly brave, put out a hand and stroked his muzzle. "Lie down, Coronel!" And Coronel's legs would double beneath him, while the children climbed on to his broad back heaving up and down with the bellows-like movements of his heavy breathing.

One day, after much hesitation, the Marqués had sold him to the Pamplona bull-ring, and went himself to see the corrida. His eyes became dim with emotion as he remembered the occasion. Never before had such a bull been seen. He rushed gamely out into the arena, then stopped still in the middle, dazed by the sudden change from darkness to light and from silence to uproar. But as soon as he had his first jab from a picador, he seemed to dominate the whole ring by his magnificent bravery.

"He cared nothing for men, nor horses, nor anything. In a few moments he had knocked over all the horses, and their riders were flying through the air. The peons were running; everything was in confusion. The audience called for more horses, while Coronel stood in the middle, just waiting for all comers. You'll never see such courage and strength as his again, I promise you. As soon as anyone challenged him he charged with such vigour and dash that the crowd went mad with excitement. When the signal for the kill was given, he had fourteen wounds, and was carrying a complete set of banderillas, yet he was as fresh and brave as if he'd just come from the pasture. Then. . . ."

When the cattle-breeder reached this point in his story he always stopped, to steady his quavering voice.

Then the Marqués de Moraima, who had been sitting in one of the boxes, had found himself, he knew not how, behind the barrier, amongst the agitated bullring servants and quite close to the matador, who was preparing his muleta with an appearance of calm, as if he wished to postpone the moment when he must meet his formidable adversary face to face. "Coronel!" cried the Marqués, leaning as far as he could over the barrier and beating the planks with his hands.

The animal didn't move, but lifted his head to listen to this cry reminding him of a far-off place he would never see again. "Coronel!" Turning his head he saw a man calling to him over the barrier and at once rushed forward to attack. But in the middle of his charge he pulled up, and came on slowly till his horns touched the arms stretched out towards him. He was streaked with crimson streams of blood from the banderillas fixed in his neck, and the muscles showed blue where the picadors had torn wounds in his flesh. "Coronel! My son!" And as if he understood this tender summons, the bull raised his muzzle and wetted the breeder's whiskers with his slaver. "Why have you brought me here?" his fierce bloodshot eyes seemed to be asking. And the Marqués, still unaware what he was doing, repeatedly kissed the bull's damp nose.

"Don't kill him!" shouted some kind-hearted member of the audience; and as if his words expressed the feelings of the whole crowd, shouts came from every part of the amphitheatre, while white handkerchiefs fluttered from every tier of seats. "Don't kill him!" For the moment the onlookers were in the grip of a confused emotion which made them despise their own favourite sport, feel hatred for the bullfighter in his gaudy suit with his futile heroism, and admire the courage of the bull—feeling themselves inferior to this poor animal, who seemed to represent nobility and understanding better than the thousands of reasoning beings around him.

"I took him away," said the Marqués with emotion. "I gave the impresario back his two thousand pesetas. I would have given him all I had. After a month at pasture on my ranch there wasn't a scar left on his neck. I wanted the brave fellow to die of old age; but it's not always the good who prosper in this world. He was killed by a treacherous sideways blow from a cunning bull who would never have dared to face up to him."

The Marqués and the other cattle-breeders now quickly changed the subject from their affection for their bulls to their pride in their ferocity. With what scorn they spoke of the enemies of bullfighting, of those who clamoured against it in the name of cruelty to animals! Foreign foolishness! The ignorance of those who thought all horned animals must be the same, and couldn't tell beef oxen from fighting bulls! The Spanish bull was a wild beast; the bravest wild beast in the world. And they recalled various fights between bulls and lions or tigers, in which the national animal had always triumphed.

The Marqués laughingly remembered how a fight was once arranged in a certain bull-ring between a bull on one side and a lion and tiger belonging to a famous animal-tamer on the other. He had sent Barrabás, a vicious creature which had had to be kept apart on the ranch, because he attacked and killed so many of his companions.

"I saw this with my own eyes," Moraima said. "There was a huge iron cage in the middle of the arena, and inside it was Barrabás. First they loosed the lion, and the wretched brute took advantage of the bull's unsuspiciousness and sprang on his hind quarters and tore at him with teeth and claws. Barrabás tried furiously to free himself and get at his enemy with his horns. At last he succeeded in throwing the lion in front of him, and then—man alive!—it was just like a game of ball! He tossed him from one horn to another for quite a while as if he were a toy, then threw him on one side as if he despised him; and there lay the so-called king of beasts rolled in a ball like a cat that has just been beaten. Next they loosed the tiger, and this was a much shorter affair. As soon as he showed his face Barrabás caught him and tossed him, and after giving him a good shaking threw him in a corner too, curled up like the lion. Then Barrabás, who was a spiteful brute, walked up and down and relieved himself over the two wild cats. When the tamers came to take them away a basket of sawdust was not enough to clean up with, because in their terror they had emptied their bowels of everything they contained."

There were always shouts of laughter when these stories were told at the Forty-Five. There was no other animal like a Spanish bull! Their exclamations of delight expressed a sort of patriotism, as if the proud courage of their national animal were evidence of the superiority of their country and race over all others.

When Gallardo began to frequent the club, a new subject of conversation had arisen to interrupt the endless talk of bulls and agriculture.

Everyone at the Forty-Five as in the rest of Seville was discussing the doings of Plumitas, a bandit celebrated for his audacity and for the utter failure of all attempts to capture him. The newspapers were full of stories of his extravagant and humorous doings; he had become a national character. Questions were asked about him in the Cortes, and a speedy capture was promised, but never realized. A concentrated force of the Civil Guard were mobilized to take him prisoner, and meanwhile Plumitas, quite alone with his horse and his gun, contrived to slip past his pursuers like a phantom, only confronting them a few at a time, when he would leave several dead on the ground. He was adored and helped by the poor peasantry, wretched slaves of the great landowners, who saw the bandit as the avenger of the starving and dispenser of summary and savage justice, after the fashion of the armour-clad knights-errant of long ago. He extorted money from the rich, and now and again gave help to some poor old woman or labourer with a large family, in a theatrical manner as though watched by a large audience. These acts of generosity were exaggerated by the gossip of the country people, who always had Plumitas' name on their lips but became blind and dumb when questioned by the soldiery.

He moved from one province to another with the ease of one who knew the country well, and the landed proprietors of both Seville and Córdova contributed to his support. Weeks might go by when nothing was heard of the bandit, and then suddenly he would appear at some farm or make a bold entry into a village.

The Forty-Five always had the latest news of him, just as if he were a matador.

"Plumitas was at my farm the day before yesterday," said a rich agriculturist. "My overseer gave him thirty duros and some lunch and he went away."

They put up with these exactions fairly patiently, and told no one except their friends. If they gave information to the authorities there would be forms to sign and all sorts of trouble. What was the use? The Civil Guard couldn't catch him, and he would certainly vent his rage on the informers by taking revenge on their property.

The Marqués talked about Plumitas' adventures calmly and with a smile on his face, as though they were natural and inevitable misfortunes.

"These brigands are often poor fellows who have been in trouble of some sort, and taken to the mountains. My father (may he rest in peace!) knew the famous José Maria and twice had a meal with him. I myself have run into several less well known evil-doers. They're just like bulls—simple-hearted noble creatures. They only attack when they're provoked, and the more you punish them the more formidable they get."

He had given orders to all his farmers and shepherds to give Plumitas whatever he asked for; with the result that the bandit showed him a peasant's respect for a kind and generous master, sang his praises and threatened to kill anyone who committed the slightest offence against the 'Señor Marqués'

—or so his foremen and drovers told him. Poor fellow! It wasn't worth provoking him to anger and revenge. Better give him the miserable sum he asked, tired and hungry as he was.

The cattle-breeder often galloped quite alone over the plains where his bulls were grazing, and he suspected that he had met Plumitas more than once, without recognizing him. He was probably one of those disreputable-looking horsemen whom he came across in the loneliest part of the country, without a village in sight, who would raise their hands to their greasy hats and say respectfully:

"Good day, Señor Marqués."

Sometimes when he spoke of Plumitas, Moraima would look fixedly at Gallardo, who was showing a novice's vehement indignation towards the authorities for not protecting public property.

"One of these days he'll turn up at La Rinconada, my boy," he said in his slow Andalusian drawl.

"That won't please me at all, curse him. Good heavens! Is this what I pay heavy taxes for?"

No, it wouldn't please him at all to run into the bandit on one of his visits to La Rinconada. He could be brave enough and careless of his life when he was killing bulls in the arena; but these professional killers of men inspired him with nameless fear.

His family were at the farm. Señora Angustias had taken a fancy to country life, after the squalor of her earlier days in the town. Carmen enjoyed it too; her housewifely instincts were gratified by close contact with the various tasks that went on there. Besides, the saddler's children were still with her, filling the vacuum left by her own sterility, and the country air did them good.

Gallardo had sent his family to the farm for a while, promising to join them later; but he made every sort of excuse to postpone his departure. He went on leading a bachelor existence in his town house, alone with Garabato, with complete freedom to spend as much time as possible with Doña Sol.

It seemed to him the happiest time of his life. Sometimes he almost forgot the existence of La Rinconada and its inmates.

He and Doña Sol used to go out riding on spirited horses, wearing the same clothes as the day they first met, sometimes alone together and sometimes with Don José, whose presence seemed to mollify those who were scandalized by this exhibition. Occasionally they went to look at the bulls on ranches near Seville or to try out the Marqués' yearlings; and Doña Sol, always eager for danger, was delighted when a young bull turned on her instead of running away from the garrocha, so that Gallardo had to come to her rescue.

At other times they used to go to the station of Empalme to see bulls put into trucks to go off to various bull-rings where special corridas were to be held at the end of the winter. This was one of the most important centres of export for the taurine industry, and Doña Sol took a great interest in it. There were vast enclosures close to the railway lines, and dozens of great boxes made of grey wood, raised on wheels and with sliding doors, stood in rows waiting for the busy summer season.

These boxes had travelled all over the Peninsula, taking a brave bull to some distant bull-ring and returning empty, only to take in another and repeat the journey over and over again all through the summer.

Human ingenuity had devised a trap by which these wild animals, used to a life of freedom, could be as easily handled as any other merchandise. The bulls who were to be entrained arrived at a gallop along a wide dusty road between barbed-wire fences. They had come from distant ranches, and when they got to Empalme they were driven along into the enclosure at full speed. The overseers and drovers galloped in front with their pikes over their shoulders, and behind them came the wise old bell-oxen making a barrier with their huge horns. Next came the brave bulls, the beasts destined to die in the ring, well surrounded by domestic cattle, who prevented them from straying, and by cowherds, with their slings ready to throw a stone at any pair of horns which showed signs of leaving the herd.

When they reached the enclosures the foremost riders drew up on either side of the gate, and the whole herd—a dusty, kicking, snorting, jostling avalanche—rushed in like an irresistible torrent. The gates were closed immediately the last animal had passed through, and they were egged along by men sitting astride the walls or shouting and waving their hats from the galleries. They galloped through the first enclosure without even noticing that they were trapped. As soon as they were past the first gate, the obedient well-trained bell-oxen moved to one side, letting the mass of bulls who had been snorting behind them go by into the second enclosure. Here, to their amazement and bewilderment, they found themselves alone, with walls in front of them, and when they turned they saw a shut door behind.

Now the boxing operations began. One by one the bulls were driven with shouts, waving of cloths and blows from garrochas, into a passage at the end of which stood the truck with its doors raised. It seemed to them like a small tunnel, beyond which they could see an open enclosure with grass and bell-oxen quietly grazing—a mirage of their distant pastures.

Each bull advanced slowly and suspiciously up this passage, reluctant to tread on the smooth wooden ramp which led up to the truck, sensing some danger in this forced entry, and in the constant jabs urging it on from behind. Men standing two deep on the balconies added to its agitation by their clapping and whistling. From the roof of the truck, where the carpenters were hiding ready to let down the doors, a red cloth was hanging and swinging in the rectangle of light framed by the exit. At last the garrochas, the cries, the dancing red shape and the sight of its companions quietly grazing ahead, forced it to a decision. It dashed along the passage making the wooden ramp shake under its hoofs—but the further door immediately shut with a bang, and before it could turn and retreat the door behind shut also.

The bolts were pushed home with a loud clank and the animal found itself in total darkness and silence, a prisoner in a space so small that it had to lie down with legs doubled under it. Armfuls of fodder were thrown down through a trap-door in the roof, and the movable dungeon was rolled away on little wheels to the railway line nearby. At once another truck took its place at the end of the passage, and the trap was baited again, until all the animals needed for the corrida had been successfully entrained.

Doña Sol's passion for local colour was gratified by these glimpses of the great national industry at work, and she was keen to try her hand as overseer or herdsman. She loved the life of the open air, galloping over the vast plains pursued by a great head and a sharp pair of horns which could inflict sudden death with the slightest movement. There seethed within her that craving for a pastoral life which is our inheritance from our remote ancestors, from the time when man was unable to exploit the fruits of the earth, but lived by joining his fate with animals and feeding on their dead bodies. To own a herd—but of wild beasts—seemed to Doña Sol the most interesting and splendid of all professions.

After his first intoxicating enjoyment of his good fortune, Gallardo used to gaze in amazement at his lady-love in their moments of greatest intimacy, wondering whether all great ladies were like this one.

Her caprices and fickleness of character bewildered him. He didn't dare call her *tu*; no, that was impossible. She had never invited him to such a familiarity, and once when he had tried hesitatingly to do so, he saw such an expression of amazement flash from her golden eyes that he had beat an ashamed retreat and returned to the old manner of speech.

She spoke to him as *tu* (as did the aristocratic men of his acquaintance), but only when in their moments of privacy. If she had to write him a note telling him not to come to see her as she was going out with her relations, she always addressed him as *Usted*, and there would be no expressions of affection in her letter, nothing more than the cold politeness used to a friend of an inferior social class.

"It looks almost as if she'd been about with cads who

showed her letters to every one," Gallardo muttered despondently. "She's afraid. One would think she can't trust me to behave like a gentleman because I'm a matador."

Many of her eccentricities left the bullfighter sad and frowning. Some days, for no apparent reason, he would find his way coldly barred when he went to see her, by one of her magnificent-looking servants, saying: "The Señora is not at home. The Señora has gone out." He guessed that this was a lie, and felt aware of Doña Sol's presence quite near him on the other side of doors and curtains. She must be growing tired of him, or had felt some sudden aversion for him, so that she had given orders to the servants that he was not to be admitted.

'Well—she's cooling off, I suppose,' the matador said to himself as he went away. 'I shan't go back. I'm not going to have her laughing at me.'

But when he did go back he was ashamed of having ever thought it possible not to see Doña Sol again. She flung her strong white arms around him, and looked at him with large dreamy eyes shining with an almost lunatic light, while her mouth contracted with passion.

"Why do you wear scent?" she asked with a look of disgust. "It's unworthy of you. I want you to smell of bulls and horses. Such good, rich smells! Don't you love them? Say yes, Juanin, you splendid brute!"

One night in the soft semi-darkness of her bedroom he felt almost afraid of the look in her eyes as she said:

"I should like to go down on all fours. I should like to be a bull, with you standing in front of me sword in hand. I'd give you a fine goring! Here . . . and here!"

And in her excitement she struck him several violent blows with her clenched fist on his chest, which was covered only with a thin silk vest. Gallardo drew back, not wanting to admit that a woman could hurt him so much.

"No, not a bull. No, now I want to be a dog—a shepherd's dog with long sharp teeth, to leap out and bark at you and say: 'You see that conceited fellow who kills bulls, and everyone thinks so brave? Well I'm going to eat him up! Like this! Mmm!'"

And with hysterical delight she fixed her teeth in the matador's powerful biceps, causing him acute agony. He swore violently and shook himself free of the beautiful half-naked woman, who looked like a drunken bacchante with her golden snakes of hair.

Doña Sol seemed suddenly to come to her senses.

"My poor darling! I've hurt you! Yes, I know, I'm quite mad sometimes. Let me kiss the bite and make it well. Let me kiss all your beautiful scars. My poor darling, I made you cry."

And from a beautiful fury she became a loving gentle woman, rubbing herself against the torero like a kitten.

Gallardo had an old-fashioned view of love, believing that it implied intimacy as great as that of married life, but he was never allowed to spend a whole night with Doña Sol. When he thought he had reduced her to submission by the prodigality of his love-making, she would show a sudden physical aversion to him, and burst out imperiously:

"Go away. I want to be alone. I can't bear you, you know. Nor anyone else either. Men! . . . how revolting they are!"

And Gallardo had to take flight, saddened and humiliated by the caprices of this incomprehensible woman.

One evening, seeing that she was in a confidential mood and feeling some curiosity about her past, he asked her about the kings and other important people who were said to have figured in her life.

She replied to his question with a cold stare from her pale-coloured eyes.

"And what has it got to do with you? Are you jealous by any chance? And if it were all true, what then?"

She was silent for some time with a strange expression in her eyes: that almost insane look which accompanied her most extravagant fantasies.

"You must often have hit women," she said, looking at him curiously. "Don't deny it. I'm very much interested. No, not your wife; I know how good she is. Other women, I mean; the sort you toreros mix with; women who love more fiercely when they are beaten. No? Haven't you really struck any of them?"

Gallardo protested with some dignity that a brave man couldn't ill-treat those who were weaker than himself. His exclamations seemed to disappoint Doña Sol.

"You must beat me some day. I want to know what it's like," she said firmly.

Then a shadow crossed her face, she frowned, and her eyes flashed blue through their flecks of gold.

"No; don't listen to what I say. You'd better not try. You'd certainly be the loser."

It was good advice, and Gallardo had occasion to remember it. One day a rather rough caress from his strong hands was enough to rouse a fury of rage in this woman whose feeling for him was half love, half hate. "Take that!" And she gave him a blow with her closed fist which hit him as squarely on the jaw as if she had taken lessons in boxing.

Gallardo was stunned with pain and shame, while Doña Sol tried to justify her unprovoked attack, but in a cold hostile manner.

"I wanted to teach you a lesson. I know what you toreros are like. If I once let you knock me about, you'd soon be treating me as if I were a gypsy from Triana. I had to do it. You must keep your distance in future."

One evening in early spring the two of them were returning with a party of other riders from a trial of yearlings on the Marqués' estate. Doña Sol, followed by the matador, turned aside into the fields, enjoying the soft yielding turf beneath their horses hoofs.

The dying sun had stained the green plain a vivid crimson, dotted over with white and yellow flowers. Over this vast expanse tinged with red as by a distant fire lay the long narrow shadows of the horses and their riders. The garrochas on their shoulders seemed so enormous that the ends of them were lost in the distance. On one side ran the river, like a strip of reddened steel.

Doña Sol gave Gallardo an imperious glance.

"Put your arm round my waist."

The matador obeyed, and they rode on with their horses side by side and their bodies united as one from the waist upwards. Doña Sol gazed at the blended shadows advancing at a slow, jogging pace over the magically lit fields.

"We might be in another world," she murmured. "A legendary world: it's like the meadows you see in tapestries. A scene out of some old romance: the knight and his lady travelling along with their lances over their shoulders, in love with each other and in search of adventures and danger. But you can't understand that, my darling idiot. You can't, can you?"

The bullfighter smiled, showing his strong white shining teeth. She pressed closer to him, as if attracted by his boorish ignorance, and laid her head on his shoulder, shivering with pleasure as she felt the muscles of his neck pulsate to each breath.

They rode on in silence; Doña Sol seemed to have fallen asleep. Then she suddenly opened her eyes, with that strange expression which was the precursor of the most extraordinary questions.

"Tell me, have you never killed a man?"

Gallardo started away from her in astonishment. Who? . . . He? . . . Never! He had followed his profession without doing any harm to anyone, like any other fellow. He had hardly even fought with his comrades of the capea days, when they hung on to all the money they got because they were the strongest. There had been a few blows among his fellow bullfighters; a row in a café; that was all. He had a deep respect for human life. Bulls were different.

"So you mean you've never even wanted to kill a man? I always thought toreros. . . ."

The sun sank below the horizon, the fantastic illumination vanished from the fields, the river glittered no more, and the tapestry landscape Doña Sol had thought so beautiful became suddenly dark and ordinary. The other riders were some way ahead, and she put spurs to her horse to catch them up, without saying a single word to the matador or seeming to notice whether he was following her.

Gallardo's family returned to Seville for the fiestas of Holy Week. The maestro was due to appear in the Easter corrida. It was the first time that he would fight in front of Doña Sol since he had got to know her, and this fact worried him and shook his confidence in his own powers.

Moreover, there was always a special anxiety attached to Seville bullfights. A failure in any other bull-ring in Spain would not be so bad; after all, it might be long before he returned there. But in his home town, among his worst enemies!

"I want to see you distinguish yourself," his manager said. "Think who will be watching you. Remember you're the best man of them all!"

On Easter eve, during the small hours, the animals for the following day's corrida were to be put in their pens, and Doña Sol was anxious to take part in this operation which had the added charm of taking place in darkness. The bulls had to be brought from the Tablada ranch to the bull-ring enclosure.

Gallardo did not go, although he would have liked to be with Doña Sol, for his manager was against it, saying that he must have a good night's rest so as to be fresh and strong the following afternoon. Round about midnight the road leading from the ranch to the bull-ring was as full of life as if a feria was going on. The windows of all the country-houses were brightly lit, and dancing shadows passed across them to the music of pianos. The doors of the wayside inns stood open, throwing rectangles of light on to the dark earth, and from inside came the sound of shouts, laughter, the thrumming of guitars and clink of glasses, showing that wine and Manzanilla were circulating in abundance.

At about one o'clock a rider trotted slowly up the road. It was the *aviso*, a herdsman who stopped at every house or inn where lights were showing, to warn them that the herd would be passing in less than a quarter of an hour, and to ask them to put out their lights and keep perfectly quiet.

141

This order, issued in the name of the national fiesta, was obeyed more promptly than any from the Government. The houses were immediately darkened, their white walls merging with the obscure shapes of trees; people stood grouped in absolute silence behind the window-grilles and fences, waiting for what was to come. The gas-lamps along the riverside paths were put out one by one, as the herdsman came by shouting his warning.

All was silence. Above the dark massed shapes of the trees stars were twinkling in the tranquil expanse of the sky; at ground level only a very slight movement could be detected, a restrained rustling, as if swarms of insects were moving in the darkness. The time of waiting seemed very long, but at last through the cool silence came the distant deep tolling of bells. They were coming! They would soon be here!

The sound of bells grew louder, and with it a thunder of hoofs which shook the ground. A few men on horseback were the first to gallop past, looking immense in the darkness, with their pikes held low. These were the drovers. Then came a party of aficionados with garrochas, among whom was Doña Sol, thrilled by this wild gallop through the shadows, when a single false step by her horse or a fall would mean certain death, crushed under the powerful horns of the fierce herd galloping blindly on behind.

The bells jangled wildly now; dust whirled into the open mouths of the onlookers standing hidden in the darkness, and the frenzied herd rushed by like some dreadful nightmare— shapeless monsters of the darkness, great mountains of moving flesh, heavy yet active, giving terrifying snorts, lowering their heads at shadows, frightened and enraged by the shouts of the drovers following them on foot and the horsemen with pikes who brought up the rear.

The heavy, noisy cavalcade had gone by in a moment. There was nothing more to be seen. Quite satisfied by this fleeting spectacle after their long wait, the crowd came out from their hiding-places, and some started running after the herd hoping to see them put into the enclosures.

When they reached the bull-ring the leading riders moved aside, letting the bulls rush on after the bell-oxen straight into the narrow fenced-in passage which led to the enclosures.

The aficionados congratulated each other on the successful performance of the operation. The herd had been rounded up without a single bull going astray. They were all well-bred animals, most of them from the Marqués' ranch. Great things could be expected next day, if the maestros lived up to their reputations. And riders and peons dispersed, happily looking forward to the fiesta. An hour later the bull-ring and its surroundings were completely deserted, and silent darkness had swallowed up the fierce animals within, who lay peacefully in the enclosure enjoying the last night's sleep of their lives.

Juan Gallardo was up early next morning, after a bad night disturbed by nightmares.

Why did they make him fight in Seville? In other towns he could lead a bachelor life, forgetting his family for the moment, in a completely strange hotel room which 'said nothing' to him, since there was nothing in it belonging to him. But here he had to put on his fighting suit in his own bedroom, where everything on the chairs and tables reminded him of Carmen. Leaving this house, which he had built himself and which contained all that was closest to his heart, to go out and face danger, filled him with as much distress and anxiety as if it had been the first time he had to kill a bull. Besides, he was afraid of his fellow-townsmen, the people he would have to spend the rest of his life with, whose good opinion was more important to him than the applause of the whole of the rest of Spain. What a terrible moment it was when dressed by Garabato in his fighting suit he went down into the silent patio! His little nephew and niece would come to see him and touch his gorgeous clothes with wondering admiration, too intimidated to speak; his moustachioed sister would kiss him with a look of terror, as if he were doomed to die; his mother hid herself in the darkest room in the house. No; she didn't want to see him, she was feeling ill. Carmen would be deathly pale, over-animated, biting her lips till they turned blue, blinking her eyes nervously to keep back the tears; but when she saw him in the porch she would quickly press her handkerchief to her eyes while her whole body shook with the sobs and moans she tried to suppress, and without the supporting arms of the other women she would have fallen to the ground.

It was enough to make a coward even of Roger de Flor!

"Damnation take it!" Gallardo would say. "Why, I wouldn't fight in Seville for all the money in the world, except that they like to see me, and that I won't have them saying I'm afraid of my own people!"

After he got up that morning, the matador wandered about the house with a cigarette in his mouth, stretching his sinewy arms to test their suppleness. He drank a glass of wine in the kitchen, where his mother was busying herself at the stove in spite of her age and corpulence, giving orders to the servants and supervising the running of the house.

Gallardo went out into the cool brightness of the patio. The early morning silence was broken by the singing of the birds, hopping from perch to perch in their gilded cages. A shaft of sunlight fell on the marble pavement, making a golden triangle which included the leafy border of the fountain, and the gold-fish sending streams of bubbles from their small round mouths.

There was a woman dressed in black, with a pail by her side, washing the marble floor, whose colours shone more brightly under her damp cloth. She looked up.

"Good morning, Señor Juan," she said with the affectionate familiarity every popular figure inspires.

And she looked at him admiringly with her solitary eye. Where the other should have been, a maze of wrinkles seemed to meet in the dark hollow of the socket.

Señor Juan made no reply. He hurried to the kitchen, calling for Señora Angustias.

"But, Mamma, who is that woman—the one-eyed creature who's scrubbing the patio?"

"Why, who d'you think, my boy? Just a poor woman. Our usual cleaner is ill, so I got this poor thing to come; she's got a family to support."

The bullfighter seemed agitated, and his expression was full of worry and fear. Devil take it! With a corrida in Seville, it was really the last straw that the first person he should run into should be a one-eyed woman! Good heavens, such things never happened to anyone else! Nothing could possibly be more unlucky. Did they want him to be killed?

Alarmed by his dramatic prognostications and the violence of his anger, his poor mother tried to excuse herself. How could she have known what he would feel? The woman was desperately poor and wanted to earn a peseta for her children. Juan must pluck up courage, and give thanks to God for taking care of them all and delivering them from poverty as great as hers.

His mother's words calmed Gallardo, and the thought of the hard times of long ago made him more tolerant towards the poor one-eyed woman. Very well; she should stay, come what might.

And he crossed the patio with his back turned so as not to catch sight of the terrible eye of the unlucky bird of ill omen, and took refuge in his study, close to the hall.

Above the deep dado of Moorish tiles, the white walls were hung with announcements of bullfights printed on silk of different colours. Diplomas headed with the grandiose titles of charitable societies recorded the corridas in which Gallardo had given his services free for the benefit of the poor. Innumerable photographs of the maestro, standing, sitting, spreading his cape or going in to kill, bore witness to the zeal with which the newspapers represented him in every possible attitude. Over the door was a portrait of Carmen wearing a white mantilla which made her eyes look darker than ever, and with a bunch of carnations in her black hair. From the opposite wall, above the arm-chair which stood in front of the writing-table, an enormous black bull's head seemed to preside over the orderly room, with its glass eyes, brilliantly varnished nostrils, a white spot on the forehead, and huge horns, pale as ivory at the base and gradually becoming darker till the sharp points were as black as ink. Potaje the picador used to break out into rhapsodical praise of this animal's horns when he

145

looked at them, saying that they were so large and so widely spread that a blackbird could sit and sing on the point of one of them without being heard from the other.

Gallardo sat down in front of his beautiful writing-table with its brass fittings. Except for a layer of several days' dust, everything was as it should be. The wells of the enormous inkstand, decorated with two brass horses, were white and empty. There were no pens in the handsome tray supported on dogs' heads. The great man never had to to do any writing. His manager Don José dealt with all his contracts and other professional documents, and all he had to do was to sit down at a table in the club in the Calle de las Sierpes, and add his slow, complicated signature.

On one side of the room stood his 'library': an oak bookcase, with its permanently shut glass doors through which could be seen rows of large important-looking volumes in handsome bindings.

When Don José began to talk about his matador as the 'torero of the aristocracy', Gallardo felt he must try and live up to the description and acquire some education, so that his distinguished friends shouldn't laugh at his ignorance as had happened to some of his comrades. One day he walked into a bookshop with a determined air.

"Send me three thousand pesetas-worth of books."

And when the bookseller hesitated and seemed not to understand, he repeated energetically:

"Books, you understand? Large books; and if possible with gilt bindings."

Gallardo was pleased with the appearance of his library. When they talked at the club about things he didn't understand, he used to smile knowingly and say to himself:

"That must be in one of the books in my study."

One wet afternoon when he was feeling poorly and wandering round the house not knowing what to do with himself, he opened the bookcase as if performing some religious rite, and took out the largest book he could see, like some mysterious god from its shrine. He stopped reading after a few lines and turned over the pages, taking a childish pleasure in the pictures of lions, elephants, horses with fiery eyes and flowing manes, and zebras with coats as regularly striped as if they had been drawn with a ruler. The bullfighter advanced recklessly along the path of knowledge, until suddenly he came upon a picture of a snake with its brightly-coloured coils. Ugh! a snake—the ill-omened creature! And he quickly closed the middle fingers of his hand, leaving the index and little fingers standing up like two horns to avert the evil eye. He turned a few more pages, but all the pictures were of horrifying reptiles, and in the end he shut the book with trembling hands and put it back on the shelf, muttering: "Lizard, lizard!" to dispel the unfortunate impression left by this incident.

After this the key of his library lay forgotten in a drawer of his writing-table covered over with old papers. He could get along very well without reading. When his admirers brought him a copy of a bullfighting newspaper hot from the press, generally because it contained an attack on one of his rivals, Gallardo gave it to his brother-in-law or Carmen to read to him, while he listened with a beatific smile, puffing at a cigar.

"That's good! Those chaps know how to write!"

But when the journalists criticized Gallardo himself there was no reading aloud, and he talked with disgust about people who wrote about bullfighting when they wouldn't know the first thing to do with a cape if they found themselves in the ring.

On the morning of the Seville corrida he could find no peace of mind in his study. He sat staring at the bull's head, without quite knowing why, and the most painful memory of his whole career came to his mind. It gave him a real sense of victory to be able to look at the head of that malignant brute any time he wanted to. How that bull had made him sweat in the bull-ring at Zaragoza! It was almost human in its cleverness. It had stood still waiting for the matador to advance with an expression of diabolical wickedness in its eyes, and had ignored the red cloth altogether, making always for his body.

Several swords had been tossed through the air, without inflicting any wound. The audience had begun to get impatient, whistling and making insulting remarks; he had come up behind the bull, following it from one side of the ring to the other, and knowing that if he faced up to it to attack he would be the one to be killed; at last, exhausted and dripping with sweat, he had taken a chance and finished the brute off with a treacherous thrust in the side of its neck, to the indignation of the crowd, who pelted him with bottles and oranges. The recollection of it made Gallardo hot with shame, and he began to feel that for him to be sitting there looking at his worst enemy was as unlucky as his meeting with the one-eyed woman.

Garabato came to tell him that some friends were waiting to see him. They were enthusiastic supporters of his who always visited him on bullfight days. The matador shook off his worries immediately and came smiling out of his study with his head held high, as if the bulls waiting for him at the ring were personal enemies and he could hardly wait to get at them and bring them to the ground with a thrust of his sword.

He ate a light meal, and alone as usual, and when he went up to get dressed the women disappeared. They hated the sight of those glittering clothes, carefully wrapped away in linen bags, those brilliant implements with which the family prosperity had been forged.

The farewells were as usual distressingly painful for Gallardo. The women refused to see him go; only Carmen forced herself to keep calm and had the fortitude to go with him as far as the door. His nephew and niece looked at him with wondering amazement; everything seemed to irritate the matador, and as the hour of danger approached he became more arrogant and boastful.

"Anyone would think they were taking me to the gallows! Well, see you later! Don't worry; I'll be all right." And he got into his carriage, making his way through the crowd of neighbours and others who had come to wish him luck.

For his family the afternoons when he fought in Seville were far the most agonizing. They couldn't wait with patient resignation for the arrival of the evening telegram, as they did when he was far away. The danger was close at hand, and they were in a continual fever of anxiety, hoping for news of how the corrida was going every quarter of an hour.

The saddler went off smartly dressed in a light flannel suit and a silky white felt hat, promising to send back news to his women-folk after each bull Juan killed, by one of the small boys who hung about outside the ring; but he was furious with his brother-in-law for not offering him a seat in the carriage with the cuadrilla.

The corrida was a tremendous triumph for Gallardo. When he entered the ring to the loud applause of the crowd, his heart swelled with pride.

He knew the ground he was treading on; it was familiar, and in some sense his own. He was aware of the difference in the sand of the various arenas and his superstitious temperament responded to it. He remembered the almost white floor of the large bull-rings of Valencia and Barcelona; the dark sand in the arenas of the North, and the reddish earth of Madrid. The sand of Seville was different from all the rest: it came from the Guadalquivir and was bright yellow like powdered paint. When blood poured down on to it from a disembowelled horse, like wine from a jug with its bottom stove in, Gallardo used to be reminded of the national flag waving from the roof of the bull-ring.

The architectural styles of the different rings also had their influence on the torero's over-excited imagination. They had been built at various times; some in the Roman style; others were Moorish—with the empty, colourless banality of a new church. The Seville bull-ring was a cathedral packed with memories; each succeeding generation had left its mark on it. Its doorway belonged to the age when men had worn white wigs, and all the most famous heroes had trodden its yellow sand. Here had been seen the innovators and perfectors of the bullfighting art—from the dignified champions of the Ronda school with their correct, restrained style, to the agile, mercurial Sevillian maestros, with their tricks to delight the audience. And here, this very afternoon, intoxicated by the cheering, the sun, the noise, and the sight of a white mantilla and a blue bodice leaning over the edge of a box, Gallardo felt himself to be capable of the utmost heights of daring.

He was determined to outshine his companions; the applause should be all for him. There were no limits to his audacity and agility; he had never been in finer form. Every time he brought off some brilliant pass, Don José stood up and shouted challengingly: "Now, who's going to say he isn't the best of them all?"

When Gallardo's second bull was to be killed, he made El Nacional bring it, by means of skilful cloak-play, under the box in which was the white mantilla and the blue dress. Beside Doña Sol sat the Marqués and his two daughters.

Every eye was on Gallardo as he advanced towards the barrier holding his sword and muleta in his hand, and took off his montera to dedicate the bull to the Marqués de Moraima's niece. There were many malicious smiles to be seen. "Some people have all the luck!" He gave a half turn, threw his montera on the ground, and stood waiting for the bull which his peons were luring towards him with their capes. The matador carried the *faena*[1] to its conclusion in a remarkably short time without leaving this chosen spot. He wanted to kill the bull under Doña Sol's very eyes; he wanted her to see him defying danger, from close range. Every pass with the muleta was greeted by shouts of admiration and anxiety on his behalf. The horns appeared to graze his chest, it seemed impossible that they shouldn't draw blood. Suddenly he squared up to the bull with the sword held well in front of him, and before the audience could give cries of warning or advice he had hurled himself swiftly on the animal so that for a few seconds man and bull were merged in a single mass.

When he disengaged himself and stood still, the bull staggered forwards bellowing, with its tongue hanging out and

[1] The final stage, accomplished by the matador with muleta and sword, ending in the killing of the bull.

the red handle of the sword hardly visible, sticking out from between the blood-stained shoulders. After a few steps it fell to the ground, and the whole audience stood up as one man and burst into thunderous applause, cheering and shouting. Gallardo was the bravest man in the world! Did he even know what fear meant?

The matador stood before Doña Sol's box with wide-spread arms holding the sword and muleta, while her white-gloved hands beat together in frenzied applause.

Then a small object was passed from spectator to spectator, on its way from the box to the barrier. It was the handkerchief the lady had carried in her hand, a diminutive scented square of cambric and lace, which she had passed through a diamond ring—a present to the bullfighter in exchange for his dedication.

The giving of this present was the signal for a further outburst of enthusiasm, and the crowd, who had all been looking at the matador, now turned to gaze at Doña Sol, praising her beauty at the top of their voices, with the familiar gallantry typical of Andalusians. Then a hairy and still warm triangle of flesh was passed from the barrier to the box. It was the bull's ear, sent by the matador in confirmation of his dedication.

By the time the corrida was over, the news of Gallardo's great triumph had spread all over the town, and when he arrived home there was a crowd waiting opposite his house to cheer him, as if they had all been at the bull-ring.

The saddler, forgetting his grievance against his brother-in-law, seemed to admire him even more for his friendship with the great and rich than for his success in the arena. There was a certain job that he had his eye on, and now that Juan was friendly with the élite of Seville he felt sure he should get it.

"Show them the ring. Look, Encarnación, what a fine present! Worthy of Roger de Flor!"

And the ring was passed round for everyone to see and admire. Carmen was the only one who looked askance at it. "Yes, it's very pretty," she said, and passed it quickly to her sister-in-law as if it burnt her fingers.

After the Seville bullfight the travelling season began for Gallardo. He had more contracts than in any previous year. When the Madrid corridas were over he was engaged to fight in every bull-ring in Spain. His manager was deep in railway time-tables, making out interminable schedules of his matador's movements.

Gallardo went from triumph to triumph. He had never felt more self-confident; he seemed to have acquired some new strength. Before the corridas began he was always assailed by cruel doubts and anxieties, worse than those of the early days before he had made his name; but once he was in the ring his fears vanished and a sort of savage courage took possession of him, which always brought him success.

At the end of an afternoon fighting in some provincial bull-ring he would go back to his hotel with his cuadrilla, and sink into a chair with the agreeable weariness of triumph, still in his fighting suit and covered in sweat. Then the local aficionados would come and congratulate him. He had been terrific! He was the first torero in the world! That estocada which had finished off the fourth bull! . . .

"You really thought so?" Gallardo would ask with childish vanity. "It wan't too bad perhaps. . . ."

Interminable conversation on the subject of bulls made the time pass quickly, and neither the matador nor his admirers got tired of talking about the afternoon's corrida and others of past seasons. Darkness fell, the lights were lit, and still the aficionados didn't go. The cuadrilla listened silently from the other end of the room. According to the rules of bullfighting etiquette they couldn't go and change their clothes or have a meal until the maestro gave them leave. The picadors, exhausted by falls from their horses and the heavy armour on their legs, moved their beaver hats restlessly between their knees; the banderilleros, whose tight silk suits were soaked in sweat, were famished after their afternoon's violent exercise. All had the same thought, and were casting looks of rage at the enthusiasts: "Why the hell don't those tiresome idiots go away?"

At last the matador noticed their impatience. "You may go," he said. And the cuadrilla pushed each other in their hurry to get out of the room, like schoolboys set free after class, while the maestro went on listening to the adulation of the aficionados, forgetting all about Garabato who was silently waiting to undress him.

On his days of rest, when he was free from preoccupation with danger and glory, his thoughts would return to Seville. Now and then he would receive a brief scented letter, congratulating him on his success. Ah, if only Doña Sol were with him now!

As he travelled from one audience to another, his adoring admirers were anxious to make his stay in their town pleasant for him, and wild parties with women were arranged in his honour. He always came away from these festivities with his head confused by drinking and in a state of ferocious gloom which made him impossible to deal with. He was aware of a violent desire to ill-treat women, an irresistible need to avenge himself for the aggressiveness and caprice of Doña Sol on others of her sex.

At times he was impelled to unload the heavy burden of his sadness by confiding in El Nacional. And when he was away from Seville he felt more affection for the banderillero, a sort of reflected emotion. Sebastián knew about his love affair with Doña Sol; he had seen her from afar, and she had often laughed at stories about the banderillero.

El Nacional received his master's confidences with a severe expression.

"What you have to do is to forget all about that lady, Juan. To my way of thinking, peace at home is worth everything to the likes of us, who have to go all over the world and may be brought back helpless and done for any day. And Carmen knows more than you think she does. She knows all about it. Why, she's already asked me one or two questions about you and the Marqués' niece. Poor little thing! It's a shame to make her unhappy! She's got plenty of spirit too, and may give you an unpleasant surprise one of these days."

But when Gallardo was away from his family, thoughts of Doña Sol obsessed him, and he hardly seemed to understand the dangers El Nacional was talking of. He shrugged off such sentimental scruples. He wanted to make his memories more real and solid by sharing his past happiness with his friend, and with the shamelessness of a successful lover longed for his good fortune to be understood and admired.

"But you've no idea what that woman is like, I tell you, Sebastián! Put all the beautiful women in Seville together. Nothing, compared to her. Take all the women from all the towns we've been to. Nothing. Doña Sol is the only one. When you've got a woman like that you don't care about any others. If only you knew her as I do, old man. Women of our sort smell of clean flesh and white linen. But this one, Sebastián, this one! Think of all the roses in the Alcázar Gardens, put together. No—better than that—jasmine, honeysuckle, every flower combined; all those sweet scents seem to come from her as if they were in her blood, not as if she put them on from a bottle. And she's not one of those silly girls with everything in their shop window. With her there's always something more, something you want, or hope for, but it doesn't come. . . . I can't explain it, Sebastián, but there it is. The fact is you don't know what a real lady is like; so stop preaching and shut your mouth."

Gallardo got no more letters from Seville. Doña Sol had gone abroad. He saw her once when he was fighting in San Sebastián. She had come from Biarritz with some French-women who wanted to meet the bullfighter. Then she went away and he only had vague news of her all that summer, either from her few letters or from what his manager had heard from the Marqués de Moraima.

She wrote from smart resorts, places whose names the torero had never heard before and didn't know how to pronounce; then came news that she was travelling in England; later, that she had gone to Germany to hear some operas in a marvellous theatre which was only open for a few weeks in the year. Gallardo began to despair of seeing her again. She was a restless bird of passage, and there seemed small chance of her returning to her nest at Seville even for the winter.

The possibility that he might never see her again plunged the matador into despair, and revealed to him what an ascendancy this woman had gained over his body and soul. Never to see her again! Then what was the point of risking his life and becoming famous? Of what use were the acclamations of the crowd?

His manager reassured him. She would certainly come back. Even if it were only for a year. In spite of all her wild ideas Doña Sol was a practical woman at heart and knew how to run her life. She needed her uncle's help to disentangle the confusion in which her own fortune and what her husband had left had been involved, ever since their expensive and luxurious stay abroad.

The matador returned to Seville at the end of the summer. He still had a number of engagements for corridas in the autumn, but he looked forward to about a month's rest first. His family were away at Sanlúcar, enjoying a seaside holiday which had been recommended for the children's health.

It was with a thrill of emotion that Gallardo heard from his manager that Doña Sol had just arrived unexpectedly in the town. He went to see her at once, but after a very few words had been exchanged her aloof amiability and the expression in her eyes had succeeded in intimidating him.

She was looking at him as if he were someone else. He detected in her glance a certain surprise at his rough appearance, a consciousness of the difference between herself and this young man whose profession it was to kill wild beasts.

He too was aware of the gulf which seemed to have opened between them. He looked at her with new eyes, as a grand lady of a different race and country.

They talked quietly. She seemed to have forgotten the past and Gallardo dared not remind her of it nor venture on the slightest advance, for fear of one of her outbursts of temper.

"Seville!" Doña Sol said. "It's very beautiful, very delightful. But there are other places in the world! I warn you,

Gallardo, I shall be off for good one of these days. I have a feeling I'm going to be bored here. Seville has lost its charm for me."

She no longer addressed him as *tu*.

Several days passed, and still the bullfighter was not brave enough to make any reference to the past. He often sat in silence, gazing at her with dark, adoring eyes, on the verge of tears.

"I'm bored. I shan't stay here much longer," Doña Sol exclaimed whenever they met.

Sometimes the torero would be stopped at the front door by the dignified manservant, saying that the Señora had gone out, when he knew for certain she was in the house.

One evening Gallardo told her that he had to pay a short visit to his farm at La Rinconada. He must look at an olive plantation which his manager had bought for him during his absence, and see how things were going on the estate.

The idea of accompanying the matador on this expedition made Doña Sol smile. The absurdity and outrageousness of going to the farm where he spent half the year with his family appealed to her. She relished the idea of this sinful and eccentric invasion of the poor fellow's peaceful country home.

The very preposterousness of the idea decided her. She would go with him; she wanted to see La Rinconada.

Gallardo was afraid. He thought of all his farm workers, of the gossips who might pass on the news of her visit to his family. But his scruples were powerless against the expression in Doña Sol's eyes. How could one tell? Perhaps this excursion would restore him to favour again.

However, he tried to put one obstacle in the path of her wish.

"What about Plumitas? From what I hear he's wandering about near La Rinconada at present."

Ah! Plumitas! The look of boredom cleared from Doña Sol's face, which seemed to light up with an inward flame.

"How very interesting! I hope you'll be able to introduce him to me."

Gallardo made arrangements for the journey. He had meant to go alone, but since Doña Sol was coming he had to find an escort, in case they encountered any trouble on the way.

First he asked Potaje, the picador. He was a tough character, afraid of nothing in the world except his gypsy wife, who when she got tired of being beaten would fly at him and bite him. He wouldn't need any explanations, only plenty of wine. What with alcohol and some terrible falls in the ring, he seemed in a perpetual state of confusion, as if there was a constant buzzing in his brain which made his words come out slowly and gave him a muddled view of things.

He also told El Nacional to come with them; he would make one more, and his discretion could be relied on.

The banderillero had to obey orders, but he grumbled when he heard Doña Sol was to be of the party.

"Good heavens! What do you want to get mixed up in such ugly doings for, and you a family man! What will Carmen and Señora Angustias think of me if they find out?"

But when he found himself driving through the country in a motor-car, sitting beside Potaje and opposite the matador and his lady, his annoyance gradually simmered down.

He couldn't see her very well, as her face was covered by a blue veil which fell from her travelling hat and was fastened to her yellow silk coat; but she was certainly very beautiful! And how she talked! And what a lot she knew!

Before the journey was half over El Nacional, in spite of his twenty-five years of conjugal fidelity, had forgiven the matador his weakness and understood his infatuation. If he ever found himself in the same position he would do the same!

Such is the power of education, which can infuse even the worst sins with respectability.

CHAPTER FIVE

"TELL him to say who he is or go to the devil. Damn it all, can't you let a fellow sleep in peace?"

El Nacional received this answer through his master's bedroom door and passed it on to one of the farm hands who was waiting on the stairs:

"Make him tell you who he is. Otherwise, the master won't come down."

It was eight o'clock. The banderillero went to the window and watched the man run down a path opposite the house as far as the fence which bounded the estate. Close to the gate in this fence he saw a figure on horseback; both man and horse looked so small at this distance that they might have come out of a box of toys.

A little later, after a talk with the rider, the farm hand returned, and El Nacional went to meet him at the foot of the stairs, intrigued by these comings and goings.

"He says he must see the master," the man panted out hurriedly. "Looks like he's up to no good. The master must come down at once, he says, and hear what he's got to say."

The banderillero knocked again at the matador's door, and paid no attention to his grumbling. He must get up; it was already quite late according to country standards, and the visitor might have some important message.

"All right, I'll come," Gallardo said crossly, without getting out of bed however.

El Nacional looked out of the window again, and saw the horseman riding up the path which led to the house.

The farm hand went out to meet him. He had struck the banderillero as seeming uneasy, and had stammered out his message with a look of fear and uncertainty on his face, as though not daring to voice his thoughts.

El Nacional saw him stand listening for a few moments to what the rider had to say and then start running quickly back towards the house. There was the sound of steps hurrying upstairs and he appeared pale and trembling before the banderillero.

"It's Plumitas, Señor Sebastian! He says he's Plumitas and that he must see the master. . . . I was frightened out of my wits as soon as I saw him."

Plumitas! The farm hand's voice seemed to ring through the whole house, stammering and out of breath though he

158

was. The banderillero was speechless with surprise. From the matador's room could be heard a volley of oaths, followed by the rustle of bedclothes and the sound of someone jumping out of bed. Movements in Doña Sol's room showed that she too had heard the astonishing news.

"But what does he want, damn him? Why has he come to La Rinconada? And just at this moment . . .!"

Gallardo came quickly out of his room, with a jacket and trousers pulled over his night clothes. He ran past the banderillero and dashed downstairs with all the impetuous energy that was natural to him. El Nacional followed.

The rider was in the act of dismounting in front of the house. One of the farm labourers was holding the reins and the others stood in a group a short distance away, looking at the new arrival with curiosity and respect.

He was a man of average build, not very tall, with short strong limbs, a round face and fair hair. He was dressed in a grey blouse trimmed with black braid, breeches of dark striped material reinforced with patches of leather inside the knee, and leather gaiters, cracked by the sun and rain and covered in mud. A wide sash and a cartridge-belt with a revolver and a sheath-knife stuck in it combined to bulk out his waist. In his right hand he held a carbine. On his head he wore a hat that had once been white, with its brim stained and drooping from the inclemency of the weather. A red handkerchief knotted round his neck was the brightest item of his clothing.

His broad, plump face looked like a pale full moon. The bristles of a several days' blond beard encroached on his cheeks, whose pallor was visible under their tan, giving them a glint of gold in the sunlight. The only disquieting feature of this face, which might otherwise have been that of a good-natured country priest, was the eyes: they were like a pig's eyes, malignant, small and buried in folds of fat. They were grey-blue, with dilated pupils.

When Gallardo appeared at the front door Plumitas recognized him at once, and raised his hat from his bullet head.

"May God grant us a good day, Señor Juan," he said with the grave politeness of the Andalusian peasant.

"Good morning."

"Are the family well, Señor Juan?"

"Quite well, thanks. And yours?" the matador asked automatically, from force of habit.

"Well, so far as I know. I've not seen them for some time."

The two men were standing close together, looking each other over as naturally as if they had met on a country walk. The matador's face was pale, and he compressed his lips to hide his feelings. Did the bandit suppose he was afraid of him? Perhaps in different circumstances he might have been alarmed by this visitation; but now that a certain person was in his house he felt capable of fighting him exactly as if he had been a bull, if he should make any hostile move.

Several moments passed in silence. All the farm hands who had not gone out into the fields—more than a dozen in number—gazed with almost childish amazement at this terrifying personage, whose name carried such an aura of drama and ill-fame.

"Can you take the mare to the stables to cool off a bit?" the bandit asked.

Gallardo signed to the man who was holding the reins, and he led her away.

"Take good care of her," said Plumitas. "I think the world of her, more than I do of the wife and kids."

Another person had now joined the matador and the bandit in the middle of the group of interested farm hands. It was Potaje the picador, who came out of the house with his shirt open at the front, stretching himself with all the animal strength of his athletic body. He rubbed his eyes, still inflamed with drink, and going up to the bandit, dropped his huge hand on his shoulder with studied familiarity, seeming to enjoy making him start and at the same time expressing a rough sort of friendliness.

"How are you, Plumitas?"

He had never set eyes on him before. The bandit stiffened

160

under the unceremonious caress, and he raised his rifle menacingly in his right hand. Then his small blue eyes, looking fixedly at the picador, showed signs of recognition.

"You're Potaje, aren't you? I saw you in the ring at Seville the other day. My God! what a fall you had! You must be tough all right! Made of steel!"

And he returned the picador's greeting by seizing his arm in his horny hand, and squeezing the biceps with an admiring smile. The two men stood looking at each other with friendly expressions. Then Potaje burst into a loud guffaw.

"Why, I thought you'd be a bigger man, Plumitas. Never mind, you're a fine fellow, just the same."

The bandit turned to the matador.

"Can you give me some lunch?"

"No one goes away from La Rinconada without lunch," said Gallardo in his grandest style.

They all went into the kitchen, an enormous room with an open fireplace, which was the centre of life in the farm-house.

The matador sat down in an arm-chair, and a girl, the foreman's daughter, ran to put on his boots for him, for he had come down in slippers in his hurry.

El Nacional, wanting to show some sign of life and reassured by the visitor's courteous manner, came in with a bottle of the local wine and some glasses.

"I know you too," said the bandit, treating him as familiarly as he had the picador. "I've seen you place the banderillas. You can do it well enough when you want to, but you ought to come closer, you know. . . ."

Potaje and the maestro laughed at this piece of criticism. When Plumitas stretched out for his glass of wine he was hampered by his carbine which he was holding between his knees.

"Put it down, man," the picador said. "You don't want that thing when you're paying a visit, surely?"

The bandit immediately looked serious. It was quite all right where it was; he was used to it. The rifle went with him everywhere, even to bed. And this allusion to his weapon, which was like an extra limb attached to his body, made him look round rather uneasily, with the suspicious expression of a man who lives ever on the alert for danger and trusts nobody and nothing but his own strength.

One of the farm hands crossed the kitchen on his way to the door.

"Where's that man off to?"

As he said this he sat up straight in his chair, drawing the loaded rifle to him with his knees.

Hearing that he was going to join the other labourers in the fields, Plumitas calmed down again.

"Listen here, Señor Juan. I came here because I wanted to see you and because I know you're a gentleman and won't split on me. Besides, you know what people say about Plumitas. It isn't easy to catch him, and anyone who tries is going to pay for it."

The picador broke in before his master could answer.

"Don't be a fool, Plumitas. You're among friends here, so long as you behave yourself."

Now completely reassured, the bandit talked to the picador about his mare, praising her good qualities. The two men became absorbed in their common interest in horses, for which they both felt more love than they did for human beings.

Gallardo still seemed uneasy and paced up and down the kitchen, while the swarthy, masculine-looking farm women stoked up the fire and cooked the lunch, stealing sidelong looks at the famous Plumitas as they did so.

In one of his turns round the room the matador went up to El Nacional. He must go up to Doña Sol's room and ask her not to come downstairs. The bandit was sure to go after lunch. Much better that she shouldn't show herself to such a sinister individual.

The banderillero went away, and Plumitas, noticing that the maestro was taking no part in the conversation, went up to him and asked about his forthcoming corridas with great interest.

"I'm a Gallardist, you see. I've applauded you more often than you know. I've seen you at Seville, at Jaén, at Córdova— lots of places."

Gallardo was astonished. How could this man, who was pursued by a whole army, go quietly off to watch a bullfight? Plumitas gave a superior smile.

"Bah! I go wherever I like. I'm all over the place."

Then he told the matador how he had seen him on his way to his farm, sometimes with friends, sometimes alone, and how Gallardo had passed him by without a glance, as if he were a wretched labourer taking a message to some shepherd's hut near by.

"When you came from Seville to buy those two mills down yonder, I met you on the road. You had five thousand duros on you, didn't you? That's right, isn't it? You see I'm well informed. Another time I saw you in one of those animals they call motor-cars, with another fellow from Seville—your manager I think. You were going to sign the purchase deeds for Olivar del Cura, and you had even more money that time—bags of it."

Gallardo was gradually convinced of the accuracy of what Plumitas said, and stared in surprise at this man who seemed to know everything. The bandit wanted to emphasize his generosity to the bullfighter on these past occasions, by making light of all the obstacles that often came his way.

"These motor-cars, now. Piffling things! I can stop one of these animals with nothing but this"—and he pointed to his rifle. "I had an account to settle in Córdova with a Señor who was my enemy. I drew up my mare by the road, and along came this animal in a cloud of dust and stinking of petrol. 'Halt!' I said. He wouldn't stop, so I let him have a bullet in the wheel. To cut the story short: the car stopped a bit further on and I galloped up and settled that gentleman's hash. If a man can put a bullet where he wants to, he can stop anything on the road."

Gallardo listened in amazement while Plumitas spoke about his adventures on the high road with professional directness.

"I didn't want to hold you up. You're not a rich man. You're a poor man like me, only you've had more luck; and if you've made money, well—you deserve it. I think a lot of you, Señor Juan. I like you because you're a fine matador and I've got a weakness for brave men. We're the same sort, you and I; we both live by risking our lives. That's why, although you didn't know me, I let you pass without asking so much as a cigarette of you. . . ."

An unexpected apparition cut short the bandit's speech, and brought a look of exasperation to the bullfighter's face. Doña Sol! Damn it all, hadn't El Nacional given her his message? The banderillero came into the room behind her and signified in dumb show from the door of the kitchen that all his appeals and advice had been useless.

Doña Sol came down in her travelling-coat, without a hat and with her golden hair hastily combed and fastened up. Plumitas at the farm! How wonderful! She had been thinking about him half the night in a state of delicious apprehension, deciding that she would ride over the solitary plains around La Rinconada the next morning, in the hopes of being lucky enough to meet him. And now, just as if her thoughts had had some magnetic power, this interesting bandit had obeyed her wishes and arrived at the farm.

Plumitas! The name had called up a vivid picture to her imagination. It was hardly necessary to see him in the flesh, nothing about him could possibly surprise her. He would be tall, slim and olive-skinned, wearing a broad-brimmed hat over a red handkerchief, under which could be seen jet-black curls; his strong, active body would be dressed in black velvet, his supple waist belted with a purple silk sash, his legs in brown leather gaiters: a knight-errant of the Andalusian hills. something like the elegantly dressed tenors in *Carmen*, who when crossed in love leave their military uniforms behind, and become smugglers.

Her eyes wandered all round the kitchen, wide with excitement, without seeing anything at all like a broad-brimmed hat or a blunderbuss. All she saw was a strange man standing there: a sort of gamekeeper with a rifle, much like those she often came across on her uncle's estate.

"Good morning, Señora Marquesa. Is your uncle the Marqués keeping quite well?"

Then she saw that every pair of eyes in the room was fixed on this man, and she guessed the truth. Oh dear, so this was Plumitas!

He had taken off his hat with awkward politeness, and stood with his carbine in one hand and the old felt in the other, obviously abashed by Doña Sol's presence.

Gallardo was amazed that the bandit seemed to know everyone. Not only did he know who Doña Sol was, but by an excess of respect he had given her the benefit of the family title.

Recovering from her surprise, the lady indicated that the bandit could sit down and put on his hat again; he obeyed, the first injunction, but laid his hat beside him on a chair.

"The Señora Marquesa needn't be surprised I know her," Plumitas went on, seeming to read the question in her eyes. "I've seen her often enough, going with the Marqués and other gentlemen to the yearling trials. And I've watched the Señora with a garrocha. The Señora is the bravest and hand-somest woman on God's earth. It's a very fine thing indeed to see her ride on horseback wearing her wide hat and sash. No wonder that men are ready to come to blows for those lovely blue eyes."

The bandit delivered this flood of Andalusian eloquence as if it were the most natural thing in the world, and seemed to be searching his mind for new ways to flatter her.

Doña Sol turned pale and her eyes opened wide with pleasurable fear. She began to be more interested in the bandit. Was it on her account he had come to the farm? Perhaps he meant to carry her off to his hiding-place, like some rapacious bird of prey swooping down on the plains from his nest among the mountains.

The bullfighter also heard this outburst of crude admiration with alarm. Damn the man! In his own house, and before his very face! If things went on like this he would go upstairs and get his gun, and they would soon see which was the better man, Plumitas or no Plumitas.

The bandit suddenly appeared to realize the uneasiness his words had caused, and became more respectful.

"You must excuse me if I let my tongue run away with me, Señora Marquesa. I've a wife and four children, and the poor thing sheds more tears on my account than the Virgin of Sorrows. I'm a peace-loving man. It's only bad luck that's made me what I am."

And, evidently trying to make himself agreeable to Doña Sol, he broke into warm praise of her family. He had as much respect for the Marqués de Moraima as for any man alive.

"I wish there were more rich men like him. My father used to work for him, and told us how good he was. Once in the hot season I hid in one of his shepherd's huts. He knew all about it, but he never said a thing. He gave orders on his farms that they should give me what I asked for and leave me in peace. A man doesn't forget a thing like that, and so many rich scoundrels as there are in the world! Every so often I'll meet him riding along by himself, sitting his horse like a youngster, not the old chap he is. 'Good-day, Señor Marqués.' 'Good-day, my lad.' He doesn't know me, hasn't an idea who I am, because I hide my friend here"—and he pointed to his rifle—"under my coat. I'd like to stop him and take him by the hand—not to shake it, no. (How could a good man like him shake hands with someone with so much trouble and murder on his conscience?) No, I'd kiss it, and kneel down, as if he was my father and thank him for all he's done for me."

Doña Sol was unmoved by the vehemence of his gratitude to her uncle. So this was the famous Plumitas? . . . A poor wretch; just a rabbit of a man who was mistaken for a wolf because of his reputation.

"There are some very bad lots among the rich," the bandit went on. "How some of them treat the poor! There's one living near my village who lends out money at interest—a regular Judas. I sent him a message to stop bothering people for their payments, and instead of doing what I said the dirty blackguard put the Civil Guards on to me. So what did I do? I set fire to one of his barns and for more than six months he never dared go to Seville or even leave the village, for fear of running into Plumitas. Then another of them was going to turn a poor old girl out of the cottage she'd lived in all her life, because of her not paying the rent. So I went to see that Señor one evening, when he was just sitting down to supper with his family. 'I'm Plumitas,' I said, 'and I want a hundred duros.' He gave me the money and I took it to the old woman. 'Here you are, Grannie. Pay the Jew what you owe him, and keep the rest and good luck to you'."

Doña Sol was looking at the bandit with more interest.

"How many men have you killed?" she asked him.

"We won't talk about that, Señora," the bandit answered gravely. "Or you might take against me, and I'm only a poor unlucky chap who has to save himself from being caught and shut up."

There was a long silence.

"If you knew what a life I led, Señora Marquesa," he went on. "Worse than a hunted animal's. I sleep where I can or not at all. I wake up one end of the province and go to bed the other. You have to keep your eyes open and your gun ready if you want to be treated right. The poor people are good at heart, but poverty's an ugly thing and makes the best of them bad. Except that they're scared of me they'd have handed me over to the Civil Guards many a time. The only real friends I've got are my mare and this"—he pointed to his rifle. "Sometimes I get lonely for my wife and kids; I go back to my village at night and the neighbours wink at it. But that'll end badly one of these days . . . Sometimes I get tired of being on my own and want some company. I've wanted to come to La Rinconada for quite a while. 'Why don't I go and see Señor Juan Gallardo? I've admired him in the ring and clapped him often enough.' But you always had your friends with you, or your mother and wife and the children. I know how it would have been: they would have died of fright to see Plumitas come along. But now it's different. When I saw you'd brought the Señora Marquesa here with you, I said to myself: 'I'll go and see those Señores and have a chat with them'."

167

The sly smile which accompanied these words at once established the difference between the bullfighter's family and Doña Sol, making it quite clear that the bandit was well aware what the latter's relations were with Gallardo. He had a peasant's basic respect for legitimate marriage, and felt entitled to take more liberties with the torero's aristocratic mistress than with the women of his family.

Doña Sol ignored his attitude, and began pressing the bandit with questions as to how he had come to be what he now was.

"Not by my own choosing, Señora Marquesa. It was just one of those misfortunes which happens to us poor people. I was one of the sharpest boys in my village, and they always sent me to ask if they wanted anything from the rich gentry. I can read and write; I acted as sacristan when I was a lad and they called me Plumitas because I used to run after the hens and pull out their tail feathers to write with."

A clap on the back from Potaje interrupted him:

"I thought as soon as I set eyes on you that you were a church rat or something of the sort!"

El Nacional said nothing, but smiled to himself. A sacristan turned bandit! What would Don Joselito say when he told him?

"Then I got married and the first child came along. One night the Civil Guards came to our house and took me away to the threshing-floor. Some fellow had fired a shot or two at the door of a rich man and they made up their minds I was their man. When I said no, they beat me with their rifles. I said no again, and they beat me again. To cut a long story short: they went on beating me all night long, first with the butt and then with the barrel, all over my body, until they were tired out and I lay on the ground senseless. My hands and feet were tied and they beat me as if I was a sack of grain, and said: 'Aren't you the bravest man in the village? Well, get up and defend yourself. Come on! Show us what you can do.' That's what I couldn't stand: their making fun of me. My poor wife did what she could for me, but after that I couldn't rest; I couldn't go on as I was, remembering how they'd beat me and made fun of me. To cut a long story short again: one of these Civil Guards was found dead on the threshing-floor one day soon after, and to spare myself any trouble I made off into the mountains . . . and I've been there ever since."

"Well done, old fellow!" cried Potaje admiringly. "And what about the other?"

"Can't say. He'll be somewhere about. He left the village, that I do know, and asked to be moved to some other place, but I've not forgotten him. I shall settle with him one day. Sometimes I hear he's at some place the other end of Spain, and off I go. I'd follow him to hell itself. I leave my mare and my rifle with a friend and I take the train like a gentleman. I've been to Barcelona and Valladolid and lots of other towns. I go and stand near the barracks and I watch the Civil Guards going in and out. 'That's not my man; nor that one neither.' What I was told couldn't be true, but no matter. I've looked for him for years now and I'll find him in the end. Unless of course he's dead, and that would be a pity."

Doña Sol had listened to this story with interest. What an extraordinary character Plumitas was! Not a rabbit after all.

The bandit fell silent, frowning, as if he was afraid of having said too much and had decided to refrain from further confidences.

"With your permission," he said to the matador, "I'll go to the stables and see how they've treated my mare. Coming, friend?" he added to Potaje. "You'll see something worth looking at."

And the picador accepted his invitation and left the kitchen with him.

When the bullfighter was left alone with Doña Sol his ill humour burst out. Why had she come downstairs? It was rash to come and show herself to such a man: a bandit who was the terror of the district.

But Doña Sol was well pleased with the way the meeting had gone, and laughed at the matador's fears. She thought the bandit a good sort of man who had been unlucky; his crimes had been exaggerated in people's imagination.

"I thought he'd be quite different; all the same I'm delighted to have seen him. We'll give him some money when he goes. What an amazing country this is! What original characters one meets! And what a fascinating story about chasing the Civil Guard all over Spain! It could be the plot of a short story."

The farm women were lifting two great frying pans from the fire, and an appetising smell of pork sausages spread into the room.

"Lunch-time, gentlemen!" cried El Nacional, who had taken upon himself the function of major-domo in his master's house.

In the middle of the kitchen stood a long table covered with a cloth, with round loaves of bread and bottles of wine upon it.

Plumitas and Potaje and some of the farm workers came in answer to the summons: the foreman, the bailiff and all those who held posts of responsibility. They began to sit down on the benches alongside the table, while Gallardo looked at Doña Sol uncertainly. She had better eat upstairs in the room usually occupied by the family. But she laughed at this suggestion and sat down at the head of the table. She enjoyed this rustic life of the farm, and thought it would be fun to eat with all these men. She ought really to have been a soldier! And in a free-and-easy masculine way she invited the matador to join her, wrinkling up her pretty nose with pleasure as she snuffed up the succulent aroma coming from the sausages. What an excellent meal! How hungry she was!

"This is fine," Plumitas said sententiously as he looked round the table. "Masters and servants eating together, as they used to in the old days. I never in my life saw it happen before."

And he sat down beside the picador, but without letting go of his rifle which he still held between his knees.

"Shove up a bit, old fellow," he said pushing up against Potaje.

The picador, who had been treating him with a sort of rough geniality, answered with another push, and the two men went on laughing and pushing each other, amusing the whole table with their horse-play.

"But for Christ's sake put that thing away from between your knees," said the picador. "Can't you see it's pointing straight at me? Anything might happen."

The bandit's rifle had in fact slipped sideways, and its black muzzle was pointing straight at the picador.

"Put it down, man," Potaje insisted. "You don't want it to eat with."

"It's all right where it is. Don't you worry about it," the bandit replied shortly, frowning and seeming resentful of any reference to his precautions.

He seized a spoon and a large hunk of bread and looked round at the rest to see if the moment had come when it would be polite to start eating.

"Your health, Señora!" and he began to attack the large dish which had been put in the middle of the table for himself, Potaje and El Nacional. Another large dish for the farm workers sizzled at the other end of the table.

But he suddenly seemed ashamed of his own greed, and after a few mouthfuls he stopped eating and began excusing himself.

"I've not touched a thing since yesterday morning except a crust of bread and a little milk in a shepherd's hut. A good appetite to you all!"

And he began to tuck in again, receiving all Potaje's jokes about his appetite with winks and steadily munching jaws.

The picador wanted to make him drink but was chary of reaching for one of the flasks of wine that stood on the table in the presence of his master, who had good reason to fear his drunkenness.

"Have some wine, Plumitas. It's a bad thing to eat dry food. You must wash it down with something."

Before the bandit could accept his invitation the picador had poured himself out a drink, and followed it with a second. Plumitas only touched his wine at long intervals, and after considerable hesitation. He was afraid of wine; he'd lost the habit of drinking it. It was often impossible for him to get it, and, besides, wine was the worst enemy of a man like him, who must always be alert and on guard.

"But you're among friends here," said the picador. "Remember you're in the province of Seville, Plumitas, under the protection of the Virgin de la Macarena. No one can touch you here. And if any Civil Guards happen to turn up, I'll be beside you with a garrocha in my hand, and we won't leave one of the blackguards alive. It wouldn't take much to make me ride off into the mountains—I've always fancied the idea."

"Potaje!" cried the matador from the end of the table, anxious as to what the picador would say next under the influence of wine.

The bandit had only drunk a little, but his face was flushed and his small blue eyes sparkled with pleasure.

He was sitting facing the kitchen door through which he could see the gate into the farm and part of the road leading to it. Now and again a cow, a pig or a goat would cross this strip of road with their dark shadows projected in front of them on to the yellow ground. This was quite enough to startle Plumitas and make him drop his spoon and clutch at his rifle.

He talked to his neighbours at the table, but without ever taking his attention from what was going on out of doors, for it was a point of honour with him never to be caught by surprise.

When he had finished eating he accepted one more glass of wine from Potaje and sat with his chin resting on his hand, staring out of the door in silence, stupefied by his digestive processes. He had the digestion of a boa constrictor, a stomach which was used to irregular meals, with bouts of over-eating separated by long fasts.

Gallardo offered him a Havana cigar.

"Thanks, Señor Juan. I don't smoke, but I'll keep it for a friend of mine in the mountains; the poor chap would rather smoke than eat. He's a young man who's been in trouble, and he helps me whenever there's work for two."

He put the cigar away under his blouse, smiling with savage glee as he thought of his distant friend. The wine had had its effect on Plumitas. His face had changed. There was a disturbing steely glitter in his eyes, and his round face was

172

contracted by a rictus which contradicted his usual amiable expression. It was clear that he wanted to talk, to boast of his adventures and to reward his hosts by astonishing them.

"Did you hear what I did last month on the road to Fregenal? You didn't? Well, my comrade and I were waiting by the road for the bus to come along, as I had a bone to pick with a rich man who was in it and who wasn't likely to forget me in a hurry. He was a bossy sort of chap, who was used to ordering everyone about from the mayor to the Civil Guards. I sent him a message asking for a hundred duros, and what did he do but write to the Governor of Seville and set things buzzing as far as Madrid, so that they chased after me more than ever. Thanks to him I had a brush with the Civil Guards and got a bullet in my leg; even that wasn't enough, he asked them to put my wife in prison, as if the poor woman knew where I was. This Judas didn't dare leave his village for fear of Plumitas; but just about then I went off on one of those journeys I told you about. So my man plucked up courage one day and went to Seville on business, and also so as to set things going against me. It was the bus back from Seville we were waiting for, and all in good time along it came. My mate is a good man for a hold-up and he yelled to the driver to halt. I stuck my head and my carbine in at the door. Screams from the women, children crying; and the men said nothing but their faces turned white as a sheet. I said to them: 'I don't want anything from you. Don't be frightened, Señoras. Good day, gentlemen, and a good journey . . . but make that fat man get out.' And my man, who had been crouching down as if he wanted to hide under the women's skirts, had to get out, with his face as white as if he hadn't a drop of blood left in his body, and staggering as though he was drunk. The bus drove off and there we were alone together in the middle of the road. 'I'm Plumitas, d'you hear me? And I'm going to give you something to remember me by.' And I did. But I didn't kill him outright. I let him have it in a certain place so that he should last another twenty-four hours, and when the Civil Guards found him he could tell them it was Plumitas who'd

173

done for him. I didn't want there to be any mistake about that' nor for anyone else to take the credit."

Doña Sol listened, intensely pale and nervously biting her lips; a strange light in her eyes was the only expression of her secret thoughts.

Gallardo frowned, disturbed by this horrifying story.

"Every man has his own trade, Señor Juan," Plumitas said, seeming aware of his thoughts. "You and I live by killing: you kill bulls and I kill men. The difference is that you're rich and famous and can get beautiful women, and I'm often half dead with hunger, and if I don't look out I'll end up riddled with bullets, for the crows to eat. I don't do so well out of my trade as you, Señor Juan! You know where to give it to the bull so as to bring him to the ground at once. I know where to let a Christian have it so as to finish him there and then, or so as he should last a bit longer, perhaps spend weeks raging against Plumitas—who doesn't meddle with anyone's business, but knows how to deal with those who meddle with his."

Again Doña Sol returned to the number of his crimes.

"And how many men have you killed?"

"You won't like it if I tell you, Señora Marquesa; but since you want to know . . . I may have forgotten some, although I try not to. Perhaps it would be about thirty or thirty-five; I'm not sure. You can't keep accounts leading the life I lead. But I'm an unhappy man, Señora Marquesa, and everything's been against me. The men who did me wrong are the guilty ones. Killing men is like eating cherries. Pull one down and the others come tumbling in dozens. I have to kill so as to go on living, and if I feel any pity I must swallow it."

There was a long silence. Doña Sol looked at the bandit's broad strong hands with their broken fingernails. But Plumitas took no notice of the Señora Marquesa. All his attention was for the matador, for he was anxious to show him his gratitude for the way he had entertained him, and to dispel the bad impression his words might have made.

"You're a man I respect, Señor Juan," he added. "When I

saw you in the ring the first time I said to myself: 'That's a brave chap!' You've a great many aficionados who admire you, but none more than I do! Just think, I've often had to disguise myself so as to see you fight, and then go to towns where I might easily be caught. There's an aficionado for you!"

Gallardo smiled and nodded; his professional pride was flattered.

"Another thing," the bandit went on. "No one can ever say I came to La Rinconada to ask for food. I've often been hungry or in need of five duros or so when I was passing by here, but up to today I've never thought of coming in. 'Señor Juan is sacred', I always say to myself. 'He earns his living like me, risking his life. We ought to be good friends.' Because you'll agree, Señor Juan, that though you're a famous man and I'm only a poor wretch, we're both the same, we both live by playing with death. Now here we both sit quietly together, but one of these days, when God gets tired of protecting us, they'll pick me up at the side of the road shot to pieces like a mad dog; and as for you, in spite of all your money, they'll carry you out of the ring feet foremost, and though the papers will write about the accident for a week or so, a damned lot of good that'll do you in the next world!"

"It's true . . . it's quite true," said Gallardo, turning suddenly pale.

The superstitious dread which often assailed him as the time of danger grew near was reflected in his face. There seemed to him at that moment no difference between his own destiny and that of this formidable outcast, who was bound sooner or later to succumb to unequal odds.

"But if you think I'm afraid of death, you're wrong," Plumitas went on. "I don't regret anything, and I go my own way. I've got my pride and my pleasures, just as you have when you read in the papers that you did well with such and such a bull and they gave you the ear. They talk about Plumitas all over the country, you know, and the papers are full of lies about me; they take me off in the theatres, and in that palace in Madrid where the deputies meet, not a week passes but they talk about me. On top of that, I've the gratification of having a whole army after me, of knowing that I plague the life out of hundreds of men drawing Government pay and wearing a sword—I, all by myself! The other day, it was a Sunday, I went into a village during Mass and tethered my mare in the square near some blind men who were singing and playing the guitar. People were gaping at a poster they had with them, with a picture of a well-dressed man in a big hat, with side-whiskers, riding on a splendid horse, with a blunderbuss on his saddle-bow and a fine girl behind him. It took me some time to realize that this handsome fellow was meant to be Plumitas. Well, that was pretty good, it seemed to me. While I was going about starving and half-dressed, these people thought I was quite different. I bought the piece of paper they were singing from, and I've got it here: it's the life of Plumitas, all in poetry, and full of lies. Pretty good, eh? When I was up in the mountains I learnt it off by heart. Some very clever man must have written it."

The terrible bandit spoke with a childish pride in his fame. The quiet restrained manner he had had when he arrived at the farm was all gone now. Then he had seemed anxious that everything should be forgotten except that he was a poor hungry wayfarer. Now he dwelt with pleasure on the notoriety attaching to his name and deeds.

"If I'd gone on living in my village, no one would ever have heard of me," he went on. "I've thought about that quite a bit. There's only two ways for us unlucky ones: either we must eat our hearts out working for other people, or we must take the only road to money and fame: murder. I wouldn't be any good at killing bulls. My village is in the mountains and we don't have brave cattle there. Besides which, I'm slow on my feet and heavy too. That's why I kill men instead. It's the best a poor chap can do to get himself respected and make his way in the world."

El Nacional, who had been listening attentively to what the bandit said up till now, thought the time had come to break in.

"What a poor man needs is education: reading and writing."

176

Everybody who knew El Nacional's obsession on this subject burst out laughing.

"Now you've had your say, old chap, let Plumitas get on with his," Potaje said. "He's talking sense."

The bandit paid very little attention to the views of the banderillero, of whom he had a poor opinion after seeing his cautiousness in the bull-ring.

"I can read and write, and what good has it done me? What a poor man wants is justice, to get his rights; and if they aren't given him he must take them, that's all. You have to turn into a wolf and make everyone afraid of you. The other wolves respect you and the cattle let you eat them with pleasure. If they see you're cowardly and weak, even the sheep will spit in your face."

Potaje was by now quite drunk, and he agreed enthusiastically with everything Plumitas said. He didn't understand his actual words, but he seemed to see the bright light of great wisdom shining through the dense mists of his own intoxication.

"That's quite true, old man. Fine! Go on."

"I know what people are like," the bandit continued. "There are two sorts of people in the world: the sheep and the sheep-shearers. I don't want to be a sheep; I was born brave and I'm not afraid of any man. You're the same, Señor Juan. You've pulled yourself up by your boot-straps. But you're better off than I am."

He looked thoughtfully at the matador for a while and then added in a tone of conviction:

"I think you and I came into the world too late, Señor Juan. What couldn't we have done in the old days, two fine fellows like us? You wouldn't have been killing bulls, and I wouldn't have been wandering all over the country, hunted like a wild beast. We'd have been governors of some province or great panjandrums of some sort or other. Have you ever heard tell of Pizarro, Señor Juan?"

Señor Juan made a vague gesture, not wanting to reveal his ignorance of the name, which he now heard for the first time.

"The Señora Marquesa knows more about him than I do; she must excuse me if I get it wrong. I found out about him when I was a sacristan and used to read the old books in the priest's library. Well this Pizarro was a poor man like us, who crossed over the sea with a dozen or so other stout fellows and came to a country just like paradise. The mines of Potosí were in it; I needn't say any more. They fought I don't know how many battles with the American savages who wore feathers and carried bows and arrows, and in the end they had won it all for themselves, and had got hold of the king's treasure. Every man had his house full of gold coins right up to the roof, and was made a Marqués, a general or a judge. And there were others who did the same. Just imagine if we had lived in those days, Señor Juan! We could have done as well as Pizarro or better with a handful of these fine fellows who are listening to us now!"

The farm hands listened in silence, but their eyes sparkled with excitement and they nodded their heads in agreement with the bandit.

"Yes, we were born too late, Señor Juan. The gates are shut for us poor men; there's nowhere left for us Spaniards to go and conquer. Anything there was has been grabbed by the English or other foreigners. The door is shut I say, and a brave man has to stay inside this cattle-yard and be shouted at for not doing what he should. I might have been a king in America or some other place, and instead I'm hunted down like a thief. You're a brave man and you kill bulls; but I know lots of gentry who think it's low to be a torero."

Doña Sol interrupted to ask the bandit why he didn't become a soldier, and go to far countries, fight in wars and make good use of his talents?

"I might have done that, Señora Marquesa; I've often thought about it. When I sleep in bed like a Christian in a farm-house or even at home for a few days, and eat hot food at a table like this one, I enjoy the comfort, I won't say I don't; then I get tired of it and I long for the mountains, and wish I was sleeping on the ground with my coat over me and a stone for a pillow. Yes, I might have been a soldier, and a good one too. But where should I go? There are no real wars these days where one can take one's chance along with a few friends. Now it's just herds of men, all the same colour and marked with the same brand, who fight and die like a lot of idiots. It's the same as in the rest of the world: sheep and shearers. You do some fine thing and the colonel takes the credit; you fight like a tiger and the general gets a medal. . . . No; I was born too late to be a soldier."

Plumitas was silent for some time, with lowered eyes, reflecting how unfortunate he was to be living in the present age.

Suddenly he stood up, grasping his rifle.

"I'm off now. Thanks very much, Señor Juan. Good-bye, Señora Marquesa."

"But where are you going?" Potaje said, catching hold of him. "Sit down, you fool. You're better off here than anywhere else."

The picador would have liked the bandit to stay; he was enjoying talking to him like an old friend, and looking forward to describing this interesting meeting later on in the town.

"I've been here three hours; time to go. I never stay so long anywhere as open and flat as La Rinconada. The news of my being here may have got around by now."

"Are you scared of the Civil Guards?" asked Potaje. "They won't come; and if they do, here am I beside you."

Plumitas made a gesture of contempt. The Civil Guards indeed! They were just men like the rest; some brave, some not; but all of them fathers of families, who weren't anxious to meet him, and would arrive late on purpose when they heard of his whereabouts. They only attacked him when they came upon him by chance and there was no avoiding him.

"One day last month I was at Five Chimneys farm, eating just as I did here but not in such good company, when I saw six Civil Guards walking up to the house. I swear they didn't know I was there and they just came for something to drink. Bad luck; because neither of us could turn tail before all the farm people, for them to say we were cowards. The farmer shut the gate and the Civil Guards started kicking it to get him to open it. I told him and one of his men to stand each side of it. 'When I say "Now!" open it wide.' Then I mounted my mare with my revolver in my hand. 'Now!' They opened the gate and I galloped out like a flash. You don't know how my mare can go. They fired I don't know how many times, but never a hit! I let off my revolver as I went, and wounded two of the Civil Guards, so I heard. To cut a long story short: I got away crouching on the mare's neck, so as not to give them a target, and the Civil Guards gave the farm hands a beating to relieve their feelings. So it's better to say nothing about my visits, Señor Juan. Or along'll come the three-cornered hats and drive you silly with questions and signed statements, as if they were going to catch me with them!"

The people of La Rinconada silently signified their assent. They knew the truth of what he said well enough. It was better to hold their tongues and save themselves bother, as all the other farms and ranches did. This general silence was the bandit's most potent ally. Besides, all these peasants admired Plumitas and thought of him as an avenging hero. They had nothing to fear from him; it was only the rich he threatened.

"I'm not scared of the Civil Guards," went on the bandit. "It's the poor people I'm afraid of. They mean me no harm, but poverty's an ugly thing! I know those three-cornered hats won't get me. If any one kills me it'll be some poor man. I let them come close because they're my sort, but some day they'll take advantage of me. I've got my enemies; people who've sworn to get their own back on me. Or sometimes some wretch thinks he'll make a few pesetas by telling on me. If you want to be respected you must come down hard on people like that. If you settle with one of them, there's always his family to pay you out. But if you decide to be forgiving and just take his trousers down and give him a little stroke with some nettles and thistles he remembers the joke for the rest of his life. It's the poor, my own sort, that I'm afraid of."

Plumitas stopped speaking and then, looking at the matador, added:

"And also my aficionados and followers, the young lads who want to tag along behind. It's true, Señor Juan. Who gives you more trouble, the bulls or those hungry young novilleros who want to do better than the maestro? Well, it's the same with me; I told you we were the same, didn't I? In every village there's some young chap that would like to step into my shoes; if he found me asleep under a tree he'd blow my brains out there and then."

He went off to the stables followed by Potaje, and a quarter of an hour later rode into the courtyard on his powerful mare, his inseparable companion. The raw-boned animal looked larger and glossier after her short enjoyment of the abundance of the Rinconada mangers.

Plumitas paused to pat her flanks as he arranged the blanket on the saddle-bow. She wasn't often treated as well as at Señor Juan's farm. She must make the most of it, for there was a long day ahead of them.

"And where are you going, old chap?" Potaje asked.

"That's a question no one asks me. Out into the world! I don't know myself. Wherever anything turns up."

And putting one foot in the rusty muddy stirrup, he leapt into the saddle.

Doña Sol was watching the bandit's preparations for departure with a strange expression in her eyes, and pale, compressed lips. Gallardo left her side for a moment, searching in the inside pocket of his jacket, and then came up to Plumitas and surreptitiously handed him some crumpled pieces of paper.

"What's this?" the bandit said. "Money? Thanks, Señor Juan. I suppose someone told you you have to give me something when I visit a farm; but that's only for the others, the rich men whose money drops into their laps. You earn yours by risking your life. We're comrades. Keep it, Señor Juan."

Señor Juan kept the notes, though slightly put out by the bandit's refusal and insistence on treating him as an equal.

"If we see each other in the bull-ring some day, you shall

dedicate a bull to me," Plumitas added. "That would be worth more than all the money in the world."

Doña Sol stepped forward and stood close to the rider's leg, and taking an autumn rose from the front of her dress she offered it to him silently, looking at him with her green and yellow eyes.

"Is this for me?" the bandit asked, in a voice of surprise. "Is this really for me, Señora Marquesa?"

When he saw her nod her head, he took the flower with clumsy embarrassment, as if it were heavy and he didn't know what to do with it; then he put it in the buttonhole of his shirt between the ends of the red handkerchief he wore round his neck.

"That's fine!" he exclaimed, his round face expanding into a wide smile. "It's the first time that ever happened to me."

The rough bandit seemed both moved and embarrassed by this feminine gift. Roses, to him!

He gathered up the reins.

"Good-bye to you, gentlemen all. Till we meet again. Good-bye, old chap. One of these days I'll send you a cigar if you do well in the arena." And he shook the picador by the hand, receiving in reply a thump on the thigh which made him jump. Plumitas was a man after Potaje's heart, and in his drunken affection he would have liked to go with him to the mountains.

"Good-bye! Good-bye!"

And he spurred his horse and trotted out of the courtyard.

Gallardo seemed relieved to see him go. Then he glanced at Doña Sol, who was standing quite still following the bandit with her eyes as he vanished into the distance.

"What a mad creature she is!" he murmured in dismay.

It was lucky that Plumitas was so ugly, ragged and dirty, otherwise she would have gone with him.

CHAPTER SIX

"I wouldn't have believed it of you, Sebastián. A man like you, with a wife and children, to act no better than a pimp! And I've always thought you so different and trusted you when you went on journeys with Juaniyo! I've been happy thinking he had such a good man with him. What's happened to all your theories, and your religion too? Is this the sort of thing you pick up among the Jews at Don Joselito's house?"

Appalled by Señora Angustias' indignation and distressed to see Carmen silently weeping into a handkerchief, El Nacional had been defending himself feebly. But at the last words he pulled himself together and said solemnly:

"Please don't attack my theories, Señora Angustias, and please leave Don Joselito out of it. All this has nothing to do with him. Good heavens! I went to La Rinconada because my master told me to. You know well enough what a cuadrilla is? Well it's a matter of discipline and obedience, just like the army. The matador gives his orders and we have to obey. Bullfighting started in the days of the Inquisition, and it's the most reactionary profession in the world."

"You great idiot," cried Señora Angustias. "This nonsense about the Inquisition and reaction is all very fine! Among the lot of you you're killing this poor child, who spends the whole day in tears like La Dolorosa. What you're trying to do is cover up my son's wickedness, because he gives you your daily bread."

"Just as you say, Señora Angustias, Juaniyo gives me my daily bread. That's it; and because of that I have to do what he tells me. But look here now, Señora, put yourself in my place. The maestro tells me I must go to La Rinconada. Very well. When it's time to start I find a beautiful lady in the motor-car. What am I supposed to do? The maestro gives the orders. Besides I wasn't alone. Potaje was there too, who is a respectable middle-aged man, even if he is rough in his ways."

The bullfighter's mother was infuriated by this excuse.

"Potaje! If Juaniyo had any shame he wouldn't have that bad man in his cuadrilla. Don't talk to me about that drunkard, who beats his wife and starves his children!"

"All right. We'll leave Potaje out of it. I tell you I saw this grand lady. What was I to do? She wasn't a whore, she was the Marqués' niece and the maestro's friend. Toreros have to keep in with the nobility, as you know. They mustn't offend their public. Where's the harm in that? Well then later on at the farm, there was nothing, I swear it. Nothing at all! I'm a decent man, Señora Angustias, and it's not right to call me the bad names you did just now. Nothing happened, I tell you. They talked just as you and I are doing; each spent the night in their own room; there was nothing bad in words or deeds. Decent behaviour all the time. And if you like, I'll fetch Potaje; he'll tell you the same. . . ."

But Carmen interrupted between gasps and sobs, with a look of horror on her face:

"In my own house! Here at the farm! And she slept in my bed! I knew all about it too, long before, and I held my tongue! I said nothing! But this! Jesus! There's not another man in Seville who would dare do such a thing!"

El Nacional interposed kindly: "Calm yourself, Señora Carmen. It's nothing, really it isn't. A lady who admires the maestro has visited the farm, wanting to see the way he lives in the country. These half-foreign ladies are full of strange ideas. You should have seen how the Frenchwomen went on when the cuadrilla was fighting at Nîmes and Arles! What does it all amount to? Nothing at all. Just rubbish! By jingo, I should like to know what cheeky scoundrel came telling tales. If I were Juaniyo and it was one of the farm hands, I'd show him the door; and if not I'd have him up before the judge and send him to prison for slander."

Carmen went on weeping, without hearing the banderillero's protests, while Señora Angustias sat with her bulky person overflowing her arm-chair, frowning and pursing up her hairy, wrinkled lips.

"Hold your tongue, Sebastián and don't tell lies," the old woman said. "I know all about it. That trip to the farm was a shameful, wicked business. They had a gang of gypsies in—a regular fiesta; they even say that thief Plumitas was there!"

This remark fairly took El Nacional by surprise, and filled him with sudden anxiety. In his mind's eye he saw a disreputable-looking rider, wearing a stained hat, come into the patio, bring his mare to a standstill on the marble flagstones and take aim at him with his rifle, calling him coward and informer. Then he seemed to see many three-cornered hats made of shining oil-cloth, moustachioed mouths asking endless questions, hands busy writing down the answers, and the whole cuadrilla in their fighting suits being marched off to gaol in chains. The time had come to deny everything emphatically.

"Rubbish! All rubbish! What's all this about Plumitas? Everything was quiet and decent I tell you. Good lord! they'll be saying next that I'm a friend of Plumitas—a respectable citizen like me, who carries over a hundred votes from my suburb to the ballot box!"

Señora Angustias was convinced by El Nacional's protestations, and as she had never thought this last piece of news very probable she now rejected it altogether. Very well; no more about Plumitas. But as for the other business—Juan's visit to the farm with that . . . female! And with the stubborn blindness of a mother she threw all the responsibility for the matador's actions on to his companions, and went on pitching into El Nacional.

"I'm going to tell your wife what sort of man you are! There's the poor thing killing herself with work from morning to night in the wine shop, while you go on the spree like a youngster. You ought to be ashamed of yourself. At your age! With all those children of yours!"

In the end the banderillero left the house to escape from Señora Angustias' wrath. Her indignation had restored the fluency and freedom of speech of her old days in the tobacco factory. He vowed he would never go back to his master's house again.

185

He met Gallardo in the street. He seemed out of humour, but when he saw the banderillero he smiled and assumed an air of cheerfulness as if unaffected by the troubles at home.

"It's a bad business, Juaniyo. I'm not going to your house any more, not at any price. Your mother has been insulting me as if I was a gypsy from Triana. Your wife cries her eyes out and looks at me as if it was all my doing. Leave me out of it next time, for heaven's sake. Take someone else with you when you're planning to go away with a woman."

Gallardo smiled. It would all be over soon, nothing would come of it. He had been through worse storms before.

"Come back home with me now, that's what you must do. When there are plenty of us, there'll be no squabbling."

"Me?" exclaimed El Nacional. "No thanks. I'd sooner turn priest."

After this the matador thought it was no use pressing him. He spent the greater part of the day away from home, out of range of the sullen and tearful silence of his women-folk; and when he returned to the house it was in the company of his manager and some other friends.

The saddler was a great support to Gallardo at this juncture. For the first time he had a genuine fellow-feeling for his brother-in-law, admired his good sense and thought he deserved better treatment. He had taken upon himself to pacify the women, including his own wife, during the matador's absence, and had reduced them to the state of exhausted furies.

"Let's see what all the fuss is about," he said. "Just an unimportant girl. It all depends who one is, and Juaniyo is a celebrity and naturally has to mix with influential people. And if the Señora did go to the farm with him, what of it? He has to entertain his friends; how else can he ask favours of them and help his family? There was nothing wrong between them; that's all lies. El Nacional was there, and he's an honest man. I know him well."

It was the first time in his life he had praised the banderillero. He was constantly in the house now, and seemed to be the only person who could reduce the women to silence with his endless chatter. The bullfighter was not ungrateful. The saddler had shut up his shop, as business was going badly, and he was hoping to get a job through his brother-in-law. Meanwhile the matador supplied all the wants of the family, and finally invited them all to move into his own house. Poor Carmen would worry less if she were not so much alone.

One day El Nacional got a message from the maestro's wife, asking him to go and see her. It was his own wife who delivered it.

"I saw her this morning. She'd been to San Gil. Her eyes were swollen with crying, poor thing. Go and see her, do. Ay! these handsome men! What a plague they are!"

Carmen received El Nacional in the matador's study. They could be alone there, without fear of being disturbed by Señora Angustias with her endless tirades, or Gallardo's sister and her family who were now installed in the house and taking every advantage they could of the domestic disagreement. Gallardo was at the club in the Calle de las Sierpes. He was out as much as possible and often ate away from home, going with his friends to the inn at Eritaña, so as to avoid meeting his wife.

El Nacional was sitting on the sofa, with his hat in his hands and his head hanging, unable to look his master's wife in the face. How she had altered! Her eyes were red, with deep, dark circles round them. Her cheeks and nose were red too from constant rubbing with a pocket-handkerchief.

"Please tell me the truth, Sebastián. You're an honest man, and you're the best friend Juan has got. You mustn't mind the things his mother said the other day. It's just her way. You know what a good soul she is really. Her tantrums are soon over. Don't worry about that."

The banderillero nodded, waiting for the questions which must follow. What did Señora Carmen want to know?

"Please tell me what really happened at La Rinconada, both what you saw and what you guessed at."

Ah! this was not so bad. The kind-hearted Nacional lifted

his head, pleased to think he could be of some help to this unfortunate woman. He had seen nothing wrong.

"I swear it by my dead father. I swear it by . . . my theories."

He was content to support his oath on such sacred testimony as his theories, because in fact he had seen nothing whatever, and that being so he held the logical belief founded on pride in his own perspicacity and common sense that nothing wrong could have happened.

"It seems to me they're just friends. Perhaps there was something more between them once, that I don't know. People will talk, you know. They make up such lies! You mustn't worry about that, Señora Carmen. You've your life to live, and you must be as happy as possible, that's the thing!"

But she stuck to her point. Exactly what had happened at the farm? The farm was her own home, and that was what made her particularly indignant; it was more than infidelity, it was a sort of sacrilege, a direct and personal insult.

"Do you think I'm a fool, Sebastián? I saw it all; from the moment he first got interested in the Señora, I knew what was in Juan's mind. The day he dedicated a bull to her and came back with that diamond ring, I guessed what there was between them, and I wanted to take it and stamp on it. Afterwards I knew everything that happened, everything! There are always people ready to carry tales and make others unhappy. Besides they never tried to hide what they were up to; they went about everywhere just like husband and wife in front of everybody, like those gypsies who go about from feria to feria. When we were at the farm I used to hear about everything Juan did; and afterwards at Sanlúcar too."

El Nacional saw that Carmen was becoming upset by her own recollections, and on the point of tears. He felt he must say something.

"And you believe all those lies, child? Don't you see that they're made up by people who want to hurt you? Jealousy, that's all."

"No; I know Juan. You don't imagine this is the first time do you? He can't help being what he is. It's his hateful profession—it seems to turn men's heads! Two years after we were married he had an affair with a pretty girl who worked at the butcher's stall in the market. What I suffered when I heard about it! But I never said a word. He still thinks I didn't know. And afterwards, how many more! Music-hall dancers, whores from low taverns or even out of brothels. I don't know how many there were—dozens! And I said nothing, so as there should be peace at home. But this woman is different from all the others. Juan's crazy about her; she's made a fool of him. I know he's been ready to do anything so that she shouldn't throw him out of her house, ashamed of having a torero for a lover. Now she's gone away. Didn't you know? She was bored in Seville, so she's gone. I've heard it from lots of people. She left without even saying good-bye to Juan, and when he went to see her the other day he found her door shut. So he goes round as gloomy as a sick animal, with a face like a funeral, and gets drunk with his friends to cheer himself up, and comes home gloomier than ever. No, he can't forget that woman. He was proud that a female of her class could love him and now his feelings are wounded because she's left him. Ay! I'm disgusted with him! He's not my husband any more; he's changed. We're like strangers; we hardly speak to each other except to quarrel. I'm all alone upstairs, and he sleeps downstairs in a room off the patio. We'll never come together again. I swear it! I used to put up with everything; it was part of his profession; all toreros have this crazy idea that they're irresistible to women. But now I never want to see him again; he disgusts me."

She was talking excitedly, and her eyes shone with hatred.

"Ay! how that woman has changed him! He's a different man! He only wants to go about with rich people, and all our neighbours and the poor people of Seville, who used to be his friends and helped him when he was a beginner, complain of him now; some fine day they'll start a disturbance against him in the bull-ring. At present he's raking in the money by bucketfulls, there's no counting it. Even he doesn't know how much he's got. He gambles heavily so as to impress his new friends, and he loses so much that what comes in at one door goes out at the other. I never say a word. After all he's earned it. But he's had to borrow from Don José to meet expenses on the farm, and I know the olive groves he added to the property this year were bought with someone else's money. Practically everything he makes next season will have to go to pay off his debts. And supposing he had an accident? Or has to retire, like they all do in the end? He's even tried to make me different, just as he's different himself. I know his lordship thinks his mamma and me very dull and dowdy in our shawls and dressing-gowns when he comes back from visiting his Doña Sol or Doña She-devil. That was why he made me wear those hats from Madrid, which make me look such a fool; I felt like an organ-grinder's monkey in them. And a mantilla is such a pretty thing! Then he bought that dreadful motor-car, which frightens the life out of me and stinks to heaven. If he had his way he'd make poor Mamma wear a hat with feathers in it. He's always thinking of that woman and he wants to make us look like her so as not to be ashamed of us. He's just a snob."

The banderillero burst out in protest. No, that wasn't true. Juan was a kind-hearted man and he did these things because he loved his family and wanted them to have every comfort and luxury.

"Say what you like about Juaniyo, Señora Carmen, there's one thing you must allow. There are lots of women dying with envy of you, remember that! Isn't it something to be the wife of the bravest bullfighter in the world, with plenty of money, a splendid house, and the maestro wanting you to be mistress of it all and do just what you like with it?"

Carmen's eyes filled with tears and she dabbed them with her handkerchief.

"I'd rather be a shoemaker's wife. I've thought so many a time! If only Juan had kept on with his trade instead of taking to this accursed bullfighting! I'd be a lot happier dressed in my old shawl taking him his lunch under the archway where his father used to work. There wouldn't be all these pretty girls trying to take him away from me; he'd be mine; we might be hard up at times, but on Sundays we'd go out and lunch at an inn in our best clothes. And then I'm frightened out of my wits every time he's fighting in that horrible arena. It's no sort of a life! Plenty of money, yes indeed, but I tell you Sebastián it's just poison to me, and the more comes into the house the worse I feel. It's as if it were killing me. What do I want with hats and things like that? People think I'm the happiest woman in the world and envy me, and all the while I'm looking at poor women with babies in their arms. They may be short of everything else, but when they're unhappy they look at their little ones and smile. Ay! I know what's wrong with my life! If only I had a child! If Juan could see a little boy in his house who was all his own, not just a nephew!"

Carmen burst out crying, and the tears streamed from under her handkerchief, wetting her reddened cheeks. Hers was the anguish of a barren woman who envies every mother; the desperation of a wife who pretends to put her husband's estrangement down to various causes, but in her heart of heart attributes it to her own sterility. A son would bring them together again! And Carmen, who had in the course of time become convinced that her longing was useless, raged against the cruelty of fate, and looked with envy at the man who listened to her in silence, who had been blessed by Nature with what she most longed for.

The banderillero came away from the interview in a melancholy mood and went in search of his master. He found him outside the Forty-Five Club.

"Juan, I've just seen your wife. Things are going from bad to worse. See if you can calm her down, and put yourself right with her."

"Damn it all! She'll make herself ill in the end, and you and me as well. I hope to God a bull gets me on Sunday and makes an end of it all. Life's not worth living these days!"

He was rather drunk. The sullen silence which greeted him at home was driving him to desperation, and he brooded even more—though this he would not confess to anyone—over the fact that Doña Sol had gone away without a word, not so

191

much as four lines in farewell. He had been sent away from her door like a servant. He didn't even know where she was. The Marqués hadn't shown much interest in his niece's travels; the mad girl hadn't said anything to him about her departure, but that didn't mean she'd disappeared for good. Some sign of her existence was sure to arrive from foreign parts—wherever her whim might have taken her.

Gallardo couldn't conceal his despair, even when he was at home. Confronted by a silent wife, frowning or lowering her eyes and refusing to reply to his attempts at conversation, the matador openly expressed his desire for death.

"Oh, this is too much! I hope to God a Miura bull gets me on Sunday and finishes me off for good, and they bring what's left of me home in a basket!"

"Don't you say such wicked things!" cried Señora Angustias indignantly. "It's tempting fate! It'll bring you bad luck."

But the saddler intervened sententiously, glad of a chance to flatter the matador: "Don't worry, Mamma. There's no bull alive that can hurt him!"

Sunday's bullfight was the last Gallardo was engaged to appear in that year. The morning passed without any of the vague superstitious fears that usually troubled him. As he got dressed he was in good spirits, buoyed up by a nervous excitement which seemed to increase his physical energy. How splendid it would be to be treading the yellow sand again, and astonishing twelve thousand spectators by his grace and reckless daring! His art was the only thing that mattered, that consummate skill which gained him the crowd's applause and plenty of money to burn. Everything else—family, love affairs—was just a source of trouble and complication. Ah, what estocadas he would bring off today! He felt he had a giant's strength; he was a new man, his fears and worries were behind him. He was impatient for it to be time to go to the bull-ring, instead of trying to postpone the dreaded moment as he usually did. His anger over his domestic difficulties and the indignation caused by that sudden wounding departure would all be vented on the bulls.

When the carriage arrived, Gallardo went across the patio to it without noticing his womenfolk's agitation. Carmen didn't come down. Bah! these women! What use were they except to embitter one's life? It was only men who could be trusted, who were cheerful companions. There was his brother-in-law, preening himself in a suit of the matador's which had been altered to fit him before it had been worn by its rightful owner. He was a ludicrous charlatan; all the same he was worth more than the rest of the family put together. His loyalty could be counted on.

"You look finer than Roger de Flor himself," said the saddler gaily. "Get in, and I'll come with you to the ring."

He sat down beside the great man, bursting with pride as they drove through the streets of Seville and all the world saw him sitting amongst the toreros with their silk capes and gold embroideries.

The amphitheatre was full. This last corrida of the autumn had attracted a large audience, not only from the town itself but from the surrounding country-side. The benches on the sunny side were crowded with people from the neighbouring villages. From the first Gallardo displayed the intense nervous energy which possessed him. He went out far from the barrier to meet the bull and engage it with cloak-play, while the picadors waited for the moment when the brute would turn and attack their wretched horses.

A certain predisposition against the matador could be noticed in the audience. They applauded him as usual, but much more enthusiastic and prolonged demonstrations came from the seats in the shade (where there were regular rows of white Córdovan hats) than from those in the sun, which were full of a lively, mixed crowd, many of them sitting in their shirt-sleeves in the scorching heat.

Gallardo soon became aware of this state of things. If he had a bit of bad luck, half the audience would be on its feet shouting abuse, and taunting him with letting down the people who had first launched him. The killing of his first bull was only a moderate success. He threw himself between the horns with his usual recklessness, but the sword hit a bone. His supporters applauded. The thrust had been well placed and it was not his fault that it had not been effective. For the second time he came in to kill; the sword struck the same spot, and as the bull charged the muleta the weapon was jerked from the wound and flung to some distance. Then, taking another sword from Garabato, he advanced again to meet the bull, which stood waiting for him, its weight heavily on all four feet, its neck spouting blood, and its foaming muzzle almost touching the sand.

Spreading his muleta before the animal's eyes, the maestro quietly moved aside the banderillas which fell across its head with the point of his sword. He was going to administer a *descabello*.[1] With the steel resting between the horns he felt about for the right spot, and then tried to drive the sword home. The bull shuddered but remained on its feet and managed to toss away the sword with a quick movement of its head.

"One!" came a mocking shout from the seats in the sun.

Why did they attack him so unfairly, damn them?

Again he aimed the point of the sword at the vulnerable spot and this time successfully. The bull fell to the ground as if shot, mortally wounded at the centre of its nervous system, and lay belly upwards with its horns in the sand and its stiff legs in the air.

The people in the shady seats applauded, from class solidarity, while the crowd on the sunny side broke out into whistling and taunting shouts.

Gallardo turned his back on their outcry and saluted his supporters with sword and muleta. These insults from the common people who had always been his friends hurt him deeply, and he clenched his fists.

What on earth did they want? There was nothing else he could have done with that bull. This looked like organized hostility.

[1] *A coup de grâce* given by the matador to a bull still on its feet but wounded by an estocada; the point of the sword is driven between the base of the skull and the first vertebra, severing the spinal cord. A descabello on a bull that is still strong and needs another estocada is thought ill of.

He spent the greater part of the corrida standing by the barrier, watching his comrades with a scornful expression and inwardly accusing them of having set going this show of enmity against him. He cursed the bad luck that had landed him with such a bull. To come so well prepared, resolved to do great things, and then meet with an animal which gave him no chance to shine! Breeders who sent in such brutes ought to be shot.

When he took his sword and muleta in hand for the second time that afternoon, he gave instructions to El Nacional and the other peons to bring the bull by their cloak-play close to the part of the amphitheatre where the cheaper seats were.

He knew his public. He must do something to flatter the occupants of the seats in the sun—that formidable and clamorous proletariat, who brought their class hatred with them to the bull-ring, but who could be induced to convert their whistling into applause by the slightest titillation of their vanity.

Flourishing their capes before the bull, the peons tried to draw it towards the sunny side of the arena. This manœuvre was greeted with pleased surprise by the mob. The supreme climax, the death of the bull, was going to take place under their very eyes, instead of a long way off as almost always happened, for the benefit of the rich people sitting in the shade.

Left to its own devices for a moment at this side of the ring, the bull charged at the dead body of a horse. It buried its head in the gaping stomach, and lifted the wretched carcass on its horns like a limp rag, scattering entrails and excrement in every direction. Then the corpse fell to the ground, doubled in two, and the bull moved away undecidedly, but soon turned round and sniffed at it again, snorting loudly and burying its horns in the stomach, while the public roared with laughter at its stupid obstinacy in trying to reanimate the lifeless body.

"That's the way! . . . Show us how strong you are, old boy! Go on, give it him again!"

But now the attention of the whole audience turned from the furious beast to watch Gallardo who was crossing the ring

195

with short steps, his body swaying lightly from the waist; in one hand he carried the folded muleta, in the other he was swinging the sword as if it were a walking-stick.

The spectators in the sunny seats roared applause, delighted to see the matador approaching them.

"You've got them where you want them now," said El Nacional who was standing not far from the bull holding the cape.

The crowd clapped and called out, "Here! Here!" Each one of them wanted the bull to be killed right in front of his seat, so that he shouldn't miss a thing, and the matador hesitated between the contradictory commands of thousands of voices.

Standing with one foot on the step of the barrier he was considering which was the best place to kill the bull. A little further on, perhaps. He was bothered by the eviscerated remains of the horse, which seemed to fill one whole side of the ring and might get in his way.

He was just going to tell El Nacional to remove then, when he heard a voice he knew coming from behind him, a voice he didn't at once recognize but which made him turn round suddenly.

"Good evening, Señor Juan! Are you going to show us the real thing this time?"

In the first row, underneath the ropes of the inside barrier, he saw a folded jacket, two arms in shirt sleeves crossed on top of it, and between the hands a round clean-shaven face, with a hat pulled down over the ears. It might have been an amiable rustic come in to town from his village to see the corrida.

Gallardo knew him now. It was Plumitas.

He had been true to his promise, and here he was, among twelve thousand people who might recognize him at any moment, boldly greeting the matador, who couldn't help feeling pleased by this mark of trust.

Gallardo was astounded at his temerity. He had left the safety of his lonely mountains and come all the way to Seville, into the bull-ring, without his two faithful companions—his mare and his carbine, and all for the sake of seeing him kill bulls. Of the two of them, Plumitas was the braver man.

It flashed through his mind that his farm lay completely at the bandit's mercy, and that his peaceful country life was only possible so long as he kept on good terms with this extraordinary character. This bull should be dedicated to him.

He smiled at the bandit, who was still staring calmly at him; he took off his montera, and with his eyes fixed on Plumitas shouted at the restless crowd:

"This bull is for you!"

Then he threw his montera towards the front rows and dozens of outstretched hands fought to catch the coveted object.

Gallardo signed to El Nacional to bring the bull towards him.

As he spread his muleta the bull charged with a loud snort, passing under the red cloth. "*Olé!*" roared the crowd, again delighted with their old idol and prepared to find everything he did admirable.

Pass after pass with the muleta followed, while the crowd cheered and shouted, watching each move from close range and offering him their advice. "Careful, Gallardo! The bull's not tired yet. Don't get between him and the barrier. Keep your retreat open!"

Other enthusiasts incited him to greater feats of daring:

"Let him have it! You know how! You've got him now! Kill him and put him in your pocket!"

But the bull was much too large and full of fight to be put in anyone's pocket. It was excited by the proximity of the dead horse, and kept returning to it, as if intoxicated by the smell coming from the animal's stomach.

After a pass with the muleta, the bull seemed to tire and stood motionless for a moment. The dead horse was behind Gallardo. It was a bad position, but he had come out of worse ones triumphantly.

He wanted to take advantage of the bull's immobility, and the audience were inciting him to action. Amongst the other men who were leaning over the inside barrier determined not to lose a single detail of the climax, he recognized several plebeian aficionados who had lately begun to desert him but were now applauding him, pleased by his flattering attentions to them.

"Now's your chance, my boy! Now for the real thing! Let him have it!"

Gallardo turned his head slightly to salute Plumitas, who was still smiling away, with his moon face propped on his arms and his jacket.

"For you, my friend!"

He profiled with the sword, preparing for the kill; but at the very same moment the earth seemed to tremble, and heave, throwing him to a great distance, the bull-ring seemed to be falling upon him, everything turned black and a furious hurricane seemed to be raging round him. His body throbbed with pain from head to foot as if it was being torn asunder; there was a buzzing in his brain as if his head was bursting; a fearful pain seared his chest . . . and he felt himself falling into endless, murky nothingness, and knew no more.

At the same instant that the matador had been preparing to come in and kill, the bull had made an unexpected rush at him, attracted by the body of the horse behind him, which it had made its querencia. The collision was terrific, sending the silk and gold-clad figure rolling to the ground under the cruel hoofs. He was not gored; but the shock was horrifying and crushing, as the great head and horns, and all the powerful forepart of the creature came down upon him like a steam hammer.

The bull had only seemed to see the horse, but now became aware of some obstacle between its feet; it ignored the carcass and turned to attack the brilliantly coloured figure lying on the ground. It lifted him on one horn, shook him and threw him several feet away; then prepared to charge again.

The crowd sat with bated breath, struck dumb with horror at the rapidity with which all this had happened. The bull would kill him! Perhaps he was already dead? Suddenly this agonizing silence was broken by a shout from the whole audience. Someone was flourishing a cape between the bull and its victim; strong arms were holding the cloth so close to the animal's head that it almost blinded it. It was El Nacional, who had hurled himself at the bull in the desperation of the moment, ready to be tossed himself if he could save the maestro from peril. The creature turned away from the fallen man and charged at this new adversary. The banderillero was caught between the horns, and ran backwards waving the cape, unable to extricate himself from this dangerous position but relieved at having drawn the bull away from his wounded master.

This new development absorbed the attention of the crowd so that they almost forgot the matador. El Nacional would be down, too, in another moment, he couldn't possibly escape from between the horns; the bull was carrying him along as if it had already impaled him. Men shouted, as if their cries could have been of any assistance to him; women gasped with fear, turning away their faces and wringing their hands; then suddenly the banderillero took advantage of the bull's lowering its head to toss him, to slip from between the horns and step quickly aside, while the brute rushed blindly on, carrying the torn cape on its head.

The tension of the audience found relief in a burst of deafening applause. The fickle spectators could be moved only by the danger that was actually before their eyes, and they cheered El Nacional enthusiastically. It was one of the finest moments of his life. They were so busy shouting and clapping him that they hardly noticed the matador's inanimate body being carried out of the ring with head hanging.

Gallardo's accident was the sole topic of conversation in Seville that night; it was far the worst he had ever had Special editions of the newspapers were published all over Spain describing and commenting on what had happened. The telegraph offices were as busy as if a politician had been assassinated.

Dreadful rumours, coloured by the exaggeration natural to

Southerners, were circulating in the Calle de las Sierpes. Poor Gallardo had just died. The person responsible for this piece of news had seen him lying in the bull-ring infirmary, white as a sheet, holding the cross between his hands. Another man came forward with a less dismal report. He was not dead, yet.

"But every part of his body is damaged: his heart, kidneys, everything! The brute has left him riddled like a sieve."

Civil Guards were stationed round the bull-ring to prevent people breaking in to the infirmary in their anxiety for news. A large crowd collected outside, and everyone who went in or out was questioned about the matador's state.

El Nacional came out several times, still wearing his fighting suit, frowning and glum; he flew into a rage because no means of transferring the maestro to his own house seemed to be forthcoming.

When they saw the banderillero the crowd forgot about the wounded man in their eagerness to congratulate him.

"You were magnificent, Señor Sebastián! If it hadn't been for you. . . !"

But he would have none of their praise. What did it matter whether he had acted bravely or not? It was all . . . rubbish! The important thing was that poor Juan was lying in the infirmary fighting for his life.

"And how is he, Señor Sebastián?" the crowd wanted to know.

"Very bad. He's only just come to his senses again. One of his legs is ground to powder, and he's been gored under the arm, and I don't know what besides, poor fellow. We're going to take him home."

As night fell, Gallardo was carried out of the bull-ring infirmary on a stretcher. The crowd walked behind in silence. The journey took a long time. Every few minutes El Nacional bent anxiously over the oilskin cover of the stretcher and told the bearers to stop. He was carrying his cape over his arm and his brilliant fighting suit contrasted with the drab clothes of the crowd.

The bull-ring doctors walked behind, and with them were

the Marqués de Moraima and Don José the manager, who was almost fainting, supported by some friends from the Forty-Five Club; their common horror and anxiety united them with the disreputable and ragged crew following the stretcher.

It was a melancholy procession. It seemed as if some national disaster had just happened, cancelling out all class distinctions and making all men equal under the pressure of general misfortune.

"What a terrible thing, Señor Marqués!" said a round-faced fair-haired peasant, who was carrying his coat over his shoulder.

This man had twice roughly tried to push aside one of the stretcher-bearers and take his place. The Marqués looked at him sympathetically. He must be one of the villagers who often greeted him when he was at his cattle ranch.

"Yes, it's a shocking affair."

"Do you think he'll die, Señor Marqués?"

"I'm afraid so; it'll take a miracle to save him. He's been terribly mangled."

And the Marqués put his hand on the unknown man's shoulder, and seemed grateful for the sadness he read in his face.

Gallardo's arrival home was extremely distressing. Cries of despair could be heard issuing from the patio. A group of women who lived near by, or were friends of the family, were wailing and tearing their hair in the street, believing that Juanillo was already dead.

Potaje and some of the others had to stand in the gateway, blocking the entrance with their bodies and using physical force to prevent the crowd trying to make its way into the house behind the stretcher. The street outside was full of people muttering gloomily about the accident, and staring up at the house as if they could guess what was happening behind its walls.

The stretcher was carried into a small room giving on to the patio, and with infinite precautions the matador was transferred to his bed. He was swathed in bloodstained bandages and cloths smelling strongly of antiseptics. All that he still wore of his fighting suit was one pink stocking. His underclothes had been torn and cut with scissors.

His pigtail hung loose and tangled on his neck; he was as pale as a ghost. He opened his eyes when he felt a hand in his, and smiled feebly as he saw it was Carmen, but a Carmen with a face as white as his, dry-eyed, but with bloodless lips and an expression of terror as if his last moment had come.

The matador's friends prudently intervened. This musn't be allowed to go on: Carmen must leave him. So far the wounded man had only received first aid, and there was a great deal still for the doctors to do.

In the end Carmen left the room unwillingly, almost pushed out by the friends of the family. The injured man made a sign that he wanted to speak to El Nacional, who bent over him to catch his faintly murmured words.

"Juan wants us to telegraph for Doctor Ruiz," he said, going out into the patio.

The manager was pleased to be able to tell him that it had already been done. He had telegraphed himself, earlier in the afternoon, as soon as he saw how serious the accident was. The doctor was almost certainly at this moment on his way and would be here next morning.

Don José questioned the doctors who had attended the matador at the ring. After their initial dismay, they had become more optimistic. He had a chance of survival. He had such amazing powers of resistance! The thing most to be feared was the shock he had suffered—which must have been quite enough to kill a man outright; but he had already come through the stage of collapse and recovered consciousness, although he was still terribly weak. As for the actual damage, they didn't consider it dangerous. The wound in his arm was slight, though perhaps it might result in some loss of agility. The leg was not so hopeful. The bone was fractured; Gallardo might be lame.

Don José had controlled his feelings with a great effort some hours earlier when everyone had believed the matador's death inevi able; he broke down when he heard this news. 'His matador' lame? That meant he would never fight again?

He was indignant at the calm way the doctors discussed the possibilty that Gallardo might become useless as a torero.

"It's impossible! Do you really think it logically conceivable that Juan could continue to exist and not fight? He's the best of them all . . . and you want him to retire!"

He spent the night sitting up with the rest of the cuadrilla and Gallardo's brother-in-law. The saddler kept going from the wounded man's room to the upper floor, to console and pacify the women and prevent them from trying to see the matador. They must carry out the doctors' orders, and avoid agitating the sick man. Juan was very weak, and it was this that was causing the anxiety, not his wounds.

Next morning the manager hurried off to the station. The Madrid express arrived, and with it Doctor Ruiz. He had no luggage, and was as carelessly dressed as ever; but he was smiling behind his yellowish-white beard, as he ambled unsteadily along on his short legs, swinging his great stomach like a Buddha. He had heard the news in Madrid as he came away from a novillada which had been arranged to give a chance to a boy from Las Ventas. It had been an absurd affair, and even after an exhausting night in the train he laughed at the memory of this farcical corrida, as if he had forgotten the object of his visit.

When the matador saw him come into the room where he lay, sunk in the limbo of his own weakness, his face was illumined by a smile full of trust. After a whispered consultation with the other doctors in the corner of the room Ruiz went up to the wounded man with a confident air.

"Courage, my boy! They've not done for you this time! You've been lucky!"

And he added, to his colleagues: "Juanillo is such a magnificent physical specimen! Otherwise our work would be over by now."

He examined him with the greatest care. There was a nasty horn wound, but he had seen so many! In cases of ordinary or chronic illness he was often undecided, and loth to give a definite opinion; but gorings were his speciality, and he knew that the most spectacular cures could be expected of them, as if the horn dispensed a remedy along with the wound.

"If a man doesn't die outright in the ring, you might almost say he's sure to recover," he used to say. "It's only a matter of time."

For three whole days Gallardo had to submit to a series of agonizing operations, and though he cried out with the pain his weak state made the use of anaesthetics inadvisable. Doctor Ruiz extracted several pieces of the fractured tibia from his injured leg.

"Who said you wouldn't be able to fight any more?" he exclaimed, satisfied with his own skill. "You will, my boy; the public will soon be cheering you again."

The manager nodded his head. Wasn't that just what he had been saying? This couldn't possibly be the end of 'his matador's' career.

On Doctor Ruiz's orders the bullfighter's family had all moved to Don José's house. The women were a nuisance; it was impossible to have them about while the operations were going on. A groan of pain from Gallardo would produce wails from his mother and sister, like a dismal echo from the other end of the house, while Carmen fought like a mad thing to get to her husband and had to be restrained by force.

Her anxiety had produced a complete change in the matador's wife; her grievances were forgotten. She often wept from remorse, feeling that she had unconsciously been responsible for the accident.

"It's all my fault, I know it is," she said to El Nacional in a voice of despair. "He kept on saying he wished a bull would get him and put an end to his troubles. I've not done right by him; I've embittered his life."

In vain the banderillero went over all that had led up to the accident, so as to convince her that it had depended entirely on a series of unlucky circumstances. No; she was sure that Gallardo had wanted to make an end of it all, and if it hadn't been for El Nacional he would have been carried out of the ring dead.

When the operations were finished, the family came back to the house.

Carmen entered the wounded man's room on tiptoe, with her eyes cast down, as if ashamed of her former hostility.

"How are you feeling?" she asked, taking one of Juan's hands between both of hers.

And there she sat, silent and timid, in front of Ruiz and the matador's friends, who never left the injured man's bedside.

If she had been alone with him she would have gone down on her knees and asked him to forgive her. Poor darling! She had driven him to despair by her cruelty, so that he had lost all desire to go on living. She must make up to him for it all. And she looked at him with an expression of self-abnegation, mixed with wifely love and a mother's tenderness.

Gallardo seemed to have shrunk under the pain he had suffered, and he looked pale and weak, like a frightened child. There was nothing in him now of the arrogant young man who used to set the audience on fire with his bravery. He repined against his immobility and the crushing weight of the splints on his leg. The terrible operations he had had to bear in full consciousness seemed to have made a coward of him. His former power to endure pain had gone, and he groaned at the smallest discomfort.

His room had become a sort of meeting-place for the foremost aficionados of the town. Cigar smoke was mixed with the smell of iodoform and other pungent odours. There were bottles of wine for the entertainment of his visitors standing about among the medicines and rolls of cotton wool and bandages on the tables.

"This is nothing," his friends would exclaim, trying to rally the torero with their noisy optimism. "You'll be fighting again in a couple of months. You're in good hands. Doctor Ruiz always performs miracles."

The doctor was equally hopeful.

"He's much more himself, you see. He's begun to smoke again. And when a sick man starts smoking . . . !"

The doctor, the manager and some of the cuadrilla sat with the injured man until far into the night. When Potaje was of the company he was always to be found close to one of the tables, with a bottle within reach.

The conversation between Ruiz, Don José and El Nacional was invariably about bulls. It was impossible to talk about anything else in the manager's presence. He criticized all the other matadors, discussed their merits and the amount of money they earned, while the sick man lay listening in enforced immobility or fell into a drowsy torpor lulled by the hum of voices.

It was usually the doctor who held forth, while El Nacional hung on his words and watched him with serious admiring eyes. What that man knew! The banderillero was so much impressed that he withdrew some of the implicit confidence he usually accorded to Don Joselito, and asked the doctor when the Revolution could be expected?

"What does it matter to you, eh? What you want to think about is getting to know the bulls better, and becoming a better banderillero."

El Nacional protested against this attempt to limit his interests. He was a citizen like the rest of them, an elector whose favour was sought by candidates on polling-day.

"It seems to me I've a right to my opinions. I'm on the committee of my party, that's a fact. What if I am a torero? I know it's a reactionary low sort of profession, but it doesn't prevent me having my own theories about things."

He insisted on the qualification 'reactionary', ignoring Don José's teasing jokes, for although he respected the manager his remarks were all directed at Doctor Ruiz. It was Ferdinand VII who had been responsible for all the trouble; yes indeed, he was a tyrant, who had made bullfighting hateful and ridiculous by closing down the universities and opening the School of Tauromachy in Seville.

"A plague on all tyrants, doctor!"

206

El Nacional thought of the political history of his country in terms of bullfighting, and just as he detested El Sombrerero and other matadors who had been supporters of the absolute monarchy, he was in favour of Juan León, who had proudly and defiantly appeared in the ring in a black fighting suit at this time, and had fearlessly faced the threats and anger of the crowd. Bullfighting was a thing of the past, El Nacional insisted, and an uncivilized profession; all the same its practitioners had their rights just like other men.

"And where do you get this idea of its being reactionary from?" the doctor asked. "You're a good fellow, Nacional, and wish no harm to any man; all the same you're an ignoramus."

"That's true enough," exclaimed Don José. "His wits have been completely fuddled by all the ranting and preaching that goes on in that committee of his."

"Bullfighting is a stage in our national progress," went on the doctor, smiling. "You understand, Sebastián? It belongs to our national customs, it's an improvement on the popular amusements of the old days in Spain—those days your Don Joselito is always telling you about."

And Ruiz talked on and on, with a glass of wine in one hand, only stopping to take a sip.

"All that about bullfighting being a thing of the past is absolutely untrue. They used to kill wild beasts in Spain long ago, for the amusement of the crowd, but bullfighting as we know it simply didn't exist. The Cid used to spear bulls, true enough; both Moors and Christians used to be seen in the arena; but there was no such thing as professional bullfighting, nor were the animals put to death in a dignified manner, according to rules."

And the doctor went on to outline the development of the national sport throughout the ages. Only on very rare occasions were such events as royal marriages, treaties of peace or the inauguration of a church or a cathedral celebrated with corridas. These fiestas obeyed no rules, and no professional toreros took part in them. Gentlemen riders entered the arena handsomely dressed in bright coloured silks, and attacked and killed bulls with spears before an audience of ladies. If the bull succeeded in dismounting them they drew their swords, and with the help of their servants in livery killed the animal as best they could, without rules of any sort. If it was a corrida for the common people, the crowd often surged into the arena and made a massed attack on the bull, until they managed to drag it down and finish it off with their knives.

"Those weren't bullfights," the doctor went on, "but cattle hunts. . . . Come to think of it people had other things to do, and other sorts of fiestas in those days; there was no need for them to perfect this special sport."

Spaniards of warlike temperaments could always find a means of advancement in one of the endless wars in various parts of Europe, or by sailing to America. Brave men were always in demand. In the name of religion too, there were exciting and dramatic spectacles allowing them to enjoy the thrill of seeing others face imminent death, while at the same time earning indulgences for their souls. *Autos-da-fé* and burning of men alive provided stronger meat for the spectators than such simple amusements with wild animals. The Inquisition became the great national fiesta.

"But then came the day when the Inquisition began to falter," said Ruiz with an ironical smile. "Nothing lasts for ever in this world. It died of old age, before the new laws came to suppress it. It had nothing more to live for; the world had entirely changed, and the fiestas it had sponsored were rather like a bullfight in Norway would be, under a grey sky and with frost on the ground. The atmosphere was no longer sympathetic to it. People began to feel ashamed of burning heretics, with all the business of sermons, ridiculous vestments, recantations and so on. They didn't dare hold *autos-da-fé* any more. When the Inquisition felt it necessary to give some signs of life, it made do with a few whippings behind closed doors. Just about the same time the Spaniards got tired of traipsing all over the world in search of adventures, and came home;

there were no more wars in Flanders or Italy; the conquest of America was complete. Now it was that the real art of bull-fighting began to develop; permanent bull-rings were built, cuadrillas of professional toreros formed, and the rules were drawn up, both for banderilleros and matadors, much as we know them today. The crowds liked this new sort of fiesta, and bullfighting became democratic and professional at one and the same time. Instead of gentlemen the performers were now working class men and gained their living by risking their lives; and the public who crowded into the amphitheatre were their lords and masters and could insult them with perfect freedom from the benches. The sons of those men who had watched heretics and Jews being fried to a cinder with intense religious enthusiasm, now took a noisy delight in seeing struggles between a man and a bull, which only very rarely ended in the death of the man. Don't you call that progress?"

Ruiz elaborated his theme. About the middle of the eighteenth century, when Spain had retired into her shell, abandoning colonization and wars in far off lands, when the cold cruelty of religious persecution had died out for lack of a soil in which it could thrive—that was the moment when bullfighting began to flourish. The courage of our race needed new paths of access to fame and fortune. The savagery of the crowds reared on the spectacle of violent death and torture needed a new escape valve. Bullfights took the place of *autos-da-fé*. A man who in past centuries would have been a soldier in Flanders or a colonist in the solitudes of the New World now became a torero. The Spanish race, finding all their previous avenues to fame closed, worked to make this new national fiesta a glorious outlet for men of ambition and courage.

"It was progress," said the doctor. "Surely that's obvious? That's why, although I'm a revolutionary through and through, I'm not ashamed of saying I enjoy going to bullfights. A man needs a spice of devilry to alleviate the monotony of life. Alcohol is bad for us too, we know that, but we nearly all drink it. A little savagery now and then renews one's energies.

We all enjoy turning the clock back occasionally and living like our remote ancestors. Indulging our brutality brings to life some mysterious force within us which it's not advisable to let die. Bullfights are uncivilized affairs you say? Certainly they are; but they're not the only uncivilized fiestas in the world. Going back to barbarian and violent pleasures is a disease every nation suffers from, and it makes me angry when foreigners talk as if Spain was the only country where such things happened."

And the doctor declaimed against horse-races, which caused the death of more men than bullfights did; against the hunting of rats by trained dogs in front of a smart audience: against all forms of modern sport which led to broken legs, fractured skulls and flattened noses; and against duelling, which was more often than not caused by an unhealthy craving for notoriety.

"These foreigners shed tears of sympathy for our bulls and horses," Ruiz went on, "but we hear no cries of grief from them when one of their own race-horses falls going at full gallop and breaks its legs. And they consider that every large town needs a zoological garden, where all the most dangerous and useless animals in the world are shut up and kept in princely comfort and warmth in the name of civilization. What's the point? Science knows all about them and has them thoroughly catalogued. If some people are revolted by the killing of bulls, why shouldn't the rest of us complain about the sinister tragedies which are going on all the time inside the cages of zoos? The terrified, bleating goat with her useless horns we see put into the panther's lair, to be leapt upon and devoured with a horrifying crunching of bones, while the savage brute buries its claws in its victim's entrails and its muzzle in its steaming blood. . . . The wretched rabbits taken from their peaceful sweet-smelling mountain pastures, to tremble with fear as they feel the breath of the boa constrictor advancing with hypnotic eyes fixed on them, to catch them in its coloured coils and crush them with its icy pressure. Hundreds of poor weak, useful animals have to die to provide food for the ferocious and completely useless brutes which are kept and cared for in some of the cities considering themselves most highly civilized; yet from these cities pours abuse of the barbarous Spaniards, because in our country brave, agile men face and kill a proud and terrible wild beast, according to strictly laid-down rules, under a blue sky, in front of a noisy many-coloured crowd—thus adding delight in beauty to the emotion caused by danger. Thank God it is so!

"They insult us because we don't count for much in the world today," said Ruiz, becoming indignant as he thought of this general injustice. "We're like monkeys; we imitate the behaviour and pleasures of anyone we feel to be superior to us. Because England rules the roost at present, horse-racing flourishes in both hemispheres, and people sit bored to death watching a few nags running round a track—the stupidest sight in the world. The trouble is that real bullfights began too late, when we were already past our best. If they had been as important in the days of Philip II as they are now, there would have been bull-rings all over Europe. Don't talk to me about foreigners! I admire them because they have revolutions, and we owe many of our beliefs to them; but when it's a question of bulls—good God! They'd better stop talking nonsense!"

The zealous doctor made no distinction in his blind fanaticism among all the nations of the earth which disapproved of the national sport; he dealt out his execration impartially.

After ten days in Seville, Doctor Ruiz returned to Madrid.

"You don't need me any more, my boy," he said to the sick man, "and I've a great deal to do. Don't do anything foolish. In two months you'll be strong and well. Perhaps you'll feel your leg a little, but you've got an iron constitution, and it'll mend in time."

Gallardo's restoration to health followed the course Doctor Ruiz had foretold. At the end of a month he began to use his leg a little, and was able to go out and sit in the patio, still weak and limping slightly, where his friends visited him.

During his illness, when his fever ran high and gloomy nightmares troubled him, a single thought was always present in the midst of his delirious wanderings. Had Doña Sol heard of his accident?

One day, while he was still confined to bed, he asked his manager about her, when they happened to be alone together.

"Good heavens, yes!" said Don José. "Of course she's been thinking of you. She sent me a wire from Nice asking how you were three days after the accident. No doubt she read it in the papers. They've all been writing about you, as if you were royalty."

The manager had replied to her telegram, but had heard nothing since.

Gallardo was satisfied by this piece of news for a few days, but then he returned to the subject with the persistence of an invalid who imagines that the world revolves round the state of his health. Had she written? Hadn't she inquired after him again? The manager tried to make reassuring excuses for Doña Sol's silence. The matador must remember that she was always on the move. She might be anywhere on earth at that very moment!

But the bullfighter was so obviously saddened to think himself forgotten that Don José was forced into pious lying. He had had a short letter from Doña Sol from Italy, he said, asking for news.

"Let me see it," the matador begged.

And when the manager pretended he had left it at home, Gallardo inplored him to bring it. "I should so much like to see her letter, and convince myself she's not forgotten me."

To avoid further complicated deceit, Don José thought of the idea of a correspondence which didn't pass through his hands. According to him, Doña Sol wrote to the Marqués on financial business, and at the end of every letter she asked how Gallardo was. There were other letters to a cousin, and these also contained inquiries after the torero.

Gallardo listened, apparently satisfied, but shaking his head with an expression of doubt. When was he going to see her again? Would he ever see her? Oh, what a capricious and extraordinary woman she was, disappearing suddenly like that without any apparent reason!

"What you must do is forget all about the female sex," the manager said, "and think about business matters instead. You're out of bed now, you're nearly well. How do you feel about it? Shall we start fighting again, or not? What do you say? You've got the rest of the winter to recuperate in. Shall we accept contracts, or do you want to give them up for this year?"

Gallardo raised his head proudly, as if something dishonourable were being proposed to him. Give up fighting? Let a whole year go by without appearing in the ring? What would his public say to such a desertion?

"Accept contracts, Don José. There's plenty of time between now and next spring for me to get perfectly strong again. I'll take any engagement that offers. You can sign me up for the Easter corrida. This leg will still take some mending, but by then it should be like steel, please God."

It was two months before the torero felt really strong again. He still limped very slightly, and his arms were not yet as limber as before; but he made light of these minor troubles, because he felt his physical vigour returning to him.

One day when he was alone in the conjugal bedroom—he had returned to it now from the sick-room—he stood in front of the looking-glass and squared up to his own image as if it had been a bull, crossing one arm over the other as if he held the sword and muleta. He made a thrust at the imaginary enemy. Up to the hilt! And he smiled as he thought how he would disappoint his enemies, who used to prophesy that his skill was sure to fall off after a bad goring.

He longed for the time when he could return to the ring, for the excitement of the clapping and cheering, almost as if he were a beginner again at the outset of his career; as if his goring had in some way given him a second lease of life.

He decided to complete his convalescence by spending the rest of the winter at La Rinconada with his family. His leg would be strengthened by long walks and hunting. He would superintend the farm work on horseback, go and see his herds of goats and pigs, visit the cowsheds and the mares out at pasture. Things weren't going well on the farm. Everything cost him more than it did other landlords, and his receipts were less. His estate had suffered from being the property of an open-handed bullfighter, accustomed to make enormous sums of money and unused to economies. The fact that he always spent part of the year travelling, together with all the confusion resulting from his accident, had not improved things.

His brother-in-law Antonio had taken over the farm for a while in a very dictatorial fashion and tried to put things straight, but all he had succeeded in doing was to disturb the routine of work and enrage the farm hands. It was lucky Gallardo could count on a secure income from bullfighting, and this inexhaustible supply should recoup the effects of bad management and extravagance, with something to spare.

Before leaving for La Rinconada, Señora Angustias wanted her son to go and kneel before the Virgin of Hope. It was in fulfilment of a vow she had made on that dreadful evening when she saw him lying on the stretcher, pale and motionless as a corpse. How many times she had knelt weeping before La Macarena, the beautiful Queen of Heaven with her long eyelashes and dusky cheeks, imploring her not to desert her poor Juanillo!

It became the occasion for a general fiesta.

The matador's mother got all the gardeners of the district to fill the church of San Gil with flowers, making pyramids of tall sprays on every altar, hanging garlands between the arches and bunches from the lamps.

The ceremony took place on a sunny morning. Although it was a working day, most of the people from the neighbouring suburbs crowded into the church; there were fat women with black eyes and short necks, bulging out of their black silk dresses and wearing white mantillas over their pale faces; workmen with freshly-shaved faces, wearing new suits, round hats and gold chains over their waistcoats. Beggars arrived in hordes, and stood in two rows outside the church door as if it was a wedding. The poor women of the district stood about in groups, with untidy hair and babies in their arms, impatiently waiting for Gallardo and his family to arrive.

A Mass was to be sung, with orchestral accompaniment—something quite out of the ordinary, like the operas performed at Easter in the theatre of San Fernando. Afterwards there would be a Te Deum of thanksgiving for the recovery of Señor Juan Gallardo.

The party arrived, and made their way through the crowd. First came the matador's mother and wife with friends and relations, walking with a rustling of stiff black silk skirts, and smiling under their mantillas. Then came Gallardo himself, followed by a large escort of friends and bullfighters, all dressed in light-coloured suits and wearing gold chains and flashing diamonds; their white felt hats set off the black dresses of the women.

Gallardo looked serious. He was a true believer. He didn't think often of God, and he automatically took His name in vain at moments of stress like most other men; but this was different: here he was going to return thanks to the most sacred Virgin of the Macarena, and his expression was reverent and repentant as he went into the church.

Everyone followed, except El Nacional, who left his wife and children to go in without him, and stayed outside in the little square.

"I'm a freethinker," he thought it necessary to explain to a group of friends. "I respect other people's beliefs, whatever they may be; but the one going on inside there is all . . . rubbish, to my way of thinking. I don't want to say anything against La Macarena, nor take away any of the credit they're giving her, but I'd like to know what you think would have happened if I'd not been there in time to take the bull away, when Juaniyo was on the ground?"

Through the open doors of the church floated the wail of stringed instruments and the voices of the choir blending in a sweet, sensuous melody, accompanied by whiffs of the scent of innumerable flowers and the smell of wax.

The bullfighters and aficionados waiting outside the church smoked cigar after cigar. Now and again one or two would go off to pass the time away at the nearby tavern.

When the matador's party came out the beggars scrambled and quarrelled over the handfuls of money he threw them. There was enough for everybody, for Gallardo was in a generous mood.

Señora Angustias was weeping, with her head on a friend's shoulder.

The maestro stood in the door of the church, smiling and radiant, arm in arm with his wife, who was trembling with emotion.

Tears of joy were gathering under her downcast lids Carmen felt she had just been married to him for the second time.

CHAPTER SEVEN

WHEN Holy Week came round Gallardo did something which gave his mother great pleasure.

In previous years the matador had walked in the procession sent out by the parish of San Lorenzo, as a devotee of Our Lord Jesus of Great Power, wearing a long black tunic and pointed hood with a mask which left only his eyes visible. This was the Brotherhood to which most of the aristocracy belonged, and the torero had joined it when he became rich and famous, deserting the popular Brotherhoods, whose devotions were generally accompanied by wild and drunken behaviour.

Gallardo used to speak with pride of the seriousness of his religious fraternity, which was as well-disciplined as an army. As the clock of San Lorenzo sounded the second stroke of two on the night of every Maundy Thursday, the church doors would open, and the crowd collected in the dark square outside could see the brilliantly-lit interior and the brethren drawn up ready to start the procession.

The silent, sombre figures, with no sign of life about them but their eyes shining through their masks, advanced slowly two by two, each holding a long wax candle and leaving a wide space between each pair for their long sweeping robes.

The impressionable Andalusian crowd watched this hooded train—of Nazarenes, as they were called—with deep interest; these mysterious masks might hide the faces of great noblemen, whose devotion and respect for tradition had induced them to join this procession, which would go on all night until dawn.

The Nazarenes were pledged to keep silent, and an escort of municipal guards used to walk beside them to protect them from annoyance. There were countless drunks among the crowds, who had begun to celebrate Christ's Passion by going from wine shop to wine shop on Wednesday night and were still at it on Saturday, by which time they had fallen down times without number in the narrow streets, and had often been taken in charge.

When the Brotherhood passed by in obligatory silence, these godless characters, whose last moral scruple had vanished in the fumes of alcohol, used to walk alongside them whispering the most atrocious insults against the disguised brethren and their families. The Nazarenes suffered in silence, accepting these outrages and offering them up as a sacrifice to Our Lord Jesus of Great Power. Their meekness often seemed to increase the audacity of these bluebottle flies, who buzzed all the louder in their ears, until at last perhaps a masked figure would reflect that although silence was obligatory action was not, and raising his candle would deal some vigorous blows with it, somewhat upsetting the pious restraint of the ceremony.

As the procession moved along, the men carrying the heavy platforms with their figures and lanterns, needed to rest from time to time. A soft hiss was the signal for the hooded marchers to stop and turn face to face, standing with their candles resting on their feet, and watching the crowd with eyes that gleamed mysteriously through their masks. These sinister, theatrical beings might have come straight from some *auto-da-fé*, and dark waves of incense and the reek of burning faggots seemed to emanate from them. A metalic lament from long copper trumpets tore through the silence. Above the pointed hoods floated the square pennons of the Brotherhood, made of black velvet fringed with gold, with the letters S.P.Q.R. embroidered on them as a reminder of the part played by the procurator of Judea in the condemnation of Christ.

The *paso*[1] of Our Lord Jesus of Great Power was a heavy platform made of wrought iron, with black velvet hangings which reached to the ground, completely hiding the twenty sweating and almost naked man who carried it. At each corner were groups of lanterns held by golden angels, and in the centre was the tragic figure of Jesus bowed beneath the cross, blood-stained from the crown of thorns, with cadaverous face and eyes full of tears, dressed in a full velvet tunic so richly embroidered with golden flowers that little of the stuff remained visible.

The appearance of the Lord of Great Power was always greeted with a sigh from hundreds of breasts.

"Father Jesus!" murmured the old women with their eyes hypnotically fixed upon the image. "Our Lord of Great Power! Do not forget us!"

When the paso and its hooded escort stopped in the middle of the square, the devotion of the Andalusian people found vent, as did all their emotions, in song; the crowd saluted the image with interminable laments and birdlike trills.

A girl who pushed her way to the front of the crowd was the first to break the silence with a *saeta*[2] to Jesus, sung in a childish voice of tremulous sweetness. There were three verses: to Our Lord of Great Power, to the beautifully sculptured figure, and to the sculptor Montañés whose creation it was.

[1] A large platform supporting life-sized figures carved in wood and magnificently dressed, representing the Virgin Mary, the Apostles or scenes from the Life of Jesus.
[2] A religious song, often improvised.

This saeta was like the first shot fired in a battle; it gave rise to an endless series of explosions. Hardly had the singer finished when another struck up, and another, and another, as if the square were a huge cage of lunatic birds, who awoke at the sound of the voice of one of their companions, and burst out singing all together in wildest confusion. The harsh deep voices of the men mingled their graver note with the roulades and trills of the women. All sang with their eyes fixed on the holy image, as if they stood alone before it, forgetful of the crowds around them, deaf to the voices of the rest, without faltering or losing themselves in the complicated musical embroidery of the saeta. The hooded brethren stood listening in silence, gazing at the figure of Jesus weeping under the weight of His burden and the pain of the thorns. Then the dignified leader of the procession, feeling that the pause had lasted long enough, would strike a silver bell on the front of the platform. "On again!" And Our Lord of Great Power swayed once or twice and then rose unsteadily, while the feet of the invisible porters began to move like tentacles along the ground.

Next would come the Virgin, Our Lady of the Greatest Sorrow; for every parish sent out two pasos, one of the Son of God and one of the Virgin. Her golden crown was surrounded by flickering candles under a velvet canopy. Her ample cloak hung over a sort of wooden crinoline which displayed the full gleaming, rich splendour of its heavy embroidery, on which a whole generation of patient workers had exercised their skill.

The Virgin too had her escort of hooded brethren carrying candles, whose reflected light flashed from the gold embroidery of her regal mantle, illuminating the surrounding darkness. Behind her, to the rolling of drums, walked a troop of women, their bodies in shadow but their faces showing red in the light of the tapers they carried. There were old women in mantillas walking barefoot; young girls wearing the white garments which were to have served them as shrouds; women who dragged themselves painfully along as if they carried with them some hidden and agonizing disease; a whole battalion from the ranks of suffering humanity, who had escaped from death through the favour of Our Lord of Great Power and His Blessed Mother, and were following their images in fulfilment of their vows.

The procession of the Brotherhoods made its way slowly through the streets, with many long pauses for the singing of canticles, and then entered the Cathedral, whose doors stood open all night long. The lines of tapers wound through the vast naves, making the huge columns emerge from the shadows, with their crimson velvet hangings trimmed with gold; but their light was not strong enough to dispel the blackness gathered in the vaulted roof above. Then they came out again from this tomb-like darkness, under the starlit sky, and at last the rising sun caught the procession as it made its way along the streets, extinguishing the light of the candles, and shining upon the gold of the vestments and the tears and sweat of the images.

Gallardo was a serious upholder of Our Lord of Great Power and His silent Brotherhood. People might laugh at some of the other pasos with their irreligious and unruly followers; but not at this one! Good heavens, no! He felt a thrill of emotion as he looked at the massive figure of Jesus, 'the finest piece of sculpture in the world', and at the hooded figures walking with such dignity behind Him. This was a Brotherhood of men of importance.

Nevertheless, this year the matador decided to abandon the Brotherhood of Our Lord of Great Power and join that of La Macarena, the Virgin of Hope.

This decision gave great pleasure to Señora Angustias. He owed it to the Virgin, who had saved him from this last accident. Besides, it gratified her feelings of solidarity with her humble neighbours.

"Everyone should stick to his own sort, Juanillo. Of course you have to go about with the gentry, I know that; but remember it's the poor people who really love you, and already they're beginning to think you look down on them."

The torero knew it all too well. The noisy proletarian

crowds who sat on the sunny side of the bull-ring were
beginning to show signs of hostility to him, thinking he had
forgotten them. They were critical of his fondness for rich,
important people and desertion of his first supporters.
Gallardo was ready to use every method of combating their
growing animosity; the applause of the public was necessary
to him and he would stoop to the most unscrupulous servility
to regain it. He informed the most influential members of the
Brotherhood of La Macarena that he would be taking part in
their procession this year. No need to tell the rest; it was an
act of devotion on his part, and he wanted it to remain a
secret.

However in a very few days the whole neighbourhood was
talking of nothing else. La Macarena would have a fine
procession this year! They were not interested in the rich
Brotherhood of Great Power, with its silent well-disciplined
followers, but only in their rivals across the river—the
disorderly people of Triana, who were so pleased with their
Virgin of Protection and Christ of the Blessed Death.

"La Macarena will be a sight worth seeing this year," said
the gossips, discussing the matador's decision. "Señora
Angustias wants to cover the paso in flowers. At least a
hundred duros' worth. And Juaniyo is to hang all his jewellery
on the Virgin—a fortune in diamonds!"

It was quite true. Gallardo collected together all his
jewellery, and his wife's as well, to decorate La Macarena.
She would wear some ear-rings of Carmen's, that the matador
had bought in Madrid with the proceeds of several corridas.
Round her neck would hang the torero's double gold chain,
with all his diamond rings and the studs he wore in the front of
his shirt suspended from it.

"Jesus! How smart our dark beauty will look!" said the
neighbours, speaking of their Virgin. "And Señor Juan is
paying for everything."

When he was questioned on the subject the matador smiled
modestly. He had always been deeply devoted to La Macarena.
She was the Virgin of the suburb where he had been born;

moreover his poor father had never failed to walk in her procession dressed as a Roman legionary. It was a privilege belonging to his family, and had things been different he himself would have put on the helmet and carried the lance like so many former Gallardos now mouldering underground.

He was flattered by this new popularity; he wanted everyone in the suburb to know that he was taking part in the procession, yet at the same time he dreaded the news spreading to the rest of the town. He believed in the Virgin, and he wished to insure his future safety by standing well with her; but he trembled at the thought of the mockery of his friends in the cafés and clubs of the Calle de las Sierpes.

"They'll make fun of me if they find out," he said. "After all, one must keep on the right side of people."

On the evening of Maundy Thursday he and Carmen went to the Cathedral to hear the Miserere. The only light in the huge building with its incredibly high Gothic arches came from a few wax candles fixed to the columns: barely enough for the crowd to find their way. The nobility and gentry were shut in behind the iron grilles of the side chapels, avoiding contact with the sweating crowds jostling each other in the nave.

In the blackness of the choir the lights for the singers and musicians shone like a constellation of rosy stars. The serene Italian melodies of the Miserere floated out into the awe-inspiring and mysterious darkness. It was a typically Andalusian Miserere, graceful and gay like the beating of a bird's wings, with arias like lovers' serenades and choruses like drinking-songs, conveying the joy of life in a country which is forgetful of death and revolts against the gloomy drama of the Passion.

When the last aria was over, and the voice of the tenor apostrophizing Jerusalem had faded away into the vaulted roof, the crowds began to disperse, eager to get back to the liveliness of the streets, which now presented the appearance of a theatre, with electric-lighting, rows of chairs on the pavements and wooden platforms in the squares.

Gallardo went home to put on his Nazarene dress. Señora Angustias had made ready his clothes with tender reminiscent care. This was the night when her poor dear husband used to put on his warrior's array, and go out with his lance over his shoulder, not to return till the following day, with his helmet dented and his tunic covered in dirt after visiting every wine shop in Seville with his brothers-in-arms!

The matador was as particular as a woman about his clothes and took as much care of his Nazarene costume as if it had been his fighting suit on a bullfight day. He put on silk stockings and patent leather shoes. Next came the white satin robe his mother had made for him, and over that a tall pointed hood of green velvet which fell over his face and shoulders like a mask and hung down to his knees like a chasuble. On one side of the breast was the coat of arms of the Brotherhood, embroidered in richly coloured and elaborate detail. He pulled on white gloves and took up a tall staff covered in green velvet with a silver knob, which was a sign of distinction in the Brotherhood.

It was after midnight when Gallardo made his way through the crowded streets to San Gil, wearing this elegant attire. The lights from wax candles, or thrown by the open doors of the wine shops, cast quivering reflections and shadows on the white walls of the houses, as if from a conflagration.

In the narrow street leading to the church, Gallardo came across the procession of the Jews (as they were called) a fierce-looking body of armed men who were marking time to the ceaseless beating of a drum, impatient to be off.

There were young lads and old men, all with their faces framed by the chin-strap of their helmets, wearing wine-coloured tunics, flesh-coloured cotton stockings and high sandals. At their belts they carried a Roman sword and over one shoulder, like a modern rifle-strap, was the cord supporting the lance. At the front of the column a Roman standard, with the senatorial inscription, was waving in time to the beating of the drum.

A magnificently dressed individual was swaggering along, sword in hand, in front of this army. Gallardo recognized him as he passed.

223

"Damn the fellow!" he said to himself, laughing under his mask. "He's going to have it all his own way tonight. I shan't cut any ice at all!"

He was a man known as Captain Chivo, a gypsy singer, who had arrived that very morning from Paris to take command of his troop of soldiers.

If he had failed in his duty he would have had to renounce the title of Captain which was to be seen on the Paris hoardings, when he danced and sang there with his daughters. These girls were charming little creatures, with enormous eyes and bright colouring, and their grace and fantastic agility turned everybody's heads. The eldest had run away with an immensely rich Russian prince, and for several days the Parisian papers spoke of the despair of a certain 'brave officer of the Spanish army', who was determined to avenge his honour by murder, and whom they even compared to Don Quixote. One of the theatres on the boulevards had even put on an operetta with the gypsy's elopement for its theme, and ballets of bull-fighters, choruses of friars and other scenes of faithful local colouring. In the end El Chivo made it up with his left-handed son-in-law in exchange for an indemnity, and went on dancing in Paris with the other girls in hopes of another Russian prince coming along. Many foreigners who thought they understood the ways of the world were left pensive by his rank as captain. "Ah, Spain. . . ! Such a decadent country! Officers in the army get no pay, and noblemen have to let their daughters exhibit themselves on the boards."

As Holy Week approached, Captain Chivo couldn't bear to stay away from Seville, and he said good-bye to his daughters in his severe, uncompromising way.

"Well, girls, I'm off. Be good and behave yourselves properly. My company's expecting me. What would they say if I left them in the lurch?"

And he travelled back from Paris to Seville, thinking with pride of his father and his ancestors, all of whom had been captains of the Jews of the Macarena, and of the new lustre he himself was going to give to the family reputation.

224

He had once won a prize of ten thousand pesetas in the national lottery, and spent the entire sum on a uniform worthy of his rank. The people of his suburb came hurrying to see the captain dressed in his corselet of burnished metal, his tunic with its gold embroideries and helmet with its cascade of white flowers, so brightly polished that the lights of the tapers were mirrored in it. He seemed to have the fantastic gorgeousness of a Red Indian. The women fingered his velvet tunic, admiring the border design, made up of nails, hammers, thorns—all the attributes of the Passion. His boots flashed as he walked, from the brilliance of the spangles and artificial jewellery which covered them. His brown face, darker still in contrast to the white plumes of the helmet, was framed by grey whiskers. His appearance could hardly be called military, as the Captain himself confessed; but he would soon be returning to Paris, and something must be conceded to art.

He turned his head with a proud gesture and fixed eagle eyes on the legionaries of his company.

"No one is to leave the ranks! We must have decency and discipline!"

And he issued his orders through his teeth in the same harsh and coarse voice which he used to encourage his daughters when they were dancing.

The company advanced at a slow regular marching pace, to the rhythmical beating of the drum. There were wine shops in every street, and in their doors stood cheerful citizens with their hats on the backs of their heads and their waistcoats unbuttoned, who had quite lost count of all the glasses they had drunk to drown the memory of Our Lord's martyrdom and death.

As soon as they saw the impressive figure of the Captain approaching from afar, they held up glasses of fragrant amber-coloured wine. The captain tried to hide his distress, turning away his eyes and holding himself still more stiffly inside his metal corselet. If only he hadn't been on duty!

Someone more enterprising than the rest crossed the road and pushed a glass under the cascade of feathers, hoping that the aroma would tempt him; but the incorruptible centurion drew back and raised his sword. Duty was duty. He was determined that this year should be different from others, when the company had fallen into disorder very soon after the start, staggering along quite out of time.

His progress through the streets of Seville became a *via dolorosa* for Captain Chivo. He was very hot in his armour; surely a drink of wine would not be the end of all discipline? So he accepted a glass, and then another, and in a short while his company had gaps in its ranks, and stragglers were being dropped at every tavern they passed.

The procession marched with traditional slowness, waiting for hours at every crossroads. There was no need to hurry. It was only midnight, and La Macarena would not return home till noon on the following day; it would be possible to get from Seville to Madrid in the time that was left for her journey round the streets.

At the head of the column was the paso of the Sentencing of Our Lord Jesus Christ, a platform covered with figures. Pilate was seated on a golden throne surrounded by soldiers in bright-coloured tunics and plumed helmets, guarding the sorrowful figure of Jesus about to go to His death, wearing a tunic of embroidered purple velvet and with three golden feathers—representing the three aspects of ₐHis divinity— radiating from His crown of thorns. But although this paso contained so many figures and was so richly ornamented, it did not attract much attention from the crowds, but was overshadowed by the one following it: the queen of the working class suburbs, the miraculous Virgin of Hope, La Macarena.

When this Virgin with her rosy cheeks and her long dark eyelashes left San Gil under a velvet canopy which swayed with every movement of the hidden porters, a deafening roar of acclamation went up from the crowd collected in the square outside. Ah, how beautiful she was, their beloved Virgin! And it was a beauty which never aged!

Her voluminous and splendid cloak, with its wide gold border embroidered to imitate the meshes of a net, fell down behind the paso like the tail of a gigantic peacock. Her glass eyes shone as if she responded to the shouts of the faithful with tears of emotion, and there was a brilliant glitter from the jewels which made a corselet over her velvet dress. There were hundreds of them, perhaps even thousands. It was as if she had been sprinkled with sparkling drops, each flashing with all the colours of the rainbow. Round her neck were strings of pearls, and golden chains threaded with dozens of rings, which shot out their magic fire as she moved. Her tunic and the front of her dress was covered in gold watches, diamond and emerald pendants, and rings with stones as big as pebbles. All had shown their devotion by sending their jewels to deck the most Sacred Macarena for the procession. Women went about with bare hands on this night of religious mourning, so that the Mother of God should wear the rings which were their proudest possessions. The crowds knew all her ornaments well, for they saw them every year, and were able to point out any that were new. Those which the Virgin wore on her breast, hanging from a gold chain, came from Gallardo the bull-fighter. But there were others which competed for the admiration of the public. Women gazed with interest at two enormous pearls and a string of rings. They belonged to a girl from the suburb who had gone to Madrid two years ago and now returned from the fiesta with an elderly cavalier. What a lucky girl!

Gallardo walked in front of the paso among the dignitaries of the Brotherhood, with his face masked and the staff of authority in his hand. Other hooded figures carried long trumpets hung with green pennons fringed with gold. Now and again they lifted the mouthpiece to the slits in their masks, and a sound of torment—a heart-breaking funereal fanfare— rent the air. But this terrifying blast roused no echo in the hearts of the crowd, nor did it make them think of death. From every little dark side alley were coming wafts of the spring night air, loaded with the scent of gardens, of orange blossom and the pot plants in every balcony and patio. The sky grew paler under the caress of the moon, floating over its feather-bed of clouds and peering down between the eaves of the houses. The melancholy procession seemed to be advancing against the current of Nature, and at every moment it lost something of its funeral solemnity. In vain did the trumpets utter their lament, the singers weep as they intoned their religious chants, and the soldiers march grimly on, frowning like executioners. The spring night was smiling, spreading the perfumed breath of a thousand flowers, and no one thought of death.

The people of the Macarena quarter swarmed around their Virgin. There were market gardeners from the outskirts with their dishevelled wives and a string of children who would follow the procession till dawn; young men in new felt hats, with their black curls smoothed over their ears, brandishing sticks as if someone might show disrespect to their beautiful Virgin and they would have to defend her. They all herded along together, flattening themselves between the huge paso and the street walls to get through the narrow alley-ways; all with their eyes fixed on the image, talking to her, paying compliments to her beauty and her miraculous power, with the carefree lightheartedness that came from wine and their own pleasure-loving temperatments.

"*Olé* La Macarena! . . . The most marvellous Virgin in the world!"

Every fifty paces the paso came to a halt. There was no hurry; there was a long journey ahead. Many people insisted that the Virgin should stop by their houses, so that they could admire her properly; and every wine-seller wanted a pause at the door of his shop, claiming his rights as an inhabitant of the district.

Perhaps a man would cross the road, and go up to the masked Brethren who walked in front of the paso:

"Hi! Stop a moment! Here's the best singer in the world, who wants to greet the Virgin with a saeta!"

Then the 'best singer in the world' would pass his glass of wine to someone else, advance towards the image supporting his unsteady legs by leaning on a friend, give a cough, and pour forth his harsh voice in a torrent of song, the words of which disappeared in a cascade of roulades. All that could be made out was that he was singing to the Mother of God, and as he uttered these words his voice trembled with that poetical emotion of the common man which is inspired by love of his mother.

Before the singer was halfway through his slow refrain, another voice had struck up, and soon another followed; it was as if the street were full of invisible birds engaged in a singing contest; some voices were hoarse and quavering, as though coming from shattered lungs; others piercing and strident, suggesting a purple-faced singer with a bursting throat. Most of the singers remained hidden among the crowd, their simple devotion having no need of exhibiting itself to view. Others, proud of their voice and style of singing, stood right in La Macarena's path.

A thin girl, dressed in a limp faded frock, and with hair thickly plastered in oil, crossed her hands over her hollow stomach, and fixing her eyes on the face of the Virgin, sang in a tiny thread of a voice about the misery of the Mother when she saw her Son bleeding from his crown of thorns and staggering under the weight of the cross.

A few steps further on, a bronzed young gypsy smelling of dirty clothes and disease, stood as if in an ecstasy with his hat in his hands; he too burst into song to the universal Mother ('Little Mother of my Soul', 'Little Mother of God',) while a group of friends listened with nods of admiration for the beauty of his style.

Meanwhile the drums went on beating behind the image and the trumpets uttered their plaintive cry, and hundreds of discordant voices mingled together without any singer ever losing his place in his song, each saeta beginning and ending without mishap. They might all have been deaf, their religious fervour cut them off so effectively from the outside world; their whole existence was concentrated in a voice of trembling adoration and eyes fixed on the image with hypnotic tenacity.

When the singing was over, the crowd broke out into

shouts and ribald cries, glorifying La Macarena in a new fashion. She was the most beautiful of all the Virgins; she was unique. Glasses of wine were passed around and the more excitable threw their hats before her as if she were a pretty girl. It wasn't possible to tell where religious fervour ended and the mood of pagan orgy began.

A young man dressed in a purple robe with a crown of thorns on his head was walking barefoot in front of the paso. He was bowed under the weight of a cross twice as large as himself; and when, after a long rest, he set off again, good-natured people helped him shoulder his burden again.

Women groaned sympathetically as he came by. Poor boy! He was carrying out his penance with such holy fervour. They all remembered the sacrilege he had committed. It had been drink as usual—the curse of mankind! Three years ago on the morning of Good Friday, when La Macarena was returning to her church after her long progress through the streets of Seville, this poor sinner who had spent the night carousing with his friends made the procession stop in front of a wine shop in the market-place. First he sang to the Virgin and then, carried away by enthusiasm, he burst out into compliments and flattery. Olé! How beautiful she was, La Macarena! He loved her more than he did his sweetheart! He wanted to demonstrate his devotion by throwing at her feet what he believed to be his hat, but unfortunately it was a glass he was holding in his hand, and it smashed to pieces on Our Lady's beautiful face. They took him off to prison in tears. He loved La Macarena as if she were his mother! It was all that damned wine, which had made him lose his senses! He trembled with fear as he thought of the years of imprisonment he must expect for desecrating a religious image, sobbed out his penitence, and in the end succeeded in impressing even the most indignant of his judges in his favour and was let off on promising to perform some extraordinary penance, as a warning to other sinners.

Gasping and sweating, he dragged along the cross, shifting the weight when his shoulders became bruised and painful under the burden. Women wept aloud, with the instinct for drama of the passionate southern temperament. His friends offered him glasses of wine, from no desire to mock at his penance but out of compassion. He was dropping with exhaustion, he was in sore need of refreshment.

But he turned his eyes away and looked up at the Virgin, seeming to ask her to bear witness to his martyrdom. He would drink as much as he wanted next day, without fear, when La Macarena was safe in her church again.

The paso was still in the La Feria district, while the head of the procession had already reached the centre of the town. The green-hooded Brotherhood and the Roman legionaries now advanced with circumspection, like an army marching to the attack. They wanted to occupy La Campana and so take possession of the entrance to the Calle de las Sierpes before any other Brotherhood arrived. Once the vanguard was master of this position, they could wait quietly until the Virgin caught up with them. Every year it was the Macarenos who took the lead in this famous street, and then passed slowly along it, enjoying the impatient protests of the Brotherhoods from other suburbs—a very inferior lot, whose images couldn't compare with the Virgin of La Macarena, and who were therefore obliged to wait humbly till she had passed.

Captain Chivo's company sounded the drums at the entrance to the Calle de la Campana at exactly the same moment that another Brotherhood, dressed in black hoods and masks, appeared from a different direction, equally anxious to be first in this street. There was a crowd of interested onlookers moving about between the heads of the two processions. A clash was inevitable! The black-hoods had no great respect for the Jews and their redoubtable Captain, who was maintaining an attitude of cold haughtiness. His company must not get involved in brawls. It was the Macarenos who fell upon the black Nazarenes, hitting them with sticks and candles in defence of the honour of their suburb. The police came running up and led away two young men, who were complaining loudly that they had lost their hats and sticks, and several Nazarenes without hoods were taken to the nearest chemist's shop, holding their heads with expressions of anguish.

Meanwhile, Captain Chivo had shrewdly carried out a tactical movement and occupied La Campana as far as the entrance to the Calle de las Sierpes, to the noisy and triumphant accompaniment of drums and the shouts of delight of his brave auxiliaries from the suburb. "No one can come through here! Long live the Virgin of La Macarena!"

The Calle de las Sierpes looked like an immensely long drawing-room. The balconies were full of people, electric lights were hanging from cables stretched across the street, and all the shops and cafés were brilliantly lit with rows of heads at every window. Hundreds of people were sitting on chairs along the pavements, and got up and stood on them whenever the distant sound of trumpet or drum announced the approach of a paso.

No one slept in Seville that night. Even old ladies of regular and cautious habits, who never left their lodgings, sat up to see the processions go by just before the dawn.

Although it was three o'clock in the morning there was nothing to show the lateness of the hour. People were eating in cafés and taverns. The succulent odour of frying-oil came from the doors of the fish shops. Sweets and drinks were being sold in the middle of the street. Whole families, who never made their appearance except on the most important holidays, had been waiting since two in the afternoon to see the processions pass; processions and more processions; splendidly dressed Virgins whose long veiled mantles drew cries of admiration from the crowd; Redeemers with golden crowns and brocaded vestments; a whole world of fantastic images, whose theatrical and magnificent garments contrasted strangely with their tragic faces, dripping with blood or tears.

The Sevillians sitting in front of the cafés pointed out the pasos by name to any foreigners who had come to see this extraordinary Christian festival with its pagan gaiety. No sad faces except those of the images were to be seen.

One after another came the pasos of the Holy Decree, the Blessed Christ of Silence, Our Lady of Bitterness, Jesus with the Cross on His shoulder, Our Lady of the Valley, Our Father Jesus of the Three Falls, Our Lady of Tears, Christ of the Blessed Death and Our Lady of the Three Necessities; and this procession of images was accompanied by escorts of Nazarenes dressed in black, white, red, green, blue and purple, all masked, and giving no sign of the mysterious individualities hidden under the tall pointed hoods, except the eyes which looked out through the slits in them.

The heavy platforms moved slowly and laboriously on through the narrow street; but when they came out into the Plaza de San Francisco, opposite the boxes which had been set up against the town hall, each paso gave a half turn so as to bring the images to the front, and the porters bowed their knees in salutation to the distinguished foreigners and royal personages who had come there to see the fiesta.

Boys carrying pitchers full of water walked beside the pasos. Whenever the catafalque halted a corner of the velvet hangings was raised, and twenty or thirty sweating men were seen, purple with fatigue, half naked, with handkerchiefs knotted round their heads, looking like exhausted savages. These were the Galicians, as all those porters engaged in specially heavy work were called whatever province they came from, as if men from the rest of Spain were not credited with any powers of endurance. They gulped the water thirstily, and if there happened to be a tavern near by they clamoured mutinously for wine. Obliged as they were to stay in their confinement for hours on end, they had to squat down when they wanted to eat or satisfy their other needs. Often when the holy paso moved on after a long pause, the crowd would burst out laughing to see what had been left behind in full view on the pavement, while the municipal cleaners hurried forward with their baskets.

All through the night that astonishingly gay, sumptuous and theatrical procession, with its stream of scaffolds covered with cadaverous-faced figures in brilliant clothes, wended its

233

way through the town. In vain did the trumpets blare their lament for the most dreadful of all injustices, the shameful execution of a God. There was no response from Nature to this traditional ceremony of mourning. The river still murmured under the bridges, and spread a sheet of silver between the fields; the orange trees—those incense-burners of the night-time—opened a thousand white orifices and filled the air with their voluptuous scent; the palm trees waved their tufts of plumes above the Moorish battlements of the Alcázar; the Giralda soared among the stars like a blue ghost, cutting out a piece of the sky with its slender minaret; and the moon's face smiled down (as if intoxicated by the perfumed darkness and swollen with the sap of spring) on the city with its brightly-lit, intersecting furrows, at the bottom of which people moved hither and thither like ants, glad to be alive, to drink and sing and take a death that happened centuries ago as the excuse for endless merry-making.

The cheerful crowds in the Calle de las Sierpes pressed forward eagerly or stood on their chairs, to see the pasos of La Macarena, as they advanced along the street headed by a band of musicians and escorted by a compact procession of the people of the suburb: men with shirts opened to the waist brandishing sticks and shouting; miserably-dressed, untidy women waving their arms; all excited to find themselves in the centre of Seville and being curiously looked at by the grandest and richest people of the town.

On this night of all nights, poor as they were, they could have their say; and as they approached the cafés full of wealthy people and the clubs where the nobility gathered together, they shouted:

"Here come the Macarenos! Come and see the finest Virgin in the world! Long live La Macarena!"

Some of the women were leaning heavily on their husbands, dropping with fatigue after three hours of walking in the procession.

"Let's go home!" one of them would say.

But the man staggering along beside her would reply in a voice thick with wine:

"Leave me alone, woman! I must sing another verse to La Macarena."

Then he would cough and put his hand to his throat, fix his eye on the image and burst out singing in a voice so hoarse that no one but himself could hear it, and which was anyway quickly lost in the confused hubbub of music, shouting and trumpet blasts. A hundred voices were singing at once, each in a different key and rhythm. Pale, sweating, ragged youths, looking as if their last hour had come, approached the paso leaning on the shoulders of their friends, chanting saetas in the voices of dying men. At the entrance to the street several Macarenos were lying stretched on the pavement, like corpses—the casualties of this glorious expedition.

El Nacional was standing with all his family at the door of a café to watch the Brotherhood pass. "It's all reactionary superstition!" Nevertheless he came every year to watch the noisy invasion of the Calle de las Sierpes by the Macarenos.

He recognized Gallardo immediately, from his fine figure and the style with which he wore his Inquisitorial vestments.

"Juaniyo! Make the paso stop! There are some foreign ladies here who want to see La Macarena!"

The platform halted, and the band struck up a lively march tune, such as delights the public at bullfights. The hidden porters at once began to lift first one leg then the other, in a strange dance which made the catafalque sway violently, nearly crushing some of the crowd against the walls. The Virgin and all her load of flowers, jewels and lights—even the heavy canopy—danced in time to the music. This was a performance which required some rehearsing, and of which the Macarenos were very proud. The young men who held on to both sides of the paso and followed its violent oscillations shouted proudly:

"Come and see, all of you! Everyone come and see! This is really worth seeing! Only the Macarenos can do this!"

When the music stopped and the paso stood still, a tremendous roar of irreligious, profane applause broke out, in praise of the Holy Macarena, the one and only, the best.

the most sacred of all Virgins ever known or possible to know.

So the Brotherhood's triumphal march went on, leaving stragglers in every street. They were at the opposite side of Seville, as far as possible from their own district, when the sun rose, sparkling on the Virgin's corselet of jewels and lighting up the lividly pale faces of her escort and of the Nazarenes, who had now taken off their masks. They looked like a dissolute rout returning from an orgy.

The two pasos were now abandoned in the middle of the street near the market-place, while all the marchers went to the nearest taverns for glasses of the local wine or aguardiente. The white skirts of the Brethren were covered in disgusting stains. Most of them had lost their gloves. A Nazarene was bending over at a corner, retching noisily in the attempt to relieve his overloaded stomach, his burnt-out taper in one hand and his hood in the other.

All that remained of the splendid company of Jews was a small band of stragglers, who looked as if they were returning from a defeat. Their captain walked sadly and unsteadily along, with his bedraggled plumes hanging over his ashen face, still trying to keep his magnificent costume from damage and dirt. The uniform must be respected at all costs!

Gallardo left the procession soon after sunrise. He felt he had done enough by escorting the Virgin all night long, and that she would give him the credit for it.

Besides, the last part of the proceedings was always the most trying. People who had been refreshed by several hours' sleep came out and made fun of the hooded brethren, who did indeed look absurd in the brilliant sunlight, with all the traces of the night's dirt and drunkenness still upon them. It wouldn't be advisable for the matador to be seen with this troop of inebriates.

Señora Angustias was waiting for him in the patio and helped him out of his Nazarene costume. He had paid his debt to the Virgin; now he must rest. There was to be a bullfight on Easter Sunday, the first since his accident. There was no respite in his hateful profession! After this peaceful interval his poor womenfolk were to be plunged in anxieties and dread once more.

The matador spent all Saturday and the morning of Sunday receiving visits from aficionados from other parts of Spain who were in Seville for Holy Week. All of them were smiling and full of confidence.

"We shall see how you are after your rest! It'll be fine to see you in the ring again. Have you got back all your strength, d'you think?"

Gallardo was confident in his own vigour. The months he had spent in the country had made him more robust, and he now felt as well as he had before the accident. The only trace that remained of the catastrophe was a slight feeling of weakness in the broken leg, but this was only noticeable after a long day on foot, shooting at the farm.

"I'll do my best," Gallardo murmured with false modesty. "I don't think I shall be too bad."

His manager interrupted on his usual note of blind confidence:

"You're as fresh as a daisy and you'll fight like an angel! You'll put the bulls in your pocket!"

Then the aficionados forgot about the corrida for a moment and began to talk of a piece of news which was all over the town.

Up in the mountains in the province of Córdova, the Civil Guards had come across a decomposed body with the head almost blown to pieces by a shot fired at point blank range. The face was unrecognizable; but from the clothes, the carbine and the rest they believed it was Plumitas.

Gallardo listened in silence. He hadn't seen Plumitas since the day of his accident; but he thought of him with friendly feelings. His farm labourers had told him that while his life was in danger the bandit had twice arrived at La Rinconada to ask for news of him. And when he had been at the farm himself with his family, his shepherds and workmen had several times taken him aside to tell him they had met

237

Plumitas out in the country and that he had sent messages of greeting to Señor Juan.

Poor fellow! Gallardo felt really sorry, and remembered the bandit's ominous predictions. It was not the Civil Guards who had killed him. He had probably been murdered in his sleep by one of his own sort—some envious rival.

The matador's departure for the bull-ring that Sunday was even more agonizing than usual. Carmen tried to keep calm and even came to watch Garabato dress his master. She smiled at him with a mournful smile, pretending to be cheerful, and fancying she noticed a similar anxiety and a similar attempt to disguise it in her husband. Señora Angustias hovered outside the room, waiting to see her Juanillo, as if it were for the last time.

When Gallardo went out into the patio with his montera on his head and his cloak over his shoulder, his mother flung her arms round his neck and burst into tears. She didn't utter a word, but her noisy sobs expressed her thoughts. This was the first time he had fought since his accident, and it was to be in the same ring! Her superstitious nature rebelled against such imprudence! Ay! When could he retire from his hated profession? Surely he had made enough money?

But the saddler intervened in his capacity of family adviser. There was nothing very terrible to make a fuss about. It was just a bullfight, like any other. The best thing they could do was to leave Juan in peace and not rattle him with this snivelling just as he was due to start for the ring.

Carmen was braver. She didn't cry, she went with her husband to the gate; she tried to encourage him. There had been a reflowering of their love as a result of the accident, and Juan and she now lived peacefully together in mutual devotion; she couldn't believe that any fresh disaster could come and disturb their happiness. She saw the hand of God in Juan's accident, which had been the means of bringing them together again. Now Juan was off to the ring, as he had gone so often before, and he would come home safe and sound.

"Good luck!"

With loving eyes she watched the carriage drive away, followed by a crowd of ragged little boys. But when she was alone, the poor woman went up to her room and lit candles before a statue of the Virgin of Hope.

El Nacional sat in the carriage beside the maestro frowning and sullen. It was the day of the elections, but of course none of the rest of the cuadrilla had taken the least notice of the fact. Everyone was talking of Plumitas' death or the afternoon's bullfight.

The banderillero had been with his fellow-members of the committee until after midday, helping 'to spread the light'. And now this confounded corrida would prevent his carrying out his duty as a good citizen, and taking several friends to the ballot-box who would certainly not vote at all if left to themselves! Only those who had 'seen the light' would register their votes; most of the town seemed ignorant of the very existence of the elections. There were large groups of people standing in the streets, deep in passionate discussion, but they were talking of nothing but bulls. What a country! El Nacional remembered with indignation the treacherous and violent actions of the other party. Don Joselito was in prison as a result of his political eloquence, and so were some of his friends. The banderillero would have liked to share their martyrdom, but instead he had felt obliged to put on his fighting suit and go off to the ring with his master. Was this assault on the liberty of the citizen to go unnoticed? Would nothing make the people rise?

As the carriage approached La Campana, the toreros saw a large gathering of people, waving sticks and shouting excitedly. The police were charging the crowd, sword in hand, and something very like a battle was in progress.

El Nacional stood up in his seat and seemed about to jump out of the carriage. Ah, at last! The moment had come!

"It's the revolution! It's begun!"

But the maestro pushed him down into his seat again, half smiling, half angry.

"Don't be an idiot, Sebastián. You see revolutions everywhere."

The rest of the cuadrilla guessed the truth, and laughed. Some heroic members of the public who had been unable to get seats for the bullfight in the office in la Campana were trying to take it by storm and set it on fire, and being held back by the police. El Nacional hung his head sadly.

"Ignorance and reaction everywhere! It's because they can't read and write!"

They arrived at the bull-ring. A tremendous ovation, frantic rounds of clapping and shouts, received the cuadrillas as they entered the arena. It was all for Gallardo. The public was welcoming his first reappearance after the appalling tossing which had set the whole of Spain talking.

When the moment arrived for Gallardo to kill his first bull, there was another burst of applause. Women in white mantillas were following his movements through opera-glasses from the boxes; people sitting in the sun cheered as loudly as those in the shade. Even his enemies were carried away in the general enthusiasm. Poor fellow! He'd had a shocking time of it! The whole amphitheatre was on his side to a man. Gallardo had never seen an audience which was so completely his own.

He stood before the president's box, montera in hand, to dedicate the bull. *Olé! Olé!* No one heard a word, but everyone was delighted. He must have said something splendid. And the applause followed him as he advanced towards the bull, fading away into expectant silence as he closed in upon it.

He unfolded his muleta, but standing at some distance from the animal, instead of firing the ardour of the audience by spreading it almost on its muzzle as in the past. A feeling of surprise was to be detected in the silent bull-ring; but no one said a word. Gallardo stamped on the ground several times to incite the bull to charge, which at last it did, rather half-heartedly, only just touching the muleta, when the torero drew back with noticeable haste. Many glances were exchanged among the audience. What did this mean?

El Nacional stood beside the matador, and another peon was a few steps further back; but this time there was no shout of "Out of the ring all of you!"

A muttering was beginning to be heard among the audience in the benches. People were discussing the situation; and the matador's friends were making excuses for their hero.

"He's not really well yet. He's not fit to fight. That leg of his! Did you notice?"

The two peons helped the matador pass the bull, with their cape-play. The beast was bewildered by this profusion of red cloths, and as soon as it charged the muleta it was distracted away by the activities of one of the other toreros.

Gallardo seemed to want to put an end to this disagreeable state of things and he squared up, with the sword held high, and threw himself on the bull.

A murmur of stupefaction greeted this move. The sword went in to about a third of its length, and stuck there quivering, as if about to fly out. Gallardo had come away from between the horns without plunging it in to the hilt, as he used to do.

"It was well placed, all the same," his supporters shouted, clapping as loudly as they could to make up for those who were silent.

The connoisseurs smiled pityingly. This boy seemed to have lost the only quality he had ever possessed: his courage, his reckless daring. They noticed the way he instinctively drew back his arm at the moment of striking; they saw him turn his head aside with the impulse of a man who fears to look danger in the face.

The sword fell to the ground, and Gallardo took another and again turned towards the bull with his peons behind him. El Nacional's cape was constantly spread, and he kept shouting to distract the animal and prevent it from approaching the matador too closely.

The second estocada was hardly more successful than the first, the sword only going in half way.

"He's not leaning on it," came protestingly from the benches. "He's afraid of the horns."

Gallardo stood in front of the bull with his arms wide open like a cross, so as to indicate to the audience behind him that the animal had had enough and would fall at any moment.

But the bull still remained on its feet, waving its head uneasily from side to side.

El Nacional managed to get it on the move again, and took the opportunity to hit it on the neck with his cape, using the full strength of his arms. The audience realized what he was up to, and and protested loudly. He hoped that the sword would work its way in further as the animal moved, and was also trying to drive it in deeper with blows from his cape. Abusive epithets were hurled at him from all sides; reflections on his mother and on the legitimacy of his birth; sticks were waved threateningly; oranges and bottles landed in the arena —but he put up with this hail of insults and missiles like a man who is both deaf and blind, and went on doggedly doing what he believed to be his duty, and trying to save his master.

Suddenly a stream of blood gushed from the bull's mouth, and its legs slowly doubled under it; but its head was still high as if it meant to get up and charge again. The puntillero advanced to finish the animal off and get the matador out of his predicament; while El Nacional leant surreptitiously on the sword and drove it in up to the hilt.

The people on the sunny side of the ring detected this manoeuvre and rose to their feet, shouting in a fury of rage: "Thief! Assassin!"

They were furious because the poor bull hadn't had a fair deal—as if it weren't doomed to die in any case; they seemed to think that El Nacional had just committed a crime under their very eyes, and waved their fists at him so angrily that he retired behind the barrier with a crestfallen expression.

Meanwhile Gallardo went to salute the president, and those few in whose eyes he could do no wrong applauded loudly.

"He had bad luck!" they said, their belief in him unaffected by what they had just seen. "And did you notice how well-placed his estocadas were? No one can deny that."

The matador went over to the seats where his most fervent admirers were sitting, and explained that it had been a very bad bull. Impossible to make a good job of it.

His supporters, led by Don José, eagerly backed up his

excuses, which were the same as those they had invented themselves.

Gallardo spent a large part of the corrida standing by the barrier. It was all very well making such explanations to his own friends, but a cruel doubt was gnawing at his mind, and he was assailed by a lack of confidence that was entirely new to him.

The bulls appeared larger than usual, and seemed to possess a reserve of vitality which made them difficult to kill; why didn't they fall under his sword-thrust with the same marvellous ease as before? They must have given him the worst of the herd on purpose. That was it; no question about it. Some plot on the part of his enemies.

Another suspicion was dawning in the dark confusion of his thoughts, but he hardly dared drag it to the light of day to examine it more closely. When he had sighted with the sword, his arm had seemed shorter than before. In the old days it would reach the bull's neck with the speed of a flash of lightning; now suddenly he was aware that his hand must traverse a long, terrifying space which he felt unable to bridge. His legs, too, did not behave as they used to. They seemed to possess an independent life of their own. He made an effort of will and ordered them to remain still and steady—but they did not obey him. They seemed to have eyes which saw their danger, and as soon as they felt the wind made by the bull's charge, they leapt aside with unnecessary speed, instead of firmly standing their ground.

Unable to accept his shame at his failure and weakness, Gallardo turned it against the public. What did they expect? Did they want him to be killed for their amusement? There were plenty of scars on his body to bear witness to his mad recklessness in the past. There was no need to prove his courage. He was only alive today because of the protection of God, and the prayers of his mother and his poor little wife. Nobody had looked so closely into the fleshless face of Death as he had done, and nobody knew the value of life better than he did. "They're not going to make a fool of me!" he thought, looking round at the audience.

He decided that from now on he would fight as most of his comrades did. Some days he would do well, other days badly. Bullfighting was only a profession after all, and once he had reached the first rank the important thing was to preserve his life, carrying out his commitments as well as possible. He was not going to let himself be gored just so that the crowd should praise his courage.

When the time came for him to kill his second bull, this train of thought had been succeeded by a state of calm courage. No bull was going to kill him! He would do his utmost not to get within reach of the horns.

As he advanced towards the animal he gave the same arrogant order to his peons as in the old days: "Out of the ring all of you!"

A murmur of satisfaction went through the crowd. He had said, "Out of the ring!" They were going to have one of his finest faenas.

But the public didn't get what they hoped for; nor could El Nacional be persuaded to desist from walking behind his master with his cape over his arm, for he was too astute and experienced a peon not to detect the theatrical falseness of the order.

Gallardo unfolded his muleta at an appreciable distance and passed the bull a number of times with obvious nervousness, never close to his body and always with the help of Sebastián's cape.

Once when he was standing still for a moment with the muleta trailing on the ground, the bull lowered its head as if to charge. The matador, tensely on the alert, was taken in by this movement and took several quick jumps backwards, though in fact the animal made no move to attack him.

This unnecessary retreat left him in a ridiculous position, which brought exclamations, laughter and whistling from the crowd.

"Hey! Look out! He'll catch you!" shouted an ironical voice.

"Cissy!" cried another, in an assumed feminine squeak.

Gallardo turned crimson with rage. To be talked to like

244

this! And in the Seville bull-ring! He felt his heart leap up with the courage of his early days, and a mad desire came over him to hurl himself blindly on the bull, and leave the rest to God. But his body refused to obey him. His arm seemed to be thinking; his legs saw the danger and mocked at the orders issued by his will.

However the audience reacted against these insults and came to his assistance by imposing silence. This was no way to treat a man who had only just recovered from a serious horn-wound. It was unworthy of the Seville bull-ring.

Gallardo took advantage of this wave of sympathy to get out of his difficulty as best he could. He approached the bull from the side and delivered a treacherous cross-thrust with the sword. The creature fell like a butchered ox, with a jet of blood gushing from its mouth. Some of the audience applauded, hardly knowing what they were doing, others whistled, but most of them sat in silence.

"They've given you nothing but impossibly tricky brutes this afternoon," cried his manager, ignoring the fact that they all came from the Marqués' herds. "They weren't real bulls! Wait till you have some brave animals worthy of you!"

As he left the ring Gallardo was aware of the silence of the crowd. Groups of people passed him by without a greeting or a cheer. Nor did the miserable collection of loiterers outside the gates follow his carriage as he left; they had heard about everything that had happened to the maestro in the ring before the corrida was over.

Gallardo tasted the bitterness of failure for the first time in his life. Even his banderilleros sat frowning and silent, like soldiers after a defeat. But when he got home and felt his mother's arms round his neck, and the embraces of Carmen, his sister and her children, the oppression on his spirits began to lift. Damn it all, the important thing was to live, to keep his family contented, and to make money out of the public as other bullfighters did, without going in for his old recklessness which must inevitably lead to death.

During the days that followed he made a point of showing

245

himself in public, and being seen talking to his friends in the cafés and clubs of the Calle de las Sierpes. His presence reduced people to polite silence and cut short any unkind criticism of his recent fiasco. He spent whole afternoons among the poorer aficionados whom he had neglected ever since he had become friends with the rich and great. Afterwards he would go to the Forty-Five, where his manager was shouting and thumping on tables to enforce his opinions and support the reputation of 'his matador'.

What an admirable man Don José was! Nothing could shake him; his enthusiasm was bomb-proof; it never even occurred to him that his hero could diminish in stature. Not a word of criticism or reproof for his failure; on the contrary, he had taken upon himself to make excuses for it, at the same time adding a little good advice.

"You're still feeling your wound a bit. As I tell people: 'Wait till he's completely well again; then you'll see something!' Just do as you used to. Go straight up to the bull with that God-given courage of yours, and plunge in the sword up to the hilt! Then you can put him in your pocket."

Gallardo listened, smiling enigmatically. Put the bulls in his pocket! He asked for nothing better. But they seemed to have become so large and so difficult to handle! They had been growing so enormously fast during the time he'd been away from the ring!

He consoled himself by gambling. It was the only way he could forget his troubles, and he returned again and again to the green baize table, to squander his money in the company of young men who were prepared to forgive him his failure because he was one of the few toreros who behaved like a gentleman.

One night these friends took him to dine at the inn at Eritaña, in a gay party with some foreign women they had got to know in the Parisian *demi-monde*, who had come to Seville for Holy Week and the Feria, and wanted to see everything that was Spanish and picturesque. Their beauty was fading, but they had done what they could to restore it by artifice and

246

elegance, and the rich young men found their exotic charms attractive, and pursued them in hopes of favours which were seldom refused. These women were excited at the idea of getting to know a famous bullfighter, and one of the handsomest too— that same Gallardo, whose portrait they had often admired on posters and matchboxes. After seeing him in the ring they had begged to be introduced to him.

The party took place in the large dining-room at Eritaña—a pavilion in the garden, decorated in the worst possible taste with vulgar imitations of the Moorish splendours of the Alhambra. It was a room where political banquets and wild parties were often held: where fiery speeches were made and toasts drunk to the regeneration of Spain, while attractive female bodies swayed to the rhythm of the tango, guitars thrummed, and from the dark corners came the sound of kisses, feminine shrieks and breaking bottles.

The three women received Gallardo like a demi-god; they forgot all about their other admirers and had eyes only for him, quarrelling for the right to sit beside him, and gazing at him with large acquisitive eyes. Their golden hair and smart clothes inevitably reminded him of his lost—his now almost forgotten love; and the voluptuous sophisticated perfume which emanated from them began to exercise a powerful charm. The presence of his friends from the club brought Doña Sol all the more vividly to his mind. They had all been friends of hers; some were even relations.

They fell upon the food and drink voraciously, abandoning themselves eagerly to excess, and longing to plunge headlong into the wild pleasures of drunkenness.

At the end of the room some gypsies were thrumming on their guitars and singing a melancholy song. One of the three women suddenly leapt on to the table, carried away by a novice's enthusiasm, and began slowly rolling her magnificent haunches in an attempt to imitate the national style of dancing, and also to show off what she had learnt in the course of a few lessons from a Sevillian master.

"Rotten! No good at all!" shouted the young men ironically,

at the same time encouraging her with rhythmical hand-clapping.

They thought her clumsiness ridiculous, but they looked with lustful eyes at her attractive body. Meanwhile she took their incomprehensible remarks for compliments, and went on rocking her hips to and fro, with her head high and her arms in the air like the two handles of an amphora, highly satisfied with her own skill.

By midnight they were all drunk. The women had lost all traces of modesty and were besieging the matador with their attentions. Gallardo was unresponsive to their caressing hands and the burning kisses pressed on his cheeks and neck. Intoxication had only plunged him in melancholy. Ah! if only someone else was here! Someone whose head was crowned with real gold! The tresses that were becoming loose and dishevelled beside him were coloured a synthetic yellow, and the hair itself was coarse and strong, made stiff by chemicals. The lips pressed to his tasted of scented grease. The feminine curves languishing at his side were hard as steel. His dazed imagination seemed to perceive a rank smell of vulgarity beneath all their sophisticated perfumes. Oh, if only that other someone were here!

It seemed to Gallardo's confused mind that he was following a winding path through a leafy garden under the silent stare of the stars, and that between the fronds of the trees he saw the windows of the dining-room like blazing mouths of Hell, crossed and re-crossed by the black shapes of fiends.

One of the women was tugging at his arm, and Gallardo let her pull him along, hardly looking at her, and with his thoughts very far away.

An hour later he returned to the dining-room. His companion was talking to her friends with bright hostile eyes, and her dishevelled hair hung round her face. They all burst out laughing, looking at the matador with expressions and gestures of contempt. Ah, Spain! It was a country of disillusion! Everything about it was fictitious—even the courage of its heroes!

Gallardo drank deeper and deeper. The women who had

248

been quarrelling over him before now turned their backs, and fell into the arms of the other men. The guitarists bent drowsily over their instruments, too drunk to play properly.

The bullfighter was dropping asleep on a bench when one of his friends offered him a lift to his home; he had to get home before his mother the Countess got up to hear Mass at dawn, as she did every day.

Even the night wind couldn't dispel the fumes of alcohol from Gallardo's brain, and when he found himself at the corner of his own street he staggered unsteadily towards his house. He stopped for a moment outside the gate, leaning his folded arms and his head against the wall, unable to bear the heavy weight of his own thoughts.

He had forgotten all about his friends from the Club, and the supper party at Eritaña with the three foreign women with painted faces, who had first quarrelled over him and then insulted him. There still floated in his mind some residue of his ever recurrent thoughts about the other fair-haired charmer. But even this memory soon dwindled and faded altogether. And then his mind took one of those strange sudden leaps which come with drunkenness, and he became obsessed with thoughts of the bull-ring.

He was the first matador in the world. So his manager and his friends said, and it was the truth. His enemies would have to recognize the fact when he next appeared in the ring. What had happened the other day was just carelessness and bad luck.

The wine he had drunk gave him a momentary feeling of omnipotence, and he saw all the bulls of Andalusia and Castile like poor feeble goats, ready to fall over at a single blow of his hand.

No; what had happened the other day was nothing. "Rubbish!" as El Nacional would say. "Even the best singer's voice cracks sometimes."

And the recollection of this aphorism (which was often on the lips of the old wiseacres of his profession after disasters in the ring) gave him a sudden desire to fill the silent street with the sound of his own voice.

With his head still pillowed on his arms he began softly singing a verse of his own invention, in outrageous praise of his skill. "I am Juan Gallardo. . . . And I have more courage than God." As he could think of nothing better, he repeated these words over and over in a hoarse monotonous drone, which disturbed the silent street and set an invisible dog barking.

It was an inheritance from his father; he was reproducing afresh the shoemaker's mania for singing when he returned from his weekly drinking bouts.

The front door opened, and Garabato's head appeared, sleepily investigating the identity of the drunken man, whose voice he thought he recognized.

"Oh, it's you?" said the matador. "Wait while I sing you the last verse."

And he repeated his unfinished masterpiece several times over, until at last it seemed to him time to go indoors.

He had no desire to go to bed. Dimly aware of his condition, he put off the moment of going upstairs to the bedroom where Carmen was waiting for him, very likely still awake.

"You go to bed, Garabato. I've a lot of things to do."

He had no idea what they were; but he felt drawn to his study, with all its confident-looking portraits, rosettes taken from bulls and posters proclaiming his fame.

He switched on the electric light and stood swaying unsteadily in the middle of the room, surveying the walls with amazement, as if he had never seen this museum of his past triumphs before.

"Splendid!" he murmured. "Yes—really splendid! That handsome young man is me . . . and so is that one . . . all of them! Yet people say—damn them! I'm 'the best of them all'; Don José says so, and he's right."

He threw his hat on to the sofa, as if it were a triumphal crown too heavy to be worn with comfort, and staggered over to lean with both hands on his writing-table, fixing his gaze on the enormous bull's head which hung on the opposite wall.

"Hullo there! Good evening old boy! What are you doing up there?"

He began idiotically imitating the lowing and bellowing of bulls out at pasture or in the ring. He couldn't remember why the great hairy head with its threatening horns was hanging on his wall; he had no recollection of having seen it before. Then gradually his memory filled in the blank.

"Ah! I know you now, you rascal! I remember how angry you made me that day. People whistled at me and threw bottles. They even insulted my poor mother! And you didn't care, did you? You were enjoying yourself, weren't you? Eh?"

He was so drunk that he thought he saw a quiver of amusement pass over the varnished muzzle and light up the glass eyes. He even believed the great head moved, nodding its assent to his question.

Up till now he had been smiling and genial, but suddenly he felt his anger surge up, as he remembered that frightful afternoon. So the brute was still amused at the thought of its triumph? It was bulls like this, malignant and wily—seeming to mock their opponents—who were responsible for a brave man being insulted and made fun of. Good God, how he hated them! He looked with detestation at the great head with its glass eyes.

"Are you still laughing, you son of a bitch? Damnation take you! Damn the cow who bore you and the master who put you to pasture on his land! He ought to be in prison. Are you still laughing? Still making grimaces at me?"

He leant over the table, in a drunken passion of rage, opening and shutting drawers. Then he stood up and raised his hand towards the bull's head.

Bang! Bang! Two revolver shots.

One of the glass eyes was shattered, and in the bull's forehead was a round black hole surrounded by singed hair.[1]

[1] This anecdote is said to have been true of Frascuelo.

CHAPTER EIGHT

In the middle of the spring there was a sudden drop in the temperature of Madrid—one of those freakish manifestations so typical of its unreliable climate.

It became bitterly cold. Torrential rain, sometimes mixed with snow, poured from a grey sky, and people who had been wearing their thin clothes began searching in cupboards and chests for wraps and overcoats. The white summer hats of the men looked dark and shapeless under the rain.

For two weeks there had been no corridas in the Madrid bull-ring. Sunday's fight had been postponed until the first fine week-day. This enforced inactivity put the manager and employees of the ring in a very bad temper, and they gazed up at the sky as anxiously as farmers worrying about their harvests. A patch of blue, or the appearance of a few stars at midnight when they were leaving the cafés, immediately raised their spirits.

"The weather's lifting. We shall have a corrida the day after tomorrow."

But the clouds joined up again, rain went on falling from the leaden, louring sky, and the aficionados raged against the climate, which seemed to have declared war on their national sport. What a wretched country! Even bullfighting was becoming impossible in it.

Gallardo was obliged to take a fortnight's rest. His cuadrilla complained of their inactivity. In any other town they would have accepted the delay with resignation, for the matador paid their hotel expenses everywhere except in Madrid, according to a precedent established some time ago by maestros who lived near the capital. The supposition was that every torero must have his abode there, and the poor peons and picadors, who put up in a lodging-house kept by a banderillero's widow, had to eke out their resources by means of all sorts of economies, smoking hardly at all and keeping out of cafés. They thought longingly of their homes and families. They only received a handful of duros for risking their lives, and by the time the two corridas had been held their earnings would all have been spent.

The matador's spirits were as low as theirs, but it was his bad luck, not the weather, which depressed him.

His first corrida in Madrid had been deplorable. The public had completely changed towards him. There were still some whose faith in him was unshaken and who hurried to his defence, but not with the noisy and aggressive enthusiasm of a year ago. They now seemed dejected, and when they found a chance to applaud him they did so timidly. His enemies, on the other hand, and most of the public (who hankered for the sight of danger and death) had become horribly unfair to him. How ready they were to shout insults at him! What was permissible to other matadors was unforgivable in him.

Because they had seen him in the past hurl himself blindly into danger, they expected him to go on doing so until death cut short his career. In the old days when he was building up his reputation his behaviour had been suicidal, but he had been lucky; and the audience had no patience with his present caution. Whenever he showed respect for his own safety insults were hurled at him. As soon as he spread his muleta, standing at some distance from the bull, protests broke forth. Why didn't he go closer? He was afraid! And he had only to take one step backwards for the crowds in the cheap seats to start shouting abuse at him.

The news of what had happened in the Easter corrida at Seville seemed to have travelled all over Spain. His enemies took their revenge for the long years they had spent envying him. Rival toreros, who had often been driven to take risks out of a desire to emulate him, now spread the news of Gallardo's decline with hypocritical expressions of pity. He had lost his courage. That last horn-wound had made him over-cautious. And the audience were influenced by these rumours, so that as soon as he came into the ring they watched him expecting to find everything he did bad, just as they had formerly applauded even his faults.

The natural fickleness of crowds had much to do with this change of attitude. People had had enough of admiring Gallardo's courage, and now they were enjoying his timidity and caution—as if by doing so they became braver themselves.

They would never believe that he kept close enough to the bull. He should come nearer in! And when he made a tremendous effort of will and forced his body to obey him and not shrink back from danger, with the result that he killed a bull in his old style, the applause was not as loud as it should have been. It was as if the electric current which had formerly flowed between him and his public had now been cut. His meagre successes only made them pester him with advice and criticism. "That's the way to kill! Why don't you always do it like that, you old fraud?"

His faithful band of supporters accepted his failures, but made excuses for him, harking back to his dazzling exploits in the past.

"He's got a bit careless," they said. "He's tired. But he can do it when he wants to, all right!"

Gallardo was only too eager to regain the favour of the public, but his successes were usually the result of luck or a combination of circumstances; the sudden spurt of courage of the good old days now visited him very rarely.

He had already been whistled at in several provincial bull-rings. The people in the sunny seats mocked him by jingling cow-bells or hooting on horns whenever he was slow to kill a bull, or thrust the sword only half-way in without bringing the animal to its knees.

In Madrid the audience "waited to pounce on him" as he described it. As soon as the onlookers at the first corrida saw him pass the bull with the muleta and come in to kill, a hullabaloo broke out. The 'boy from Seville' was not the same as he used to be! This was not their Gallardo. He was quite different. He shortened his arm, turned away his face, and ran away from the bull's horns like a hare, instead of calmly waiting for it to charge. There had been a catastrophic decline in his courage and ability.

That first corrida was a fiasco for Gallardo which was much discussed when the aficionados met together afterwards. The old men, who thought everything new was bad, deplored the feebleness of modern toreros. They began their careers with mad recklessness, but as soon as they felt the touch of a horn on their flesh . . . they were done for!

Compelled to rest by the bad weather, Gallardo waited impatiently for the second corrida, when he fully intended to do great things. His enemies' mockery had opened a wound in his *amour-propre* which caused him great pain. If he returned to the provinces with the stigma of a failure in Madrid he was a lost man. He must somehow or other get the better of his nerves, and master the obsession which made him shrink from the bulls and see them as larger and more terrifying than they really were. He believed he had it in him to achieve the same successes as in the past. There was still a trifling weakness in his arm and leg, but that would soon pass.

His manager suggested a very profitable contract to fight in bull-rings in America. No, he was not ready to cross the Atlantic yet. First he must show Spain that he hadn't lost his skill as a matador. There would be time to think of such a journey afterwards.

With the anxiety of every popular hero who feels his prestige is in danger, Gallardo frequented all the places where aficionados gathered. He went into the Café Inglés, the special haunt of supporters of Andalusian toreros, hoping to bring their relentless criticism to a halt; and he opened the subject of his performance himself, smiling with a humility that disarmed the most intransigent:

"Of course I didn't do well; I know that. But wait till the next corrida, when the weather clears. I promise you I'll do my best."

He hadn't the courage to enter the cafés where the poorer aficionados congregated, in the Puerta del Sol. These men were hostile to Andalusian toreros; they were Madrileños through and through, and bitterly resented the fact that all the matadors came from Córdova and Seville, and there was not a single representative of the capital. The memory of Frascuelo, who had been a son of Madrid, was cherished among them like some sort of patron saint. There were some who hadn't been to the bull-ring for years—not since El Negro retired in fact. What was the point? They read the newspaper reports and remained convinced that there had been no real bulls nor real toreros since Frascuelo died. Just Andalusian boys, that was all, cutting capers like ballet dancers, but without any notion of how to stand and 'receive' a bull.

Every now and then there had been a rumour which revived their hopes. Madrid was going to have its own matador again. A novillero had just been discovered in the suburbs, who had covered himself with glory in the bull-rings of Vallecas and Tetuán, and was now to be seen in the cheap Sunday corridas in the capital. For a while his name was on everyone's lips. In the barber's shops in the working-class districts people talked enthusiastically about him, prophesying great triumphs. The hero himself was to be seen in all the wine shops, collecting new supporters. He was backed by the poor aficionados, who couldn't afford a ticket for the important bullfights and had to wait for the evening papers to discuss events they had not seen.

"We can spot a future star; that's more than the rich do," they said proudly.

But time passed and their prophecies didn't come true. Perhaps their hero fell a victim to a fatal horn-wound, and his death was noticed by a bare four lines in the newspapers; or else he got a bad tossing and disappeared from view among the wearers of pigtails who hung around the Puerta del Sol, waiting for imaginary contracts. Then the aficionados turned their attention to other beginners, always passionately hoping for a matador who would be the glory of Madrid.

Gallardo didn't dare go near these proletarian enthusiasts; they had always hated him and were now rejoicing in his fall from favour. Few of them even went to see him in the ring. They thought little of all the toreros of the day and were waiting for their expected Messiah.

In the evenings he used to wander through the Puerta del Sol and the Calle de Sevilla, and get into conversation with the stragglers of the bullfighting profession who were to be found there, collected in groups, boasting of their past exploits, and grumbling enviously about the success of others.

They addressed Gallardo as 'Maestro' or 'Señor Juan', and though they often had a half-starved appearance and produced elaborate reasons why he should lend them a few pesetas, they were flamboyantly dressed, wore clean linen and a surprising quantity of cheap imitation jewellery, and put on a bold front, as if they had had their fill of worldly pleasures.

Some were honest enough young men, who were trying to make a career as bullfighters so as to support their families on something better than a workman's wage. Other less scrupulous characters lived on the immoral earnings of women who were ready to sacrifice their bodies to buy food and clothes for a handsome young man who would one day be famous, if what he said was to be believed. They spent their days swaggering about in the centre of the town, talking of contracts which they had refused, and watching each other to see which of them was sufficiently in funds to treat the rest. When one of them had a stroke of luck and was engaged to fight in a novillada somewhere in the provinces, he first had to redeem his fighting suit from the pawnbroker's. It would be an ancient garment which had belonged to various heroes of the past, with its gold embroidery dull and tarnished, and the silk full of mends and tears from glorious wounds, and covered with yellow stains—the undignified traces of fear.

Amongst this bullfighting rabble, embittered by failure and kept in obscurity by their own fear or stupidity, there were a few men of stature, who were treated with general respect. A man who had run from the bulls might still be feared for his skill with his knife. Another had been in prison for killing a man with his fists. Then there was Tragasombreros[1] who had been famous ever since he had eaten a Córdovan hat, cut in pieces and fried, washed down with wine in a tavern in Vallecas.

[1]Literally 'hat-eater'.

One or two smooth customers, always decently dressed and clean-shaven, used to attach themselves to Gallardo, and walk along beside him in the hopes of being invited to dinner.

"I'm all right, Maestro," said one pleasant-looking fellow. "I don't get many contracts, times are bad; but I've always got my patron—the Marqués, you know."

And as Gallardo smiled enigmatically, he searched for something in his pocket.

"He thinks a lot of me. Look at this cigarette case he brought me from Paris!" And he proudly displayed a small metal box with the lid decorated with naked cupids in enamel and an amorous inscription.

Other handsome, arrogant young men, whose bold eyes seemed full of pride in their own virility, entertained the matador with stories of their adventures. On sunny mornings they used to go out to La Castellana at the hour when the governesses employed by grand families were taking their charges for a walk. There were English misses and German fräuleins, who had recently arrived in Madrid with their heads full of fantastic ideas about this romantic country; and as soon as they set eyes on a good-looking young man with a clean-shaven face and a broad-brimmed hat, they were sure he must be a bullfighter. A bullfighter for a sweetheart!

"Those girls are as dull and stupid as bread without salt, you know, Maestro. Big feet, hair like straw; but they've got the goods all right. Oh yes! I'll say they have. A chap has only got to say something nice and they're all smiles and showing their white teeth and opening their big eyes. They don't talk like Christians but they understand all right when you make a sign that it's a question of the cash—and as I'm a man, and strong and healthy (thank God), they give me enough to buy tobacco and the rest of it. So I don't do so badly. I've got three of them on hand at the moment." And he swelled with pride as he boasted of the way his inexhaustible virility attracted the governesses' savings.

Others concentrated on the foreign singers and dancers who arrived at Madrid music-halls, anxious to start straight away enjoying the delights of having a bullfighter for a lover. There were vivacious Frenchwomen with little pointed noses and flat chests, so ethereal and thin that there hardly seemed to be anything tangible between their curly heads and their rustling, scented petticoats; solid Germans, as blonde and magnificent as Valkyries; Italians with oiled black hair, olive skins and tragic eyes.

The young men laughed as they remembered their first *tête-à-têtes* with these devoted female admirers. The girls always seemed afraid of being tricked, as if they were disconcerted to find that this mythical hero behaved like an ordinary man. Was he really and truly a bullfighter? And they looked for his pigtail, smiling with pleasure at their own sharpness when they took this identifying ornament in their hands.

"You don't know what those women are like, Maestro. You'd be surprised. They want to spend the whole night kissing, as if there was nothing better to do. And such fancies as they have! A fellow has to jump out of bed in the middle of the night and show them how he fights bulls with a chair, and the sheet for a cape. Then, because they're used to going all over the world getting presents out of any chap who comes near them, they start begging and wheedling in their crazy lingo (which even God can't understand): 'Please give me one of your capes, all trimmed with gold, to wear when I'm dancing!' Did you ever hear anything like it, Maestro? As if a man bought a cape like a newspaper! As if he had dozens of them!"

Yes, she should have a cape. Of course all toreros were rich. And while the splendid present was on the way, the relationship would become more intimate; the bullfighter would beg small loans of his sweetheart—if she had no money some jewellery would do; and as he gained her confidence he might start laying hands on anything he found within reach; and when she showed signs of emerging from her amorous dream and protested against such liberties, the young man would show the violence of his passion and act up to his character of mythical hero by giving her a beating.

Gallardo was delighted with this story, especially when it reached this point.

"You did, did you? Fine!" he said with savage satisfaction. "That's the way to treat those girls. You understand them all right. They'll love you all the more. It's the worst thing that can happen to a man to get mixed up with some of those women. You have to make them respect you."

He openly admired the complete unscrupulousness of these young men, who made a living by using the romantic illusions of foreign women to hold them to ransom.

He had other distractions besides his conversations with these shady characters. There was a Galician innkeeper from Las Ventas, a powerfully built man with a short neck and a high colour, who had made a small fortune from the soldiers and servants who went to dance at his tavern on Sundays; he was an admirer of Gallardo's, and importuned him with persistent requests.

He had only one son, an undersized, weakly youth whom his father had destined to be a famous bullfighter, as a result of his admiration for Gallardo and other matadors.

"That boy's got it in him," he said. "I understand these matters, you know, Señor Juan. I'm quite ready to spend a bit of money to give him a start but if he's to get on he must have a patron, and there couldn't be a better man than yourself. If you could only arrange a novillada for the boy! People would go in hundreds, and I'd stand all the expenses."

The readiness with which he let himself in for 'standing all the expenses', so as to help his son in his career, had already caused the innkeeper heavy losses. But he persisted, encouraged by his commercial instincts, which made him hope for a rich financial reward when his son had become a successful matador.

The poor young man, who had been interested in bull-fighting in his early years like any other small boy of his class, now found himself driven along by the eager enthusiasm of his father, who seriously believed in his vocation and was always discovering new signs of his aptitude in him. The boy's

260

diffidence was taken for laziness, his timidity for lack of ambition. A cloud of parasites—low-class aficionados and obscure toreros with nothing left of their profession but their pigtails—clustered round the innkeeper, drinking at his expense, and begging small loans in return for their advice; and they joined him in his project of introducing this unknown bull-fighting star from Las Ventas to the public.

Without consulting his son, the innkeeper had arranged for corridas in the Tetuán and Vallecas bull-rings, 'standing all the expenses' himself. Anyone who wanted to be trampled or gored by a bull in front of several hundred spectators could do so in these two suburban arenas. But the pleasure couldn't be had for nothing. He had to put up the money to cover the value of all the seats and arrange for the distribution of tickets, in order to have the satisfaction of being rolled in the sand with his breeches torn to ribbons and covered in blood and dung.

The optimistic father filled all the seats with his personal friends and poor aficionados, and paid a handsome fee to the members of his son's cuadrilla, the peons and banderilleros he had selected from those to be found hanging round the Puerta del Sol. They were to wear ordinary clothes, while the matador was to be resplendent in a fighting suit. Nothing was too much trouble to give the boy a good start!

"He's got a brand new fighting suit, made by the best tailor, who dresses Gallardo and the other matadors. It cost me seven thousand *reals!*[1] He ought to look his best in that, it seems to me! I'm determined to spend my last peseta if necessary, on the boy's career. There aren't many toreros with a father like me!"

During the corrida the innkeeper stood between the barriers to encourage the young matador by his presence, and also by waving a large stick. Whenever the boy came over to the barrier for a rest, the fat red face of his father and the knob of his thick stick confronted him like some horrifying apparition.

"I didn't spend all my money for this sort of thing, my lad—

[1] A quarter of a peseta.

to see you carrying on like a young lady. Go on out and get along with it! Good God, if only I was your age and not so stout and heavy. . . ."

When the boy stood before the bull holding the sword and muleta, his face ashen and his legs trembling beneath him, his father followed his every movement from behind the barrier, ready to come down on him like a captious schoolmaster if he made the slightest mistake in his lesson.

What the poor matador was dreading most, as he stood there in his red silk suit embroidered in gold, was the return home that evening and having to face his father's disapproval.

Wrapped in his magnificent cloak, so as to hide the pieces of shirt protruding through the rents in his breeches, he entered the inn that night, aching all over from the rolling and trampling the young bulls had given him. His mother, a large ugly woman, hurried anxiously forward with arms outstretched.

"Here's your duffer of a son back again!" roared the innkeeper. "He's made a proper fool of himself. All my money wasted!"

He raised his terrible stick threateningly, and the young man dressed in silk and gold, who had just managed to assassinate two small bulls, tried to make his escape hiding his face behind his arm, while his mother got between the two of them.

"But can't you see the poor boy's been wounded?"

"Wounded!" his father cried bitterly, regretting that it was not the truth. "Only real toreros get wounded! Put a few stitches in his breeches and see they're washed. They'll need it."

But a few days later the innkeeper had recovered his optimism. Everybody had a bad day now and again. He had seen famous matadors do no better than his son. There must be no looking back now! And he organized corridas in the bull-rings of Toledo and Guadalajara, with some of his friends as impresarios, but 'standing all the expenses' himself as usual.

The boy's novillada in the Madrid bull-ring had been one of the best ever seen, according to the innkeeper. By a lucky chance he had succeeded in killing two young bulls moderately well, and was applauded by the audience, who had most of them been given free seats.

As he came out of the arena the young man was met by his father, at the head of a noisy bunch of street-arabs. He had collected any he could find hanging round the bull-ring and had managed to smuggle them in through the gates. Always methodical in his dealings, he had offered them fifty centimos each if they would shout at the top of their voices: "Long live El Manitas!" and carry the successful novillero on their shoulders out of the ring.

El Manitas, still somewhat shaken from the dangers he had been through, found himself surrounded, pushed, and finally raised aloft by this noisy gang; and in this manner he was carried in triumph from the bull-ring to Las Ventas by way of the Calle de Alcalá, followed by surprised and curious glances from the people on the trams, whose way was ruthlessly barred by this glorious procession. The matador's father walked along with his stick under his arm, delighted, but pretending all this excitement had nothing to do with him; however, whenever the shouting grew less, he hurried to the front determined to get his money's worth, and throwing caution to the winds started it up again with: "Long live El Manitas!"

All this had happened months ago, but the innkeeper still remembered it with emotion.

"They brought him home on their shoulders, Señor Juan, just as they have so often brought you, if you'll forgive the comparison. So you see there's good stuff in the boy. All he needs is a bit of a push. Now, if only you could give him a hand...."

To quiet the innkeeper Gallardo made some vague promises. Perhaps he could do something for the boy. They could settle it later on; there was plenty of time before the winter.

One evening, as it was getting dark, the matador was just turning into the Calle de Alcalá from the Puerta del Sol, when he started back in surprise. A fair-haired lady was getting out of a carriage at the door of the Hotel de París.

It was Doña Sol! A foreign-looking man gave her his hand as

she stepped down, said a few words to her and then went away, while she entered the hotel. It was Doña Sol; there was no question of that. Nor did the bullfighter have any doubts what her relations with the stranger must be, after seeing the expression in her eyes and the smile with which she had said good-bye to him. She used to smile at him in just that same way in the happy days when they used to ride together through the lonely country-side, in the soft rosy light of the setting sun. Damn the woman!

He spent the evening with some friends, in a disgruntled mood; afterwards he slept badly, his mind occupied with scenes of the past. When he awoke, the dull grey light of a melancholy morning was coming in at his windows. Rain mixed with a few snowflakes was falling from the sky. Everything looked black: the sky, the walls of the houses opposite, the dripping gutters, the muddy pavements, the glistening hoods of the carriages, the moving domes of umbrellas.

It was eleven o'clock. Should he go and see Doña Sol? Why not? Last night he had angrily rejected the idea. It would be humbling himself. She had left him without a single word of explanation, and afterwards, when she heard his life was in danger, she had hardly bothered to inquire after him. One telegram soon after the accident, that was all; she hadn't even sent him a few lines, and writing came so easily to her! No, he wouldn't go and see her. He was too much of a man for that. . . .

But his strength of will seemed to have evaporated during the night. "Why not?" he asked himself again. He must see her. She still stood first among all the women he had known, her attraction for him had a special potency, quite different from that of all the rest. "I'm not free of her yet," the torero said to himself, realizing his own weakness. How cruelly he had suffered from that sudden separation!

The intense physical pain from his terrible wound in the Seville bull-ring had broken in upon the misery of disappointed love. His long illness, and his tender reconciliation with Carmen during his convalescence, had finally resigned him to

264

his misfortune. But he would never forget her. He had made great efforts not to think about the past, but Doña Sol's image returned to his mind on the slightest provocation—if he happened to find himself in some country lane where he had galloped beside her, if he met a fair Englishwoman in the street or any of her relations. Oh no! He would never find another woman like her! When he lost her, Gallardo felt he had taken a step backwards in his life. Things had never been the same since. He had gone down several rungs in the social ladder. He even attributed his failures in the ring to her desertion. When she was his, he had more courage; when she left him his luck went also. Always at the mercy of the mirages of superstitition, he believed that if only she came back to him the days of his glory would return once more.

Perhaps his desire to see her was a happy inspiration, like those which had so often carried him on to triumph in the ring. Why not? His easy successes with women had given him great confidence in his own irresistibility. Perhaps after so long an absence . . . who could tell? That was how it had been the first time they were alone together.

So, trusting in his lucky star, and confident that he could arouse desire in any woman he cast his eyes upon, Gallardo set off for the Hotel de París, which was not far from his own.

He was kept waiting for more than half an hour, sitting on a sofa in the hall, under inquisitive glances from the hotel staff and other guests, who turned to look at him when they heard his name.

At last a servant showed him into the lift and up to a small sitting-room on the first floor, from whose windows he could see the Puerta del Sol, with its black roofs, opposing streams of umbrellas moving along invisible pavements, cabs speeding across the shining asphalt under the lashing rain, and trams criss-crossing the square and tinkling their incessant warning to pedestrians.

A little door concealed by wallpaper opened, and Doña Sol came into the room with a rustling of silk and a waft of fresh perfume, in the full radiance of the summertime of her beauty.

265

Gallardo devoured her with his eyes, taking in all he saw with a connoisseur's attention to detail. She was exactly the same as when he had last seen her in Seville. No, perhaps she seemed even more beautiful from the added glamour lent by absence.

She was dressed with elegant casualness in an exotic style, and wore the same strange jewellery which he had last seen in her house in Seville. There were low-cut gold-embroidered slippers on her little feet. She held out her hand, with a distant smile.

"Well, how are you, Gallardo? I knew you were in Madrid. I saw you."

She no longer used the familiar *tu*, to which he used to respond in the formal style appropriate to a lover of an inferior class. It was *Usted* now. That *Usted* seemed to make them equals, and filled the matador with despair. He had hoped to be treated like a servant whose love has raised him to a great lady's arms, and instead she greeted him with cold politeness, like an ordinary friend.

She explained that she had seen him in the Madrid bull-ring when he fought at his only corrida since the accident. She had gone with a foreign friend who was anxious to see everything that was typically Spanish. He was staying at another hotel.

Gallardo nodded. He knew her foreigner; he had seen him with her.

There was silence, neither knowing what to say next. Doña Sol was the first to break it.

She thought the bullfighter was looking well; she seemed to remember he had had a nasty wound; she was almost certain she had telegraphed to Seville for news of him. But really, with the life she led, so constantly on the move and with so many new friends, she couldn't be sure of anything! But he looked just the same as ever, and had seemed quite restored to strength and confidence in the arena, though it was true he hadn't been at all lucky. She didn't understand much about bulls herself. . . .

"So you weren't badly hurt that time?"

Gallardo was irritated by the indifferent tone of voice in which she asked the question. And when he was hanging between life and death he had thought of no one but her! In a rather surly manner, attributable to his wounded feelings, he described his accident and his convalescence which had taken the whole winter.

She listened with assumed interest but with an expression of indifference in her eyes. What were the troubles of this bullfighter to her? They were the ordinary accidents of his profession, and could be of no importance to anyone but himself.

As he talked of his convalescence at the farm, Gallardo remembered the man who had seen Doña Sol and himself together.

"And Plumitas? Do you remember that poor fellow? They killed him in the end; I don't know if you heard about it?"

Doña Sol vaguely thought she remembered that also. Perhaps she had read about it in the Paris newspapers; they had been full of articles about the bandit at one time, as a picturesque Spanish character.

"A miserable specimen," Doña Sol said offhandedly. "I just remember him as an uninteresting, loutish peasant. One sees things more accurately from a distance. What I do recollect though is his lunching with us at the farm."

Gallardo also remembered it well. Poor Plumitas! With what obvious emotion he had taken the flower Doña Sol gave him! Had she forgotten giving the bandit a flower when he went away?

Doña Sol's eyes widened with genuine surprise.

"Are you sure?" she asked. "Did I really? I swear to you I don't remember anything about it. Ah well! The sunny south, so delightfully picturesque! What follies it makes one commit!"

There was a note of regret in her voice. Then she burst out laughing.

"And I expect the poor oaf kept that flower till he died. Don't you think so, Gallardo? Don't say no. No one had ever given him a flower before. They probably found it lying withered on his dead body—a mysterious relic that nobody could account for. Didn't you hear something of the sort, Gallardo? Wasn't it in the newspapers? Do say it was; don't shatter my illusions. It must have been; I like to think so. Poor Plumitas! What an interesting character! And to think I'd forgotten all about giving him the flower! I'll tell my friend about it; he's thinking of writing a book about Spanish customs."

This was the second time in a few minutes that Doña Sol had mentioned her friend. It cut the torero to the heart, and he gazed at her with sad dark eyes full of tears, which seemed to beg for mercy.

"Doña Sol! Doña Sol!" he murmured in a voice of desperation, as if reproaching her for her cruelty.

"What's the matter, my friend?" she asked smiling. "What are you trying to say?"

Gallardo sat silent with his head bent, intimidated by the ironical light in those pale eyes flecked with gold. Then he looked up, with a more resolute expression.

"Where have you been all this time, Doña Sol?"

"All over the world," she answered simply. "I'm a bird of passage. To hundreds of places you've never heard of."

"And this foreigner who is with you now, is he . . . is he? . . ."

"He's a friend of mine," she said coldly. "A friend who has been kind enough to come with me, and who wants to get to know Spain; an interesting, clever man who bears an illustrious name. We're going on from here to Andalusia, after he's visited all the museums. What more do you want to know?"

The haughty manner in which she asked this question showed an imperious desire to keep the bullfighter at arm's length, to emphasize the social distinction between them. Gallardo was disconcerted.

"Doña Sol!" he burst out, suddenly dropping his reserve. "What you have done to me is unforgivable. You've treated me badly, very badly. Why did you go away without a word?" His eyes filled with tears, and he clenched his fists in his despair.

"Don't take it like that, Gallardo. I really did you a great service. Haven't you discovered what I'm like yet? Hadn't you had enough? If I was a man I'd run away from women like me. It's suicide for a man to fall in love with me."

"But why did you go away?" Gallardo insisted.

"I went away because I was bored. Is that plain enough for you? And when one is bored, one has a perfect right to look for amusement elsewhere it seems to me. I'm bored to death wherever I go; you ought to be sorry for me."

"But I love you with all my heart!" cried the bullfighter with a dramatic earnestness which would have been laughable in another man.

" 'I love you with all my heart'!" repeated Doña Sol, mimicking his voice and manner. "And what of it? Oh, you selfish men who are used to public applause! You think the world has been made specially for you! 'I love you with all my heart, that's sufficient reason for you to love me.' No, Gallardo. I don't love you. You're a friend, nothing more. All the rest—what happened in Seville—was a dream, a mad escapade which I can scarcely remember, and which you had better forget."

The torero got up and came towards her with outstretched arms. He was too ignorant and clumsy to find words to convince this woman. He would put his trust in action, in the impulsive vehemence of his hopes and desires; he would take her in his arms and so bridge the cold gulf yawning between them.

"Doña Sol!" he said imploringly.

With a quick movement she freed herself from the matador's arms. Her eyes blazed with indignation and she drew herself up proudly as if she had been insulted.

"That's quite enough, Gallardo! If you go on like this, you aren't my friend any more, and I shall have you turned out of the hotel."

The bullfighter stood humiliated and ashamed for several minutes, until at last Doña Sol took pity on him.

"Don't be so childish," she said. "What's the use of remembering things which are over and done with. Why don't you forget me altogether? You've got your wife, who everyone says is beautiful and good, and a kind companion for you. If not

269

her, there are others. There are plenty of pretty girls down in Seville, with flowers in their hair and shawls over their shoulders—the sort I used to be so charmed with—who would be delighted to have Gallardo for a lover. As far as I'm concerned it's all over. It hurts your pride because you're a famous man and used to success, but that's how it is—over. Friends, that's all. Once I get bored I never go back over my tracks. My illusions are short-lived and when they're over they leave no trace. I'm to be pitied, you know "

She looked at the matador with commiseration and a certain surprise, as if she suddenly saw all his defects and lack of polish.

"I don't suppose you would understand, but you seem different from the Gallardo I knew in Seville," she went on. "Are you really the same? Of course you must be, but not for me. How can I explain? When I was in London I got to know a rajah. . . . Do you know what a rajah is?"

Gallardo shook his head, smiling at his own ignorance.

"An Indian Prince."

The ex-Ambassadress thought of her Hindoo admirer, with his brown face and black moustache, his huge white turban with a large and dazzling diamond in the front, and the rest of his body enveloped in floating white garments, made of soft gauzy stuff, like the petals of a flower.

"He was beautiful, he was young; he worshipped me with inscrutable eyes like some forest animal. But I found him ridiculous and made fun of him when he stammered out his oriental compliments in bad English. He shivered in the cold, the London fogs made him cough; he was like a bird flapping its wings in the rain. When he told me he loved me, looking at me with those liquid gazelle's eyes, I wanted to buy him an overcoat and cap to keep him from shivering. All the same I realize he was a handsome man, and I dare say he could have made some woman who had exotic tastes very happy for a few months. It was a question of environment, of atmosphere. You don't understand that sort of thing, Gallardo."

Doña Sol was silent, thinking about the poor rajah,

trembling with cold in his ridiculous clothes in the misty London air. She imagined him in his own country, transformed by the majesty of power and the brilliant sunlight. His brown face, with its green reflections suggesting a tropical forest, would look like some splendid bronze image. She pictured him riding on his state elephant, with its splendid gold caparison sweeping the ground, escorted by horsemen and slaves carrying censers of burning perfume; his great turban crowned with white feathers and studded with precious stones; his chest covered in diamonds; a belt of emeralds and a golden scimitar at his waist; and all around him nautch-girls with painted eyes and firm breasts, tame tigers, forests of spears. There would be pagodas with roofs piled one on another, ringed round with bells which chimed a mysterious tune at the lightest breath of wind; cool palaces; bosky woods, in whose depths fierce many-coloured animals leapt and clambered. Oh yes, that was the proper setting for him! If she had seen her poor rajah thus, as proud as a god, under a deep blue sky and amid splendours lit by a blazing sun, it would never have entered her head to buy him an overcoat. In fact she would almost certainly have gone straight to his arms and offered him her love.

"You remind me of my rajah, Gallardo my friend. You were a fine fellow in Seville, in your country clothes with your garrocha over your shoulder. You fitted into the landscape. But here! Madrid has become completely European, like any other city. You don't see anyone wearing Spanish costume these days, nor any Manilla shawls, except on the stage. Don't be offended, Gallardo, but you remind me of my Indian friend, I don't know why."

She looked out of the window at the sad rainy sky, the few snow-flakes falling on to the damp asphalt, and the crowds hurrying along under their dripping umbrellas. Oh, how melancholy Madrid looked under the rain! Her friend had come here expecting unchanging blue skies; he would be disappointed. When she looked out at the groups of toreros standing on the pavements below, she was irresistibly reminded of wild animals from tropical countries, caged in zoos under grey clouds and rain. Then she turned to the matador again, noticing with surprise his pigtail, his hair-cut, his hat—all the signs of his profession which contrasted so oddly with his smart town suit. She saw him as it were out of his frame. In Andalusia Gallardo had been a hero, the finest product of a cattle-breeding country. Here he seemed like an actor, with his clean-shaven face and his self-conscious manner: an actor whose role it was to freeze the blood of his audience by fighting with wild beasts.

Ah, what seductive illusions she had found in that country where the sun always shines, where the colours and light spread their own intoxicating enchantment! For several months she had loved this rough uncivilized man, taking his ignorance for wit, and even revelling in the smell of bulls and horses which hung about him, and insisting that he shouldn't drown it in scent. What foolishness it had all been!

She remembered the mortal danger she had been in at the bull-baiting; she remembered lunching with the bandit, and how she had listened to his stories in amazement and given him a flower. How far away, and how absurd it all seemed now!

All that was left now of that remote and ridiculous past was the man who stood motionless before her, looking at her with imploring eyes, full of childish longing to return to his lost happiness. Poor fellow! As if it were possible to recapitulate those wild frenzies, now that the blindness of illusion and enchantment were gone and her head was cool and clear.

"It's all over," Doña Sol said. "The past had better be forgotten for good and all, its brilliant colours have faded. I wish I could see it as I used; but when I came back to Spain from abroad everything seemed different. You seem to have changed too; when I saw you in the ring the other day I thought you had lost some of your daring . . . and that the crowd applauded you less."

She said this quite simply, without a trace of malice, but Gallardo thought he detected a note of mockery in her voice and bent his head, while his cheeks flushed scarlet.

His professional anxieties rose again in his mind. All his troubles came from the fact that he no longer hurled himself recklessly on the bulls. That was what she was telling him now, as plainly as possible. He 'seemed different'. If he could once again become the Gallardo she used to know, perhaps she would be kinder to him. Women can only love brave men.

And the matador let himself be carried away by this illusion, taking what was in reality the death of a caprice for a temporary estrangement, which could be ended by his own prowess.

Doña Sol got up. The visit had lasted some time and the torero showed no signs of taking his leave; he felt vaguely that if he stayed beside her ·some chance circumstance might reunite them.

However he had no choice but to get up also. She made the excuse that she had to go out. She was expecting her friend; they were going to the Prado together.

She invited him to have lunch another day, in her private suite. She would ask her friend; he would very much like to meet a bullfighter, though he hardly spoke any Spanish.

The matador pressed her hand, mumbling a few incoherent words, and left the room. He was so angry that everything swam before his eyes and there was a buzzing in his ears.

So she had sent him away, coldly, like a mere acquaintance —and an importunate one at that! Was she really the same woman he had known in Seville? And he was to come to lunch to meet her friend, who would be amused to have a close view of such a rare insect as a bullfighter.

Damn her! He would show her he was a man. It was all over. He would never see her again.

CHAPTER NINE

WHILE he was in Madrid Gallardo received several letters from Don José and Carmen.

The matador's manager did his best to encourage him and

always added the same advice: that he should fling himself straight at the bull. "An estocada, and you can put him in your pocket!" But a faint note of despondency was beginning to make itself felt, as if cracks were appearing in his hitherto steadfast belief that Gallardo was 'the best of them all'.

He had got wind of his bad reception by the public on various occasions; and the Madrid corrida was the last straw for poor Don José. No, Gallardo was not like some other matadors who could ignore the whistling and jeers of the audience so long as they earned their money. 'His matador' took a pride in his profession, and the enthusiasm of the crowd was necessary to him. A fair success was as bad as utter failure. People were used to seeing him fight with his old astounding dash and courage, and anything less seemed to them a disaster.

Don José tried to make up his mind what was wrong with his matador. Lack of courage? Impossible. He would die rather than admit such a defect in his idol. Probably he was tired, and had not fully recovered from his wounds. "That's why I think it would be better for you to take a rest for a season," he wrote, "and come back at the top of your form afterwards." He offered to arrange everything. All that was needed was a medical certificate to justify his temporary inaction, and Don José would come to some agreement with the impresarios as to all pending contracts, by which Gallardo would pay a moderate salary to a young matador who should take his place.

In this way he would still make money.

Carmen wrote more emphatically and with less beating about the bush. He ought to retire at once, 'cut off his pigtail' as they said in the profession, and go and live quietly at La Rinconada or his house in Seville with his family—the only people who really loved him. She could bear it no longer; she lived in greater fear now even than in the early years of their marriage, when her happiness had been torn to pieces between anxiety and hope. She felt in her heart, with that feminine intuition which seldom failed her, that some dreadful thing

274

was going to happen. She couldn't sleep; she lay awake brooding for hours, slipping now and again into horrifying dreams.

She was enraged by the fickleness of the public, and the speed with which they had forgotten the matador's successes when he had his full strength. They were an ungrateful, black-hearted lot, and all they wanted was to see him killed for their amusement—just as if she didn't exist, as if he had no mother. "Juan, Mamma and I beg and implore you to retire. What's the point of going on fighting? We've enough to live on, and I can't bear to hear of your being insulted by people who are worth far less than you. And suppose you had another accident? Oh God! I think it would drive me mad."

Gallardo was very thoughtful for some time after reading these letters. Retire? What nonsense! Women's notions! It was understandable that Carmen should ask him, out of her love for him, but impossible for him to do it. Cut off his pigtail at the age of thirty? How his enemies would laugh! He had no right to retire as long as his limbs were sound and he could still fight. It would be ridiculous. And money wasn't everything: what about his professional pride? What would all his thousands and thousands of loyal supporters have to say? What could they answer when his enemies threw it in their teeth that Gallardo had retired because he was afraid?

The matador paused to consider whether or no his finances would in any case make retirement a possible solution. He was rich and yet he was not. What he now possessed had mostly been acquired in the first years of his marriage, when one of his greatest pleasures had been to save, and then surprise Carmen and his mother with the news of his latest investments. Afterwards he had gone on making money, perhaps in even larger amounts, but it had disappeared down innumerable channels which had been opened by his new mode of life. He had gambled heavily, and lived extravagantly. Some of the farms which had been added to his extensive estate at La Rinconada, to round off the property, had been bought with money advanced by Don José and other friends. He had

275

borrowed from several aficionados to pay off his gambling debts. He was rich, but if he were to retire and lose the magnificent salary he got from corridas—between two and three hundred thousand pesetas a year—he would have to reduce expenses, after paying his debts, and live like a country gentleman on the income from La Rinconada, economizing and superintending the farm himself, for at present it was run by a paid manager and showed very little profit.

The thought of leading a life of obscurity as a farmer, endlessly pinching and saving, filled Gallardo with gloom. He was used to having plenty of money, to lavishness and display. Though his wealth had steadily increased as he advanced in his career it had never seemed more than he needed; yet what he now possessed would have made him feel like a millionaire in his early days. If he gave up bullfighting he would be a poor man. He would have to give up offering Havana cigars to all his friends, and buying expensive Andalusian wines; he would have to stop behaving in his lordly fashion and calling out: "I'm paying for everything!" in cafés and wine-shops—make an end of all the wild extravagances, in fact, appropriate to a life of constant danger. He would have to send away all the flatterers and parasites who crowded to his door and made him laugh with their absurd requests; and if a handsome woman of the working classes came his way—even after his retirement, which was unlikely—he could no longer indulge himself by seeing her turn pale with pleasure when he hung gold and pearl drops in her ears, nor by pouring wine over her Chinese shawl so as to replace it with a much finer one. That was how he had lived hitherto, and he couldn't bear to change. He was a torero of the old sort—extravagant, ostentatious, lavish, always ready to help people in trouble with princely generosity if they succeeded in touching his heart.

Gallardo used to jeer at many of his comrades in the profession, who went from bull-ring to bull-ring like commercial travellers, keeping careful accounts of all their expenses. Some of them, hardly more than boys, kept notebooks in their pockets in which they even noted down the five centimos they spent on a glass of water at the railway station. They were glad to accept a glass of wine, but never dreamt of standing treat to anyone else. There were others who had large quantities of coffee made and put in great bottles before they started on a journey, and took this black brew about with them so as to avoid paying for any in hotels. The members of some cuadrillas even went hungry, and grumbled in public of the meanness of their maestros.

Gallardo did not regret his extravagant life. And now they wanted him to give it up!

His whole household enjoyed and took for granted their easy unconstrained life, free from financial worries, with money pouring in in an endless stream. Beside his mother and his wife, he had taken on an extra family, his sister and his garrulous brother-in-law (who did no work, seeming to think his relationship to a famous matador gave him a right to be idle) and the ever-growing tribe of little nephews and nieces. Was he expected to introduce order and economy into the lives of all these people, who had got into the way of living a cheerful, thriftless life at his expense? All of them, even poor Garabato, would have to work on the farm and turn themselves into sunburnt peasants. And his poor mother would no longer be able to gladden her last years with her charity to the poor women of the district, nor look like a shamefaced little girl when her son pretended to be angry because nothing was left of the hundred duros he had given her a fortnight before! And Carmen, who was economical by nature, would be the first to make sacrifices and deprive herself of many frivolities which added to the charm of life.

Damn it all! It would mean a step down in the world for his family: it would be a shame to deprive them of the comforts they had grown accustomed to. And what must he do to avoid this disaster? Simply throw himself on the bulls! Fight as he had fought in the old days! And that was what he intended to do.

He answered Carmen and his manager with short, laboriously

written letters, announcing his decision. Retire? No, certainly not.

He told Don José that he was determined to be as good as in the past. He would follow his advice: "An estocada, and you can put him in your pocket." He felt his courage rising and that he was capable of facing any bulls, however big.

To his wife he wrote cheerfully, but as if slightly offended that she should doubt his strength. She would soon have news of the next corrida. He was going to astonish the public and make them ashamed of their behaviour to him. If the bulls were all right he'd be equal to Roger de Flor himself—that individual his idiot of a brother-in-law was always talking about.

If only the bulls came up to his expectations! That was Gallardo's main preoccupation. In the past he had prided himself on being uninterested in them, and in never going to look at them before the corrida.

"I kill whatever they give me," he used to say conceitedly. And the first time he set eyes on the animals was when they rushed into the arena.

Now he wanted to look them over from close range, and prepare for success by a careful study of their characteristics.

At last the weather had cleared, and the sun was shining; the second corrida was fixed for the following day.

That evening Gallardo went alone to the bull-ring. The red brick amphitheatre with its Moorish windows stood out against a background of low green hills. On a distant slope beyond the wide, monotonously rolling plain, he saw something white which might have been a herd of cattle. It was the cemetery.

As the matador approached the bull-ring some dirty ragged men came up to him—parasites of the ring who were allowed to sleep in the stables, and lived on charity from the aficionados and scraps of food left over from the neighbouring taverns. Some of them had come from Andalusia with a consignment of bulls, and had been hanging about ever since.

Gallardo put a few coins into their outstretched caps and went in by the door leading to the stables.

In the courtyard a group of aficionados were watching the picadors trying out their horses. Potaje was preparing to mount, with a garrocha in his hand and great cowboy spurs on his boots. The stable-lads were talking to the contractor who had supplied the horses, a stout man in a wide felt hat, who answered the insults and jokes of the picadors in a slow, imperturbable voice.

The monosabios, with their sleeves rolled up, led out the miserable crocks for the riders to try. They had been training them for several days, and their spur marks still showed red on the wretched animals' flanks. They had forced them to trot with fictitious energy in the open space round the bull-ring, and taught them to turn quickly, so as to get them used to their work in the arena. They came back to the stables with their sides covered in blood and were washed down with buckets of water to refresh them. The water running between the cobble-stones round the drinking-trough was dark red like spilt wine.

Those to be used in the next day's corrida were dragged out of the stables, to be examined and passed by the picadors.

These scraggy relics of equine wretchedness came forward with their trembling legs and tortured flanks, presenting a living picture of the tragedy of old age and decrepitude, and of human ingratitude and forgetfulness of past services. Some of them were incredibly thin, mere skeletons whose prominent ribs looked as if they must break through the shaggy hides tightly stretched across them. Others, with shining coats and bright eyes, held themselves proudly, pawing the ground with strong legs; they were splendid animals such as might have come straight from drawing a smart carriage, and seemed quite out of place among their miserable companions. However they were the most dangerous to ride, being afflicted with some incurable disease like the staggers, which meant that they might come down at any moment, sending their riders flying over their heads. Behind these wretched or diseased animals clattered sadly a group of casualties from industry: cab-horses and horses from mills, factories, and farms, all worn out from long years spent dragging carts and ploughs:

unfortunate outcasts who were to be exploited to the very last moments of their lives, so as to entertain human beings by their leaps and kicks of agony when they felt the bulls' horns pierce their bellies.

It was a procession of galled necks on which bloated green flies were battening; dim eyes, with yellowish whites but trustful expressions; long bony heads, whose skin was swarming with vermin; angular flanks with coats matted like wool; narrow chests shaken by deep whinnies; feeble legs, looking as if they must break at any moment, with the hair growing so long on them right down to the hoof that they seemed to be wearing trousers. Their stomachs were unused to the rich fodder they had been given to fortify them, and they left behind them a trail of smoking and ill-digested droppings. To mount one of this trembling, miserable, crazy cavalcade required as much courage as to face the bull. There were some animals whose legs almost doubled under them when they felt the weight of the heavy, high-pointed Moorish saddles, with their cow-boy stirrups.

Potaje took a very high and mighty tone with the contractor, and made even the monosabios laugh with his gypsy oaths. He and the other picadors knew how to treat these horse-dealers.

A stable-boy came out leading an old crock with a hanging head, long matted coat and painfully prominent ribs.

"What's that you've got there?" Potaje shouted to the contractor. "That's not fit for service. Nobody's going to get on an animal like that!"

The dealer replied with phlegmatic calm. If Potaje didn't dare get on it, that was because nowadays picadors had no courage at all. With a gentle, docile horse like this, Señor Calderón, El Trigo, or any other rider of the good old days, would have fought two afternoons running, and not had a single fall, nor the animal so much as a scratch. But nowadays! People seemed to have plenty of timidity but no pride in their profession.

The picador and the contractor went on abusing each other

in the friendliest fashion, as if the most appalling insults lost their sting through force of habit.

"You're an old fraud, that's what you are!" Potaje shouted again. "A worse thief than José Maria el Tempraniyo. Go on and put your grandmother up on the old hack; it'll do instead of the broomstick she rides every Saturday night."

Everyone roared with laughter but the contractor only shrugged his shoulders.

"Well, but what's the matter with the horse?" he said calmly. "Just look at him, you scoundrel! He's a lot better than some of those with glanders or the staggers who chuck you over their heads before you get anywhere near the bull. He's as sound as an apple. He's worked in a mineral-water factory for the last twenty-eight years like a decent fellow, and no one's ever complained of him, and now you come along shouting and abusing him and trying to take away his character!"

"I won't have him, see? You can keep him yourself!"

The contractor walked slowly over to Potaje with the deliberation of long experience in such transactions, and whispered something in his ear. The picador pretended to be angry, but finally went up to the horse. He didn't want to be taken for a difficult man, ready to do anyone a bad turn, so he put his foot in the stirrup and let his weight fall on the poor animal's back. Then he took his garrocha under his arm and pushed it against a large post built into the wall, attacking it several times with all his strength as if he had a huge bull at the end of his pike. The poor horse's legs shook and nearly doubled under it with each impact.

"Not so bad," said Potaje in a conciliatory tone. "It's a better animal than I thought. Good mouth, good legs. Well, have it your own way. Put him aside for me."

And the picador dismounted, apparently ready to accept anything that was offered him, since the contractor's mysterious aside.

Gallardo left the group of aficionados, who had been watching this scene with some amusement. He went through a gate leading to the bull-pens. The enclosure was surrounded on three sides by a stone wall reaching to the height of a man's shoulders, strengthened by thick posts which supported the balcony above. At intervals in it there were doors so narrow that a man could only get through them sideways. In this spacious corral were eight bulls, some lying down, others standing and snuffing at heaps of grass.

The matador walked all round outside the walls, looking at the animals. From time to time he slipped through one of the slit-like doors into the enclosure. He waved his arms, giving loud challenging yells, which roused the bulls from their immobility. Some jumped up quickly, lowered their heads, and charged the man who had ventured to disturb the peace of their prison. Others stood four-square, with heads high and menacing expressions, waiting to see if the intruder would come any closer.

Then Gallardo slipped quickly behind the wall again, and studied the appearance and behaviour of the creatures, without however being able to decide which two he should select.

The head drover was standing beside him. He was a big athletic man, wearing a suit of thick cloth, gaiters and spurs, and a wide hat with a strap under the chin. His nickname was Lobato,[1] and he spent most of the year out on the pastures with his herds; in Madrid his appearance and behaviour seemed outlandish and out of place.

He never wanted to go and look at the city streets, nor did he in fact ever leave the immediate neighbourhood of the bull-ring.

For him, the capital of Spain consisted in an amphitheatre surrounded by waste land, while further away lay a mysterious collection of houses which he had no desire to investigate. From this point of view the most important establishment in Madrid was the Gallina tavern, quite close to the bull-ring, a place which offered all sorts of pleasures—an enchanted palace where he could eat at the expense of the management

[1] Wolf-cub.

before riding back to the ranch, with his blanket on the saddle-bow and his pike over his shoulder. He enjoyed terrifying the inn servants by his friendly greetings: terrible handshakes which crushed their bones and made them cry out with pain. Delighted with his own strength, and pleased at being called a brute, he sat down to his daily ration—a dish as big as a basin, full of meat and potatoes, and more than one jug of wine.

The bulls bought by the management were looked after by him on the pastures of Muñoza or of the Sierra de Guadarrama. He brought them to the bull-ring at midnight, two days before the corrida, after driving them through the outskirts of Madrid with an escort of riders and cowherds. He grew desperate when the bad weather prevented the corrida taking place and kept the bulls in their pens, for he longed to return as quickly as possible to his peaceful solitudes.

Slow of speech and dull-witted though he was, this centaur smelling of leather and manure became almost eloquent when he talked about his life on the pastures with his bulls. He thought the Madrid sky was too narrow and had too few stars. He used to describe in his laconic but picturesque way the nights out in the open, with his bulls sleeping under the faint light of the stars, and the dense silence broken by mysterious forest noises. In the silence you could hear the strange song of the mountain snakes. Oh yes, they could sing all right. No one dared dispute the point with Lobato; he had heard them thousands of times, and if anybody doubted it they were calling him a liar and would probably feel the weight of his fists. Just as snakes sang, so did bulls talk, though he hadn't yet mastered all the mysteries of their language. They were very like human beings, although they had horns and walked on four legs. You ought to see them wake up at dawn. They bounded about as friskily as children, pretending to fight or mount each other, as if they were greeting the rising of the sun and the glory of God. Then he would describe his slow journeys across the Sierra de Guadarrama, following the beds of the crystal-clear rivulets which came down from the melting snow of the summits to feed the rivers; the flowery meadows; the birds which flapped down from the trees to perch on the horns of sleeping bulls; the wolves howling in the darkness—but always keeping their distance, apparently terrified of these large wild animals which had followed the tolling bell-oxen into their wild solitudes. No use talking to him about Madrid, that suffocating town! The only tolerable things to be found in that vast forest of houses were Gallina's wine and savoury stews.

Lobato gave the matador his advice about his choice of bulls. He had no awe or respect for the idols of the public, he was rather inclined to despise them for killing such noble animals by means of trickery and deceit. He himself was the braver man, living as he did alone among them, walking between their horns every day, with no defence except his bare hands and no public to applaud him.

As Gallardo was leaving the enclosure another figure joined them, greeting the maestro respectfully. It was an old man who had been employed for years to clean the bull-ring, and who had known all the famous bullfighters of his day. He was shabbily dressed, but was often to be seen wearing feminine-looking rings; and when he wanted to blow his nose he would pull out of his blouse a small monogrammed cambric handkerchief, trimmed with fine lace and faintly scented.

During the week he alone was responsible for cleaning the huge arena and the tiers of seats and boxes; nor did he complain of the work being too heavy. If the impresario was dissatisfied with him and wanted to punish him, he used to open the doors to the rabble always to be found outside the ring, and the poor man would promise to improve his ways if only they shouldn't be given his job.

Occasionally he took on half a dozen boys to help him— usually toreros' apprentices who worked faithfully for him in exchange for being allowed to watch corridas on fiesta days from the 'dog kennel' as it was called, a door with an iron grille situated close to the bull-pens, through which wounded bullfighters were removed from the ring. The boys used to hang on to the iron bars for dear life and fight like monkeys in a cage for the best place.

The old man shared out the work according to a plan of his own. The boys worked on the sunny side of the amphitheatre, where the poorer, dirtier spectators sat, who left behind a whole rubbish-heap of orange-peel, paper and cigarette ends.

"Be sure to put aside all the cigar ends!" he said to his squad of cleaners. "Anyone who keeps a single one won't see the bullfight next Sunday."

He himself worked industriously on the shady side, crouching down like a treasure-seeker in the darkness of the boxes to stow away his finds: ladies' fans, rings, handkerchiefs, coins, ribbons, anything which might be left behind by an army of fourteen thousand people. He carefully collected cigar and cigarette ends, chopped them up and dried them in the sun, to be sold later for tobacco. His more valuable finds, which the audience had dropped or forgotten in their excitement, he sold to a pawnbroker.

Gallardo replied to the old man's obsequious greeting by giving him a cigar, and took leave of Lobato, who had agreed to put aside the two bulls he had chosen. The other matadors wouldn't object. They were easy-going young men, full of daring, and would kill whatever was put before them.

When he came out again into the courtyard where the horses were being tried, Gallardo saw a tall, thin, sunburnt man in torero's clothes leave the group of spectators and came towards him. Tufts of grey hair showed under his hat, and there were deep lines around his mouth.

"Pescadero! How are you?" said Gallardo, grasping his hand with genuine emotion.

He was an ageing ex-matador who had had his youthful days of triumph, but whose name was now remembered by few. Other matadors had come upon the scene to eclipse such poor fame as he had achieved, and after fighting for a while in America and getting gored once or twice, he had retired on his small savings. Gallardo knew he owned a wine shop not far from the bull-ring, but seeing him was a surprise.

"What d'you expect!" said Pescadero sadly. "I don't come to corridas often, but the sport's in my blood, so I drop in now and again in a neighbourly sort of way. I'm only an innkeeper now you know."

Gallardo looked at this melancholy figure and thought of the Pescadero he had known in his childhood, one of his most admired heroes: a confident man, beloved by many women, and often to be seen in La Campana when he came to Seville, smartly dressed in a velvet hat, wine-coloured jacket and striped silk sash, with an ivory gold-knobbed stick in his hand And this was how he himself would look—shabby and ordinary—if he were to retire from the bull-ring!

They talked for a long time about professional matters Pescadero was pessimistic, like most old men who have been embittered by bad luck. There were hardly any good toreros nowadays—real men of spirit. Gallardo and one or two others were the only matadors who killed in the proper way. Even the bulls seemed less powerful than before. Between these complaints he pressed the matador to come back to his house with him, if he had nothing special to do.

Gallardo agreed, and they turned into a little wine shop, just like all the rest, in a long street not far from the bull-ring; the façade was painted red, and in the window were dingy-looking cutlets and pieces of fried chicken lying on dusty plates, and jars of pickled vegetables. Inside the shop was a counter made of zinc, some large wine barrels, bottles, circular tables with wooden stools round them, and a great many coloured pictures of toreros and scenes in the bull-ring.

"Bring us some Montilla," said Pescadero to the young man behind the counter, who smiled when he saw Gallardo.

The matador studied his face, and noticed the empty sleeve of his jacket which was pinned to his breast.

"It seems to me I know you," he said.

"I should think you did!" interrupted Pescadero. "It's Pipi."

The nickname immediately reminded Gallardo of the young man's history. He had been a plucky youngster, with a

masterly hand with the banderillas, and some of the aficionados
had singled him out as 'the torero of the future'. One day in
the Madrid bull-ring he had been so badly gored in the arm
that it had had to be amputated, and that was the end of his
bullfighting career.

"I took him in, Juan," Pescadero went on. "I've got no
family and my wife's dead, so I look on him as a son. If a
man's got no good feelings for his fellows, on top of all his
other troubles, then I don't know what's the use of him!
Pipi and I aren't rich of course. But everything I have is his
and we make do as best we can, thanks to our old friends who
sometimes come and have a meal here or play a game of
cards, and above all thanks to the school."

Gallardo smiled. He'd heard about the school of tauromachy
which Pescadero had started near his wine shop.

"Well, what can a man do?" the latter said, as if excusing
himself. "We had to live, and the school brings in more than
the wine shop. A good class of people come there: young
gentlemen who want to learn how to cut a dash at the yearling
trials; foreigners who get excited by going to corridas, and take
it into their heads to become toreros in their old age! I've got
one here now, who comes every afternoon. Come and see him."

They crossed the street to a plot of ground surrounded by a
high wall. Painted across the planks of the door in large black
letters were the words: School of Tauromachy.

They went in. The first thing that attracted Gallardo's
attention was the bull: an animal made of wood and bamboo,
mounted on wheels, with a tail of tow, head of plaited straw, a
cork neck and a pair of enormous and genuine horns, which
struck terror into the hearts of the pupils.

A boy, naked to the waist, wearing a cap and his hair in
two curls over the ears, gave life and intelligence to the
strange creature by pushing it about when the pupils stood in
front of it with the cape in their hands.

In the middle of the plot stood a fat elderly man, with a red
face and bristling white moustache, dressed in his shirt-sleeves
and holding a banderilla in each hand. In a chair close to the

wall, a lady of about the same age and no less corpulent sat with her arms folded, wearing a hat covered all over with flowers. Each time her husband put up a creditable show she laughed, and the roses in her hat and her false curls (dyed an impossible yellow) shook wildly. She clapped and threw herself back in her chair, separating her legs and spreading her skirt so as to reveal some of her portly and faded charms.

As they stood at the door, Pescadero explained to Gallardo who these people were. Probably they were French—he wasn't certain, nor did he greatly care—anyway they were a married couple who travelled a lot and seemed to have lived everywhere. The man had done everything in turn: mined in Africa, colonized some remote island, hunted wild horses with a lasso in America. Now he wanted to fight bulls for a living, and came to school every afternoon like an obstinate child; but he paid generously for his lessons.

"What a fool! A torero with a phiz like that! And he must be past fifty!"

When the two men came into the yard, the pupil dropped his arms holding the banderillas, while the lady arranged her skirts and her flowery hat, and exclaimed "Oh, *cher maître!*"

"Good evening, Mosiú. My compliments, Madame," said the maestro, raising his hand to his hat. "Let's see how you're getting on, Mosiú. You remember what I told you? Stand your ground firmly, challenge the animal and let him come on; then when he's close to you, just bend over and place the banderillas in his neck. There's nothing to worry about; the bull will do it all for you. Now! Are you ready?"

The maestro stood aside and made a sign to the terrible bull, or rather to the youth who was pushing it from behind.

"Eeeeh! Come on, Morito!"

Pescadero gave a terrifying yell and stamped on the ground to incite this creature with the straw head and entrails full of air to charge. Morito rushed to the attack, with a loud creaking of wheels, bumping along over the uneven ground, with the boy hanging on behind. No bull from the most famous herd could compare in intelligence with this immortal animal, who had received thousands of banderillas and estocadas without suffering any wounds that the carpenter couldn't put right. He seemed as wise as a human being. When he reached the pupil he altered his course a trifle so as not to touch him with his horns, and then went off with a pair of banderillas stuck in his cork neck.

This feat was loudly applauded, while the banderillero stood planted where he was, straightening his braces and his shirt cuffs. His wife threw herself backwards again in her delight, laughing and clapping, and again her skirt got pulled up, revealing the lower part of her anatomy.

"Splendid, Mosiú," shouted Pescadero. "You couldn't have done it better."

And the foreigner, delighted by the professor's approval, struck himself on the chest and said modestly:

"I've got the most important thing—courage, and plenty of it!"

Then to celebrate his success he called to Morito's animating spirit, who was already coming up as if he anticipated the order, to fetch a bottle of wine. There were already three empty ones on the ground beside the lady, who was getting more purple in the face and more obstreperous every moment, as she laughingly applauded her husband's bullfighting skill.

When she heard that the man with the maestro was the famous Gallardo, and recognized his face from his portraits in newspapers and on matchboxes, the foreign lady became almost pale with emotion. "Oh, *cher maître!*" She smiled and rubbed herself up against him, and would gladly have thrown her large flabby body into his arms.

Glasses of wine were clinked to the future success of the new torero; even Morito had to share in the celebration—the boy who had pushed him, drinking in his name.

"Within two months, Mosiú," said Pescadero with Andalusian gravity, "you will be placing the banderillas in the Madrid bull-ring like God himself, and getting money, and glory, and women too . . . if the lady will excuse me."

The lady, who had never taken her sentimental gaze from

289

Gallardo's face, seemed to be convulsed with delight, and a burst of laughing shook all the loose flesh on her body.

The pupil went on with his lesson, with a pertinacity which showed him to be a man of character. He must make good use of his time. He was longing for the day when he should figure in the Madrid bull-ring and enjoy all the delights the maestro had promised him. His red-faced consort, seeing the two toreros go, sat down again with the remains of the bottle of wine for company.

Pescadero walked with Gallardo to the end of the street.

"Good-bye Juan," he said gravely. "We may see each other tomorrow at the ring. You see what I've sunk to—making a living out of telling lies to buffoons."

Gallardo walked away deep in thought. This was the man he had seen throwing his money about like a prince in the days of his triumphs, confident in his future! His savings had all vanished in unfortunate speculations. A bullfighter's life did not teach a man how to manage his fortune. And still Carmen and his mother wanted him to retire! Never! He must go on throwing himself on the bulls.

Next day his spirits were still high, and he went to the bull-ring without any superstitious fears. He felt confident of success, and that his old inspiration would not desert him.

From the very start the corrida was eventful. The first bull showed itself exceptionally persistent in attacking the men on horseback. Within a few moments it had unseated three picadors, who were waiting for it with their lances ready, and of the horses two lay dying with dark gouts of blood gushing from the holes in their chests. The other was galloping round the arena, mad with pain and terror, with its saddle flapping loose and its stomach ripped open, showing the blue and red entrails like enormous sausages. As it dragged its intestines on the ground and trod on them with its hind feet, they gradually became disentangled as a skein is unravelled.

The sight of its mad career impelled the bull to charge, and putting its powerful head under the horse's stomach it lifted it on its horns, threw it to the ground and again attacked the wretched broken body, pierced with holes. When the brute left it, kicking in its death agony, a monosabio came up to finish it off by driving his knife in at the base of its skull. In a final spasm the miserable animal buried its teeth in the man's hand; he gave a yell, and lifting the bleeding hand buried the knife again till the horse stopped kicking and lay with rigid legs. Meanwhile other bull-ring servants ran forward with big baskets full of sand which they heaped on the pools of blood and the bodies of the horses.

By this time the audience were on their feet, shouting and gesticulating. They admired the bull's ferocity, and protested loudly because there were no picadors left in the ring, shouting: "Horses! More horses!"

They knew well enough that others would appear any minute, but they couldn't bear that a single moment should be wasted without fresh butchery for their entertainment. The bull stood alone in the middle of the arena, bellowing and pawing the ground, with its bloody horns held high and the badge of its herd floating from its neck, which was marked with red and blue gashes. Fresh horsemen came into the ring, and once more the revolting spectacle was repeated. As soon as the picador approached with his tilted lance, sidling his horse along so that its bandaged eye was towards the enemy, there was the shock of impact and the sound of a fall. There was a splintering of dry wood as the pikes broke, and the next minute the horse was being tossed in the air, scattering blood and excrement, while the picador rolled in the sand like a yellow-legged doll and was quickly protected by the peons with their capes.

One of the horses, wounded in the stomach, evacuated disgusting streams of green excrement in every direction, staining the clothes of the nearest toreros.

The audience greeted the falls of the picadors with roars of laughter and shouts of delight. The dull sound of the bull's horns against their iron leg-casings rang through the arena. One of them fell as heavily as a sack, and his head struck the wall of the barrier with a sinister sound.

"That one won't get up again," yelled the crowd. "He must have cracked his nob!"

However, he did get up, and after feeling his arms and his head carefully, he picked up his beaver hat and remounted the same horse, which the monosabios had dragged to its feet with kicks and blows, and forced it to trot again, dragging an ever-increasing mass of intestines behind it on the sand. The picador again approached the bull on his wretched, dying mount.

"This is for you!" he cried, throwing his hat to some friends.

But no sooner had he driven the pike again into the bull's neck, than man and horse were in the air, parting company from the violence of the shock and each falling in a different direction.

Another time the monosabios and some of the audience shouted to a picador to dismount before the bull had struck him; but before his stiffly encased legs could follow their advice the horse had dropped to the ground, killed instantaneously, while the picador flew over its ears and landed heavily on his head in the sand.

The bull had not succeeded in goring any of the riders; but some of the picadors lay insensible on the ground, and the bull-ring servants had to carry them to the infirmary to be treated for broken bones, or concussion, which made them look like dead men.

Gallardo ran from side to side of the ring in his eagerness to win the sympathy of the public, and was loudly applauded when he pulled the bull's tail, saving a picador who was on the ground in imminent danger of being gored.

While the banderilleros were engaged he leant on the barrier and scanned the boxes. Doña Sol was probably in one of them. At last he saw her, but she was not wearing the white mantilla that had made her look like one of Goya's ladies at the Seville bullfight. With her fair hair and fashionable hat, she looked like a foreigner at her first corrida. Beside her sat her friend, the man she had said such nice things about, who wanted to see everything interesting in the country. Ah, Doña Sol! She would soon realize that her discarded lover was a fine fellow. She would have to applaud him, even in front of the hated foreigner; against her will she would be carried away by the general enthusiam.

When the time came for Gallardo to kill his bull, which was the second of the corrida, the audience received him well, seeming to have forgotten their recent dissatisfaction with him. The crowds had become more tolerant during that fortnight's intermission during the rain. They had waited a long time for this bullfight and they wanted it to be good. Moreover the braveness of the bulls and the number of horses they had killed had put them in a good humour.

Gallardo walked up to the bull, with his head uncovered, holding the muleta in front of him and waving the sword like a walking-stick. Behind him at. some distance were El Nacional and another peon. There were some cries of protest from the sunny side. Why so many assistants? He looked like a parish priest going to a funeral.

"Out of the ring all of you!" shouted Gallardo.

The two peons left him, because this time he said it as if he meant it.

He advanced till he got close to the animal, and then unfolded his muleta and took a few more steps forward, as in his best days, till the red cloth almost touched its damp muzzle. A pass. *Olé!* A murmur of delight ran through the tiers of seats. The 'boy from Seville' was going to be worthy of his name; he had got back his professional pride. He was going to give them a taste of his own inimitable style. His passes with the muleta were greeted with shouts of enthusiasm, and his partizans began accusing his critics of unfairness. What about this? Gallardo had been a bit careless lately—but as soon as he really took trouble, just look what he could do!

He seemed to be in his best form that afternoon. When the bull was at last brought to a standstill the audience shouted: "Now then! Give it him!"

And Gallardo threw himself on the animal, driving in the sword and then quickly withdrawing from between the terrible horns.

Applause rang out but it was short-lived, and quickly followed by a threatening murmur mixed with whistling. Gallardo's supporters turned away from the bull to look indignantly at the protesting part of the public. How unfair! And how ignorant too! He had gone in to kill magnificently!

But his critics were pointing at the bull and still protesting loudly, and the whole amphitheatre soon joined in a deafening chorus of whistling.

The sword had gone in slantwise, and its point was protruding between the ribs close to one of its forelegs.

The audience was indignant. What a shocking business! A bad novillero could have done better.

The bull took a few halting steps, with the handle of the sword sticking out of its neck and the point from its ribs, its huge bulk swaying unsteadily. This seemed to arouse the sympathy of the crowd. Poor creature! It had fought so well, so nobly. Some leant forward shouting angrily as if about to jump into the arena. Thief! Son of a whore! Torturing an animal much braver than himself! And for some reason they were all full of violent indignation at the animal's suffering, just as if they hadn't paid to see it killed.

Gallardo was stupefied by what had happened, and he bowed his head under the storm of insults and threats. Damnation take it! He'd gone in to kill just as in his best days, overcoming the nervous impulse which made him want to turn away his face from the sight of his enemy. But his desire to avoid danger and get out from between the horns as quickly as possible had led to this shockingly unskilful estocada.

People were arguing and shouting at each other in the benches. "He turns his face away. He's no good any more!" And Gallardo's supporters defended their hero with equal excitement. "This might happen to anyone. The important thing is to go in to kill bravely, and that's what he did."

After staggering a little way in a painful manner which made everyone shout protestingly, the bull stood still so as not to prolong its agony.

Gallardo took another sword and went up to it.

The audience guessed his intentions. He was going to carry out a descabello, the only thing to be done after such a criminally bad estocada.

He placed the point of his sword between the horns and waved the muleta in his left hand to make the animal lower its head. Then he leant on the sword, but the bull tossed its head and managed to eject it.

"One!" cried the crowd with jeering unanimity.

Again the matador returned to the attack and tried to drive in the sword, only causing a shudder to run through the animal's body.

"Two!" came the mocking voices from the benches.

A third time he repeated his attempt, producing a bellow of pain from the bull, but nothing more.

"Three!"

But this time the ironical chorus was accompanied by whistles and cries of protest. When was this bungler going to finish the job?

At last he succeeded in severing the spinal cord with the point of his sword, and the bull fell instantly, lying on its side with rigid legs.

The matador wiped the sweat from his forehead and walked slowly round to the president's box, almost gasping for breath. At last he was quit of the brute; it had seemed as if he would never manage to finish it off. The public received him in scornful silence or with sarcastic remarks. There was no applause. He saluted the president amidst general indifference and retired behind the barrier like a shamefaced schoolboy. While Garabato handed him a glass of water, Gallardo looked up at the boxes and met the eyes of Doña Sol, whose gaze had followed him to his refuge. What was she thinking of him now? How she and her friend must be laughing together, to see him insulted by the audience. What the devil had put it into her head to come to this corrida?

He stayed where he was, anxious to avoid any further fatigue until the next bull for him to kill should appear. His wounded leg was painful from so much running. He wasn't the man he used to be; at last he was forced to recognize the fact. All his efforts at self-confidence, his determination to 'hurl himself on the bull' were in vain. His legs had lost their old agility and steadiness, and his right arm the boldness with which it used to thrust forward towards the bull's neck. Now it drew back, disobeying his will with an instinctive response like that of animals which roll up into a ball or hide their heads in the presence of danger.

His old superstitious terrors suddenly returned to him in full force, obsessing him utterly. "My luck's out," he thought to himself. "Something tells me that the fifth bull's going to get me. It'll get me! There's no help for it."

However when the fifth bull came into the ring the first thing it saw was Gallardo's cape. What a brute! It looked quite different from the one he had chosen in the pens yesterday evening. They must have changed the order. And the voice of fear still chanted in his ears: "My luck's out! He'll get me; I shall be carried out of the ring feet foremost."

In spite of this he went on playing the bull and saving the picadors from danger. At first his endeavours were received in silence; but gradually the audience warmed to him, and applauded feebly.

When the moment to kill arrived and Gallardo took up his position in front of the bull, his confusion of mind was apparent to all. He moved uncertainly; it was enough for the animal to shake its head for him to think it was about to charge, and his legs carried him backwards in great leaps, while the audience greeted these involuntary movements of recoil with a chorus of jeering.

"Hi! Look out! He'll catch you!"

Suddenly he threw himself on the creature with the sword, as if longing to make an end of it somehow or other; but his thrust was an oblique one, owing to his desire to get away from danger as fast as possible. There was a burst of whistling and indignant shouts. The sword had only gone in a few inches, and after quivering in the brute's neck for a while it was thrown out to some distance.

Gallardo picked it up and once more approached the bull. He was just squaring up again with the sword when the animal charged. He would have liked to fly, but his legs were not quick enough to carry him. He was caught and rolled along the ground. Everyone ran to his assistance and he got to his feet covered in sand with a long rent in the back of his trousers through which his white underlinen protruded, and minus one of his shoes and the moña from his pigtail.

This arrogant young man, whose dashing appearance the public had so greatly admired, now looked pathetic and ridiculous, with his shirt-tail sticking out, his hair ruffled and his pigtail hanging down sadly.

Capes were spread around him for his protection and assistance. Out of a generous feeling of comradeship the other matadors tried to prepare the bull so that he could finish it off quickly. But Gallardo seemed stunned; the slightest movement from the animal was enough to make him throw himself backwards, as if his recent fall had left him mad with terror. He couldn't understand what his comrades were saying to him, and with an intensely pale and frowning face he stammered out, not knowing what he said:

"Out of the ring all of you! Leave me alone!"

And all the time the voice of fear was ringing through his head: "Today you will die! Today you will get your last goring!"

The audience guessed at his thoughts from his uncontrolled movements.

"He's terrified of the bull! He's afraid!"

And even Gallardo's most fervent supporters were silent with shame, unable to explain this unprecedented behaviour.

The spectators seemed to enjoy his terror, with the uncompromising valour of those who sit in safety. Others felt defrauded of their money's worth and shouted angry abuse of this man who was refusing to give them what they had paid for, out of concern for his own safety. It was sheer robbery!

Some low-minded members of the audience insulted the matador by casting doubts on his manhood. The violence of their anger made them resuscitate memories of his childhood long buried under years of admiration, and which he had even forgotten himself. They reminded him of his night life among the ragamuffins of the Alameda de Hércules. They laughed at his torn breeches with the white underclothes appearing through the rent.

"Just look at you now!" cried high-pitched voices, in assumed feminine accents.

With the help of the other toreros and their capes, Gallardo tried to take every chance to wound the bull with his sword, but the animal hardly felt his estocadas. His fear of being caught by the horns was such that he kept too far away, only inflicting small wounds with the point of his weapon.

Some of the swords hardly penetrated the flesh and fell out almost immediately, others stuck quivering in a bone, with most of their length exposed. The bull made the rounds of the barrier, bellowing with his head low, as if complaining of this useless torment. The matador followed, muleta in hand, longing to put an end to it and yet terrified of exposing himself to danger, and behind him came a troop of peons flourishing their capes as if trying to persuade the animal to double its legs and collapse on the sand. As the bull went by with foam falling from its muzzle and its neck bristling with swords, there was a further explosion of jeers and insults.

"It's like La Dolorosa!"[1] someone cried.

Others compared it to a pincushion full of pins.

"Thief! You're no bullfighter!"

Some persisted in their reflections on Gallardo's sex.

"Juanita! Don't do anything dangerous!"

Time passed in this way, and some of the audience, wanting to discharge their wrath on someone else beside the matador, turned to the president's box.

"Señor President! How long is this scandalous display to go on?"

The president made a sign for silence and gave an order.

[1] The Virgin of Seven Sorrows, who is depicted with her heart pierced with swords.

298

An alguacil in his feathered hat and fluttering cape was seen hurrying round between the barriers to the place where the bull now was. He raised his closed fist towards Gallardo, with the forefinger outstretched. It was the first warning. If he hadn't succeeded in killing the bull before the third it would be sent back to the corral—the worst possible disgrace for the matador.

As if the threat had woken him from a trance Gallardo pointed his sword horizontally at the bull and hurled himself upon it. But it was yet another estocada which only penetrated a little way.

The matador let his arms drop to his sides, utterly discouraged. This bull was immortal; it was impervious to estocadas. Was it never going to die?

This last unsuccessful thrust enraged the crowd. They all got to their feet, whistling so loudly that the women had to stop their ears. Oranges, pieces of bread, cushions and any other handy object were thrown at the matador. From the seats in the sun came stentorian roars and noises like a steam-siren, which it seemed impossible that human throats could produce. Cowbells jingled, and from the benches near the bull-pens a powerful male chorus began to intone a funeral chant.

Many people turned to the president again. When was he going to give the second warning? Gallardo was wiping the sweat from his face with a handkerchief, amazed at the injustice of the public and holding the bull responsible for everything. He glanced at Doña Sol's box, but she was turning her back so as not to see the arena; perhaps she was sorry for him, perhaps she felt ashamed of her past kindness to him.

Once again he came in to kill, and this time so many capes were spread around him that few people could follow his movements. The bull fell to the ground with a stream of blood gushing from its mouth.

At last! The uproar from the crowd grew less, though there was still some whistling and shouting. The puntillero did his job and the animal was fastened by the head behind a team of mules and dragged out of the arena, leaving behind it a broad belt of smoothed sand streaked with blood, which was quickly effaced by the bull-ring servants with their rakes.

Gallardo retired between the barriers, shrinking from the insults his presence still provoked. There he remained, panting with exhaustion, his injured leg causing him great pain; but even through all his misery he was aware of the relief of being out of danger. He had not after all met his death on the horns of the brute—and he owed the fact to his own prudence. As for the crowd! They were just a collection of murderers longing to see a man die. Did they imagine they were the only ones who loved life and had families dependent on them?

His departure from the ring through all the pedestrians, carriages, cars and trams was agonizing.

Gallardo's carriage had to go slowly so as not to run down the people walking away from the bull-ring. They stepped aside to let the mules pass, but when they recognized the matador they appeared to repent of their politeness.

Gallardo guessed at the insults which were coming from their moving lips. Other carriages full of beautiful women in white mantillas passed close to his. Some turned their heads away; others looked at him with eyes full of pity.

The matador shrank back in his seat as if he didn't want to be seen; he hid himself behind the bulky form of El Nacional, who was frowning and silent.

Some boys began whistling and running after the carriage, and many of the crowds standing on the pavements followed suit, venting their feelings of frustration at not having been able to afford the price of a seat. The news of Gallardo's failure had spread quickly among them, and it gave them pleasure to insult a man who earned such enormous sums of money.

Their hostility roused the matador from his state of silent resignation.

"What are they whistling for, curse them? They didn't see the corrida, did they? They haven't wasted any of their money?"

A stone struck one of the carriage wheels. The boys were shouting alongside the step now; but two mounted policemen rode up and dispersed them, and afterwards acted as escort to the famous Juan Gallardo, 'the best matador of them all'.

CHAPTER TEN

THE cuadrillas had just gone into the ring the following Sunday when there was a loud knocking on the door to the stables.

One of the bull-ring servants shouted angrily that there was no entrance that way; whoever it was must go round to the other entrance. But a voice from outside continued to insist, and he opened the door.

A man and a woman came in, the man wearing a white Córdovan hat, the woman dressed in black with a mantilla.

The man shook the attendant's hand, leaving something in it which made him look more friendly.

"You know me, don't you?" said the newcomer. "Surely you do? I'm Gallardo's brother-in-law, and this lady is his wife."

Carmen looked around her at the empty courtyard. Through the massive brick walls came the faint sound of distant music, and the murmurs and shouts of the crowd. The cuadrillas were parading before the president.

"Where is he?" Carmen asked anxiously.

"Where do you suppose he is, my dear?" replied her brother-in-law roughly. "In the ring, doing his duty. It was madness for you to come here. I shouldn't have let you—but I'm always so weak!"

Carmen went on gazing round her undecidedly, as if repenting of her decision. What could she do, now that she had come?

The bull-ring servant was all politeness since Antonio's hand-shake, and was impressed also by the two visitors' relationship to a famous matador. If the lady wanted to wait till the end of the corrida she could certainly sit in the gate-keeper's house. Or if they preferred he would find them good seats in the ring, even though they had no tickets.

Carmen shuddered at the idea. See the corrida? No. It had cost her a great effort of will to get to the bull-ring, and she was already beginning to repent of having come. She had never seen her husband fight. She would wait here as long as she could bear to.

"God's will be done!" said the saddler resignedly. "We'll wait here then, though a fine lot we shall see opposite the stables!"

Encarnación's husband had been in attendance on his sister-in-law since the previous day, constantly subjected to the alarms and weeping-fits which were symptoms of a state of fear that was far from unreasonable.

At midday on the Saturday Carmen had summoned him to the maestro's study. She was going to Madrid. She had made up her mind. She couldn't stay in Seville a moment longer. For nearly a week she had hardly slept at all and her imagination had tormented her with scenes of horror. Her feminine intuition seemed to be warning her of coming disaster. She must hurry to Juan's side. She didn't know why she was going nor what she meant to do when she got there, but she wanted to be close to Gallardo, as if her love could somehow diminish his danger.

At present her life was not worth living. She had read in the newspapers about last Sunday's disastrous corrida in the Madrid ring. She knew how great was his professional pride, and that he wouldn't be able to take this set-back lying down. He was capable of any madness to regain the public favour. His last letter had made this all too clear.

"No, and again no," she said to her brother-in-law emphatically. "I'm going to Madrid this very afternoon. If you'd like to come with me, do; if not I'll go alone. But what-ever you do, not a word to Don José; he would try to stop me. He mustn't hear of it, nor must Mamma."

The saddler had to give in. After all it was a free journey to

Madrid, even though in such dismal company! On the way, Carmen found her desires taking concrete shape. She would speak firmly to her husband. Why must he go on fighting? Hadn't they enough to live on? He must retire, and at once, if he didn't want to be the death of her. This corrida must really be his last, and even so it was one too many. She hoped to reach Madrid in time to persuade her husband not to fight that afternoon. Her heart told her that being there might prevent a catastrophe.

Her brother-in-law listened with exaggerated gestures of protest.

"What outrageous nonsense! Just like a woman too! Once get a thing into their heads and it must be the truth. Do you really think there are no rules and regulations in bullfighting, and that it's enough for a woman to feel frightened and want to run and kiss her husband for the corrida to be stopped and the public disappointed? Say whatever you like to Juan, but it'll have to be after the corrida. You can't play tricks with the authorities; we should all be sent to prison."

And the saddler imagined the most dramatic consequences, if Carmen were to persist in her crazy notion of going to see her husband and preventing him from fighting. They would all be taken off to jail. To his simple way of thinking, he himself would be held guilty as an accomplice to the crime.

When they arrived at Madrid he had to exert all his powers of persuasion to prevent his companion from rushing straight to her husband's hotel. What use could that possibly be?

"You'd upset him, and he'd go off to the bull-ring in a bad humour and worried; and then if anything happened it would be your fault."

The argument carried weight with Carmen and she let her brother-in-law take her to a hotel of his own choosing, where she spent the whole morning lying on a sofa in her room weeping as though the worst had already happened. The saddler was delighted to be in Madrid in comfortable quarters, and her despair seemed to him ridiculous.

"Good heavens, don't go on like that! Just like a woman!

Anyone would think you were already a widow, instead of which your husband is happily getting ready for the corrida this very moment, and as strong and well as Roger de Flor himself. What foolishness!"

Carmen would hardly eat any lunch, and remained deaf to her brother-in-law's praise of the hotel cuisine. In the afternoon her patience again deserted her.

The hotel was close to the Puerta del Sol, and she could hear the noise of the crowds going to the bull-ring. No, she couldn't possibly stay in this room while her husband was risking his life. She must see him. She wasn't brave enough to watch the fight herself, but she wanted to feel close to him; she would go to the ring. But where was it? She had never even seen it. If they wouldn't let her in, she would stay outside. The important thing was to be near him; she felt her presence might bring Gallardo luck.

The saddler protested. For heaven's sake! He had every intention of seeing the corrida; he had already been out and bought himself a ticket. And now Carmen wanted to spoil his enjoyment by insisting on coming to the ring herself.

"But what will you do when you get there, child? How can your being there help him? Just think if Juan saw you!"

They argued for some time, but Carmen obstinately went on repeating:

"You needn't come. I'll go by myself."

In the end her brother-in-law gave in, and they took a cab to the bull-ring and went in by the door to the stables. The saddler knew the back regions of the ring fairly well, as he had accompanied Gallardo to one of the spring corridas in Madrid.

He and the bull-ring servant were at a loss what to do with this red-eyed, hollow-cheeked woman who insisted on staying in the courtyard. Both men felt drawn towards the sounds of music and shouting which came from within. Must they stay out here the whole afternoon and not see the corrida?

Then the attendant had a brilliant idea.

"Perhaps the lady would care to go to the chapel?"

The procession of the cuadrillas was over. Horsemen were

304

seen trotting past the door which led into the arena. They were the picadors who were not on duty, who were leaving the ring until it was their turn to replace their comrades. There were six more horses tied to posts in the wall, ready saddled to take the places of any that fell in the ring. Behind them some picadors were filling in the time of waiting by putting their mounts through some turns. A stable-boy was galloping an excited horse round the corral to tire it out before handing it over to the picadors.

The tethered animals were fidgeting and kicking, plagued by the flies, and tugging at their halters as if they knew the danger awaiting them.

Carmen and her brother-in-law had to take refuge under the arcades, and at last the matador's wife accepted the invitation to go to the chapel. At least it would be safe and quiet there, and perhaps she could do something to help her husband.

When she found herself in the holy place, still stuffy from the crowds which had lately been there to watch the toreros at their prayers, Carmen looked in surprise at the poorly furnished altar. There were four candles burning in front of the Virgin of the Dove—it seemed to her a meagre offering.

She opened her purse to give a duro to the bull-ring servant. Couldn't he bring some more tapers? He scratched his forehead. Tapers? Tapers? He didn't think any such things were to be found among the bull-ring stores. But he suddenly remembered that the sister of one of the matadors always brought candles when he was fighting. The last she brought had not all been used, and were probably stowed away in some corner of the chapel. After a long search he found them. There were no candlesticks; but he was a resourceful man and he brought a couple of empty bottles and stuck the lit candles in their necks, adding them to the other lights on the altar.

Carmen fell on her knees, and the two men hurried away to the arena, anxious not to miss any of the performance.

The matador's wife gazed with interest at the faded picture lit by the warm glow from the candles. She had never seen this Virgin before, but she must surely be gentle and good like the Virgin in Seville she had so often prayed to. Besides she watched over the toreros and heard their last prayers when the nearness of danger must bring forth the most genuine faith of which these rough men were capable. Her husband must have knelt here often. And this thought was enough to make her feel drawn to the image, and look at the Virgin with trust as if she had known her from childhood.

Her lips were moving rapidly, automatically repeating prayer after prayer, but her thoughts were carried far away by the noise of the crowd in the arena.

How terrible it was, the intermittent roaring of that volcano —the howling of that distant storm, broken every now and again by dramatic silences! In her imagination Carmen pictured the invisible scene. She could guess from the changing intonation of the different sounds what was the course of the tragedy unfolding itself within the ring. Once or twice indignant shouts and whistling broke out; then hundreds and hundreds of voices were uttering unintelligible words, all together. Suddenly there was a long scream of fear, which seemed to rise to heaven itself, followed by a terrified gasp which made her think of thousands of faces pale with emotion, craning forward to follow the bull's pursuit of a man with their eyes . . . then the cries suddenly ceased and there was calm again. The danger had passed.

Sometimes there were long spells of absolute silence— silence so empty that the buzzing of the flies from the stables was clearly audible; it was as if the fourteen thousand people in the arena had stopped breathing and were motionless, and Carmen was the only living creature within the bull-ring walls.

All at once the silence was broken by a terrific uproar, like the noise of hundreds of bricks falling on top of each other. It was a burst of clapping. From the courtyard outside the chapel came the sound of thwacks on the hides of the miserable horses, curses, and the clink of horseshoes on stone. A voice called out: "Who has been hurt?" New picadors were urgently summoned into the arena.

306

To these distant noises nearer ones were now added. Footsteps crossed the next room; doors were opened and the panting voices were heard of several men who seemed to be staggering under a heavy weight.

"It's nothing—only a bump on the head. You're not losing any blood. You'll be on your horse again before the end of the corrida."

A hoarse voice, weak with pain and seeming to come from the bottom of the lungs, gasped out in an accent which reminded Carmen of home:

"Virgin of Solitude! I'm sure I've broken something! Look very carefully, doctor. Oh, my poor children!"

Carmen trembled with fright. She raised terrified eyes to the Virgin. Her nose seemed thin and sharp between her pale hollow cheeks. She felt ill; she thought she was going to faint. She tried to bury herself in prayer, away from these terrible noises, but the splashing of water and the voices of doctors and nurses rallying the wounded picador came through the walls with appalling distinctness.

The man was groaning and swearing, but at the same time trying to make light of the pain his broken bones were causing him.

"Virgin of Solitude! My poor children! What are they to eat I should like to know, when their father can't fight?"

Carmen got up. She could bear it no longer. She would faint if she stayed in this dark place listening to these groans of anguish. She must have air, and sunlight. She seemed to feel the pain of the unknown man in her own bones.

She went out into the courtyard. There was blood everywhere: on the ground and round some pails full of reddish water.

The signal for the banderillas had been given, and the picadors were riding out of the ring on horses streaked with blood, with their flesh torn, and the repellent mass of their entrails hanging from under their bellies.

The riders dismounted, talking excitedly about the incidents of the fight. Carmen saw Potaje lower his strong body to the ground, moving slowly in his heavy iron leggings and firing off a tirade of oaths at the monosabio who was clumsily trying to help him. He rubbed his bruised shoulders ruefully and smiled, showing yellow horse teeth.

"Did you see how good Juan was?" he said to the others. "He's giving them the real thing today!"

When he recognized the only woman among the men in the courtyard, he showed no surprise.

"So you're here, Señora Carmen! And quite right too!"

He spoke phlegmatically, as if so dazed with wine and his own brutish nature that nothing in the world could surprise him.

"Did you see Juan?" he went on. "He lay down on the ground in front of the bull, under its very nose. He can show all the other matadors something, no fear. Go in and see him, he's in fine form today."

Then someone called him from the infirmary door. The wounded picador wanted a word with him before they took him to hospital.

"Good-bye, Señora Carmen. I'm off to see this poor chap. He's broken something, so they say, and won't be able to work any more this season."

Carmen retired under the arcades, longing to shut her eyes so as to blot out the horrible spectacle in the courtyard, but at the same time fascinated by the sickening pools of blood.

The monosabios led along the terrified wounded horses dragging their entrails on the ground and leaving a trail of droppings behind them.

When he saw them the head stable-man sprang to life, waving his arms in a sadistic frenzy.

"Steady there!" he shouted to his lads. "Down with them!"

One of the lads cautiously approached a horse that was kicking about with pain, removed some of the harness, and quickly tightened it round the animal's four feet, throwing it to the ground.

"That's the way! Come on now!" the head man shouted, gesticulating wildly.

And the stable-lads rolled up their sleeves and bent over the horse's ripped-up stomach, from which blood and urine were streaming, and tried to push back the heavy mass of entrails by handfuls into the ghastly aperture.

Another man held the reins and put a foot on the poor animal's head to keep it on the ground. Its nostrils twitched with pain, the long yellow teeth rattled together, but its whinnies of agony were lost in the dust. With bloody hands the workers tried to push back the slippery bowels; but the victim's gasping breaths kept forcing them out again, and the enormous bladder refused to be stowed away.

"Harder lads! Come on there!" shouted the head man.

And at last the bladder and the rest of the entrails disappeared into the horses's belly, and the stable-lads deftly stitched together the sides of the wound.

When the horse had been thus barbarously and speedily 'mended', they threw a bucket of water over its head, untied its legs and whacked it with a stick to make it scramble to its feet. Some of the animals that had been so treated took only a few steps and fell to the ground, with a torrent of blood streaming from the stitched wound. Death had been instantaneous as soon as the entrails were back in place. Others were kept on their legs by their incredible reserves of animal vitality, and were taken after their 'mending' to be 'varnished' —which consisted in their stomachs and legs being strenuously washed down with buckets of water. After this their white or chestnut coats glistened, while a pink fluid (a mixture of water and blood) trickled down their legs to the ground.

The horses were repaired just like old shoes; the utmost use was to be got out of them, though this prolonged their torment and postponed the moment of death. Pieces of intestine which had been cut away to facilitate the 'mending' lay on the ground. There were other remnants inside the ring, covered over with sand until they could be removed in baskets after the death of the bull. Very often the spaces in their bellies left by these lost organs was stuffed with bunches of tow by their rough-and-ready surgeons.

The chief thing was to keep the horses on their legs a few

minutes longer, until the picadors had re-entered the ring, when the bull would soon take over and finish his work. And the miserable, dying animals endured their tragic rehabilitation uncomplainingly. A horse that was by nature docile opened its mouth to bite one of the monosabios who came close to it, and there were seen to be fragments of skin and reddish hairs between its teeth. When it had felt the horns pierce its stomach it had bitten the bull's neck in its frenzy.

The wounded creatures whinnied mournfully and lifted their tails to relieve their stomachs of wind. A stench of blood and vegetable excrement filled the courtyard; blood ran freely between the stones, dyeing them red and turning black as it dried.

The noise of the distant crowd was distinctly audible. Sometimes there were anxious exclamations, which told of the flight of a banderillero hotly pursued by the bull. Then absolute silence. The man had turned on his adversary, and a loud burst of applause greeted the skilful placing of two more banderillas. Afterwards the trumpets announced the beginning of the faena, and more applause followed.

Carmen longed to go away. Virgin of Hope! What was she doing here? She didn't know the order of events in the ring. Perhaps that trumpet blast had been the signal for her husband to face the bull. And she was here, only a few yards away, yet she couldn't see him! She longed to get away, to escape from this torment.

Besides, she was horrified by the pools of blood in the courtyard, and the sufferings of the poor horses. Her feminine delicacy revolted against this torture, just as it made her hold her handkerchief over her nose to keep away the stench of the butcher's shop.

She had never watched a bullfight. She had spent a large part of her life hearing corridas talked about, but all that had been called up by these discussions was what the audience saw: the feats of skill in the arena in the sunlight; the brilliance of the silks and gold embroidery; the sumptuous ritual and display. She had known nothing of the hateful preparations which went on in the secrecy of the wings. And she and all her family had lived on these fiestas and the revolting torture of weak animals they involved. Their fortune had been made by spectacles such as these!

Tremendous applause came from the arena. Orders were issued in an imperative voice in the courtyard. The first bull had just been killed. The gates at the end of the passage-way communicating with the ring were thrown open, and the voices of the crowd and the blare of the music became louder.

The mules were in the ring: one team to drag away the carcass of the bull, another for the dead horses.

Carmen saw her brother-in-law approaching through the arcades, still quivering with excitement at what he had seen.

"Juan! He's stupendous! I've never seen him so good as today. Don't worry. He's eating the bulls alive!"

Then he looked at her anxiously, lest she should have any plans that might make him miss this splendid afternoon's entertainment. What did she want to do? Did she feel brave enough to come into the ring?

"Take me away!" she cried in agonized tones. "Please get me out of here quickly! I'm ill. Take me to the nearest church."

The saddler frowned. Good heavens! Must he leave this magnificent corrida? And while going with Carmen to the door he was wondering where he could deposit her, so as to get back to the ring as soon as possible.

When the second bull entered the arena Gallardo was still leaning on the barrier, receiving congratulations from his admirers. What courage he had shown! The whole audience had applauded his first bull, forgetting their dissatisfaction at last week's corridas. When a picador fell from his horse and lay senseless from the shock, Gallardo had hurried forward with his cape and carried the bull off to the middle of the ring. Then he had executed a magnificent series of veronicas, leaving the animal exhausted and motionless from rushing after the deceptive red cloth. Finally he had taken advantage of the bull's bewilderment to stand a few steps from its muzzle,

311

presenting his stomach as if to defy it. He felt his heart leap up as it did before his greatest feats in the past. He must win the audience by some act of outrageous daring, and he knelt down in front of the horns—albeit with a certain caution, ready to leap up at the first sign of a charge.

The bull stood perfectly still. Even when the matador put out a hand and touched its muzzle, it made no movement. Then he did something which reduced the audience to breathless silence. He slowly lowered himself to the ground and lay with the cape between his arms like a pillow, and there he remained for some seconds stretched under the very nose of the bull while it sniffed at him mistrustfully, seeming to suspect some hidden danger.

When the animal again lowered its head as if to attack, the torero rolled quickly over towards its front legs, thus putting himself out of its reach, and the bull rushed over his body without touching him, blindly seeking for some solid object to charge.

Gallardo got up and brushed the sand from his clothes, while the public roared its applause of his daring with as much enthusiasm as they had ever showed him in the past. It wasn't only his bravery they were applauding but the dignity with which he was making this bid to be reconciled with them—to regain their affection.

"He's sometimes careless," they said to each other, "but he takes a real pride in his work, and he's certainly making his come-back now."

Their excitement and delight at this feat of Gallardo's, and at the confident estocada which had finished off the first bull, turned to dismay and expostulations when they saw the second bull enter the arena. It was a huge, splendid-looking beast, but it ran into the middle of the ring and gazed round in fear and astonishment at the noisy crowd who were trying to excite it with shouts and whistling; it seemed to suspect traps everywhere and was ready to run away from its own shadow. The peons came forward spreading their capes and it made as if to attack, but instead gave a snort of surprise and turned tail and rushed off in the opposite direction in a series of wild leaps. Its readiness for flight enraged the audience.

"That's not a bull—it's a monkey!"

At last the maestros succeeded in enticing it close to the barrier, where the picadors sat waiting motionless on their horses, with their garrochas under their arms. The bull made for one of them with its head down, snorting fiercely; but before the rider could drive his pike into its neck it gave a bound and rushed away, passing between the outstretched capes of the peons. When it was confronted by another picador it repeated the whole performance—snort, leap and flight. Then it came up to a third rider who caught it fair and square in the neck with his pike; the pain only seemed to increase its fear and desire to escape.

The whole audience were by now on their feet, waving their arms and shouting. The bull was a coward! What an outrage! They all turned towards the president's box protesting loudly: "Señor President, this can't go on! It must be stopped!"

From some of the benches came a chorus of voices repeating the same words over and over in a monotonous chant:

"*Fuego!*[1] *Fuego!*"

The president appeared to be hesitating. The bull still rushed about the ring followed by the toreros with their capes over their arms. If one of them managed to get ahead of it and tried to stop it, the animal sniffed at the cloth and made off in the opposite direction with kicks and bounds, snorting loudly.

The indignation of the audience grew more vociferous. "Señor President, do you see what's happening?" Bottles, oranges and cushions began to hurtle into the ring around the fugitive bull. The spectators detested it for being so cowardly. Some of them leaned over the barrier looking as if they meant to attack the wretched brute with their bare hands. What a disgraceful business, that the breeders should send animals only fit for butcher's meat to the Madrid bull-ring!

"*Fuego! Fuego!*"

[1] Fire.

At last the president was seen to wave a red handkerchief, and a round of applause greeted his gesture.

The fire banderillas[1] were seldom seen in the ring and increased the excitement of the corrida. Many people who had been shouting themselves hoarse in their indignation were secretly delighted at what had happened. They were going to see the bull roasted alive, rushing about maddened by the thunderbolts fasted in its neck.

El Nacional came forward holding with their points downward two thick banderillas which seemed to be wrapped in black paper. He approached the bull boldly, as if its cowardice hadn't earned it any respect, and planted his infernal weapons, while the crowd cheered vindictively.

There was a loud crack as if something had broken, and two coils of white smoke rose from the animal's neck. The sun was so bright that the flames were invisible, but a black scorched patch began to spread over its hide.

The bull rushed forward, surprised by this unexpected attack and trying to get away from it by flight; but then there began a volley of short sharp explosions like rifle fire, and a shower of fragments of black paper scattered round its head. The terrified beast leapt into the air with all four feet at once, and twisted its head, trying in vain to pull out these devilish instruments of torture with its teeth. The spectators laughed and clapped, finding its antics amusing. It looked like a clumsy circus animal trained to perform this elephantine dance.

"That's made him sit up a bit!" they cried with savage satisfaction.

The banderillas had stopped exploding and little bubbles of roasted fat were forming on the bull's neck. The animal no longer felt the sting of the fire and stood still panting, with its head low and its dark red tongue hanging from its mouth.

Another banderillero came up with a second pair of darts. Again smoke rose from the charred flesh, the gunpowder exploded, and the bull rushed madly about twisting its

[1] Banderillas with firecrackers fixed to their shafts, which are used to excite a cowardly bull.

massive body to reach the spot with its mouth; but now its movements were less violent, it seemed to be getting accustomed to its martyrdom.

A third pair of darts were fixed and a nauseous odour of melted fat and singed hair rose from the arena.

The audience were still applauding frenziedly, as if this poor beast was a heretic and they were performing an act of piety by burning it alive. They laughed to see its trembling legs, heaving flanks, bloodshot eyes and hanging tongue, and to hear it bellowing with pain.

Gallardo was leaning on the barrier near the president's box, waiting for the signal to kill. Garabato held the sword and muleta ready to hand him.

The corrida had begun so well, but now ill luck had provided him with this bull—or rather it had been of his own choosing. He had picked it out for its fine appearance, and now it had turned out to be a coward, damn it!

He made excuses for himself in advance to the aficionados in the front seats!

"I'll do what I can, but it won't be much," he said shrugging his shoulders.

Then he looked at the boxes, singling out the one occupied by Doña Sol. She had applauded his daring feat of lying down in front of the bull. He had seen her gloved hands clapping enthusiastically when he had turned towards the barrier and saluted the audience. When Doña Sol saw that he was looking at her she smiled charmingly at him, and even her companion —odious fellow that he was—made a stiff bow as if he were breaking in half at the waist. Afterwards he had several times been aware that her opera-glasses were fixed on him, even following him when he went behind the barrier. Perhaps his courage had revived the attraction he once had for her. He would go and see her next day, in case the wind had changed.

The signal to kill was given, and after a short dedication the matador advanced towards the bull.

The experts shouted their advice.

"Finish him quickly! He's not worth any trouble!"

315

Gallardo spread his muleta and the bull charged, but slowly and warily. It seemed that the torment it had been subjected to had aroused all its latent ferocity and it was out to wound and crush—to achieve victory at all costs. The matador was the first man who had come within reach of its horns since its martyrdom began.

The crowd felt their indignation against the bull waning. It wasn't turning out so badly, after all, it was attacking well now. *Olé!* And everyone applauded the passes with the muleta, seeming to express equal approval of the torero and the bull.

At last the beast stood still with lowered head and hanging tongue. The silence which always precedes an estocada fell on the ring: a silence more intense than that of absolute solitude, because it was produced by thousands of people holding their breath. A silence so profound that the tiniest noise in the arena was audible in the topmost benches. The sound of pieces of wood lightly hitting against each other was heard by everyone. Gallardo had thrown back the charred shafts of the banderillas with the point of his sword, so as to leave the space between the horns free for the mortal stroke. The onlookers craned forward, feeling that a mysterious union had established itself between their will and that of the matador. Now! One masterly estocada and the bull would be finished.

Gallardo hurled himself on the bull and the audience breathed again after their long tension. But the animal rushed away from the encounter bellowing angrily, and whistling and protesting cries broke from the audience in the benches. The same thing had happened again. Gallardo had shortened his arm and turned aside his head at the moment of killing. The sword stuck quivering in the bull's neck and after a few moments it fell out on to the sand.

Some of the crowd began shouting abuse at Gallardo. The spell with which he had been able to bind them to him at the beginning of the corrida was broken. They began to mistrust and criticize him again. They seemed to have forgotten their wild enthusiasm of only a few minutes ago.

Gallardo picked up the sword, and advanced again towards the bull, with head bent, too discouraged to protest against the crowd's injustice.

He was dimly aware that another torero was at his side. It must be El Nacional.

"Steady, Juan! Take it easy!"

Was it always going to be the same, damn it? Would he never again be able to stretch his arm between the horns, as he used to, and drive the sword in right up to the hilt? Was he going to be the laughing-stock of the public for the rest of his life?

He squared up to this 'cowardly' bull, which was standing still looking at him as if inviting the end. He wouldn't make any more passes with the muleta. He profiled with the sword held at the level of his eyes and the red cloth sweeping the ground. Now he must strike!

The audience leapt to their feet. For several seconds man and beast combined in a single moving mass. The experts were already lifting their hands to clap. He had thrown his weight on the sword as he used to in his best days. A magnificent estocada!

Then suddenly with a violent movement of its head, the bull threw the man on to the sand. It lowered its horns again and lifted the inert body for a moment, then let it drop, and continued its mad career with the sword plunged up to the hilt in its neck.

Gallardo slowly got to his feet and the whole audience broke into deafening applause, eager to make up for their former unfairness. *Olé! Olé!* Bravo the 'boy from Seville!' He had been superb!

But the matador didn't respond to their enthusiasm. He put his hands to his stomach, and bending his body in obvious pain walked with uncertain steps and lowered head towards the barrier. Twice he looked up, as if he couldn't see the exit, then he staggered on like a drunken man.

Suddenly he fell flat on the sand and lay there like a huge caterpillar made of silk and gold. Four bull-ring servants lifted him clumsily on to their shoulders, and El Nacional joined them, supporting the matador's head with its livid face and glassy eyes just showing under his closed lids.

The audience was taken by surprise, and the applause stopped. They exchanged glances, unable to make up their minds as to the gravity of the accident. Soon an optimistic rumour began to circulate, but no one knew where it had come from; it was one of those anonymous opinions which a crowd is always ready to accept and which may stir them to action or silence. Gallardo wasn't badly hurt. It was only a violent blow in the stomach, which had winded him and left him senseless. No one had seen any blood.

Quickly reassured, the onlookers sat down again, and shifted their attention from the wounded torero to the bull, which was still on its feet fighting to keep death at bay.

El Nacional helped carry his master to a bed in the infirmary. He fell on to it like a sack, with his arms hanging down on either side.

Sebastián had often seen his matador wounded and bleeding without losing his presence of mind, but now he was stricken with fear to see him lying as still as a corpse with his greenish white face.

"For Christ's sake!" he groaned. "Aren't there any doctors in the place? Isn't there anyone who can help?"

The infirmary staff had hurried back to their box in the bull-ring, as soon as the wounded picador had been dealt with.

The banderillero was in despair; every second seemed an hour, and he shouted to Garabato and Potaje to come and help, though he had no idea what to ask them to do when they came.

At last the doctors arrived, shut the door so as not to be disturbed, and stood round the matador's inanimate body. He must be undressed.

Garabato began taking out pins, unpicking stitches and cutting away the torero's clothes, by the light of a window in the roof.

El Nacional could hardly see his master, for the doctors

were surrounding the bed, exchanging glances and opinions in low voices. He seemed to be suffering a collapse due to shock. There was no blood to be seen. The rents in his clothes must have been caused when the bull tossed him.

Then Doctor Ruiz came hurrying in, and his colleagues made way for him, acknowledging his superior skill. He swore under his breath as he helped Garabato undress the matador with nervous haste.

There was a movement of horrified surprise from the group round the bed. The banderillero didn't dare ask what it meant. He peered between the doctors' heads and saw Gallardo's body with the shirt drawn up over his chest and the breeches pulled down, exposing the dark shadow above his genitals. The stomach was completely visible and right across it was a jagged wound with bleeding edges, between which the bluish viscera could be seen.

Doctor Ruiz shook his head sadly. Besides this terrible wound, the shock of the blow from the bull's head had been appalling. Gallardo was no longer breathing.

"Doctor! Doctor!" groaned the banderillero, begging to know the truth.

After a long silence the doctor shook his head again.

"It's all over, Sebastián. You must find another matador."

El Nacional raised his eyes to heaven. Was it possible that such a man should die like this, without being able to clasp his friends by the hand or say a single word—like a miserable rabbit that has had its neck broken?

He hurried out of the infirmary, frantic with grief. He couldn't stay there like Potaje, who was standing at the foot of the bed, motionless and grim, staring with unseeing eyes at the body of his master and twisting his hat in his hands.

The banderillero was crying like a child. His chest was convulsed with gasping sobs and tears blinded his eyes.

When he reached the courtyard he had to stand aside to make room for some picadors who were returning to the ring.

The terrible news was running through the audience. Gallardo was dead! Some disbelieved it, others were convinced

319

of its truth; but all remained in their seats. The third bull was just going to be loosed. There was still more than half of the corrida to come, and they couldn't be expected to forgo their enjoyment.

The voices of the crowd and the sound of music came out through the doorway into the courtyard.

The banderillero felt a fierce hatred arise in his heart for everything that surrounded him, a disgust for his profession and for the public which patronized it. The sonorous phrase which always made people laugh—'God or Nature'—rang through his mind, and seemed to have a new significance.

He thought of the bull, being dragged out of the ring at this moment, its neck burnt and bloody, its legs stiff and its glassy eyes gazing unseeingly at the blue sky.

Then he thought of his friend lying dead only a few feet away on the other side of a brick wall—motionless also, with stiffening limbs, his shirt pulled up over his chest, his stomach ripped open, and a strange leaden light in the eyes glimpsed under the half-closed lids.

Poor bull! Poor matador! Suddenly from the ring came a savage roar of delight, greeting the start of the next phase in the spectacle. El Nacional closed his eyes and clenched his fists.

It was the roaring of the only real beast.